Amanda
Prowse

A Little Love

HEAD
ZEUS

First published in the UK in 2014 by Head of Zeus Ltd
This paperback edition published in the UK in 2014
by Head of Zeus Ltd.

9 7 5 3 2 4 6 8

A CIP catalogue record for this book is available
from the British Library.

eBook ISBN: 9781781854952
Paperback ISBN: 9781781854983

Typeset by Palimpsest Book Production Ltd,
Falkirk, Stirlingshire.

Printed and bound by CPI Group (UK) Ltd,
Croydon, CR0 4YY.

Head of Zeus Ltd
First Floor East
5-8 Hardwick Street
London EC1R 4RG

WWW.HEADOFZEUS.COM

A Little Love

Amanda Prowse has always loved crafting short stories and scribbling notes for potential books. Her ambition is to create stories that stop people turning off the bedside light, with characters that stay with you long after the last page is turned.

Amanda's first novel, *Poppy Day*, was self-published in October 2011 and achieved a #1 spot in the eBook charts. She was then signed up by publishers Head of Zeus and her second novel, *What Have I Done?*, became a #1 bestseller in 2013, and gained rave reviews from readers.

Amanda lives in the West Country with her husband Simeon, a soldier, and their two sons Ben and Josh. She has now published five novels and four short stories, which share a common theme of ordinary women doing extraordinary things for love. After many years, she finally has her dream job – a full-time writer.

You can follow Amanda on Twitter @MrsAmandaProwse, become friends with her on Facebook, or visit her website **www.amandaprowse.org**

Also by

Amanda Prowse

Novels

Poppy Day
What Have I Done?
Clover's Child
Will You Remember Me?

Short Stories

Something Quite Beautiful
The Game
A Christmas Wish
Ten Pound Ticket

A Little Love is dedicated to the woman who never taught me to bake, but did teach me to climb mountains and reach for the sky. She is the person I go to for everything from a cup of sugar to good advice. She has had my back since I took my first breath and my life without her would be no life at all. My mum, Anne, who I love with all my heart.

As she paced the square room, her bare feet stuck to the wooden floorboards. The fire that burned in the grate seemed to heat the space directly in front of it, but little else. It was a tad too chilly in the room – at least, she thought it must be, as she was shaking. She wrapped her arms around her torso, but it made little difference.

She was in a state somewhere between panic and hysteria, and when morning finally came, she would be exhausted from trying not to succumb to either. The morning. It felt very far away.

The silky lotion she had rubbed into her legs made her skin shine where the lamplight touched it. It was a neat trick – one of many she had learned over the last couple of weeks, along with putting Vaseline on her eyelashes to make them seem thicker, and weaving a fat, loose plait to give her hair fabulous waves and make it look styled.

Perching on the patchwork quilt, she felt the aged mattress sag beneath her. She sighed, fingering the lace front of her nightie, checking that each little pearlescent button sat snugly through its buttonhole, and patting the front flat. She wanted to look neat, nice. She then studied her fingernails, using the thumbnail of one hand to scoop behind the nails of the other.

1

Dusk was falling and she was becoming increasingly agitated. Glancing at the clock on the bedside table, she wished she could turn back the hands to reclaim a couple of hours, give her longer to prepare. Not that more time would have made much difference; she would still reach this moment and feel exactly the same, with a churning sickness in the base of her stomach, the sound of her heartbeat loud in her ears and a layer of sweat on her palm that gathered like a little river in her lifeline. She licked it away, surprised that the salty residue wasn't unpleasant on her tongue, then wiped the hand, slick with her spit, down her arm.

She stretched out her fingers and studied the palm-wide crease more closely. It made her heart beat faster. Mrs Stanescu, who was married to the rag and bone man and wore a thick black scarf around her hair whatever the weather, had insisted on reading her palm. Lowering her bulk from her husband's rickety cart one day, she had grabbed her by the wrist, smiling with her stubby, dark teeth revealed as she twisted and then slapped to make her fingers open. She had to concentrate on every vowel to understand the woman's English with its heavy Romanian accent. Mrs Stanescu said she saw a long life, then pointed at the tiny triangles that sat on the crease, dotted almost uniformly along it.

'These,' she said as she jabbed at them with her long, dirty fingernail, 'are very interesting. There are two sorts of island on a palm and they can mean times of deep sadness or times of great joy. They define a life.'

She had looked up into the fixed eyes of Mrs Stanescu.

Her lip trembled, pupils large. 'Which sort are mine?' she'd whispered, hardly able to listen to the answer.

The woman's stare hadn't wavered. 'Yours are not the joyous kind. They mean a life which will be bound by a chain that you will wear around your heart and a sadness that will sit behind your eyes, filling your mouth with sourness. It will taint all you do. You will die old and alone and you will know deep fear.'

Crying, she had run to her mum, who petted her hair against her pinny and told her it was a load of old tosh and that she should take no notice of the loopy Mrs Stanescu, who probably said the same thing to everyone. It comforted her for a while, but still, most nights, in the seconds before she fell asleep, she would recall the old crone's words. Her tongue would tingle with a bitter sensation and a wave of panic would wash over her as she wondered what it would feel like to live with a chain around her heart.

She gasped and turned her head as the top stair creaked outside her bedroom door, drawing her into the present. Her heart leapt into her mouth. This was it.

'I'm sorry.'

She didn't know why these words left her mouth involuntarily or to whom they were addressed, but they were offered sincerely. Her palms ran with sweat once again and she thought of Mrs Stanescu. It might have been a load of tosh, but she knew the old hag had been right about one thing. Closing her eyes, she tried to smother the flames of deep fear that flickered inside her.

One

Pru donned her dressing gown over her pyjamas, stretched thick socks over her feet and crept out of the flat door, closing it quietly so as not to disturb her cousin Milly, who was sleeping soundly in her bedroom further down the hall. She slipped down to the basement. This she did on occasion when the bakery was closed, usually in the dead of night when sleep proved elusive, and always with the snap of excitement at her heels as she did so, covertly.

Her alarm would not pip-pip for another three hours, yet instead of resting her head on her plump feather pillow, here she was, wandering along corridors and punching alarm codes into locked doors, looking over her shoulder and tiptoeing like a thief.

Using only minimal lighting, eschewing both the elaborate machinery around her and the complicated recipes that she and Milly had honed over the years, she did what she always did on these night-time jaunts. She set about running up a batch of fairy cakes with nothing but a wooden spoon and a ceramic bowl, just as she had been taught.

Pru fastened the apron around her waist, then laid out her ingredients and tools in a row on the counter top. She got the familiar jolt of happiness, knowing she had everything she needed to execute her plan. It felt exactly the same now as it had all those years ago. She cast her eye over the white flour, the bowl of sugar and the greasy lump of margarine splayed on the saucer next to the shiny clean bowl, awaiting her attention.

She hummed to herself as she tipped the margarine and sugar together and began creaming them into a thick paste. She savoured the gritty crunch on the back of the spoon as it smashed the crystals against the crackle-glazed side of the china bowl, pushing and churning until the mixture billowed with tiny bubbles of air and her fingers ached. Next came the spoonfuls of plain flour, a drop of essence, baking powder, the egg and gradually more flour. Pru couldn't fully describe the lift to her spirits or the bounce to her step as she watched the dry ingredients transform themselves into a pale golden batter. There was no great science to knowing when the mixture was ready; instead she used the tried and tested dropping method, lifting the spoon and watching to see how the cake mix fell. Too quickly meant it was too thin, calling for more flour and more mixing. Whereas a blob that refused to shift from the back of the spoon required more liquid and a light mix. When the batter acquired the perfect consistency, it dropped into the bowl with jaw-clenching slowness.

As the fairy cakes baked, the anticipation filled her stomach with butterflies. While they cooled, she made a strong cup of coffee to go with them. Then she decorated them, exactly as her nan had instructed: sparsely, sprinkling hundreds and thousands on to a tiny misshapen pond of white icing. Both of which had been a luxury in her nan's house. Finally, she popped the soft, vanilla-scented sponges into her mouth, allowing the sugar to spread its warm, satisfying sweetness across her tongue and the icing to stick to the roof of her mouth. She gobbled them greedily and quickly, all of them.

'I know you are shaking your head and tutting at me, but don't judge me, Alfie! I could have far worse habits.' This she uttered into the ether with her eyes raised skywards and a smile about her mouth as she licked a stray blob of icing and a couple of sprinkles from her lip.

As proprietor of the world-renowned Plum Patisserie, Pru had access to any number of delicate iced fancies and exquisite sugar-dusted morsels each and every day. Yet none of them gave her anything like the pleasure she got from eating a warm fairy cake made to her nan's exacting recipe and wolfed down illicitly in the wee small hours. The parcels of moist cake not only made her mouth water, but if she closed her eyes, she was back in their grotty kitchen in Bow, a little girl again, working diligently at their wobbly enamel-topped table. Back to a time before she knew anything of the world beyond their front door, before drive and aspiration had yoked her to a winding uphill path. Her nan, standing at the shallow china sink dressed in a pink wrap-around overall that had worn thin at the seams; and her three brothers, with pinched cheeks and rings of grime against the backs of their necks, hovering around the large china mixing bowl, their dirty fingers scooping at the fine lines of cake mixture residue, which they deposited into their eager mouths. The smell of the fluffy little ingots baking would almost drive them to tears. Clustering around the stove, unusually silent, they waited.

Her nan would then turn the cakes out of the bun tin on to a wire rack on the sideboard. The scented steam that they gave off hypnotised them. And it would feel like an eternity before she would allow them to take one each. When they finally got one of those little cakes in their mitts, round-eyed and with a mouthful of sweet crumbs, it was a moment of bliss in an otherwise bliss-free life and it was wonderful. For Pru, nothing symbolised her success as much as her ability to eat a whole batch made in the kitchen of Plum Patisserie. She never told anyone about her trips down to the big kitchen; it was another little secret for her to keep.

Pru laughed to herself as she perched on the edge of her bed a couple of hours later and applied the Crème de la Mer moisturiser to her face and throat. It was 6 a.m. but she had the alertness of someone who had been up for many hours. Fancy! She touched her fingers to her temples, where her once lustrous locks had now thinned. It was one of several habits she had acquired now that she was sixty-six, along with pushing up her eyebrows with her finger so that she could, for a second or two, re-create the wide eyes of her youth, before gravity had done its job and given them a hooded appearance.

'I was lovely once, wasn't I? Not that I really thought so at the time, despite what Trudy said. I never had her confidence – blimey, who did? She was something else, wasn't she? So very long ago. I don't know why I'm thinking about that, Alfie; our little flat in Kenway Road, my life in Earls Court. We had some fun: tough times, but happy

8

times. A lifetime ago. You're the only one I tell everything to, but I know you're a secret-keeper, aren't you, my love?'

This she addressed to one of several silver-framed photographs on her bedside table. This particular snap was of a man astride a moped. He was looking over his shoulder, a roll-up hanging from his bottom lip. It was a black and white shot, and even though it had been taken decades later, it could have come straight out of the sixties. He had the air of James Dean about him, or maybe that was just how she preferred to think of him: an anti-hero rather than a hopeless, drug-addicted drop-out.

He smiled back at her with eyes that crinkled into laughter, peeping from behind black-framed Ray-Bans that, with his head tilted towards the camera, had slipped down to the end of his nose. Pru loved this photo. There weren't that many of her family – owning a camera had never been a priority – but his grin and the setting, on what looked like a bright, sunny day, meant that she knew he'd had this one good day. Or, more specifically, this one good moment on this one day. She hoped that when things had got bad for him, the memory of that moment might have sustained him. As usual, he didn't reply.

Pru padded around the flat in her soft grey jersey pyjamas and dressing gown, with a cup of hot black coffee balanced on her palm. She hummed as she walked from room to room, finding it calming to see that everything was just as she had left it the night before, harvesting reassurance from the order in which she lived and gaining confidence from knowing she was the owner of so many lovely things. The pictures were straight, cushions plumped and objets d'art

9

positioned just so. Though she had to admit that, barring a messy burglary or natural disaster, the likelihood of this not being the case was extremely slim.

She sat on the chair at the little walnut desk in the corner of her bedroom and let the bank statement flutter in her hand. She no longer paid heed to the black figures and their commas, lined up in neat rows; it was more of an inquisitive glance to see that payments had gone through and a reminder of where she was in the month. Gone were the days of shuffling balances and debts around to keep suppliers happy, juggling dates and orders to ensure there was enough money in the accounts to pay the wages. The business had reached the point a couple of decades ago where takings began to exceed expenditure and once the scales had tipped in their favour, they had never looked back. She unscrewed the lid of her Montblanc fountain pen and placed a tiny cross by the payment that was referenced CM; one thousand pounds had gone through on the fourteenth, just as it did every month and had done for the last ten years. If she did the maths, it caused a ball to knot in her stomach and a tide of panic to rise in her throat, so it was better that she didn't. Pru folded the paper sheets and clipped them into the leather file that she stowed back in the drawer.

After showering and blow-drying her auburn hair into its blunt bob, Pru sat down at her dressing table and applied the merest hint of taupe lip stain and a single wand-slick of mascara. She rubbed her fingers over her temples. She had never thought she would become this sort of older lady. In her youth she'd only ever imagined herself in her mid twenties, old enough to know best but still young enough to enjoy herself. Yet here she was, hardly recognising the face in the mirror. And it had happened in a heartbeat! She sighed and pulled her lower teeth over her top lip, making her neck and chin taut, the way they used to look. A liberal spritz of Chanel No. 5 and she was set for the day. She accessorised her navy trousers with a white silk blouse and two rows of pearls that hung in differing lengths against her small, high chest. She slipped her feet into navy penny loafers, her footwear of choice on days like this.

Pru held her breath and tugged the blind. She watched a white transit van pull up on to the kerb with its hazard lights flashing, delivering to Guy all that they needed for a day of baking and trading. On the opposite side of the street, two young men in dinner jackets, with ties loose about their necks and a wobble to their saunter, walked arm in arm. No doubt homeward bound at this early hour. She smiled; there it was, Curzon Street, just as she had left it.

She worried that one day she might pull the blind and see instead the traffic of Kenway Road, a few miles across town in Earls Court; as if she had dreamed her success, her home in Mayfair, her Italian marble flooring, espresso machine and walk-in closet and was still there, living that life. Back then, although her surroundings had been drab, she had been full of life: a young girl with a defiant stare and a gut full of determination.

The day that she and Milly had arrived at the six-storey terrace on Kenway Road, they had thought they were invincible, immune to the regrets and recriminations that came with old age. It was the last in a long list of rentals that she and Milly had painstakingly ringed in the small ads, and from the moment they arrived they knew it was the place for them. A statuesque, elegant woman opened the door wearing a silk kimono and smoking a thin cigar in an ivory cigarette holder. She introduced herself as Trudy; she lived in a flat on the top floor. Pru walked to one of two deep-set sash windows on the landing and gazed at the most incredible view of the London skyline, all the way out to Fulham and beyond. She let her eyes skim the horizon and red-brick chimney pots. This would be the start of their journey, here among the west London rooftops, living with this assured, worldly woman. Pru followed Trudy down a narrow hallway, noting the way she swept along on her high heels, which made her look refined and sophisticated, sexy. She was going to practise that walk and when she had enough money, buy herself a pair of high-heeled red patent leather shoes, just like Trudy's.

'Who's David Parkes?' Milly asked. She had stopped at a framed certificate that hung on the wall and pointed to it.

'David was... err... my brother.' Trudy arched a carefully plucked eyebrow. 'He died a couple of years ago.'

'I'm sorry,' Pru offered. She rolled her eyes at Milly, who was always jumping in feet first.

Pru and Milly told Trudy how they wanted to open their own bakery with a shop and a café, where they would make the most delicious cakes and bread that London had ever tasted.

Trudy didn't laugh or mock, as others had when they'd shared this. Instead, she nodded and blew large Os of cigar smoke. Then she pressed her full, carmine-painted lips together and said, 'I think people without dreams are living only half a life and that's a life I wouldn't want to live.'

Pru had been impressed, Trudy sounded like a poet.

'But it's no good dreaming unless you are prepared to work really hard. You have to dream it *and* set yourself a path to make it happen. A dream won't put food on the table or money in your purse.'

Pru had subconsciously patted the purse in her pocket, which contained their first week's rent, bus fare and a lucky coin with a hole drilled through it. It was the sum total of their combined wealth. She nodded, wondering what they would need to do to clear their path – the one that led straight to the shiny glass window of Plum Patisserie.

'What's your dream then?' Milly asked Trudy over Pru's shoulder.

Trudy gave the younger girl her full attention, and drew on her cigar. 'To have a little love in my life,' she said as she turned her back and walked forward. 'I think that's everyone's dream, really.'

Dear, dear Trudy.

Pru closed her bedroom door and popped her head into the kitchen, where she spied Milly, clad in a tiger onesie.

'What *are* you wearing?' Pru shook her head.

'It's new and quite possibly the cosiest thing I have ever owned. I might never take it off.'

'That'll be nice front of house.'

Milly dipped a large croissant into her coffee before lowering the soggy mess into her mouth.

'Gross,' Pru commented.

'It's what they do in France!' Milly spoke with her mouth full.

'Maybe, but you're not French, Mills.'

'What? You are kidding me! *Mon Dieu!* I had no idea. I thought I'd imagined growing up in Bow and I was actually from a fashionable little suburb of Paris!' She winked at her cousin.

Pru grinned as she left the flat and trotted down the stairs. Taking a deep breath, she opened the door of the café. She and Milly took it in turns to do the early check on the bakery and it was her turn this week. In truth, after two decades in these premises, and with the celebrated Guy Baudin at the helm of a trusted team, it was more a cursory nod to everyone that she was around, a reminder of who was boss and the chance to monitor quality rather than get stuck in.

The cleaners in their blue nylon tabards and with their hair scraped up into untidy knots were hard at it, buffing the brass fixtures with yellow dusters and mopping the pale, waxed wooden floor. The sun had started its creep through the large window that displayed the Plum Patisserie logo, working its way up like the revelation of a dancer's fan until the whole room was bathed in light. Tiny white rosebuds had been placed in slender, finger-sized vases on every table. The glass display unit they had re-created to mimic those found in nineteenth-century Parisian coffee houses gleamed. The tiered glass cake stands and fancy china plates whose hand-painted flowers and swirls delicately kissed their fluted edges sat shining. Soon they would be arranged with scones full of jam and cream, soft iced buns and frosted sponges; flaky-pastry masterpieces stuffed with marzipan and dotted with an almond would tempt the sweet-toothed, perfect with a cup of hand-roasted French coffee.

Pru particularly loved this time of the morning, before the customers arrived, before the problems arose, before tiredness crept over her aging joints.

'Good morning, all!' she trilled with a singsong intonation. Many of these girls spoke little English, but could glean enough from her tone to reciprocate with a nod and a smile. 'This looks lovely, thank you.'

The girls duly nodded and smiled.

Making her way down the twist of staircase, she placed her foot on the last step. The wood creaked unexpectedly beneath her weight and she gasped, putting one hand to her breast and the other against the wall, trying to steady her heart rate. She exhaled and leant on the wall, using her index finger and thumb to wipe away the tiny dots of perspiration that had gathered on her top lip. She flattened her palm against her chest, trying to calm her flustered pulse. 'Come on, you silly moo.'

It still had the power to do that to her, the flash of a memory, an image, a sound. It could transport her back to a time she would rather forget.

She waited a second and dug deep to find a smile before taking one final step and pushing on the wide double fire door with its brass-edged glass porthole of a window. Immediately, she was engulfed by the smell of fresh bread baking in the oven. She never tired of the aroma; it cocooned her in a blanket of well-being and evoked full tummies, log fires, cosy rooms and all that was homely.

'Good morning, Guy.'

'Is it? I'm not so sure!' He slammed his clipboard with its checklist on to the stainless steel counter top.

This was entirely expected; Guy lived his life with his fingers tense against his flustered, plucked brow and a sigh hovering in his throat. Whippet thin and groomed to within an inch of his perma-tan, Guy lived on caffeine and his nerves.

'What's up?' Pru refrained from adding, '*now*'. Guy was undoubtedly a worrier, a panicker and a drama queen, but all that was forgiven because of his insistence on impeccably high standards both in and out of the kitchen. His attention to detail and his innovative ideas ensured that Plum Patisserie was internationally renowned for its exquisite cake designs. He was the jewel in Pru's crown, an analogy that he particularly loved.

'I specifically ordered extra lemons for our *dessert du jour*, lemon posset with almond-crusted shortbread, and they have sent me my standard order. These people drive me crazy! Are they trying to ruin my day? How can I deliver what I promise with this?' He poked at a large net of sorry-looking yellow fruit and grimaced as though he had been presented with roadkill rather than inadequate waxed citrus.

'I doubt they set out to ruin your day intentionally, they probably just forgot or got muddled; you know how it is when an order deviates from the norm, it often gets confused somewhere along the line. We *could* always send someone up to the supermarket to grab you some more lemons?'

Guy placed his hands on his hips. 'Well, I suppose we will have to.'

Pru noted the slight flicker of disappointment that crossed his face whenever a solution was easily and quickly found.

'Also, Guy, can we get someone to fix the bottom stair that comes down from the café? It's got a creak.' She gave a small cough.

'Oh, Pru! You and your creaks! I could have a man here every day, fixing one creak or another. This building is over two hundred years old, it's going to creak!' He raised his hands to the sky with flattened palms.

'And as I've said before, I don't mind if a man – or a woman, for that matter – has to come every day or indeed every hour of every day and I don't care what it costs. I can't have the stairs making that noise. Any of them, at any time. I can't. Okay?'

'Okay.' He shrugged, then muttered something inaudible in his native French.

'How's the window display coming along?' Pru knew she could easily distract him and if she were being honest was keen to change the subject. In between the double-fronted café and the front door that led to their apartments stood a tall bow window emblazoned with the Plum Patisserie logo. The window was all that was left of the Victorian pharmacy that had been knocked through and transformed into their current corner premises. The space behind it was a little over five feet deep and with no particular purpose other than decoration it was the ideal place for Guy to showcase the latest Plum creations. The little gallery had become one of the most photographed spots in Mayfair. This pleased Pru no end: whether the photos were for a magazine or just one of a tourist's haul of snaps, the fact that her logo and cakes were being admired by a wider audience was great advertising.

Guy clapped his hands under his chin, instantly diverted from his lemon crisis and his lack of empathy regarding stair repair. 'Oh, Pru, oh my! It is beyond exquisite, it's divine. No, it's beyond divine, it's epic, it's... Words fail me.' Guy placed his middle three fingers over his pursed lips and blinked away the tears that threatened.

'That good, huh?'

He nodded slowly, unable to fully articulate. '*Mais oui*, and more!' He was quite breathless.

Pru smiled. She was used to this: each of his creations was always similarly lauded and the funny thing was, it was always entirely justified. 'I can't wait to see it. Any luck with the new trainee?'

'Don't. Even. Go. There!' He held up a palm in front of her face. 'Every single person they have sent has been completely useless. I have the same conversation with the agency after every sorry interview. I tell them repeatedly, I don't need bakers! Bakers are ten a penny – no offence intended, Pru.'

'None taken.' She was a baker and proud.

'But I don't *need* a baker, I need an artiste! Someone who has the eye, the touch and the imagination, someone who can turn sugar paste into pure fantasy, someone who can make the dreams of others into reality! Is it too much to ask?' For the second time in as many minutes he looked close to tears.

Pru stared at him in silence, fishing for a suitable response and wondering if this was the job description he had given

18

the agency. Then she gave up and abandoned the topic altogether. 'I'm nipping out this morning. Bobby has a dress fitting in Spitalfields, but Milly will be around if you need anything.'

'Oh, a dress fitting? How exciting! I saw the lovely couple yesterday afternoon, strolling hand in hand like love's young dream. Oh my goodness, so beautiful together! Can you imagine what *les enfants* will look like? They are a couple that heaven blessed for sure.'

'I know, Bobby's a lucky girl. She certainly doesn't take after me; she takes after her mum, Astrid. She was the most beautiful girl I'd ever seen.'

This wasn't a topic Pru normally discussed. Astrid had disappeared to India when Bobby was three months old, leaving Alfie, her drug-addled boyfriend, to care for their daughter. She told Alfie she needed space and enlightenment; apparently it didn't occur to her that what their little girl needed was a mummy who wasn't over six thousand miles away. Ironically, the move probably saved Astrid's life. She had been as fond of recreational drugs as Alfie, but she left before he progressed to heroin and the habit that would eventually kill him.

'Oh, Pru, she most certainly does take after you. You are beautiful inside and out. I can see you now...' Guy raised his hand as if shielding his eyes. 'You could model for denture cream or stair lifts!'

Pru threw a napkin at him and turned on her heel, smiling as she did so.

Two

It was two hours later that Pru found herself standing under the hot lights of the low-ceilinged basement room in Spitalfields. She found the pristine white walls and flooring quite dazzling and felt the beginnings of a headache stirring behind her eyes. Bella turned to her and grimaced: Bobby was not making her job any easier.

'Bobby, you are not helping Bella by wriggling!' Pru placed her hand against her forehead and un-gritted her teeth. 'You need to stand still or you are going to end up with a pin in you,' she barked at her niece, who twitched her arms and jiggled her legs as she squealed and chatted.

Pru ran her fingers through her hair and stretched out her right hand, glancing at the flawless solitaire diamond and its sister band that sat there rather loosely. She had bought the diamond herself: it was proof of her success and independence and a measure of her taste. It didn't quite compensate for never having been given a ring by a man, but it certainly helped.

She flattened the front of her navy Chanel blazer, checked her buttons were neat in their holes and pulled at the sleeves until they rested just so above her silk cuffs. She might be well into her sixties, but she still had long legs, a slim physique and designer clothes to be proud of; reminding herself of this gave her a much needed jolt of confidence and happiness, every time.

'Imightstickapininheranyway!' Bella mumbled and winked.

'Don't you dare!' Bobby shouted.

'Keep still!' Pru yelled. This whole exercise was altogether more stressful than any of them had bargained on.

She shrugged apologetically at Bella, the short, chubby seamstress who was toiling over the hem of the wedding dress. With a mouth full of bobble-headed tacks, a pincushion on the back of her wrist and a determined stare, Bella tucked, scrunched and pinned.

The bride-to-be stood on the small podium that raised her twelve inches in the air, her head only inches from the ceiling. 'I can't keep still, Aunty Pru, I'm too excited! I feel like the bride on top of one of your cakes, standing up here. I can't believe it, in just under a year I shall be Mrs William Fellsley! Eleven months, and that will fly by.'

Eleven more months of this! Pru took another deep breath.

'I've been thinking about my bouquet,' Bobby rattled on, 'and I know exactly what I want. I can see it now: white lilies with ivy trailing through them. I want it to look like they've been grabbed from the wild and bunched together in a hurry. It will be haphazard but beautiful! Won't it be wonderful?' She did a little skip and clapped her hands again.

'Yes, Bobby, wonderful. I could do with some sugar.'

'I thought you said you'd given up sweets?'

'I have, but there are certain days I wish I hadn't.' Pru didn't confess to sneaking the odd packet or two of wine gums, when things got a bit much. This was fast turning into one of those days.

Roberta Plum placed her slender, manicured hands on her tiny waist, pulled her mouth into a sideways smirk and bit her cheek, an expression she employed when things weren't going according to plan. 'You look a bit fed up. I don't feel like you are sharing my joy here, Aunty Pru.'

'Oh I am sharing your joy, darling. It's just that we've been sharing your joy for the last ten months and there's only so many times I can hear about how wonderful Billy-boy is, what he said, where you went, what you wore, what he ate, where you are going on your honeymoon and how many kids you are planning on having, starting with a boy called Harry.'

'Henry, not Harry! I knew you weren't listening.'

Pru rubbed her temples and closed her eyes, pushing her thumbs into the sockets as if trying to relieve some unseen pressure. 'I'm sorry, my love, you are right. Whenever you told me that, I can't have been listening.'

As ever, she must have been running through the to-do list in her head while her niece was talking. *Check the sugar-paste order, get the repair bloke in for the other bread hook, run the invoice over to The Dorchester, send the sample colours to Lady Miriam so she can start thinking about the birthday cake, speak to the Condé Nast design team, chase the agency for the CVs, book a hair appointment with Cleo, order the paint for the front gallery window...* 'Tell me again, Bobby. I promise I'm listening now.'

Bobby visibly brightened and Pru felt the familiar swell of happiness at seeing her niece beam.

'Well, after we are married, we are going to stay in the flat in Curzon Street, but that's just until William gets promoted and gets his next posting, which we hope will be somewhere hot. I rather like the sound of Cyprus or Belize, but I am hoping for Cyprus because, as you know, I absolutely love halloumi and taramasalata, and I don't know what they eat in Belize.'

It always made Pru smile, hearing Bobby speak with the enthusiasm of a child, taking pleasure from the little things. It was reassuring too to hear confirmation that her niece wouldn't be going away any time soon. It was bad enough that she would be leaving at some point, but at least it wasn't immediately. She and Milly would have time to adjust. Bobby would remain in the flat above theirs for some time yet, where they could keep an eye on her, as they had ever since she had come to live with her aunts above the bakery when she was eight years old.

'I shall get pregnant literally just before we move and spend the whole nine months soaking up the sunshine while the Major does whatever majors do, and then I'll come back to London to have the baby, a boy, who we shall name...?'

'Henry!' Pru came in on cue.

Bobby nodded, satisfied. 'Yes, Henry! Well done, Aunty Pru. And on the day I have him, I want you to make me a basket full of those little white-chocolate muffins that I love, with pale blue ribbons streaming from the handle, and because I'll still be a bit fat, I'll be able to eat them and it won't count!'

Pru searched in her navy satin clutch bag for a bar of

Galaxy she had lurking there, for emergency use only. She held the shiny foil wrapper between her fingers.

'Notinhere!' Bella grunted through her pins and pointed at the foil-wrapped bar, understandably nervous about the combination of hand-beaded white duchess satin and sticky milk chocolate.

'Of course not, Bella. I know! I'm not even going to eat it; it just makes me feel calmer to hold it, knowing I might eat it later, which I won't, because I've given up sweets.' She used the chocolate bar to point in the direction of her niece, who stood draped in her elegant gown. 'I don't know how she turned out like this, I really don't.' Bobby looked stunning. Her thick blonde hair hung like a wave over her left shoulder, her large eyes shone from above her sculpted cheekbones.

In truth, a lot of careful thought and loving attention had gone into making Bobby the effervescent young woman she now was. Alfie had struggled on for years after Astrid left, a single dad fighting his addiction and trying to care for his baby daughter. Finally, when he felt he was losing his battle against the toxic drugs that he craved, he had entrusted Bobby into the care of his elder sister: Pru, successful businesswoman, childless and wealthy. Some members of the family called him a heartless bastard – 'How could a dad hand over his own daughter? What kind of man is that?' They had tutted and sipped tea through lips stretched thin with disapproval. The same lips that had uttered a thousand reasons as to why they couldn't offer him help when he needed it the most. But Pru and Milly had defended his action, standing defiantly with their chins up and shoulders back. They knew what kind of man he was. Alfie was a man who had performed the ultimate act of selflessness, handing over his precious, adored child into the arms of those who could do better than he, even though it hurt like hell.

Pru would never forget the day Alfie knocked on the door of her swanky Mayfair address to deliver his little girl, who was clutching everything she owned inside a plastic carrier bag. He had looked to the left and right as if expecting to be castigated or turfed out of the postcode. His hair was dull from lack of shampoo, his skin grey and acned, and Pru noticed that he had lost more teeth, causing his mouth to pucker and making him look like the old man he would never become. The trainers on his feet had collapsed, gaping on either side to reveal his sockless, dirty instep. His tracksuit top, worn shiny on the arms, was smelly and stained.

Pru's heart tore as he bent down, and kissed Bobby's scalp goodbye.

'You be a good gel, now, promise?'

Bobby had nodded and thrown her arms around his legs as she cried huge sobs that rattled her little chest and made her gulp for air. Her tears left pale white streaks down her sallow cheeks; she had the face of someone who had absorbed the stress and sadness of life with an addict, sentenced through association to a life of darkened rooms, squalor and a topsy-turvy routine.

Alfie peeled her arms from his legs before hugging his sister and kissing his daughter one final time. He sniffed, shoved his hands into the front pockets of his jeans and walked briskly out of their lives. He didn't look back. Pru and Bobby watched until he rounded the corner and disappeared. The little girl howled and stamped her feet on the spot in frustration as her aunty placed her arm across her skinny shoulder.

'It'll all be all right, Bobby, you wait and see.'

'I... I... want my dad! I want him to come back now! I want to go home and I don't like you!' she had stuttered through her sobs.

And now here she was, eleven years later, standing on the podium with a halo of light behind her head. 'Look at her! She looks like Veronica Lake.' Pru voiced her thoughts out loud.

'Who's Veronica Lake? She better not be anything like Ricki Lake!' Bobby let her top lip curl upwards in disapproval.

Pru shook her head. 'D'you hear that, Bella? All that money spent on her education. She has the voice and poise that make you think she was born with a silver spoon up her arse as well as in her gob and yet she doesn't have the sense God gave her.'

'Oh, well, that's charming! It's not my fault you sent me to those schools. You said it was so I wouldn't sound like you and Milly, which I don't, and now you laugh at me. I would have been happy going to the same school that you two went to. I wouldn't have known any different.' Bobby folded her arms across her chest in the way she had done ever since she was little, to show her vehement disapproval.

'I'm teasing you, Bobby. You sound beautiful and you are beautiful. Besides, you wouldn't have lasted five minutes in our old school, even if it hadn't been knocked down to

26

make way for the extension to the match factory. You couldn't have lived in Mayfair and gone to a school like that without being robbed of your dinner money and your watch every day. And you never have to worry: you are worth every penny, my darling girl. I wanted you to be a lady and you are.'

'Shebetternotstartgettinfat!' Bella mumbled, nervous that there was nearly a whole year to go until the big day.

'She won't, Bella, don't worry. She eats like a horse but doesn't put on an ounce, it's sickening.'

'Ellokettle!' Bella mumbled, nodding at Pru's slender frame.

'Do you think William will always love me?' Bobby chewed her bottom lip and blinked hard, always one stomach flip away from the memory of her dad, the man who had loved her most in the whole wide world but had left her on a pavement and gone away for good without looking back. No matter the reason behind his actions, he had left her and that still hurt.

'He'd be mad not to. And if he even thinks about doing anything that makes you unhappy, he'll have me to deal with.' Pru nodded, only half in jest.

She hadn't shared her fears about William with Bobby. That he seemed a little aloof; not quite disinterested, but certainly not full of the enthusiasm that his wife-to-be displayed. Milly said she was being over-protective, reminded her that boys were different. She was probably right. But it was hard not to be over-protective. She had been chosen to look after Alfie's precious girl and she couldn't afford to get it wrong. His words would stay with her forever. As

27

Bobby howled and stamped outside the front door, Alfie had looked at the sky and then the pavement, gently patting the top of his daughter's head and her shoulders, unable to meet the eyes of his little girl, the one person in the world to whom he could not lie. He shook his head. 'I'm not coming back, Bob. But you'll be fine; Aunty Pru's got you now.'

It was as if Bobby read her thoughts. 'I wonder what my dad would say if he could see me now, dressed up like this!' She gathered up handfuls of her skirt and let it fall. 'I realised the other day, Pru, I've been alive much longer without him than with him and yet it doesn't feel like that to me. It's weird, isn't it, how you can miss something so badly that you only had for a very short time.'

Alfie had died alone, just four months later, in a dirty basement flat in Hackney. Pru had cried for days at his passing, not so much for the manner in which he had died, or even the sadness that Bobby would carry with her, but because Alfie had deserved so much more and for the want of a more stable start and a pinch of self-confidence, he just might have got it.

Bobby had been rather unresponsive to the news of his passing, which worried both Pru and Milly greatly. Sitting her down, Pru had told her it was all right to feel sad and to cry for her dad. Bobby, who was nine by then, had shrugged her shoulders, shaken her fringe out of her eyes and looked squarely at her aunt. 'I know that, but I have cried all my tears out for him. I knew I wouldn't see him again when he left me here and it already makes me sad every day – when I wake up, sometimes at school *and* before I go to sleep. I can't be any sadder, because I'm already the most sad I can be.'

It was so touching and honest and it had brought tears to Pru's eyes.

Looking at his gorgeous grown-up daughter now, Pru nodded her agreement. 'It is weird, my love. It's strange for me too. I still expect him to pop up, all smiles and with something funny to tell me. He could always make me laugh, more than anyone else.'

'I would have loved him to meet William. He'd have said he was stuck-up at first, but once they got to know each other, they'd have got on great. It wouldn't have mattered to me what my dad did or had. I would give anything for him to walk me down the aisle. I would love to have him back for just that one day!'

'Oh, love.' Pru swallowed the lump that sat at the back of her throat, a lump that she had been trying to shift for over a decade. 'He'd be so proud of you! But he's with you always, watching over your shoulder and keeping you safe. You know that, don't you?'

Bobby nodded. Yes, she knew that.

Later that evening William plonked himself down in Pru's chair, rubbed his eyes and stretched his long legs out in front of him. He crossed his heavy army boots at the ankles and knitted his palms across the back of his head. 'I'm absolutely shattered.'

'You are? I've spent the best part of my day at the dress-maker's with your intended. I reckon I deserve one of your medals. I was there for four hours, but it felt like a week!'

'Does she look amazing?'

'What do you think?'

William smiled. 'I wish I could see her in it.' He looked into the middle distance.

'Well you will of course, you wally!' She laughed.

'Yes, of course.' He nodded. Wally indeed.

William yawned. Pru had to admit he looked exhausted. She was fascinated by his confidence, his whole stance, tone and air, which left her in no doubt that he considered himself to be the leader of the pack as the only male in residence. In truth, it felt odd to have a man about their pretty little home; the last time she had shared a house with boys was when she lived with her brothers in her teens. Having never married or even lived with a man, she felt his presence keenly, noting the way he took up space, the way he walked and acted. It brought a different dynamic to the place, changed the atmosphere.

William Fellsley had the confidence that came from being born into privilege and being made a leader of men at such a young age had fine-tuned his innate self-assurance still further. Had she encountered his voice and manner in her youth, she would have scuttled for cover, hiding under a blanket of inferiority. Not now though. Pru hovered in front of the grand fireplace, in her Mayfair home. 'You seem thoughtful. Tough day at the office, Billy-boy?'

'Yes, something like that.' He tensed his jaw and raised his eyebrows, stifling another yawn. 'There's a whisper going around that the Colonel has selected me for a course. Not had it confirmed yet, but I've been given the nod.'

'Oh, that's great, well done, you!'

'Well, it is and it isn't. It's a great honour and very good for my career. I know the promotion board will look favourably on it, but it means at least three months away from home, only coming back every other weekend, which is a bit of a bugger.'

'Oh no! Really? Bobby'll be heartbroken. Couldn't she come and stay with you?' Pru was already hearing her niece's distressed reaction in her head. 'How about I book you both into a nice hotel at the weekends? You could make it into an adventure!'

William shook his head. ''Fraid not. That's a lovely offer, Pru, thank you, but there's a lot of studying to do. It's fairly intense. They run events in the evenings and at weekends, which I have to be seen at – team building and so forth, planning sessions. She'd be sitting alone and I couldn't stand the thought of that. I'd rather she was here being looked after than sitting in a lonely hotel room watching the clock and scoffing the mini-bar.'

Pru clapped her hands together. 'Well, we shall just have to make the best of it and ensure that those weekends that you are home are really special. Where is your course?'

'Ashford, Kent. Not too far, but just far enough.'

'Just far enough for what?'

'To be a pain in the arse!'

She nodded. 'You'll get through it, love. Three months is nothing in the grand scheme of things, not when you've got the rest of your lives together. And anyway, what is it they say, absence makes the heart grow fonder?'

'Yes, something like that. Although, to be honest, I wish we didn't have to test that theory.'

Pru smiled at him, happy that he didn't want to be parted from her precious girl.

Right on cue, Bobby flew into the room. 'There you are, my Captain!' She plonked herself down on his lap and threw her legs over the arm of the chair, nuzzling into his neck and kissing his face. 'I missed you.'

'You only saw me this morning!' He laughed as she covered his face with kisses like an excitable puppy.

'I know,' she purred, 'but I hate being away from you even for an hour, let alone all day.'

'This work thing really gets in the way of us having a good time, doesn't it?'

'Yes it does,' Bobby responded without recognising his sarcasm.

William glanced at Pru, both acknowledging that three months of virtual separation might be harder than they thought.

'All set for the engagement party, Pru?' William managed to ask over his fiancée's head.

'Yes, really looking forward to it,' she lied.

'It should be fun. My mother's really keen to see you again and not just to discuss plans for the wedding cake!'

'Oh, don't you worry about that. Guy has already spent hours and hours sketching and modelling. It will without a shadow of a doubt be the cake of the bloody year, if not the decade. He'll make sure of it!'

Bobby squealed. 'If I think about it, I might just burst! I can't wait to see what he comes up with. I trust Guy completely, he's a genius.'

'Yes he is,' Pru concurred.

'Mother's invited lots of her old friends and I've got chums from Sandhurst coming down. Are you sure you don't want to come up with us on Friday night? There's plenty of room in the car. You and Milly would be more than welcome to stay at Mountfield for the weekend. Mum would love it, pouring wine down your neck and getting you to spill the beans on what it's like inside all those fancy London houses that you get to nose around.'

Pru gave a small cough; it sounded like her worst nightmare. 'That's very kind of your mum, love, but I've got so much to do for work. Plum's is always extra busy at this time of year – weddings, christenings and whatnot. Seems that at the first sign of spring the whole country finds a reason for a party. Not that I'm moaning! But I really can't be away for any longer than I have to be; it's not fair on Guy. So I've booked a car for Sunday and I promise we'll be there for lunchtime.'

'Splendid!' William clapped his hands together.

Yep, thought Pru, *bloody splendid.* At least she wasn't going alone. She just hoped Milly was planning on changing out of her tiger suit before the event.

Three

Pru sidled even closer to the exit as her phone buzzed in her handbag.

'Hello-o?' She tried to sound jovial and smiled falsely into the mouthpiece.

There was a second or two of silence.

'Have you seen it yet?'

'Have I seen what yet, Milly?' Pru knew very well what her cousin meant.

'The engagement cake! What do you think?'

'No, I haven't, and I'm not actually talking to you, so this is going to be a very short conversation.' Pru sighed.

'Ha! But you're talking to me now!'

'Only because I *have* to and you know what I mean.'

'I can't believe you're having a go at me. Most people would be concerned if their loved one had taken to their sick bed, or at least they'd offer some sympathy!'

'Is that what you phoned for, Mills – sympathy?'

'No! I phoned because I want to know about the bloody cake!'

'I haven't seen it, but I promise to call you the moment I have.'

'No, don't bother. I'm not remotely interested.'

'Fine. I won't.' Pru closed her eyes.

'Actually, yes, do. I want to know what it's like. It's probably a lopsided dry sponge with uneven icing and wobbly cake toppers, ordered from a knock-off catalogue and made to look like Bobby and Billy-boy. You know the ones: not bad from a distance, but up close the faces look like they've been painted by a three-year-old in a hurry. It'll be nasty and common.'

Pru took in Mountfield, the pale stone of the Queen Anne mansion that looked like a life-sized doll's house. The carefully trained wisteria that hung in uniform bunches, clipped so as not to obscure the view from the breakfast room window, and the clusters of bistro-chic garden furniture that sat under perfectly positioned willow arbours, offering just the right amount of shade for afternoon tea. 'I doubt that very much. The only thing that's common around here is me. And we've had this conversation. You know that if it had been down to Bobby, you would have made the cake and provided the food, the whole darn lot. But it wasn't, it was down to Isabel, who Bobby says was too shy to ask us, in case we thought she was asking for the lot, gratis. And I understand that not everyone is a human bulldozer like you. It's their party and it's up to them. Is that why you stayed away, is this all a ruse, you silly moo?'

'No it bloody isn't, you daft cow. I've been puking my kidneys up since six o'clock this morning!'

'Nice.' Pru gave a gentle wave to Isabel, who was sitting in the far corner of the marquee with her cronies, furiously beckoning her over. Pru turned her head, making out she hadn't seen.

35

Milly was still mid rant. 'You've got to admit it's ridiculous, Pru. We'd have happily done it "gratis", as you put it. As it is, they'll end up having to pay a fortune for something that will be way below the standards of Plum Patisserie, just cos Mrs Never Shit—'

'Don't call her that, Milly.'

'Or whatever her bloody name is—'

'You know her name. It's Isabel.'

'All right, all right! Just because Isabel thinks she knows best – it's a bloody disgrace!'

'Milly, I love you, but you are driving me mad and I have to go. It's bad enough I am here suffering all by myself, without standing and having a row with you among the smoked salmon canapés and dyed swans.'

'Dyed swans? Oh that's just bloody naff!'

Pru laughed. There were no dyed swans, but she knew it would guarantee a reaction. 'Goodbye, Milly! I'll see you later. I won't be late.'

She placed the phone back in her bag, sipped her drink and stared into the crowded marquee. 'I'm going to bloody kill you, Milly,' she muttered. 'Who in their right bloody mind eats five-day-old chicken that's been left on the work surface for twelve hours?' Pru hoped that her words would somehow travel from the Oxfordshire countryside to W1 and float through the open window, arriving like a speech bubble, loud and clear for her cousin to hear. They had both been dreading this afternoon and had agreed they would get through it by sticking together, just like they had always done.

Ordinarily, Milly would stick by her no matter what; Pru knew that. She remembered the first time she'd realised that about her cousin. It was a summer's day and the whole of Blondin Street was out on the cobbles. They were playing stuck in the mud and kick the can when Pru got into a row with Malcolm Hughes, who had called her a weakling. Millicent was almost the mirror image of her, but without the fire in her belly or the natural darts of red and gold that shot through her hair. Their nan always said that if Pru piled up the dynamite, it would be Milly who struck the match. Pru held Malcolm Hughes while Milly punched him; she had to give him double because he flinched and that was the rule. Afterwards, their nan had stood them in front of the fireplace, tutting at their ripped frocks and grubby knees, demanding to know what had happened.

'Pru told me to hit him and so I did!' Milly had finally confessed as Pru rolled her eyes skyward.

Her nan bent in close so the sharp bristles on her chin were visible. 'And if Pru told you to jump off Tower Bridge, would you?'

Milly considered her response as she reached for Pru's hand and knotted her fingers inside her cousin's. 'Yeah. I would.' She nodded.

Their nan had placed her hands on her hips and looked confused, unsure where to go from there. It clearly wasn't the answer she had been expecting.

Pru had taken great comfort from the fact that Milly would be at this engagement party with her: her crutch, diversion and reason for leaving. And yet here she was, alone, feeling like the vegetarian option at a rugby team's end-of-season barbecue. She twisted her diamond ring nervously, hoping it would give her the strength to enter the throng alone. But it only brought flooding back the memory of the day she had bought it. She had just found a window seat in a café in Holborn and was sitting enjoying the spring sunshine after a particularly successful meeting with a publishing company. She was making notes about the centrepiece design for their upcoming sales conference, a cake in their corporate colours that would re-create their bestselling books in miniature, sitting on the tiers like open butterflies, plus a few on invisible wire, poised to land. It would be stunning. She was thinking about the gasps of delight and subsequent column inches it would garner, when she tuned into the conversation on a nearby table and realised to her fascination that they were talking about her. The couple in question were clearly unaware that she was within earshot.

'She's an attractive lady,' was the young woman's opener. 'I love that red hair thing she's got going on, and that's a good suit. She's got a great pair of legs, classy.'

Pru looked straight ahead and tried to appear oblivious. The compliment, however, rang inside her head like a klaxon.

'You'll look as good as her when you're old,' her partner said with certainty, then kissed her loudly on the mouth.

'I so won't!'

'Don't be daft! You will, you're gorgeous.'

Pru smiled against the rim of her cup, enjoying the shared intimacy. And then came the words that wiped the grin off her face.

'I won't because I'm married and I've got three kids. You will all wear me down and totally knacker me out. That woman is not married, there's no wedding ring and she certainly doesn't look like a mum. Mums are never that neat or that smart and you don't get time to sit alone and enjoy a coffee! She's in no rush because there is no one waiting for her, wondering where she is or what's for tea. No, I'm telling you, she looks that good because she is single and childless, the lucky cow. Probably spends her time being pampered and booking her next holiday!'

Pru's tears had sprung almost without warning. It was as if she had been given access to a secret dossier about herself. Suddenly she saw herself as others must – a lonely fifty-year-old woman. There would be no baby to coil its tiny fingers around hers, holding on for all it was worth because she was its mummy and it never wanted to let her go. There would be no pretty white wedding for her; no husband would beam at her over his shoulder as she walked towards him under a glittering canopy of stars. Before, there had always been a flicker of hope, a grain of belief that someone would want her. Sitting at the table, that tiny flicker was snuffed out. She resolved then and there that she would buy herself the most beautiful diamond she could find. A sign that although she might not be a wife or mother, she could afford the trinkets, the twinkling markers that often went with those roles.

Now, sixteen years later, she often touched the bauble for comfort, like a talisman, to remind herself of everything she had built. But it wasn't working today.

She took a deep breath and glanced once more around the marquee, craning her neck as if trying to locate someone. This was one of those days when to have an 'other half' on her arm would have made all the difference. The extravagant buffet was curling on a table at the far end and everyone seemed to be communicating via squeals and slaps on the back. Pru felt the beginnings of a headache. Despite having spent years paying close attention to what her smart clients wore and said in order to fit in at even the finest London addresses, she was out of her comfort zone by about sixty miles. There was something about these country affairs that gave her the collywobbles. Her nan had always told her, 'People is people, Pru, we all shit through the same hole!', but that didn't really help on days like this.

It had all started soon after she and Milly had moved into Kenway Road. There had been one memorable evening when she'd decided to try out her cut-glass accent for the first time. 'Who's for a cuppa?' Milly had yelled from the kitchen.

'I would love a cup of tea, please, Milly!' Pru had replied, enunciating every syllable as best she could.

There was a moment of silence as Trudy and Milly turned to look at Pru.

'What the bloody hell was that?' Milly laughed.

Undeterred, Pru stuck her chin out. 'I want to speak properly; I don't want to sound like ElizableedinDoolittle any more. And I've been thinking, if we're going to have a posh bakery up west, we need to sound a bit more, y'know, posher.'

Milly stared at her cousin in disbelief. 'That's it! You've finally lost the plot, girl. People will come to Plum's because we make the best bloody cakes in London, not cos of how you talk!' She raised her eyes to the ceiling.

But it was Trudy who took her seriously. 'Sometimes, Pru, becoming a new person is the only way to shake off the old one. But be careful – you don't ever want to lose yourself completely. Take it from one who knows, that would be the saddest thing imaginable.'

Pru watched as Trudy's eyes pooled with tears, the only time she would ever see this. She stored her friend's words in her head; she didn't ever want to lose herself completely.

As Pru continued to hover near the exit of the marquee, she couldn't help but wonder if she had done just that. With her tangerine leather clutch bag in one hand and a glass of champagne in the other, she smiled and tapped her fingers against her glass in time to the music, as though she was having a fabulous time.

The marquee was huge – Billy Smart's Circus on Clapham Common sprang to mind. It was, as per Bobby's prospective mother-in-law's instructions, festooned with colour-coordinated bunting, strings of coloured lights that looped back and forth across the roof and a glitter ball suspended over the wooden dance floor that would put Times Square in the shade. The whole event had been a mere ten weeks in the planning and if Pru was being honest, she couldn't wait for it to be over. She dreaded to think about the level of detail and discussion that would go into the actual wedding if this were just the engagement party.

It wasn't that she disapproved of William in any way – far from it. He made Bobby happy and that was every-thing. But the prospect of having to endure cosy meetings with the excitable Isabel, who had spent the whole of lunch shrieking, clapping and tutting at the slightest provocation, was more than she could bear. Over an after-lunch coffee, taken at their vast kitchen table, Pru had listened politely to Isabel's dilemma with downsizing; apparently a smaller kitchen wouldn't go amiss.

'There have been countless times when my meals have been ruined – it's such a struggle coordinating the hob, range, fridge and microwave with so much space in between,' she trilled. Pru had nodded sympathetically. *It must be hell.* 'From one baker to another, I don't mind telling you that this vast room plays havoc with my meringues!'

Pru had then sat in silence as Isabel and Bobby debated whether ivory or jade bows would be best on the backs of the chairs and was it too much to insist that the centrepieces of gerbera and gypsophila were wired to make sure they didn't droop, *before* being adorned with a single green butterfly? On and on it went, each detail seemingly more over-considered than the last. She didn't understand how these things could be so important to the success of a wedding, but apparently they were.

Pru was used to this level of detail – her clientele were discerning, rich and picky. But she found it odd that Bobby – her flesh and blood, whose nan had toiled in a munitions factory on the night shift and had had all her own teeth pulled at eighteen to avoid dental bills; whose own dad had died practically homeless – fell so easily into the role of spoilt cow. It was her own fault, she knew.

William's wider family were nice enough. She had been introduced to several distant cousins and a couple of school friends and army chums who all had names that would have guaranteed a good beating had they grown up in her neighbourhood. Piers Parkinson-Boater being the first one that leapt to mind. Although, in fairness to Master

Parkinson-Boater, one of William's closest friends, he had been pleasant and seemed to take a genuine interest in her as Bobby's nearest and dearest. He'd offered to get her a drink and had even enquired about the opening hours of Plum's, promising to bring his mum for a cuppa and a slice of cake, if he was passing.

'Yes, that would be nice. Are you often passing by?' Pru had asked.

Piers had looked at his rather large feet. 'No, not really and not for a while. I'm off on tour actually.'

'Oh, so you're a soldier too? Where you going?'

'The usual: somewhere hot, dangerous and dusty.' He shrugged as a nervous flicker crossed his brow.

'Well, you take care of yourself, won't you?'

'Yes,' he nodded. 'Unlike Wills I didn't manage to land a desk job. I always seem to find myself in grim corners, where the jobs are rather mucky.'

'Well, thank God you do, it keep us all safe.'

Piers grinned at the compliment. 'And when I get back, I'll be sure to pop in.'

Lovely. Of the others whose acquaintance she had made that afternoon, each had in turn shaken her hand and muttered 'How d'you do,' before exiting sharpish in search of similarly monikered beings of the same age and opposite sex, with whom they could sit and compare notes about who they knew in common and in which county.

A swell of linen, silk and tanned, sculpted limbs now crowded the dance floor and Bobby was in her element. Every time Pru glimpsed her, her left arm was extended, French-manicured fingers splayed, and a different pair of eyes was scrutinising the weighty bauble that sparkled on her hand. She was so happy to be loved. Life and luck were determined by the turn of a coin – Pru of all people knew that. Had she not insisted on staying in touch with her beloved Alfie, Bobby would have ended up in care.

Pru blinked away the image that formed in her head and turned her eyes heavenwards. 'Look at her, Alfie! I couldn't be any prouder. She's doing fine, our beautiful girl, she's doing absolutely fine.' This she addressed out through the marquee entrance, to the blue sky and the full trees that surrounded the adjacent paddock and large lake.

'It's the first sign, you know.'

His voice came from over her shoulder. She swung round to face the man, who wore a sharp grey suit and pale pink shirt. He was about her age, handsome and with thinning grey hair that was slightly too long and pushed back over his tanned forehead. He had twinkly blue eyes and the skin around them was crinkled, suggesting he laughed a lot.

She brushed invisible creases from her lime-green linen shift and ran her tongue over her front teeth, in case any lipstick or lettuce had lodged there.

'What's the first sign of what?' She wrinkled her nose, confused.

'Talking to yourself, the first sign of madness.' He sipped at his glass of red wine and nodded his head as though they were mid conversation.

'Blimey, I always talk to myself; it's the only way to get any sense in our house. And anyway, I wasn't talking to myself; I was talking to my little brother, Alfie.'

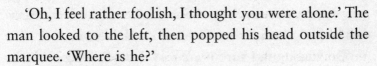

'Oh, I feel rather foolish, I thought you were alone.' The man looked to the left, then popped his head outside the marquee. 'Where is he?'

'Where's who?'

'Your brother, Alfie, the one you're talking to?'

'Oh, he's dead,' Pru said quite matter-of-factly. 'But that doesn't stop me talking to him.'

He hesitated. 'I talk to my wife, Ginny. She's dead too.'

'Does she ever answer you?' Pru cocked her head to one side, fascinated to hear his response.

'Yes. Yes she does.' He smiled. 'Or at least I hear her response. Maybe it's simply what I *think* she would say or maybe I dredge her words from a memory and cobble together an answer from all the conversations we had over the years. But that's the same thing really, isn't it?'

Pru nodded. 'Yep. I suppose it is.'

'Does your brother answer you?' The man put his hand on his hip, slipping it under his jacket and revealing a slight paunch.

Pru's voice was quieter now. 'No. No, he doesn't. But I see his face smiling at me as though he is pleased to hear my news. Mind you, he never could get a word in edgeways so that shouldn't surprise me.'

'Do you picture his face from when he was young or the last time you saw him? I only ask because when I converse with Ginny, she is in her mid thirties, but she was actually nearer fifty when she died.'

She had to think about this. 'That's strange, isn't it? I wonder why that is. I haven't really considered it before, but with Alfie it's the face he had the last time I saw him,

45

only happy, content, better.' She avoided the words 'clean' and 'sober', though they fluttered on her tongue.

'Do you know, I have never told another living soul that before.' He gave a small cough and looked anywhere other than her face.

'Well, your secret is safe with me. I think lots of people do it, I know it brings me great comfort.'

The man took a gulp of his wine. 'I don't know why I talk to my wife a lot, I really don't, stupid really. It's probably habit.' He shook his head, embarrassed.

'Probably. I think it's nice to ask for her advice or just keep her in the loop.'

'Do you?'

'Yes, otherwise she's really gone, hasn't she, if you stop talking to her. At least that's what I think.'

He held out his hand. 'I'm Christopher, by the way. Christopher Heritage.'

'Oh!' Pru recognised his name. 'You're the MP thingy. William's uncle.'

'Yep, the MP thingy, that's me.'

'I'm Pru. Roberta's my niece.'

'Hello, Pru. She's a lovely girl – we were introduced earlier. Although why she wants to get mixed up with a mob like this I'll never know!'

'Oh, Gawd, don't say that, you'll get me worrying! Everyone seems lovely.' *Even if I do feel like a fish out of water.*

'Oh, they are lovely, all of them. But it's all a bit predictable, isn't it, marrying an army officer, buying a farmhouse with an Aga, getting a chocolate Labrador called Max and

46

spending weekends in Devon. Don't you ever wish she'd go and climb the mountains of the Himalayas or backpack around Brazil and work in conservation?'

'Good God, no I don't! She gets lost if she has to go south of the river, let alone climbing Himalayan mountains. Anyway, it'd be a bit tricky in her Jimmy Choos, they'd get stuck in the mud. And actually, all I want is for her to be happy. That's all I've ever wanted, for her to be happy and safe, and with William I think she is.'

'You're right, of course. Don't listen to me, I'm just an old cynic. A lifetime in Westminster can do that to a man.'

'What is it you do in Westminster? I mean, I know you are one of the erm...' She rolled her hand as if this might help find the words that evaded her. She knew his face and his name but didn't have a clue as to his role. 'I'm sorry, I'm a bit rubbish at politics and all that stuff. I mean, I go and put my cross every four years by the best-looking candidate, but other than that it's all a bit of a mystery to me.'

'Don't apologise; actually it's a blessed relief. I've spent the whole afternoon answering questions on where these young bucks should invest next and can I give them a clue about interest rates when all I wanted was a large glass of plonk and a vol-au-vent. It's been bloody hard work.'

'Sounds it.'

'I'm the Chief Whip.' He stated this with gravitas, as if it would mean something to her.

'Well, what a coincidence, so am I! If there's a bowl of cream that needs a good lashing, they call on me! I'm a baker.'

Christopher laughed. 'You're a baker?'

'Yes, I'm Pru Plum.'

'Oh, Plum's! I know it, yes of course! Actually, I think Isabel did tell me. You've got that swanky place in Mayfair, with a little shop where you can get a coffee and a cream cake for an arm and a leg!'

'That's the one.' She smiled.

'Well I never. It's a pleasure to meet you, Pru Plum.'

'And you.'

Sir Christopher Heritage put out his hand and took hers, shaking it gently yet firmly. And it was in that moment, as his fingers grasped hers and their palms lay flat against each other, that Prudence Plum felt something new, something that she had never felt before. It washed over her from the roots of her hair to the tips of her toes. It left her feeling breathless, awkward and glowing with excitement and it was something that at sixty-six years of age, she had doubted she would ever feel.

'Can I get you a refill?' Christopher pointed at her empty glass.

She nodded, unable to speak.

He took the glass from her hand and walked towards the bar. 'Back in a mo, don't go anywhere.'

I'm not going anywhere, I'll be right here, waiting...

Pru looked skywards and laughed. 'Blimey, thank you, Alfie!'

And then she heard it, loud and clear, his response, for the first time ever. 'You're welcome!'

Christopher came back with two glasses of champagne as the band struck up 'Bye Bye Blackbird', an up-tempo version that couples bopped to on the dance floor. Men

48

twirled girls, who squealed and fell into the arms of their beaus, wobbling on legs that were one part champagne and two parts mojito.

'Fancy a dance?' Christopher asked as his cheeks coloured.

'Oh...' Pru was taken aback. 'I don't know.' She bit her bottom lip, concerned about the practicalities, like having to jiggle, sober, in front of this stranger. Where would she leave her handbag and would he have to touch her?

'You don't *know*?' He sipped at one of the glasses.

It was Pru's turn to get a little flustered. 'No, I mean, I do know, yes!'

'No, you do know, yes? You've rather lost me, I'm afraid.'

Pru laughed. 'I would like to dance with you—'

'Good,' Christopher interrupted. He set the champagne flutes down on one of the little bar tables that were dotted around the marquee.

'But I'm not sure I can,' she finished.

'Why, are you afflicted in some way? Let me guess, arthritic joints? Gammy leg? Two left feet?'

'Yes, all of the above, but that's not the reason.'

'Mmm... another reason, let me think.' He stroked his chin with pantomime theatricality. 'You've got a jealous lover hiding in the wings with a crowbar? You're about to turn into a pumpkin? Someone has super-glued your feet to that very spot?'

Pru looked at the floor. 'No, nothing like that. I'm just not sure how to dance.'

Christopher stared at her for a second. 'If you don't mind me saying, Miss Plum, I think you might be making this a tad more complicated than it needs to be. Now, put your bag on the table and take my hand.'

Pru did just that, letting him guide her through the crowd of bright young things. By the time they reached the dance floor, the song was coming to a close. The band immediately launched into the next number, 'They Can't Take That Away From Me', which was softer, slower and quite sultry.

Christopher placed one arm in the small of her back and drew her into his form, holding her closely with her hand inside his. He broke into a slow waltz. 'Don't over-think it, just let me lead you,' he breathed into her hair.

She nodded against his shoulder, feeling the soft cloth of his suit jacket against her chin. Pru hardly dared to breathe as she tried to copy his footwork. Miraculously she found the rhythm, learning the steps as they hovered together at the edge of the dance floor. The song finished too soon and the two held their pose for a second longer than was strictly necessary.

'That wasn't so bad, was it?' he whispered.

Her voice too was small. 'No. Not too bad at all.'

At 8 p.m. her car was waiting, as agreed. Pru held her shoes in her hand, having finally given up on the heels and pointy toes that had pinched her feet all afternoon, and tiptoed in her bare feet over the grass and gravel. Bobby was staying with her prospective mother-in-law for a couple of days and had kissed her aunt firmly on the cheek, hugging her tightly before being whisked away to the dance floor by a couple of her fiancé's eager friends. William and Isabel were nowhere to be seen. Christopher, however, strolled by her side.

'D'you know, I was dreading today. These things always feel like a bit of a duty on your one day off. But it's been lovely, unexpectedly lovely.'

'Yes, it has,' she agreed. 'Thanks for keeping me company. I think I'd have snuck off hours ago if you hadn't rescued me.'

'It's been my absolute pleasure.' The way he smiled into her eyes told her he was sincere. 'I was wondering...' Christopher coughed.

'Wondering what?' Pru felt her heart thud against her ribs and her cheeks flame slightly. She was torn between wanting to get away from him as quickly as possible, exhausted by the weight of emotion she was feeling, and not wanting to say goodbye.

'Well, I was wondering what route your driver takes. Tell him to take the M40; anything else will be a bugger at this time of night.'

'Will do.' She swallowed, at once disappointed as well as relieved, not quite sure what she had expected or hoped for.

Christopher opened the door of the shiny Mercedes and waited as she slid into the back. Pru stared at her hands folded in her lap and prayed that he wouldn't hug or touch her in any way, not knowing how to react if he did. She envisaged having to reach up through the car door and could picture a number of ways in which this might end awkwardly. Thankfully, he closed the door and raised his palm in goodbye. She watched him getting smaller as dusk fell on the most extraordinary day.

It was dark by the time the driver delivered her back to Curzon Street. Milly was in the sitting room, watching *An*

51

Affair to Remember on TV, curled up in her tiger suit. She nursed a healthy portion of apple *tatin* and clotted cream.

Pru nodded at the enormous bowl of pudding. 'Feeling a bit better then, Mills?'

'Much. How was it? Bobby okay? Thought you weren't going to be late – it's nearly ten o'clock!'

As usual, Pru selected which questions to answer and in what order. 'Oh, Bob was in her element, showing off her diamond and twirling on the dance floor. Isabel made a big fuss of her, she's a nice lady really, not necessarily our cup of tea maybe, but friendly enough. Apparently, since her husband died she's tended to get a bit carried away with anything that's a diversion.' *At least that's what her brother told me, Sir Christopher...* 'It made me sad to think of Alfie, what he would have said if he'd seen her. He'd have been so proud.'

Milly nodded. 'You all right, Pru?'

'Yes, why?' She almost snapped.

'Don't know. You look a bit dewy-eyed, are you sloshed?'

'No! Only had one or two early on and that was more of a prop, then I switched to cranberry juice.'

Milly waved her hand in front of her face, impatient. 'Anyway, I don't care about that, what was the cake like? Did you get a photo?'

Pru considered her response. She and Christopher had been sitting by the lake and had missed the arrival of the cake; and by the time they saw it, all that remained was a mountain of crumbs and squares of royal icing. She pondered how best to break this to her cousin.

'Ah, the cake. Well, therein lays a tale. I missed it.'

Milly was all ears, sitting forward. 'You missed it?' Her tone was accusatory.

'Yep. Sorry.'

'I've been sitting here all day, waiting to hear and you missed it?'

'Yes, Milly. And now I'm off to bed!'

'But I want to hear about their house and the buffet!' She sounded more than a little angry.

'Well, next time, don't eat five-day-old chicken and then you can see it for yourself, can't you!'

Milly huffed. 'Did you nick anything?'

'Did I *nick* anything?'

'Yeah, you know, like an ashtray or a fork?'

Pru stared at her, trying to find the words. 'Milly, I have never nicked anything in my life and if I was going to start, it wouldn't be from Bobby's future family!'

'I was only asking!' Milly tutted.

'*Only asking?* Why? Would *you* have nicked something then?'

Milly twitched her nose and sucked in her cheeks. 'Well, I'm not sure I should say now.'

'I give up. I really do. It's like living with the love child of Fagin and Tony off the Frosties box.'

Pru shook her head as she turned and walked from the room without looking back. The rustling of Milly's fake fur and tap of her ring on the bowl of pud told Pru that her exit was being followed by a hand gesture. She doubted it was a wave.

Four

Three days had passed, three days in which Pru had hardly slept and couldn't eat. Her gut was filled with a bubble of excitement that crowded her stomach. She spent most of her waking day, and a large part of the night, replaying each word they had exchanged and every second of their dance, recalling how her hand had sat inside his, the feel of his suit cloth beneath her chin and the weight of him as he moved against her. The more she tried to picture his face, the more detail she seemed to lose; she wished she had a photo. She chastised herself for any inadvertent misdemeanour: why hadn't she been keener to dance? Had he thought she was standoffish? Cool? The very idea made her laugh. She was a wreck.

'Hellooooooo!' Bobby's voice filled the staircase and was followed by thumping footsteps as she and William arrived back from Oxford.

Pru was in the kitchen. 'Hello, loves!' She turned her cheek for easy access and accepted the kiss that her niece offered. 'Have you had a lovely time?'

'Really lovely. It's been wonderful! And wasn't the cake *incredible*, but please don't tell Mills I said that.'

'The cake? Oh, I don't even know if she knew you were having one.' Pru shrugged.

'I'm still on cloud nine. Wasn't the party great?'

Pru nodded. Oh yes, it had been great. 'It really was, I sent your mum some flowers, Billy-boy. I hope she got them?'

'Yes, she did. They were beautiful and she's dropping you a line to say thanks.'

'Oh, she doesn't need to do that. In fact I should be writing to her: I promised I'd send her some of Guy's drawings and ideas for the *big* cake design. We can become pen pals!' Pru laughed. She was still ridiculously giddy for no apparent reason.

'We have been busy, you know, Aunty Pru, not just lounging in the garden and drinking Pimm's – although a lot of that, admittedly. But guess what?'

'What?' Pru asked, turning to face them, trying to show some interest.

'We've booked our honeymoon!' Bobby clapped as she jumped up and down, zigzagging across the kitchen until she ended up bashing into William, who caught her and held her still. He shook his head in an adoring but exasperated fashion.

'Ooh, lovely! Where are you going?'

'Well, the brother of William's friend Piers has a villa in Ibiza.'

'Very trendy!' Pru said, having never been to Ibiza herself, though she had heard it mentioned on the TV and in magazines.

Bobby twisted her mouth and bit the inside of her cheek. 'No. Not very trendy. We are not going to the touristy bit. This villa is on the quiet side of the island. We've hired it

for three weeks and it's got a private pool! I'm so excited!'
She clapped again, but was unable to bounce as William
had her anchored in his arms.

When he was content she wasn't about to bound off
again, he released her and stepped back, leaning on the
doorframe, filling the gap. He folded his arms across his
broad chest and watched as Pru made a cup of tea. 'You
look very well, Pru. If you don't mind me saying.'

'No, I don't mind at all! Thank you, love. I feel it.'

'Is there any reason for that, anything you want to share
with us?' He smirked and pursed his lips.

'William! I said we were not to mention it!' Bobby
thumped his chest feebly with her fist.

'I can't help it!' He caught her wrist and laughed as she
doubled over.

Pru placed the teaspoon on the granite counter top and
turned her attention to the two giggling lumps in front of
her. 'All right, let's have it!' She put her hands on her hips.

Bobby's eyes were twinkling with excitement. 'I'm sorry,
Pru, it's just that Isabel said she saw you and Christopher
chatting down by the lake on Sunday for hours and someone
told her that you'd been smooching – that's their word, not
mine! And you did seem to be getting on very well.' Bobby
paused to allow Pru to comment. She declined and so Bobby
tried again. 'Then, apparently, he called her on Monday to
say that you'd spent the most delightful time together. That
was the word he used, "delightful"!'

'Delightful!' William echoed.

'Did he now?' Pru tried to look stern but was beyond
happy that he had called Isabel and shared this. She felt

like she wanted to dance! 'Well, be sure to let me know if there is any other gossip floating around that you think I should be aware of.' She collected her mug and the newspaper from the work surface and tried to squeeze past.

'So, are you going to see him again? Come on, you can't leave it there! We need to know the details.' Bobby was inches from her aunt's face.

'Do you now? The truth is, I don't know if or when I'm seeing him again, and even if I did, I would hardly share that information with you two, just so you can laugh at us.'

'Us? Is there an "us" already? That uncle of mine is a fast worker!' William held up his raised palm for Bobby to high-five.

'Sod off, both of you!' It was the best Pru could come up with.

'Pru, I do believe you are blushing!' William sniggered.

'Well, I am now, because you are saying that!'

'Pru and Christopher sitting in a tree, K-I-S-S-I-N-G!' the two shouted before collapsing in laughter against the fridge.

'Oh, for goodness sake, Bobby, you are so childish! And anyway we didn't do any kissing and there were certainly no trees involved. We did however have a quick whizz around the dance floor, which is quite different to a smooch.' With that she swept from the room, leaving them to whoop and holler as she walked away.

Delightful!

She knocked on Milly's door and walked into her bedroom. Her cousin was in her bed, with her glasses perched on the end of her nose and *EastEnders* on quietly, with the subtitles.

'What's all the bloody noise out there? I can hear those two squawking away!'

'Oh, they're having a field day, teasing me.'

'Teasing you about what?' Milly drew her knees up under the duvet.

'What do you think? My new hair-do? Christopher, of course!'

The day after the party, Pru had finally cracked and told her all about their rather lovely afternoon. She had then fired questions at her perplexed cousin. Did Milly think he liked her? What might happen next? Milly had tried to answer but eventually, exasperated, had held a cushion over each ear and watched the news, ignoring her.

Now Milly nodded and removed her specs. 'You like him, don't you?'

'I don't know. I've only met him once, and so logically I don't know how I can like him! But this doesn't feel very logical, not at all.'

'That's not a yes or no.'

Pru sighed. Milly knew her better than anyone else, knew what she was thinking, was familiar with her every mood. 'Yes. Yes I do. I like him a lot. It's weird, Mills. We just clicked and I can't get him out of my head, not for a second, and that's never happened to me before.'

'You've got to enjoy it, every minute of it.' This was Milly's blessing. It conveyed so many things, but primarily she was saying, don't worry about me, and go grab your chance.

'D'you think so?'

Milly nodded. 'I don't think, I *know*.'

'Well, if you *know*, Mills, then I'd better just go with it, hadn't I? It's funny though. I was chatting to Alfie—'

'As you do.' Milly found her cousin's interactions with her deceased brother a little bit bonkers.

'As I do. I was telling him about Bobby, how beautiful she looked, and ping! There he was.'

'Alfie?'

'No, of course not Alfie! Christopher! But it was odd, almost as if Alfie sent him to me, like a gift. Does that sound a little bit mad?'

'No, love. It sounds a lot mad. Anyway, I thought you were still hanging on for Tom Jones?'

'No, I gave up on Tom a while ago.'

'I bet he'll be gutted, poor Tom.' Milly sniffed.

'He'll get over it.'

'It's funny, isn't it. There was you having a go at me for eating gone-off chicken, but if I hadn't, I'd have been glued to your side and you might not have met him. You should be thanking me.'

Pru slid off her cousin's bed and opened the door. 'You're right. Thank you, Mills, for nearly poisoning yourself. You silly moo.'

'You're welcome, you daft cow.'

And the two laughed, in that way that they had since they were little.

But a week passed and Christopher still hadn't called. Pru's mood soured and she snapped at Guy, which she never did. Spying a batch of bloomers that were blackened on one side and fit only for the bin, she had yelled, 'For every tray that is allowed to spoil, we lose money! Why don't I just get a handful of fivers and put them straight in the bin? Save us both the time and effort!'

He looked mortified. She pinched her nose and whispered her apology. 'I'm sorry, Guy. I don't know what's wrong with me.'

But, actually, she did know what was wrong with her. The joy at meeting Christopher had buoyed her up for the first few days, filling her with energy and a new optimism for life that took her by surprise. This had now been replaced by self-doubt and something close to embarrassment, a feeling that she might have horribly misjudged the situation. She regretted confiding in Milly and not having been more indifferent about the situation to Bobby.

The day after the party she had checked her phone every few minutes. Having exchanged numbers, she expected a call or a text. The thought of having to text a response, however, worried her. She wasn't that speedy on the little keypad and could take minutes to respond; and what if he used text speak, of which she knew very little? Eventually she reassured herself that the Government Chief Whip was fairly unlikely to pepper his written communication with LOL or C U L8R – these two abbreviations she had gleaned from Bobby. But this quickly became a moot point anyway: after three days she had received neither call nor text and she was more than a little fed up.

Pru sat at her dressing table and took a deep breath. Steeling herself, she decided to take the bull by the horns and initiate communication. After all, this was the twenty-first century: she could send the first text without being considered brazen! If he didn't respond, she would be no worse off, but if he did, then it would have been worth this excruciating awkwardness.

'This is ridiculous, Alfie. I'm so nervous! Look, my hands are sweating.' Pru held out her palm. 'I feel sick. I don't want to mess it up, but I'm worried that if we don't have contact soon, there won't be anything to mess up. What's the matter with me?' She shook her head in frustration. 'Normally I can talk to anyone, stroll into any house, however posh, and talk cake until the cows come home! And yet I can't send a simple message. I know, I know, just get on with it.'

She twisted her blouse in her hands until finally she exhaled. With her finger poised, she considered what to put.

After ten minutes, she had erased both *Hi there!* for sounding too much like a teen catching up with someone she had snogged on Prom night, and *Just wondering...* for being both too formal and too familiar. It was a minefield. Pru slammed the phone down on to the wooden surface and placed her head in her hands. 'Just give it up, Pru,' she muttered aloud. 'If he liked you, he'd have called you. Simple as.'

Her finger hovered over the delete button. She figured that if she removed his contact details, it would be easier to ignore the fact that his name wasn't flashing on her screen.

Pru and Milly were in the sitting room. It had been rather a long day and both were looking forward to an early night. It was only late April, but the unseasonably sticky London night air was so thick you could stir it with a spoon. Milly had thankfully ditched her tiger suit and was wearing cool cotton PJs. The sash windows were open and the French doors in Pru's bedroom that led to the little Juliet balcony were thrown wide, yet hardly a breeze crept in.

Pru stood and fanned her face with a copy of a glossy bridal magazine that Bobby had left on the floor. 'I think I'll turn in, Mills.' She stretched her arms over her head, instantly regretting the pull on her shoulder muscles. 'Oh I'm getting old!' she grumbled, and arched her back and dropped her chin into her chest, trying to fix her aches.

The front doorbell buzzed in their hallway.

'Who's that at this time of night?'

'How do I know, Milly? What am I, psychic?'

Pru trod the pale, carpeted stairs and slid the bolts, untwisting the double lock before opening the door on to its security chain. This happened on occasion. Living on a busy street meant they were prey to the occasional drunk and prank doorbell ringer, both of whom she found particularly unhilarious. Through the crack beneath the door chain she saw neither a drunk nor a dandy in a dinner jacket with grinning mates standing behind. Instead, she stared, wide-eyed with surprise, into the face of Sir Christopher Heritage. He stood close to the door; the toes of his shoes rested on the polished brass step and his hands were buried in his trouser pockets. Pru fumbled with the chain and released it.

'Actually, I lied to you,' he said.

'What?' Pru's heart thudded as much at seeing him again as at the prospect of an unpleasant revelation.

'I *do* know why I talk to my late wife. I talk to her

because I'm lonely and it makes it slightly better to think that I can still tell her about my day and what's going through my head. There's no one else for me to talk to. And you're right, it makes me feel that she's still around in some way.' He was almost gabbling now. Pru had to concentrate hard to keep up. 'And when you left, I wasn't wondering about your route home, I was wondering if I could see you again, but I lost my nerve and I've been kicking myself ever since. It's been over forty years since I've had to say something like that and I'm rather out of practice.'

Pru beamed. She'd caught every word. 'Well, for someone that's four decades out of practice, you seem to be doing rather well.'

'I do?'

'Yes.' She smiled.

'So, what I wanted to say was, can I see you again, Pru Plum, Chief Whip?'

'Are you asking me out?'

'Yes. Yes I am.' This time he sounded confident.

'When?'

Christopher sighed and looked up and down Curzon Street. 'Now. Right now. Let's go wandering in the park and continue our chat. That is if you're free. It'll be nice and cool in the park.'

Pru exhaled. 'Well, there *is* a cup of cocoa with my name on it, a plate of hazelnut shortbread and a pillow awaiting my tired head, but I guess they'll keep.'

She wished she hadn't rubbed at her eye make-up and removed her lipstick while she'd watched the telly. It was too late to reapply; he would just have to take her as she was. She felt a swell of excitement rush through her, banishing the tiredness that had gripped her only minutes earlier.

'I better go and get some shoes!' She wiggled her bare toes.

'Yes, sensible walking shoes, not those silly high ones you carried around for half the day; they were more useful as gloves! And you might want to lose that magazine, could give a chap the wrong idea.' He loosened his collar with his index finger to let out imaginary steam.

She giggled at the *Brides* magazine in her hand. It felt rather like he was being bossy, looking after her, and she liked it.

Christopher barely had time to admire Guy's latest window display before Pru reappeared beside him, suitably shod. They walked along Curzon Street, keeping at least a foot of pavement between them. Christopher gripped his hands behind his back as they strolled and Pru wondered if this was to stop him reaching for her hand. Her stomach lurched at the idea.

'I didn't expect to see you,' she offered.

'Oh, really? I knew I'd see you.' He winked.

'Did you?' She felt her chest cave with anticipation.

'Yes, definitely. We had such a lovely time in Oxford. I would have come sooner had I been in London.'

Would have come sooner... 'Have you been away then?'

Christopher stopped and turned to look at her. 'Yes. Do you not listen to or watch Parliament?'

'No. It's not really my thing.' She smiled.

'Not your thing? Well it should be your thing; it should be everyone's thing! If you don't listen and watch how your

64

country is being governed, you might miss something of great importance.'

'Ooh dear, I don't want to miss anything of great importance.'

'Exactly. Plus it's my job and I have a regular speaking slot. So it might be nice for you to take some interest.' He feigned hurt. 'I mean, can you imagine if I said cakes were not my thing?'

'Are cakes not your thing?'

'Dammit!' he boomed. 'Yes, cakes are my thing. I love them! However, had you been tuned in, you would have known that I have been up to my neck in beer, cold sausage and debate in Berlin.'

'And not avoiding me.'

'*Avoiding* you? Perish the thought.'

The two chuckled into the warm night air. Their conversation and demeanour were so relaxed that no onlooker would have guessed it was only the second time they'd met. They crossed Piccadilly and meandered through Green Park and across The Mall, until they found themselves in St James's Park. They strolled along the winding path, disturbing ducks that hovered on one leg trying to sleep, and ignoring lovers who sat entwined on benches. They found themselves on the bridge, where they leant on the pale blue railings. The sky had started to lose its colour and the trees took on ominous shadowy shapes. They heard but could barely see the swans that broke the surface of the water with beating wings and honks of arrival. Other couples, indistinct in the half light, walked arm in arm without giving them a second glance. Pru beamed into the encroaching darkness. She felt connected to these dreamy-eyed couples, like they were all in the same secret club.

'This is my favourite place in the whole of London.' He inhaled a deep, appreciative breath.

'Mine too!' And if it wasn't before, it would be now.

'We're lucky, aren't we, to live in the middle of a city and have this green space on our doorstep.'

'We are. I've never lived anywhere else, mind, always London, so I haven't really got anything to compare it with.'

'Have you ever wanted to live anywhere else?' he asked.

'I don't think so,' she replied. A snapshot from the day she'd moved to Kenway Road flashed into her head. Relocating from her childhood home in Bow to Earls Court had felt like a big adventure, another world. As if she had crossed oceans and not in fact less than ten miles, door to door. She remembered looking out from the sixth-floor window at the washing lines, hidden windows and secret gardens that were only visible at that height; it had felt peculiarly intimate. In this vast city, she'd thought to herself with a little jolt of pleasure, where millions of strangers co-existed without ever interacting, she would know who washed their bed linen and when because she would see it arching against the breeze.

'London's in my blood,' she continued. 'I never take it for granted.' She thought of the awe and excitement she felt each time she drove along the Embankment at night, along the curve of the river, with the buildings lit up on both sides and the different bridges. 'For me it's a city that gets more beautiful – the London Eye, the Shard. The skyline is constantly changing and that keeps my interest.' She paused and waved her hand. 'Sorry, ignore me, I'm waffling.'

'No, don't apologise. It's lovely to hear you being so positive. I spend my life replying to complaints from people who want things to stay exactly as they are, especially if any potential build might overlook their back garden. People don't like change.'

'Not all people.'

'No, quite.' He smiled at her. 'Not all people. But I think most find change frightening, especially at our age.'

'At our age? Oh my word, we sound ancient! It's funny, I don't think of myself as getting on; sometimes I look in the mirror and I'm quite shocked to see this old face staring back at me, because inside I feel the same as I always did. Having said which – at least I'm still standing! Getting old is a privilege, really, don't you think?'

Christopher nodded, slowly. 'Oh, I definitely do.'

Pru put her hand to her mouth. 'Oh God, Chris, I wasn't thinking about Ginny. I'm sorry. Me and my big mouth.'

'Not at all, it's fine!' He put his hand on her arm.

She felt the shockwave from where he had touched her; it shot through her entire body. She was sure that if she looked, his fingers would have left a glowing imprint on her skin. She gave an involuntary shudder.

'Gosh, you're getting chilly now it's dark. Come on, a brisk walk back should warm you up!'

This time she linked her arm through his and they strolled through the dark streets, grinning at each other at the end of what had turned out to be the most wonderful day.

They paused outside her front door.

'This is very strange for me, Pru. I couldn't stop thinking about you while I was away. I feel like a schoolboy with one eye on the windows in case your angry father is twitching the net curtains.'

'He'd be bloody angry if he was and understandably so. He's been dead for over fifty years and being brought back to twitch net curtains would try the patience of anyone!'

Christopher laughed and looked at his shoes. 'I would very much to see you again, if that's okay?'

'I'm not sure about that, I'll have to ask my dad.'

'In the same way that you'd ask your brother?'

'Ha! Actually, no, I don't talk to my dad in that way. That's strange, isn't it? Maybe I was too young to know him like I knew Alfie.'

'What a funny pair we are.'

She smiled up at him. She liked being considered part of a pair.

Pru slipped into sleep with a grin on her face, but only a few hours later she was drenched in sweat, claimed by a horrible nightmare. She woke up suddenly and reached with a shaking hand for the glass of water that sat on the bedside table. She clicked on the lamp and sat up, trying to shake the dream from her head. It was the same one she always had, of a man with a puckered eye weeping a solitary tear. As the man blotted his face with a starched white hand-kerchief, Pru always felt a sense of terrible fear, as if a band were tightening around her chest. Only this time the fear was even greater, for someone else had featured in the dream.

'Oh God, Alfie,' she whispered, 'I heard his horrible laugh and there he was, with his hand outstretched, introducing himself to Christopher—' She broke off and breathed deeply. 'It felt so real. I was rooted to the spot and even though I was trying to speak, no words would come out.'

Pru sank back against the pillows, her heart thumping, too scared to go back to sleep in case the dream was still lurking.

Her phone buzzed. She grabbed it and held it at arm's length – her eyes were not that good in the early hours. It was a text from Christopher! She beamed at his words: *Thanks for a lovely evening! Can't sleep!*

Pru replied with, *Me too! x* Then she wriggled down under the summer duvet, her face scarlet with embarrassment, instantly regretting the addition of a kiss. She lay under the covers until the dark filled every space inside her and her joy turned to something closer to panic. Her breath came in shallow pants. Slowly she peeled back the covers and sat up against the pillows. Her stomach lurched as she closed her eyes and imagined the moment, the conversation that she would have to have. Her bowels turned to ice. It wasn't fair. This should be a happy time and yet for her it was like walking on a beautiful cliff edge – a cliff edge from where she was unable to admire the view or feel at peace because she knew that at some point she would have to jump. And that knowledge clouded everything. Maybe it would be easier to run in the opposite direction, avoiding the jump – and the view. Was she going to have to make that sacrifice just to keep hold of what she had?

Pru looked around her beautiful bedroom. She and Milly had worked so hard for all they had achieved and her success was the one thing that gave her happiness and confidence.

The idea of it all coming crashing down around her was more than she could bear. She forced herself to think back to the first time they had seen the premises on Curzon Street, knowing the memory would distract and cheer her.

It had been Mills that had spotted the advert, running into the shop with a snippet of newspaper, which talked of a 'neglected gem in the heart of Mayfair, in need of a little redecoration'. The description alone had been enough to set their pulses racing. The shop and upstairs flat they were renting on Argyll Street, a short stroll from Oxford Street, were small and they were fast outgrowing them. Pru wanted a café, shop and showroom as well as the bakery, and she had always known that Argyll Street would be only a stepping-stone. A useful place in which to build up their custom and save hard, until they had enough to move into the sort of premises they had always dreamed of.

The funds had been in place for a year and customers continued to flock to their doors, eager to get their hands on *pain au froment*, *pain aux noix*, *beignets aux pommes*, *pain baguette* and their world-famous, flour-dusted, crusty *boules de pain*. The pleasure of hearing the ping of the till and the rustle of stiff brown paper bags filled with fresh goods baked on site hadn't waned and Pru knew that the right address and space could take Plum Patisserie to a whole other level.

Trudy, always wary of fanciful ideas that weren't grounded in good practical common sense, had insisted on coming with them to look over the Curzon Street premises. While she bantered with the cab driver, Pru and Milly sat with faces pressed against the windows. They gazed at the grand façades of W1, at the hotels and corporate offices, and the specialist businesses that sat between them – Silvers Milliner's, Tregowan's Glove Shop and Bijoux the Chocolatier among them – each with a gleaming brass front step and a brightly painted sign suspended over the door. These were just the sort of establishments they wanted to emulate. Pru turned to Milly and grinned. The taxi pulled up on the corner of Curzon Street and Shepherd Market. The brakes had hardly been applied when Pru and Milly leapt from the back of the cab. They stood in the road, taking in the entire building. Pru looked up with her hand shielding her eyes, noting the deep-set windowsills, the sash windows, the sturdy brick construction and the heavy wood-panelled front door.

The building had been empty for the last few years. The family that owned it had closed shop on their pharmacy after fifty years in business. Remnants of their history, however, still lingered. A tall Georgian bow window held a large blue glass apothecary bottle with a pointed top and a slender glass stopper. The word 'Chemist' was written across the bulge of its body in a fancy gold script, just visible through the thick layer of dust that clung to it.

Inside the shop there was the faintest whiff of chemicals and in certain corners you could smell violets, possibly one of the scents they'd sold or maybe the calling card of a loitering ghost. Mirrored panels edged in brass sat high on the walls, tilted slightly to reflect the scenes below. Pru looked up into them with her teeth biting her bottom lip: she could see reflected the shelves stacked with bread, dark wooden bistro tables with chatting customers clustered around them and ladies lifting pastry forks towards expectant mouths. The old apothecary counter would be remodelled to carry their plates of tortes, meringues, sponges and pastries. And behind the counter, on shelves also edged in brass, they would store the ornate boxes in which people would take home their wares.

As Pru looked at the crumbing plaster walls, which had taken on an orange hue, she saw vintage fruit baskets and fishermen's woven willow panniers, in which they could display a selection of loaves. She raised her hand and, squinting, used her finger to outline the shape on the walls. Then she turned to Milly, who smiled and nodded.

'Yes!' Milly spoke as if answering a question. 'With lavender sprigs interspersed in the weaving to give it a rustic feel.'

Pru laughed. The two of them had spent decades discussing and planning Plum Patisserie. No detail had been left to chance and so clear were they about their vision that they could both see it now clearly.

Milly patted the wall between the old dispensary and the shop. 'With this wall gone—'

'We'll have the right floor space,' Pru finished. 'And we'll keep the bow window—'

'Use it like a display case for our most dramatic cakes!'

The cousins rushed towards each other and gripped hands, jumping in a circle like excited six-year-olds.

'This is it, Mills,' Pru managed to utter through lips that quivered with emotion.

'Yes, Pru. This is it.'

Trudy watched the duo and wrinkled her nose at the

intricate cobwebs that looped from the mirrors to the broken chandelier, whose vast arms whispered of former grandeur. She cast her eye over the dull green brass fixtures and tried to hide her distaste.

'It's nothing a good going over with some Brasso won't fix, Trudy!' Mills reassured her.

'Well, that's good to hear.' Trudy rubbed her fingers together, trying to rid them of dust. 'And let's hope it also works on rotten woodwork, broken windows and mould.' With that she flicked her head and reached for a cigar.

Pru and Milly laughed.

'Don't you see, Trudy? This is the place! It's been waiting for us, waiting for us our whole lives.' With these words, Pru finally gave in to the tears that had threatened.

Trudy took a deep drag. 'Oh my God, you actually think that's the case, don't you?'

'No.' Pru shook her head. 'I don't *think* that's the case. I *know* it. We're home.'

Now, some two decades on, ensconced in her bedroom high above the bakery and its classy decor, Pru smoothed her crisp white bed linen and considered how far they had come. They had, against the odds, achieved all they had dreamed of. They had proved the naysayers wrong, ignored the pessimists who had told them to give up before they started. People had tried to convince them that poor East End match girls just didn't end up as the toast of the town and living in Mayfair. Well, she was proof that they did.

Suddenly Pru smiled and felt a wave of happiness wash over her. Yes! She was proof that you could achieve your dreams. No need to be dragged down by nightmares.

Picturing Christopher, she snuggled back under her duvet. There was a reason they had been led to Curzon Street on that day all those years ago and there was a reason he had come into her life. Maybe she could have it all, maybe he was the one who could forgive her past. Just maybe.

Five

The front door banged shut. Milly jumped as she always did and spread her palm over her heart at the ferocity of the slam.

'Jesus, Bobby!'

'Hellooo! It's only me!'

'Yes, I gathered that, love.' Milly smiled. Bobby always announced her arrival in a similar manner. Of course it was her, who else would it be? 'You are going to have that door off its hinges one of these days if you're not careful.'

'Sorry!' Bobby shouted from the hallway as she rummaged in a bureau drawer. 'Can I borrow some matches? I can't be bothered to go to the shop and I'm desperate for some. This could ruin my entire evening!'

Milly tutted at Bobby's definition of a desperate emergency.

Unable to find what she was looking for, Bobby headed towards the sitting room. Although she lived upstairs in a separate apartment, Bobby treated the two flats more like a single house, wandering the corridors and delving into likely-looking cupboards at will. Anything from a nail file to ketchup would be purloined, no matter in which part of the building she found it. The only areas that were off limits were the shop and bakery, which were alarmed and locked.

Bobby appeared at the sitting room door looking gorgeous: freshly showered, with perfect hair and make-up.

Milly folded the *Telegraph* and rested it on her lap. 'You know I don't like you playing with matches. What do you want them for?'

'I'm not playing with matches! God, I once accidentally set fire to a rug and you still go on about it. I'm twenty, not twelve any more!'

Milly removed her glasses, placing them on her folded paper; this required her full attention. 'Remind me, love, how old were you when you set fire to the rug?'

Bobby looked at the floor and bit the inside of her cheek. 'I was nineteen and a half, but that's not the point!'

'I thought that *was* the point – you set fire to a bloody rug! And not just any rug, but your Aunty Pru's Persian pride and joy. It was me that had to listen to her crying into her Baileys over her lost five hundred and fifty knots per square inch!'

'I said I was sorry, and anyway, I'm more sensible now. I'm going to be a married woman and not just any married woman, an army wife. I'll probably join a choir and everything!'

'Yes you are, my love, but God help any choir that has you in it. I remember the school asking you to mime at the Christmas Carol Concert.'

'They still made me stand at the front!'

'They did that.' Milly's eyes twinkled. 'Of course you can borrow some matches. They're in the kitchen drawer, but please be careful.'

'I will. I went out today and bought three beautiful new

Jo Malone candles and I'm going to have them burning when William arrives. And I've cooked dinner—'

'You've cooked dinner? Well saints be praised!' Her aunt clasped her hands in mock prayer and tried not to sound too shocked.

'Well, you know what I mean. I've heated stuff up. Asparagus tarts! Guy gave them to me, they were on the turn.'

'Ah, how lovely. I'm sure that's exactly what Billy-boy wants after a hard day's soldiering – to come home to three fabulous smelly candles and heated-up asparagus bloody tart that's on the turn.'

'He does!' Bobby bit the inside of her cheek again.

'Are you sure? Because if you are in any doubt, I've had Fortnum's deliver today, so there's lovely pâté, cheese, crackers, chutney and any amount of Parma ham – you can always help yourself, that's if you need it. Or better still, tell Billy-boy and he can come and help himself, just in case he isn't partial to a tart the size of a postage stamp.'

'He doesn't mind what he gets. As long as he's with me he's happy.'

Milly laughed. 'Oh ain't love grand! It must be lovely when all you need is the whiff of a scented candle and each other. In my day, a working man would expect a pint of stout and a big bowl of shepherd's pie or a nice fat pork chop with two veg when he got in.'

'Urgh, well in that case I'm glad it's not your day! I'm far too busy to stand cooking all day. He'll have to make do with me heating things up unless he wants to cook for himself; and if he does, I shan't stop him.'

Milly shook her head. It amazed her that Bobby was too busy despite not having a job. Her diary was full, a fatiguing whirl of get-togethers and vital shopping excursions, punctuated by hairdresser's appointments and trips to the brow and nail bar. She was one of the blessed – so beautiful that any number of men would want her, regardless of her home-making skills. It genuinely had been very different in *her* day, not that she had really had her day. No man had ever wanted her, not in that way, and she understood why. And for her part, she was too familiar with the habits of men to forgive even the smallest flaws. She viewed them as a species, a collective of silver-tongued chancers; she didn't distinguish them as individuals any more.

'Anyway, this time next year we'll be married and it'll be too late for him to mind about me being a crap cook. I'll have him trapped! But luckily he loves me and so it won't matter. In fact I might stop shaving my legs and wearing make-up, really let myself go!' Bobby squealed delightedly at the prospect and flounced from the room. She had it all figured out.

Milly returned to her crossword, tapping her pen against her front teeth.

A minute later Bobby popped her head round the door, shaking a box of matches. 'Got them! Thanks, Mills. I'm off out now, going to pick William up from work.'

Milly didn't look up but raised her pen in a wave as she studied seven across.

Pru arrived home just over an hour and a half later.

'Gosh, Mills, what a day! This is the first chance I've had

to draw breath.' She kicked off her shoes and flexed her ankles. 'Ooh, it's lovely to sit down. I think I'll have a hot bath and an early night. I haven't stopped.' She rubbed at her eyes.

'Tell me about it! The shop has been crazy. We had a rush on macaroons and cupcakes from a coachload of Japanese tourists. You know how they always love the packaging so much – they were taking photos left, right and centre. Guy said he'd been snapped so often, he felt like Kate Moss!'

Pru laughed. 'He'd have loved every minute.'

'Yes, I think he did. We were out of fresh-baked by three o'clock. We had to fill the cabinet with truffles and cookies from the freezer – once we'd given them a quick once-over in the microwave! But I think we got away with it.'

'We're just too darn good, Mills.'

'That we are.' Milly yawned and stretched. 'Bobby was in earlier, wrecking the joint as usual and nicking our matches. I think she's got a bit of a night planned with Billy-boy.' She winked at her cousin.

'Lucky Billy-boy. I had a result as well: I've had the nod on the big Condé Nast summer ball.' Pru couldn't wait to start working on this – a towering croque-en-bouche centre-piece covered in a cobweb of spun sugar, with mini lemon tarts and hand-piped brandy snaps for pudding. 'I'm getting the colour scheme as soon as they have it and we can add a garnish or something beautiful to blend. I'm thinking mint leaves if it's greens or pansy leaves for purple, that kind of thing. Or caramel strands if it's gold, of course!'

'It'll be stunning. Better get Guy to start the sketches.'

'Yes, good idea—'

They were interrupted by the beep of Pru's phone.

'No need to ask who that's from – you look like a bloody Cheshire cat,' Milly sniped.

Pru ignored her cousin, but she knew how irritating it could be. They'd had plenty of it with Bobby over the last year; she whooped and hollered every time her phone gave off its annoying little ping, then followed that by jumping up and down on the spot. And yet now Pru too cuddled her phone and read and reread the text: *Just had lonely cup of tea, wish you were here.* Who would have guessed that those ten words, delivered in such a sterile fashion, could bring such joy?

Pru was about to reply when the front door buzzed.

'That girl is a nightmare! She's forgotten her bloody key again. I told her not to set fire to anything, but I forgot to remind her to take a front door key. It's like having a child around, isn't it?'

'I'll go.' Pru stood and straightened her blouse. 'I'm not going to just buzz it open, in case it isn't her. We could have half of Curzon Street wandering up.'

'Yes, Pru, I'm sure that's why you want to go, and not because you are hoping it's a certain balding politician with an hour to kill.'

'He is not balding, jheesh!' Pru grinned as she fixed her hair and descended the stairs.

It was a few minutes later that the front door of the flat slammed. Milly jumped.

'For Gawd's sake, Bobby, that's the second time tonight you've done that!' she shouted from her chair.

'Bob?' she shouted again towards the hallway.

There was no response. That was odd: Bobby was always

a second away from issuing a witty retort or bouncing into the room like Tigger on speed.

'Bobby, is that you, love? Pru?' Milly leant forward, craning her neck.

Slowly Pru entered the sitting room. She had the wobbly gait of a drunk and leant against the doorframe for support. Her cheeks had lost their peachy blush of ten minutes ago. Her eyes were narrowed and she looked old, suddenly.

What on earth? Milly stood and walked towards her. 'Are you okay, love? What's the matter? Is it Christopher?'

Pru looked at her cousin and then over her shoulder. Milly followed her gaze and it was then that she saw the policeman standing in the hallway, hovering outside the sitting room door, unsure whether to walk in or wait for an invitation. He was blond, young and on edge, with his hat lodged awkwardly under his arm.

Pru indicated the young PC with her hand. 'I... just... they...' She couldn't get the words out.

Milly gripped Pru's shoulder and pushed the stray locks of hair from her cousin's forehead. 'Take your time. What's happened?'

Pru took several deep breaths, like an athlete preparing to perform. Her voice, when she finally spoke, was little more than a whisper. 'Hospital. We need to get to the hospital. It's William and Bobby. They've had an accident in the car. They're in St Thomas's.'

'What? Oh my God!' Milly gasped and clutched at the collar of her tunic. 'Are they all right? What happened?'

'The police have got a car downstairs, they said they'd drop us off.'

Milly couldn't take her eyes from her cousin. 'What did they say, are they hurt?'

Pru shook her head. 'I don't know. They were in the car and they've hit something—'

'Yes, that's right, Bobby went to pick him up.'

'William was driving, but I don't know anything else.' Pru's eyes brimmed with tears and her legs swayed.

Milly grabbed her handbag from the side table and addressed the young PC. 'Is she okay? Do you know if she's hurt?'

'I don't have any other details, I'm sorry.'

Milly inhaled sharply and assumed control. 'Right, well, let's not panic until we know what's what. But let's get straight to the hospital and we'll take it from there.' She smiled thinly and glanced out of the window, drawn by the blue light that swept around the sitting room, bouncing off the walls, filling the space with a menacing glare. The police car was parked directly below them, half on the pavement.

At that time of night traffic was light and they arrived at St Thomas's in fifteen minutes. Milly put her arm round Pru's shoulders as they hurried through the automatic double doors and under the large red canopy into Accident and Emergency.

Reception was busy, full of anxious relatives, the walking wounded and loud, shouty drunks. It was horribly tense. Pru and Milly half walked, half jogged to the desk and waited their turn behind an elderly man who had forgotten his postcode. The policeman stood with them. Finally they got to the front and the young PC explained who they were looking for.

'Bear with me, one second.' The receptionist tapped into a keyboard and ran her eyes down the screen in front of her. Her smile faltered and something in the way her eyebrows twitched made Pru's heart thump.

'Please, take a seat.' The woman gestured to a bank of chairs. 'Someone will be right along to assist you.'

The policeman disappeared into the bowels of the hospital and Pru watched as Milly chewed and ripped at her fingernails, something she had done since she was five years old and no amount of chastising or bitter aloes could cure. Neither woman spoke.

It was some minutes later that a bedraggled doctor appeared, in his early thirties and wearing green Converse All Stars under his blue scrubs. He was holding a clipboard and he looked nervous.

'Miss Plum?'

'Yes.' Both women stepped forward.

'I'm Dr Carmichael. Would you like to come with me?' He turned and walked quickly without waiting for a reply. The two women had to trot to keep up.

Eventually Dr Carmichael stopped in front of a small room, opened the door and flicked on the overhead strip light. It was a typical waiting room: sterile, bare and depressing. There were two red vinyl couches in an L shape along the back and side wall and the walls themselves had been painted with pale grey gloss paint. The place seemed to radiate misery.

Pru and Milly looked at each other and then the doctor; they had expected to be taken to Bobby.

'Please sit down.' The doctor gestured to the far sofa.

Pru turned to face him. 'Actually, I don't want to be rude, but I'd much rather go and see my niece first, if that's okay. I'm happy to chat or fill out forms or anything later on...' She was babbling now, determined not to listen to what her gut was trying to tell her. The doctor, the clipboard, the grey room. 'But I'd rather see her first, if it's not too much trouble.'

He gave a brief nod. 'I understand, but I think you should sit down, Miss Plum, so that we can have a proper chat.'

The two women sat close together, heads tilted, and stared at him with identical expressions of concern. Dr Carmichael put the clipboard on the sofa next to him and joined his hands before planting his elbows on his knees and placing his fists under his chin. He took a deep breath.

Milly looked at the set of his jaw and noted the nervous twitch of his eye. *Oh God! Oh dear God, no!*

'I have been on duty here all evening and at about seven o'clock your niece and her fiancé were brought in by ambulance. As you know, they had an accident in the car, which your niece's fiancé was driving; apparently they went into the back of a lorry. No one else was hurt. They were treated separately by two different teams.'

Pru glanced at her watch – it was half past ten – and stared fixedly at the doctor. It was as if he was reading from a script; like he was in an episode of *Holby City*.

'I was one of the first to see Roberta when she arrived and she was seen immediately. She also received some treatment in the ambulance. She wasn't conscious. There were significant crush injuries to her chest and her spine was damaged. She was very badly hurt.'

Pru watched the man's mouth open and close. His words

reached her brain with a split-second delay, like a badly lip-synced song. *She was very badly hurt.*

The doctor spoke slowly and deliberately. 'We took her straight into resuscitation and we tried very hard. A team of us did everything that we thought might make a difference, but it didn't.'

Milly reached out and gathered her cousin's hand into her own.

Pru struggled to focus. 'So is she still hurt? Do you need to give her an operation or something?' *I'll move her into the spare room in our flat while she recuperates, get some of her favourite things in, nice drinks and plenty of magazines.* She leant forward. 'I'd like you to do whatever it takes. I can pay for her to see a specialist, if that would make a difference?'

Dr Carmichael shook his head. 'No, it wouldn't make any difference. I am very sorry, Miss Plum, but Roberta did not regain consciousness. She was pronounced dead at nine p.m. and William shortly afterwards. She wasn't in any pain; she never woke up. I am very sorry.'

Pru sat in silence, stunned and still. Milly's face crumpled as she watched her, waiting for a reaction.

Dr Carmichael looked at the floor, still awkward at having to be the bearer of this sort of news, despite having done it many times in his career.

'Miss Plum?'

'Yes?' Pru whispered.

'Do you understand what I have just told you?' He wondered if her silence, her lack of response, might equal inattention, but he was wrong. She had heard every word.

'Yes I do. Thank you.' She tried out a small smile as she stared at the doctor's face, a handsome face. She wondered how come he was not marked, living among this misery every day. Maybe his scarring was on the inside.

'Is there anything you would like to ask me?' He spoke slowly, as if she was stupid or elderly.

'Anything that I would like to ask you?' She was sure she should have questions but right now couldn't think of a single one. *She was pronounced dead. Bobby. Bobby, my beautiful girl, my gift.*

Pru took a deep breath and when she spoke, her voice was quiet.

'She's getting married in eleven months. She's already chosen her dress, Bella's altering it right now, it's quite beautiful. She looks stunning, like Veronica Lake. They're going to Ibiza on their honeymoon, not the touristy bit, the quiet side of the island. They've hired a friend's villa and it's got a private pool. Guy's going to make her cake.' Her words grew fainter until they were almost a whisper. She turned to her cousin. 'She's not going to get married now, is she?'

'No, darling.' Milly gulped back the tears that clogged her throat.

And then Pru emitted a dreadful, deafening wail that bounced off the walls and seeped into the fabric of the building. She screamed and sobbed as she slumped down on to the dull red floor tiles, kneeling there with her head on Milly's lap. 'No! No! Please, please do something! Do something now! She's getting married! Help me, Alfie, please help me!'

Milly lowered herself on to the cold floor and held her cousin tightly in her arms.

An hour later, Milly folded her mobile phone back into her handbag. It had been horrendous giving the news to Guy, who had wept and then prayed.

The two cousins sat on the red vinyl couch with blankets around their shoulders. Neither knew what to do next, paralysed with shock and the grief that was filling up inside them until they felt they might drown in it.

'Poor Isabel,' Pru suddenly murmured.

Both women would have time to reflect that it didn't matter how many acres you had or how big your kitchen; when your heart broke, it broke. Wealth and position were no gatekeepers to tragedy. Pru pictured Christopher, wanting desperately to talk to him but knowing that was low on her list of priorities. Everything could wait. Everything would have to wait.

'Can I get you anything, Pru?' Milly, the younger cousin, assumed the motherly role as she always did, rubbing small circles on Pru's back, trying to draw her pain.

It was some minutes before Pru spoke.

'I think I would like to see her. Can we do that?'

'I don't know. But I can find out.'

Pru nodded. 'I really want to see her.'

'Well, that's entirely up to you, darling, but if you are sure, I'll go and find Dr Carmichael.'

Pru looked at her cousin with red, swollen eyes. 'I'm sure. Will you come with me?'

Milly wasn't convinced it was a good idea; she dreaded

what their beautiful niece might look like. But she wouldn't deny Pru the chance to say goodbye. 'You know I will. Always.'

Pru felt sick as she and Milly followed the young medic to the side ward where Bobby lay, on the ground floor. She wondered if the newborns were on the top floor – closest to what? God? Heaven? Although there was an argument to be made that she too was heading closer to God. The end of the cycle, the inevitable. She had never seen a dead body before; she imagined decay and rot and the bile rose in her throat.

Dr Carmichael's tone was soothing. 'This is a very personal choice. You don't have to do this, you know. No one would think any less of you.'

Pru wondered if he was trying to put her off. 'I know, but it's okay. I'm fine.' Not her real voice but that of an automaton. This voice sounded surprisingly calm, even to her own ears. But inside her head she was screaming. *She can't be dead! It's a big mistake – this is not happening! I don't believe him, he's got it wrong.* She returned his smile; ever polite, even in this situation where she had full licence to fall apart, go a little crazy. *Someone's made a mistake. Where is my beautiful niece? Where is she now? I have to touch her. I've got to see her. She can't be dead!*

She and Milly walked into the side room. The doctor closed the door behind them, quietly clicking it shut like a tired mother trying not to wake her newly settled infant. Maybe he had forgotten what floor he was on. Milly walked straight over to the trolley in the middle of the room; her loud sobs punctured the silence. Pru, however, hovered by the door. She wasn't ready. Turning swiftly with her back to the room, she gripped the handle with her right hand in readiness to escape. The grey-painted door was cool against her forehead, the shiny toes of her patent pumps flexed upwards against its base. She noticed the tears of paint where a brush had inexpertly wielded too much gloss. She could smell disinfectant and, listening to Milly's distress, could only imagine what was behind her.

She released her grip on the handle and turned back slowly. Her tongue stuck to the dry roof of her mouth, her vision blurred and her heart threatened to leap from her chest. The desire to run was strong. She swallowed and her breath came in shallow pants.

She was drawn by Bobby's face and surprised to find that it wasn't scary, just odd. Very odd and sad, so very sad.

She walked hesitantly towards the trolley, trying not to think about why her niece might need to be on a moveable table or where she might be moved to. She had to remind herself that this was Bobby because the whole situation felt surreal.

'She looks so beautiful,' Pru managed through her tears.

Milly nodded. It was true. Despite some blood dotted around her hairline and a vicious cut on her neck, she looked like she always did – beautiful, just a little pale.

'What am I going to do now, Bobby? What am I going to do without you? My precious girl.'

The two women emerged to find Dr Carmichael standing in the corridor. He looked tired.

'William is just next door.' He indicated with his palm open, as if they might want to say goodbye to him as well.

Pru was ashamed to admit that she had momentarily forgotten that William too had died, unable to see beyond the loss of her beloved Bobby. She gave a small nod.

The doctor opened the door and pulled back the curtain to reveal William. His head rested on a slim white pillow and a pale blue sheet was wrapped tightly around his body. Like Bobby, he didn't appear to be wearing any clothes. His eyes were closed and his face was pale, with blue and black bruising across his cheek and right eye. Clots of dark, dried blood were dotted along his jawline and around his nose. These details were hard to take in and would only be recalled later.

All eyes were instead on the girl who stood by the side of his bed. She was weeping as she held William's pale hand against her face, brushing her lips over the back of his fingers. She seemed to be whispering, praying with her eyes closed.

'Oh! I thought he would be alone. I'm sorry. We'll come back later.'

The girl looked up, startled.

Pru stared at her.

'No, I'm sorry, I, I didn't want to… to see anyone. I just…' Her tears made further speech difficult. She struggled to contain her distress.

'Are you okay?' Pru's tone was one of concern.

The girl dropped William's hand and staggered backwards as she wiped at the tears that coursed down her face. 'I'm just saying goodbye!' She was a cockney like them.

'Who are you? Are you a relative?' Pru asked, wanting to offer solace.

The girl sobbed even harder and fought for breath as the next wave of grief washed over her. 'No, no, I'm not a relative exactly. But I just wanted to say goodbye. I don't want to cause any trouble!'

'Of course not. We've just said goodbye to Bobby.' Saying the words aloud made Pru shudder.

'Did you know Bobby?' Milly was curious.

'No, I've never heard of him.' The girl shook her head and eyed the door; this was more contact than she had bargained on.

'Who are you, love?' Pru asked.

'I'm Megan!'

'Well, Megan, we don't want to disturb you, but we thought we might say goodbye to William.'

Megan once again focused on the body lying on the bed. Her legs bent as if she might topple. 'I don't want to cause any trouble...' she repeated, turning sideways to reveal the unmistakeable outline of a baby bump.

Pru and Milly watched as the girl swayed and gripped at the curtain that enclosed the bed, trying not to give in to the faint that threatened. Then she fled from the room, howling pitifully as she went. Pru turned to see her run the length of the corridor. She hit the wall in her blind stumbling and ricocheted to the other side, as if she were in a pinball machine. Pru followed her outside, but she was too slow and didn't see which direction she went. She flopped down on to the steps, feeling suddenly over-whelmed.

Back inside, she found Milly talking awkwardly to William's commanding officer in the corridor. Families Warrant Officer Major Sotherton of the Household Cavalry removed his hat and stepped forward. 'We are of course here to help in any way we can, Miss Plum. I shall come and see you tomorrow if you would like, but if you need me before then, here is my number.'

Pru took the piece of paper with his contact details. She placed it in her handbag for safekeeping. 'Thank you,' she said.

The man replaced his hat. 'Captain Fellsley was a fine soldier and a good man.'

It was the wee small hours when the taxi dropped the weary duo back in Curzon Street. Pru sank down into her chair without putting on the lights, preferring the darkness and the yellowy glow that came from the streetlight directly outside their window. She had gone full circle from exhaustion to hyper and was now quite numb.

Milly handed her a mug of tea. 'We need to sleep.'

Pru nodded. 'They've given me something we can take; it'll knock us out. I'll take a couple in a bit.'

She flopped back in the chair and felt curiously disorientated, like she had jet lag or had woken from a nightmare and couldn't come to. She would momentarily forget why she felt so sad and then she would remember and it was like being given the news all over again. It hurt just as bad.

Milly ran her palm over her face. 'I just can't believe it, Pru. Any of it. One minute she's flitting around looking for matches, planning her evening and the next this. Tell me it's all just a bad dream. Please! I didn't even say goodbye to her properly. I didn't give her my full attention – I was doing some bloody crossword.'

'I can't remember what the last thing I said to her was.' Pru broke down again. She turned to look at Milly. 'Do you think they're together now?' she sobbed.

'Bobby and Alfie?'

Pru nodded.

'I'm sure of it, love.' Milly sighed and mopped at her streaming face. 'And we'll get through this, just like we did before. We can get through anything, by sticking together, right?' She stared at Pru, who met her gaze and nodded.

'I just want to disappear.'

'I know. Have you spoken to Christopher?'

'Yes, very briefly. He's going straight to Oxford to be with his sister. She's in a terrible state, obviously. Her husband only died a couple of years ago and now this.' Pru cried again then, covering her face with her hands and trying to sort the jumble of information that swirled inside her head. 'I'm going to bed.'

'Don't worry about anything. Guy will have everything under control and I'll pop down, in the morning.'

'Thanks, Mills.'

'If you want a bit of company in the night or need anything at all, then just buzz me and I'll be straight in.'

'She was so happy, wasn't she? So happy.' Pru closed her eyes as she stood, picturing Bobby on the podium in Spitalfields, clapping her hands with joy and looking like a bride. She felt her way along the hallway to her bedroom.

Clicking the door shut behind her, Pru collected a framed

photo from the bedside table: Bobby and William at a party. Her niece beamed and held a glass of champagne up to the camera. The handsome Captain Fellsley was smiling too, but Pru noticed for the first time that it didn't quite reach his eyes.

'Oh, Bobby, I miss you already. Tonight I am going to make out you are asleep upstairs, tucked up safely.'

Pru held the picture to her chest and sank back against the pillows, trying to order her thoughts. She wished she could talk to Christopher, who had the knack of making everything feel better. She pictured him and Isabel and her heart went out to the woman who two years ago ceased to be a wife and had just discovered that she was no longer a mother.

Pru swallowed two of the sleeping tablets but woke after four hours of sleep with a physical pain in her chest. She sat up in the bed as though waking from a nightmare and her sobs came instantly.

'Oh, Alfie, I thought I'd dreamed it, but I didn't, did I? She's gone. She's really gone. I'm so sorry, I thought I could keep her safe for you. I tried, I really did. Is she with you now? Please, please tell me she's with you now, safe and sound.'

Pru looked past the pelmet and Liberty print curtains that framed the window of the spare bedroom at Mountfield. She hadn't wanted to stay here the night before the funeral, but had been convinced by everyone else that it would be easier in the morning. No battle with the London traffic. Milly was in the room next door.

The image of Bobby standing on the very patch of grass in front of her as a jazz band played, laughing, with her hand outstretched, showing off her diamond, popped into her head.

'Oh Bobby, where are you? Where are you right now?'

She spoke to the sky through the dappled panes of the Queen Anne window, allowing her eyes to roam over the rolling acres and come to rest on the edge of the lake where she and Christopher had spent the afternoon. Pru knew he had been due to arrive last night, but she hadn't seen him. He was probably with Isabel, who she had seen. William's mother was barely able to converse. Grief sat like a stopper in her throat. The two women had hugged briefly and parted immediately, as though their combined sadness might overwhelm everybody. Isabel had been supported by a friend and she seemed to have shrunk in stature, her eyes hollow and staring, features pinched, movements stilted. It tore at Pru to see the hurt in William's mother so visibly manifested. She barely acknowledged anyone; it took all of her strength to remain calm, centred.

Pru lay on the bed and closed her eyes. She had spent many of her waking moments this way over the last ten days, hovering between the oblivion of sleep and the dark pit of sadness that threatened to pull her in.

Milly knocked on the door and entered. 'It's nearly time to leave.'

'I'll be five minutes.'

'I'll wait here for you.'

'No, I'm okay, Mills,' Pru answered without opening her eyes or turning her head. 'Just give me a mo.'

Milly left as Pru clambered from the bed and pulled on her navy jacket, applying neither make-up nor a comb to her slightly ratty hair.

'Right then, Alfie, I'm as set as I'll ever be. You stay close and we'll get through this together.' She smoothed her skirt and left the room, to find Milly standing outside her door.

A crowd had gathered in the opulent square hallway. With her eyes lowered, Pru couldn't easily distinguish individuals, but she was aware of a mass of black cloth, repeated sharp intakes of breath and a sea of sad faces.

The front door opened to reveal a line of black shiny cars that looked grand, oddly celebratory as they sat on the gravel. William and Bobby were to have a joint funeral in the church where they were to have been married. Pru agreed with Milly, it was right that the service should be conducted in a place that had meant something to both of them.

Pru watched as Isabel stepped through the door and on to the gravel. Her body bucked as she saw the hearses. 'Oh my God!' she screeched. 'Please no! Oh my God! No! No! Someone needs to get him out of there! He can't be in there. Please, Chris, please! Tell me he's not in there! My baby, my boy!' Isabel's knees gave way and Christopher and another man caught her and kept her upright. She could barely walk, just managing a shuffle as her feet dragged along beneath her.

The two men escorted her back inside. It was best that she lie down and let the day wash over her. There was no need to put her through the torture of watching her son's coffin being lowered into the ground. It would serve no purpose. Pru was sympathetic to her distress but she envied her the escape.

She returned her attention to the shiny black hearses and the coffins within them, transfixed. Despite being early May, the day was cloaked in a dull grey blanket of rain. She and Milly slid on to the back seat of one of the cars and her eyes never left the wooden box set out behind them. Flower arrangements in a riot of colour were grouped in clusters around the coffin. Her own, a cascade of lilies interwoven with fresh ivy, sat on the top. *I can see it now: white lilies with ivy trailing through them, like they've been grabbed from the wild and bunched together. It will be haphazard but beautiful!'*

Feeling quite detached, Pru didn't register the well-wishers that had lined the route to the church. Some were there out of respect, some through morbid curiosity – it was big news in a small place. A double funeral was rare and the couple's youth made it extra newsworthy. Plus the fact that it was the son of that posh woman with the really big house.

Pru sat at the front of the church, next to Milly, their arms touching, giving mutual comfort with this simple gesture. Music began to filter through the little Norman church, not overly sombre, but classical and fitting. Pru wondered who had chosen it, who had chosen all of it? Every face turned to the door as the pall bearers entered. Christopher was one of them. Theirs was a slow progression that seemed to take an eternity.

The vicar stood at the top of the aisle and for a split second Pru thought that she might be at a wedding, but whose wedding? She was here for Bobby, was it Bobby's wedding? Where had all the time gone and where was William? But then her eyes focused on the two wooden boxes with shiny brass handles that rested on tense shoulders and she remembered that she was not here for a wedding, there would not be a wedding, not for Bobby.

Pru spoke to her in her head. 'It's all right, my darling, you go to sleep now, baby. Your dad's got you and I'm right here. I'll always be right here.'

The same handsome boys and groomed girls who only a month before had sipped at their Pimm's and danced to the jazz band in the ornate marquee now filled the dark wooden pews, sniffing into tissues that soaked up their distress. Piers Parkinson-Boater stood in full dress uniform, his medals glinting in the candlelight. Tears ran down his tanned face, which he did nothing to stem.

Pru, anesthetised, stumbled ghost-like through the proceedings, quietly watching the seconds tick by until she could return to her bed and hide. Her eyes darted, unable to focus on the Union-flag-draped coffin that stood beneath the wooden boards listing similarly titled men who had lost their lives fighting for their country. Maybe if William had passed in service for his country, it would not have felt quite so pointless. And Bobby, next to the man she loved, beneath the altar, just as she had wished. The girl with a child-like spirit who filled each room with light, gone, wiped out.

The vicar began to speak but his words became distorted inside her head, as if she was listening to them under water. Then without warning her hearing crystallised to register the line, 'These two young people united in death as they were in life, in love and before Christ's image on the cross as they would have been on their wedding day.'

A muffled scream came from the back of the church. The majority of the congregation didn't turn round – out of politeness, or respect – but Pru did, she couldn't help herself. She turned just in time to see a flash of mousy brown hair disappear through the heavy church door.

As the mourners trooped out of the church and towards the plot, freshly excavated and awaiting the young lovers, Pru scanned the graveyard. Spying what she was looking for, she padded across the spongy grass. And there she was, the girl from the hospital, peeking from behind a large cedar tree, staring into space.

'I thought I saw you. It's Megan, isn't it?' Pru spoke softly, not wanting to alarm the girl. 'I saw you before at the hospital, do you remember me?'

The girl nodded, blinking slowly. Her hair hung limply either side of her pale face, glued to her forehead in lank strands by the mist of rain that continued to settle over them. She looked exhausted and desperately sad. Pru sank down by her side.

'I didn't expect to see you today, have you come far?'

Megan whispered to the grass. 'London. I got the train, then a cab.'

'That's quite a trek. He must have meant a lot to you.'

Pru could hear the sobs coming from across the grave-yard: that would be the moment that the bodies were committed to the ground. Closing her eyes, she tried to calm her thoughts. She had no desire to see it, didn't want that image in her head. It was enough that she could picture Bobby pale and lifeless on a trolley.

'Are you that girl's nan?' Megan looked up.

'No. My name is Pru and Bobby was my niece, but I brought her up.'

'Well, you didn't do a very good job! I don't know who she thought she was! Messing up my life.'

Pru tightened her mouth and narrowed her gaze. 'Why would you say something like that? She was a wonderful girl and I loved her very much. She is not yet in the ground and I would appreciate it if you showed her a bit more respect. I thought you might need help, that's why I came over to talk to you. I was mistaken.' Pru stood and dusted off her skirt, some pine needles, sticky with sap, stuck to her palms as she did so.

'I'm sorry.' Megan shook her head and let a fresh wave of tears cascade down her face. She made no attempt to dry them or cover her sadness. 'I knew I shouldn't have come today, but I had to, I wanted to see where he was buried. I waited until the last minute to sneak in. I didn't want to see anyone. Bill said his family wouldn't be happy about the baby and that we had to keep it a secret until they got used to the idea, but I never expected anything like this.'

'The baby?'

'Our baby. Bill was my fiancé.' Megan ran her hand over her bump protectively.

'Your *fiancé*?'

'Yes. I'm due in two months. And now I've just found out he had another bird. I can't believe it!'

Pru tried to digest this new information. Billy-boy a philanderer? About to become a father? Poor, trusting Bobby. It was mortifying to hear her referred to as the other woman. Becoming William's fiancée, his future wife, had been her greatest joy. Was this girl for real? Eight weeks! In just eight weeks there would be a baby.

Megan sniffed. 'Bill said that things were going to change. That living like this would be temporary, that we'd go and get our house.' She twisted her soggy tissue into a ball and looked up at Pru. 'And I felt like I'd won the bloody lottery, not cos of the money, but because I had him, an army officer! I couldn't believe he would love someone like me, but he swore he did, he really did! I felt loved.'

Pru watched as the girl's face crumpled and the strength left her legs. She folded like a rag doll and slumped down on the grass under the tree. 'What am I going to do without him? I loved him. We're having a baby! I've got nothing without him, nothing.' Raising her knees, she placed her head in her hands and cried. 'He promised me he would take care of us. He sent me a brochure of a house in Ashford that he wanted us to go and see. It was on a little estate and it had a dishwasher and new carpets that came with it and a proper garden, with grass.'

'Ashford, Kent. Not too far, but just far enough.'

'Eh? Just far enough for what?'

Pru grimaced but did not reply.

Megan drew breath. 'I knew deep down it wouldn't really happen, not to someone like me. I knew it, but I didn't want to believe it!'

Had Billy-boy really been fooling them all? Stringing Bobby along, hurting everyone? Pru shuddered. Despite it all, her heart ached for this little girl who had been promised security and a little love – everybody's dream.

'Come on, Megan, try not to cry, love. It'll only make you feel worse.'

Megan stuttered and coughed. 'I couldn't feel any worse. If I wasn't pregnant, I swear I'd top meself and go and join him, I would. I've got nothing without him, nothing at all. And all I can think of now is that he was going to marry someone else – that was what that vicar said! I heard it and I know vicars don't lie, but that's what he said and I can't believe it. When your mate asked if I knew Bobby, I wasn't thinking straight, but I thought it was a bloke, an army mate of his or something.' She shook her head. 'Were they really going to get married?'

'Yes, Megan, they were. I don't know what to say to you, other than it all seems like a horrible mess.'

'It wasn't a mess! It was all very straightforward. We

are having a baby and we were getting a house. But now he's gone and died and everything's dissolved. Am I supposed to believe he was marrying someone else? I don't know what to believe! I can't think straight.'

'It seems like he was seeing you both and obviously neither of you knew about the other.' Pru shook her head at the improbability of it.

'I don't know what to say. I had no idea.' Megan clutched at her tummy.

'No, I can see that.'

She looked up at Pru, like a child, not a young woman about to become a mother. 'What would have happened to me, to our baby?'

Pru sat up straight. 'I honestly don't know.'

Megan howled then, not caring who heard, and collapsed into herself.

Pru edged closer. 'Please don't cry, it's all right.' It was almost as if Megan were Bobby just woken from a bad dream. Faced with this young woman in need, Pru felt her natural desire to fix things kick in. She wanted to help.

The two sat in silence for a minute until Megan stood up. 'I've got to go.' She stepped towards the gate but as Pru started to follow her she turned, angry. 'Look, you don't even know me, so just fuck off, leave me alone. Please.'

Pru nodded. 'I'm going. But if you change your mind, Megan, or you need anything at all, then I'm in Curzon Street – Plum Patisserie, you can't miss it.'

Megan turned away and carried on walking, without giving an answer or looking back.

Pru re-joined the mourners as they were about to make

their way back to Mountfield. Milly saw her across the path and grabbed her arm. 'Where have you been? I was worried sick! Are you all right?'

'I don't know.' She spoke the truth.

'We won't stay long, just show our faces and then go home, okay?' Milly spoke to her as if she was a child.

Pru nodded. 'I saw that girl, the one from the hospital. Megan.'

'When?'

'Just now, she was here. She said she was William's fiancée.' Pru smoothed the creases from the sleeves of her navy jacket and ran her hand over her face, trying to remain composed.

'What?'

'She's telling the truth, Mills. She's devastated. And she didn't know about Bob.' Pru let her tears fall, wondering if she would ever run out.

Piers Parkinson-Boater walked over to them with an older soldier by his side. He adjusted his hat as he approached. 'Miss Plum, I am so very sorry. I was fond of Bobby, I can only picture her laughing or jumping up and down.' He smiled. 'And William was a great bloke and an inspirational soldier.'

The older man stepped forward. 'I'm Sergeant Rob Gisby. William certainly was an inspirational soldier.' He smiled too; his eyes were kind, and red from crying.

Pru nodded at the two men. She couldn't speak for William's soldiering credentials, but as for being a great bloke, the presence of a second, pregnant, fiancée cast something of a shadow over that assertion. 'Thank you.'

Both women accepted their handshakes before they walked away.

'What do you make of it all, Pru? Who the hell is she?'

'I don't really know. We don't know anything, do we? Apart from her name's Megan and she *said* she was his fiancée, and she's pregnant.'

'Christ alive, I can't even think about it. Poor Bobby.'

'Poor everyone. She looked like an unfortunate little thing, you know, Mills. Reminded me of us when we were younger. It bothered me that she was on her own.'

'Well, it doesn't bother me! I think it's a bloody disgrace, coming here on the day we lay them to rest, causing trouble.' Milly folded her arms indignantly.

'She wasn't really causing trouble. I don't think she wanted to be seen.'

'I don't want to speak ill of the dead,' Milly said through gritted teeth, 'and I was fond of Billy-boy. But if she was his fiancée and he's left her pregnant... If he did do that to Bobby, it's a good job he isn't around, cos I'd bloody kill 'im!'

'You can't talk like that, Mills.'

'I know, but I'm angry. What was he playing at?'

'I don't know. I just can't make it out. If he was seeing both of them, then how the hell did he see that working out? That baby would have been about one when he was due to marry Bob! And if he wasn't involved with Megan, then who the bloody hell is she? I don't understand it, any of it.'

The two cousins walked arm in arm to the waiting car. As the limo swept them up the drive of William's family home, Pru grimaced. 'God, why so many people?' She couldn't stomach the party-like atmosphere in and around the house, the flash cars abandoned on the gravel, the sumptuous spread, the jewellery and high heels. Did they not know that her beautiful girl was dead?

There was the chink of bottle against glass as wine was poured. The hum of conversation hovered like a low cloud in the room.

'I don't want to be here,' Pru mumbled from the side of her mouth.

Milly stood in front of her. 'It's what you have to do, darling.'

Pru stared defiantly at her cousin. 'It is not what I have to do at all.' And with that she went upstairs and locked herself in the en-suite bathroom of the guest room she'd stayed in. Her own private space.

Pru had always loved the privacy and sparkle of a clean and beautiful bathroom. Even as teenagers, she and Milly had had to endure the weekly embarrassment of sitting in the tin bath in the front room of their little house in Bow. The water was always unpleasantly tepid and there was a distinct lack of privacy. Family members would traipse in and out with eyes averted. She would clamber out with pruney fingers and toes, and would then stand shivering in front of the fire, trying to get dry with a scratchy, worn towel. Worst of all though had been having to use the same water as the rest of the family, lowering herself into the carbolic-scented soap scum of the previous occupant. She had hated the way the grey bubbles, bloated with someone else's sweat, dirt and odour, clung to her skin.

When Pru and Milly first saw the bathroom at Kenway Road, they thought they had died and gone to heaven. The room was tiled in the palest pink and it sparkled so you hardly noticed the cracked sink or the stained ceiling. The tub was enormous, cast iron with a roll top, and it sat on very ornate clawed feet. The pretty cream-painted corner cupboard was crammed with Chanel No. 19 talcum powder, Sunsilk shampoo and bottles of garish red nail polish – goodies that had been in short supply in Bow. Pru had grinned at Milly. The first part of their plan was coming true: they would never be dirty or poorly dressed again.

Now Pru lay with her face against the cool terrazzo tiles of the Mountfield guest bathroom, listening to the murmur of conversation that crept up through the joists. Once or twice she heard the high-pitched trill of female laughter – how dare someone be laughing, laughing today, laughing at all.

'Who are you, Megan? What's going on?' she whispered, her eyes closed. 'Oh, Bobby, what a mess.'

She pictured the enormous bath she had run for Bobby on her first night at Curzon Street, all those years ago. Filled to the brim with bubbles.

'I ain't getting in your bath and I ain't staying here,' Bobby had shouted from the corner of her bedroom. 'I hate you!'

Pru had noted the untouched tray of food on the bed. 'Well, it's okay to hate me, but you still need to have a bath and it's far nicer to get in it when it's hot than when it's gone cold, so come on, chop chop!'

Reluctantly, Bobby had unfurled her legs and crawled from the corner on all fours. Scuttling like a beetle, she made her way across the bedroom, along the hall and into the bathroom, where she kicked the door shut behind her. Truth was, the child smelled of urine, dirt and fear-laden sweat. Pru listened at the door as Bobby's small frame plopped into the suds. She crouched down outside and heard the sound of splashing and crying. A short while later, Bobby emerged, wrapped in a large cream towel that swamped her as she scurried across the hallway and back into the bedroom, where she again kicked the door shut. Pru gathered her grubby clothes from the floor and pulled the plug, gasping at the ring of black grime that clung to the edge of the bathtub. This became their ritual, with Pru leaving clean, warm pyjamas on Bobby's bed for her to change into after her splash about. But it took another four weeks before the ice truly began to crack. One evening, clean and dry and dressed in her pyjamas, Bobby had appeared in the sitting room, popping up like a rare flower that no one had expected to bloom. Kicking her little bare feet against the edge of the sofa, she had folded her arms across her chest. 'I still hate you and I'm not staying here, but I'd like some of that cheese on toast.' Pru had had to stop herself from jumping for joy as she strolled nonchalantly into the kitchen to cut two thick slices of white bread.

Images of Bobby at all different ages, in all different pyjamas, flooded Pru's brain as she lay motionless on the cool Mountfield floor, she had loved those times, Bobby ready for bed, in the place she called home. An hour passed, then came a dull tapping at the door. Pru raised her head and glanced around the room, realising quickly that there was nowhere that she could hide.

'Pru?' It was Christopher. 'Can I come in?'

Her heart gave its familiar lift at the sound of his voice, even today. Slowly she rose from the floor on unsteady legs and slid the bolt before sinking back to the floor with her knees up and her back against the wall.

Christopher crept round the door and slid down to join her, sitting against the door on the cold floor. 'I thought you might like some company.'

Pru sidled across the tiles and placed her head against his chest. He wrapped his arms around her, stroking her hair and whispering 'Sshhhhh…' as though he could bring her some peace.

'I can't think straight, Chris,' she mumbled into the fabric of his shirt, inhaling the scent of him. 'I don't want to be awake. I don't know what I'm supposed to do.'

'You don't have to do anything. You just have to take it minute by minute, hour by hour. You don't have to make any plans or think ahead, just get through every bit of the day and see where it takes you.' He sounded wise, calm and it helped.

'I loved her so much. I couldn't have loved her any more had I given birth to her. I keep thinking she is going to walk in or phone me, but she isn't, is she?'

'No, she isn't.'

'I can't believe it. I want to speak to her one more time. I don't understand what happened. I just want five minutes, one minute. I can't believe I'm not going to see her, ever. It just won't sink in.'

'That's quite normal, Pru, but that shock fades, I promise you. It becomes easier to live with, even though you don't think it ever will, not when it's so new and raw.'

'I keep thinking that I should have made her get a cab, told her not to use the car that night. If only I'd intervened, I could have stopped it. But I didn't, I didn't know I had to.'

'We all think that. Why didn't I speak to William that day, keep him on the phone? Or say goodbye properly, tell him I was proud of him.'

Pru closed her eyes and tried to remember the last time she'd told Bobby how proud she was of her. Had she known that?

Christopher continued. 'I've asked myself for years, why didn't I make Ginny go to the doctor's when she first complained of being tired, instead of telling her to have a nap, that it would make her feel better. I should have encouraged her and yet she didn't go for another three months – three months! It might have made a difference.'

'I don't want to talk about Ginny.' Pru didn't know why she'd said it aloud, but she had.

Christopher pulled away from her. 'You're right, of course. I'm sorry.'

'No, Chris, I'm sorry.' She put her hand on his arm, which he patted. It felt brotherly, conciliatory and made her stomach twist.

Ten minutes later, Christopher made his way downstairs as Pru gathered up her overnight bag and prepared to leave. A small crowd congregated to say goodbye and offer their condolences. She watched the dark, shuffling procession approach Isabel and one by one give their love and prayers, and then they turned to her. She didn't feel like being civil to any of them, no matter how well intentioned. She hurt too much.

110

She gazed at the heavy-lidded girls and slightly sloshed boys and she couldn't help but think of Megan, who hadn't been invited. Megan, whoever she was, this ghost of a girl that appeared and disappeared, with her words that dropped like cluster bombs, heaping confusion and sadness on top of the grief. This girl who was invisible, irrelevant and yet purportedly carrying a child that had the blood of the Fellsley family running through its tiny veins. But even if Pru could have got the facts straight in her head, it wasn't her place to tell.

It took an age to say goodbye. Pru watched as William's relatives crushed his friends and colleagues into their arms, taking comfort from the connection of sorts – another young person, like him, but not him. Christopher caught her eye across the room, giving her an almost imperceptible wink that made her heart leap. *'It'll be okay, it'll all be okay.'* It told her that he too wished they were elsewhere; free to laugh, talk and continue where they had left off before this tragedy robbed them of momentum. She felt instantly guilty at the happiness that surged through her body on this of all days.

Seven

Pru didn't have the luxury of taking to her bed and wallowing in her grief; she had a business to run. The distraction was actually good for her, focusing her mind on something other than her loss. Although, in truth, concentrating on the minutiae of cake-making was difficult.

It was a busy afternoon at Plum Patisserie. She placed her teacup on the desk in front of her. The subtle lighting and tawny hues made the room seem homely and cosy; clients felt more like they were joining a friend for coffee than transacting business. The chairs in front of Pru's desk were wide and comfortable, the kind you could sink into and snooze in without too much persuasion. The vast ornate mirror behind her desk made the room appear larger than it was and in the winter the log burner gave the whole room a feeling of intimacy.

'Was dreadfully sorry to hear your sad news, Pru,' Lady Miriam said as she gulped her coffee.

'Thank you.' Pru gave a brief nod. She found it difficult to accept condolences, knowing that if she gave in to sentiment, the floodgates would open and she would be sobbing again. 'So,' she drew proceedings back to business, 'it's a cake for your daughter's birthday and she will be...?'

'Yes, my daughter Bunny and she will be fourteen.'

'Smashing, and do you have an idea of the kind of cake you are looking for, Miriam?'

Lady Miriam lapped at the cup of strong coffee and spoke through her mouthful of scone. It fascinated Pru that for all her fancy labels, privileged upbringing and pricey education, the woman still hadn't learned what a rap on the knuckles had taught Pru aged three, that a mouth full of food equalled no talking. Pru tried to listen to her words, but it took all her strength not to stare at the wet blobs that flew from her mouth and landed on the blue blotting paper in front of her, creating something that resembled an aerial shot of the Galapagos.

Pru had noticed that many of her wealthy clients seemed to calibrate differently what was polite or acceptable. She recalled one Chelsea hostess who shot her assistant a withering look when she called the downstairs cloakroom 'the toilet', but seemed to find it perfectly natural to use her bare hands to retrieve a turd from the rug, left by her rather highly strung Pomeranian. Pru had fought the urge to be sick and, unable to refuse the offered handshake at the end of their meeting, had rushed home to scrub her palm before spraying it with a liberal application of bleach.

Lady Miriam considered her response. 'I *think* I know what I want. Well... I do and I don't!'

Pru was aware that today her train of thought was fractured, her voice a monotone, but she nodded and picked up her pencil. She could go through the motions even if she couldn't muster any enthusiasm.

'What would really help would be if you could give me

an idea of a theme, a colour or anything that Bunny is particularly fond of – for example tennis or horses?' Pru was usually on safe ground with these two pastimes. 'Anything at all as a starting point and then we'll get Guy to come up with some concepts and samples that we can go through before making a final decision. How does that sound?'

Lady Miriam smiled. 'It sounds fabulous!'

Pru had learned over the years that her customers fell into two categories. There were those who picked up the phone and asked for a birthday cake, with minimal instruction. 'Something pretty, please. It's for my mother's eightieth and there'll be thirty guests.' Pru would then deliver the cake and send an invoice. In return, along with the payment, she would usually receive a brief but sincere thank you note, written on crested cream vellum. And then there were the others, who figured that as they were paying very large sums of money for extraordinary cakes, they should be involved in the intricate and time-consuming business of design, production and finish. For them, the more stages to the whole process, the better; they loved to meet over coffee, often with urgent requests for minute changes.

By the very fact of her presence, it was clear Lady Miriam fell into the latter category. She waved her arms over her head. 'I see the cake as the centrepiece, the wow moment! I want everyone to arrive and walk around it, almost in homage to Bunny reaching this incredible milestone!' Lady Miriam's hands finally came to rest under her chin.

Pru wanted to point out that becoming fourteen was not

usually considered an incredible milestone and that if this is what they were preparing for her fourteenth, what would her twenty-first look like? She gulped at this thought. Bobby would never have a twenty-first, not now. She bit back the thousand comments that wanted to surge from her throat and instead described her vision of a huge flowery cake scattered with tiny rosebuds and real gypsophila wound in, with variegated petals and teensy iced bows whose ribbons would flow over two tiers.

Would Bunny appreciate it? she wondered. She and Milly had savoured every mouthful of their own childhood birthday cakes – always a giant Victoria sponge, the middle filled with raspberry jam and buttercream frosting. They only ever received a single gift, of course – something useful like socks, mittens or knitting wool.

Guy knocked and entered and gave a sweeping bow in the direction of their customer. 'I am so very sorry to interrupt—'

'Oh, no, don't worry a jot. We haven't got down to the detail yet.' Lady Miriam sprayed Guy with scone. Pru saw him give an almost imperceptible flinch.

'But I am afraid Madame is needed upstairs in a rather urgent fashion.' He held his hands in front of his chest as though cupping a small bird inside his finger cage.

Sometimes the way Guy spoke drove Pru mad; this was one of those times. She wished he would be a bit more to the point. It was hard to tell from his demeanour and tone whether the building was on fire or they had run out of soap in the Ladies' loo.

'Do excuse me, Miriam; I'll be as quick as I can. Guy,

if you could fetch our guest another coffee.' She knew this would sweeten her absence.

They walked outside and into the corridor. 'What on earth's wrong, Guy?'

'There's a girl upstairs that says she needs to talk to you. She refuses to come inside and is sitting in your private doorway, but she can be seen from the café, hunched on the floor like a vagrant.' His nose wrinkled slightly.

Pru held her tongue. It was more important to deal with the issue than stand and debate his lack of empathy. 'Is she blonde-ish, small, pregnant?'

'Yes, yes and yes.' He nodded, looking up to his right as though picturing her.

Pru let out a breath that she had not realised she had been holding. 'Thank God. That's Megan. You'll have to take over for me with Miriam.'

Pru hurried upstairs and walked out on to the Curzon Street pavement. It was late afternoon and a busy day like any other. Businessmen walked briskly, barking into mobile phones, arranging where to go for a drink or shouting instructions to their PAs. Ladies that lunched tripped along arm in arm with their doppelgangers, sporting matching designer handbags slung over their bony décolletages and seemingly in no hurry to get home. Tourists ambled along with cameras around their necks, clogging the narrow walkways and causing much irritation to the lunching ladies and the businessmen.

In their midst Pru spied the slender back of Megan, in the same T-shirt she had seen her in twice before. Her hair was loose and hung to her shoulders. She was bending forward as if resting on her knees. Pru approached cautiously, eager not to frighten her off again. She came to a standstill a foot away from her.

'Hello there, Megan.'

The girl turned slowly and in obvious pain. 'Hello.'

Pru gasped, and tried her best not to show her shock and distress. Megan's bottom lip was swollen to twice its normal size, with a vertical split along it that oozed blood when she spoke. Her left eye was entirely bloodshot and encircled by a dark blue bruise. The lid itself was purple, shiny and swollen. She had to tip her head back slightly to get a full view.

'Oh my God, what happened to you?'

'My cousin's flatmate, he—'

'A man did this to you?' Pru interrupted, unable to keep the anger from her voice or hide the shock on her face that anyone could do this to a young, pregnant girl.

Megan shook her head vigorously and then held her jaw, regretting the ill-considered movement. 'No, Rocky is as good as gold; he lives with my cousin, Liam. I've known him a long time. It was his girlfriend.'

Pru crouched down on the pavement and put her hand on the girl's back. 'Oh, Megan. Do you need to see a doctor or go to the hospital? I can take you.'

She shook her head, more gently this time. 'No, it's just my face.'

'But we should still get you checked out, just in case.'

'I don't want to. I'm okay, honestly.' Her words were slurred, issued through her freshly misshapen mouth.

'But you're clearly not okay, love. Why did she do this? When?'

Megan spoke slowly. 'She came back to the flat last night, pissed up, and said she was sick of sleeping on the sofa while I was in Rocky's room. The two of them were arguing in the hallway and I just lay under the covers, listening. Rocky said he felt sorry for me, that he didn't mind me having his room and that was it. She went mental, said he was probably shagging me.' She closed her eyes. 'It was horrible and I felt really sorry for Rocky, he was getting all that grief just because he was doing me a favour. So I went out into the hallway, to try and tell her there was nothing going on and that they could have the room and I'd sleep on the sofa, but before I got a chance to say a word, she went crazy. She head-butted my face and punched my mouth. I think I blacked out a bit; I managed to get back in the bedroom and when it had all calmed down, I packed up my stuff and I left. I can't take any more hassle.'

'When did you leave?'

'About four o'clock this morning.'

Pru looked at her watch: it was nearly 5 p.m. 'Have you been walking around all this time?'

Megan nodded. 'I didn't know what to do. I didn't have anywhere else to go and then I remembered what you said and so I came here. I don't have to stay, I just didn't know what else to do.'

'I'm glad you thought of me, Megan. Come inside, come on.' Pru reached inside her pocket for her door key.

Megan stood and seemed to weigh up her options. She prodded her bottom lip with her thumbnail until it bled, then licked the warm trickle back up into her mouth. 'I probably shouldn't have come. I don't know what to do.'

She bit the inside of her cheek, which reminded Pru so much of Bobby that her stomach cramped.

'It'll be okay, Megan. Trust me. You can come and stay with me, there's lots of room and it'll give you a bit of space, time to get straight.' Pru hoped Milly would be kind.

'How can I trust you? I don't even know you.'

'That's true, but I know what it's like to need a break. And besides, I don't think you've got too many options at the moment, have you?'

'It still feels weird.'

'Yes, it is a bit, but this whole situation is weird. And here's the thing, Megan: you look like you are in a bit of a pickle, and I want to help you. I haven't always been as lucky as I am now, and the one thing I can tell you is that there are certain times in your life when people will offer to help you, often when you need it the most, and you should always, always take that help.'

'I'm not sure.' Megan's glance was nervous, flicking between Pru and the street, her means of escape.

Pru could see her indecision. 'I tell you what, why don't you come inside with me and have a good think about it. There are no bars on the windows, you are free to leave the second you want.'

'I wish I hadn't bothered you now, I feel really awkward. This is all bollocks – you were that girl's aunty and finding out about her is the worst thing that's ever happened to me.' Her tears fell. 'I didn't get the chance to say goodbye to him properly because you arrived and I hadn't finished. It was like you chucked me out and you didn't really have the right. All I wanted was five minutes to tell him what I

119

would do with our baby, that I'd keep all the promises we made, but I never got the chance.'

Pru patted her shoulder. 'I didn't chuck you out, Megan, you ran away. And he knew how you felt. Don't you worry. He loved you and he knew.' She swallowed the bile of disloyalty that rose in her throat.

Megan hesitated, then seemed to come to a decision. 'What can I do with my stuff?'

'How much have you got?' Pru pictured the wardrobes, chest of drawers and closet in the spare room of the flat.

'Just that.' Megan pointed to the pavement and a shallow plastic box that took up no more space than a couple of large books.

Pru's heart lurched in sympathy. 'You can bring it upstairs.' The sort of women she dealt with at the patisserie every day would be busy stocking up on baby essentials at this stage of their pregnancy and ordering towers of cupcakes in pale pink or sky blue for their baby shower. She doubted Megan even had a change of clothes. Pru resolved there and then to order her a range of stuff, from maternity wear to smart clothes. She'd have it delivered and Megan could pick what she liked.

On top of the box sat a photograph of Megan and William. They were lying on a pebble beach; Megan's head was resting on his chest and William, with one arm keeping her close and the other holding the camera at arm's length, had clearly taken the photo. They were both smiling. It shocked Pru to see him in this environment and with this girl. Where had Bobby thought he was? What lie had he told? Pru studied William's face: he looked happy. She inhaled sharply, squinting to better analyse his expression. He didn't just look happy, he looked happier than she had ever seen him. Slotted into the corner of the frame was a black and white picture, only a couple of inches in diameter but unmistakeably a scan of a baby, their baby.

'That was at Brighton. We liked it there. It's where we met – I was wandering along, minding my own business and he nearly ran me over on the seafront, that's how we first got talking.' She sniffed up her tears and her mouth twitched. 'After that we'd go in all weathers, go for a walk and then get fish and chips and eat it in the car.'

Pru absorbed this new chunk of information. Megan sitting in the car that Bobby drove, the car in which she collected him from the barracks, visited his mother, sang along to their favourite songs and planned her wedding. The car in which they had died.

'How long were you and William seeing each other?'

'A year and four months.' Megan's face crumpled.

Pru did the maths: three months longer than he had been with Bobby.

'I should have known someone like me was never going to end up with someone like him. I mean, look at me, I'm just nothing.'

Pru shivered to hear the familiar words that she herself had uttered throughout her childhood. It was more than she could bear. 'You are not just nothing, Megan.'

'Can I ask you something?' Megan looked Pru in the eye. 'Can you not call me Megan? No one calls me that. I'm Meg. When you say Megan it makes me feel like I'm in trouble and I'm nervous enough as it is.' Her mouth lifted with the beginnings of a smile.

Pru nodded as she pushed her key into the shiny brass lock and turned to her guest. 'How you doing, Meg?'

The girl gripped her plastic box tightly. 'I'm okay.' Her knuckles were white against the lid. She was petrified. 'Do you own the whole building then?'

'Yes. We have the bakery, kitchens, workroom and office in the basement; the showroom and café are on the ground floor; and there are two flats above – mine and Milly's, and Bobby's. And a room in that is yours for as long as you need it.'

Meg stepped forward and touched her fingers to the glass as she stared at the tall bow window. Its shock of red velvet fabric fell in a cascade of waves from the ceiling and over a table on which sat the most incredible cake she had ever seen. It was illuminated by dozens of flickering candle bulbs in antique brass lanterns. The cake was eight tiers high and each tier was separated by minute pillars of faux marble. The pristine white icing was covered on one side in tiny red sugar-paste rosebuds and petals that looked so real you could almost smell them. Green leaves with intricate vein detailing and lifelike jagged edges had been scattered here and there. Some poked from behind clusters of buds, others appeared to have withered and fallen. The tiny blooms looked as if they had been thrown and landed against the sponge; some looked as if they were about to fall to the tier below. They reminded Meg of confetti that had been gathered up by the wind and blown somewhere new. It was a work of art.

She was transfixed. 'Is that really a cake?'

Pru nodded.

'Can you eat it?'

'Yes, of course.'

'All of it?'

'Yes, every bit!'

'Even the petals and leaves?'

'Yes, Meg, all of it. And when it's cut, you see the red velvet sponge inside. It looks stunning.'

'It's like something out of a fairy tale. Like a Disney cake for a wicked princess.'

Pru chortled, delighted by Meg's description. Yes, that was exactly what it looked like. She recalled Guy's presentation – it had taken him half an hour to deliver and at the final slide he had described the motif as 'gothic horror meets vintage bordello with a twist of blood-red erotica'. Meg had managed to sum it up in half a dozen words.

'It's massive, but really beautiful and a bit scary. I think it's incredible. How much would a cake like that cost?' A drip of blood ran down Meg's chin from where she had inadvertently pulled open the wound on her mouth.

Pru hesitated, conscious of the girl's T-shirt and worn espadrilles and her entire worldly belongings that fitted inside a small plastic box. She pictured the cherished Bunny, who would celebrate the incredible milestone of reaching fourteen with a grand bash, and her stomach tensed. The cake would cost nine thousand pounds, but how could she explain to this girl about the man-hours and craftsmanship, the finest cochineal and celebrity-endorsed design. It would sound, in the words of Meg, like it was all bollocks.

'I'm not sure,' she lied.

'I like making cakes.'

'Do you?'

Meg nodded. 'Yeah, I used to make fairy cakes with my nan and decorate them. I was quite good at it.'

Pru nodded. 'Hey, well, that's how Milly and I got started, baking with our nan in a little kitchen. Baking is a bug and when you catch it, it takes over. I used to dream of recipes and cake designs, night after night, and I wouldn't be able to sleep until I'd got up and scribbled them down, just in case I forgot them.'

'What do you dream about now then?'

'Sorry?'

'Well, you said you used to dream about cakes and I wondered what you dream about now?' Meg rested her box on the brass lip of the windowsill.

'Oh, I don't really dream much any more.' Pru smiled and pushed open the front door. She stood back to let her guest walk in first.

'I tell you what, I wouldn't mind catching that baking bug if I ended up with a swanky place like this.' Meg flicked her head in the direction of the window.

Pru watched as she took in the plush carpet on the stairs, the sparkling chandelier and the Italian tiled flooring of the hallway.

'Welcome to our home, Meg.'

'I feel a bit sick.'

'It'll be okay, love,' she said over her shoulder.

They trod the second staircase. As Pru opened the front door of her apartment, she imagined seeing the place with

Meg's eyes for the first time. The opulent wallpaper and coordinating drapes, the antique side tables, oversized mirrors and individually lit oil paintings. She felt the need, as she often did, to excuse her inordinate wealth.

'I haven't always lived like this, you know. I grew up in a grotty two-up two-down in the East End, which I shared with three brothers, my mum and my aunt and two cousins. Milly and I worked in the match factory. We shared a single bed until we left home in our teens.'

'Blimey.' Meg was quiet for a second. 'So how did you know what furniture would look nice and what clothes to wear and stuff, if you hadn't grown up like that?'

Pru watched as the girl flattened the front of her T-shirt and looped her long fringe behind her ears. Her heart went out to her. It didn't feel like so long ago that she too had felt adrift, unable to understand how people knew how to look confident and cool.

'I copied people, stole their ideas. If I saw a woman that I thought looked nice or smart, I'd remember what she looked like and dress like her. It was the same with eating out, buying gifts and putting things in the flat, everything. I copied people that I thought got things right.'

Pru thought about her little notebook in which she had jotted furiously in the back of taxis and on the Tube. *Single variety of flowers for impact. If gold on belt and bag then gold jewellery, same for silver. A bowl of citrus fruits in kitchen looks fresh. Wide cuffs revealed on white shirts, beneath a navy jersey, v smart. Heavy eye make-up, pale lips; pale eyes, dark lips. All glasses to the right of the plate are mine; all small plates to the left are mine.*

Break bread roll at table, don't cut it. She hadn't looked at it for years.

'I'm much more relaxed now and if people don't like how I do things, that's their problem not mine. Plus I use interior designers when I need advice.'

'I guess they'll help anyone if you've got enough money.'

Pru chuckled. 'Ain't that the truth.'

'That you, Pru?' Milly called from the sitting room.

'Yep.'

Milly came into the hallway. 'Do you fancy a cup of tea? I was just going to pop the kettle on.'

Meg looked frightened and Pru noticed that she had inched closer to the front door, ready for escape.

'Ah, Mills, I was just coming to see you.' Pru drew a deep breath as she prepared her speech.

Milly looked up and did a double-take, staring open-mouthed at the girl with the beaten-up face that stood in the hallway of her home. 'You have got to be kidding me!' She put her hands on her hips. She ran her eyes over the little waif with dark circles beneath her eyes, lingering on the dirty T-shirt that strained over her enormous bump.

Meg clasped her hands across her stomach and stood facing the two cousins. It was the first time Pru noticed her likeness to Bobby. If Bobby had been there, they would have looked like the before and after shots on a fancy makeover show.

'You are not seriously suggesting what I think you are?'

'Meg needs a bit of a hand, Mills.' Pru smiled at Meg, trying to calm things.

'Is that right?' Milly shouted. 'Well, I've seen it all now!

126

Are you out of your bleeding mind?' And she flounced from the hall and disappeared into her room.

Pru pushed open the door of the spare room in the apartment above theirs, ignoring the tremor to her hand. She didn't turn her head or look at Bobby's door, which remained shut. She wasn't quite up to that yet.

'Here we are, Meg.'

Meg hesitated. 'I'm a bit worried. I don't want to cause any trouble for you.'

'Don't you worry about that. It's not the worst trouble I've faced.' She stood back. 'This is your room.'

Meg hovered by the door, taking in the room. The vast bed with its honey-coloured wooden head- and foot-board, the stack of pristine white pillows and starched white bed linen, the thick cream curtains that were draped over tiebacks to reveal the ceiling-height Georgian window. China lamps with neutral shades sat on side tables. They were already lit – all the lamps were centrally controlled and on a timer, bathing both apartments in a homely golden glow.

She turned to Pru with wide eyes. 'Is'all right, I guess.'

Pru laughed. 'Your bathroom is just through there.' She pointed to a glossy wooden door in the centre of the side wall.

'I was a chambermaid at The Savoy a few years ago – this room, this whole flat reminds me of that. I never thought I'd sleep in a room like this.'

'I know what you mean. If you'd have shown me this when I was younger, I'd have been too scared to set foot in here!'

'That about sums it up for me.' Meg placed her plastic box on the floor. 'Is it okay to put it here?'

'You can put it anywhere, love. This is your space for as long as you need it.'

'Is that right?' Milly's voice came from the hallway. She stalked into the room and looked Meg up and down. But she only had words for her cousin. 'I always thought we could rely on you, Pru. You told our Alfie that you'd always put Bobby first.' She ignored the tears that slid down her face and into her mouth. 'We've lost her, Pru. She's gone. But not yet bloody cold and you do this.' She gestured towards Meg.

'Milly, I—'

'No. Don't try and explain it. There's nothing you can say that can fix what you've done. Nothing.' She turned to Meg, who was also crying now, and pointed at her. 'You stay away from me. Do you hear me? You've got some nerve, coming here. I don't want to see you and I don't want to hear you.'

'Milly!' Pru shouted.

Meg nodded and shrank back against the wall.

Pru turned away from the upstairs flat with a heavy heart, wondering for the first time in decades whether she had done the right thing.

Eight

It was Saturday morning, two days after her row with Milly, and the sun was just peeking over the horizon. The doorbell for the flat was ringing. Pru glanced at her alarm clock: it was 5 a.m. Milly was on the early, but was clearly ignoring the doorbell, probably as part of her campaign of anger against her. There must be a problem with a delivery, who else would call at this ungodly hour on a weekend?

Pru groaned and flung back her duvet. What was it they said? No rest for the wicked? Whoever it was that was jabbing at the bell on the outside wall was not going to admit defeat and leave any time soon. Fastening her grey jersey dressing gown around herself, she descended the stairs, yawning, and poked her head cautiously around the door.

'Christopher!'

Her heart raced at the sight of him. It was two weeks since she had last seen him, at the funeral, and she had been nervous of calling, not wanting to intrude on him or his sister while they were grieving, and anxiously aware that she had snapped at his mention of Ginny. The fact was, she wanted him to like her, not use her as therapy, but she should have explained herself better. And then the longer she'd left it, the bigger deal it had become to pick up the phone.

She wanted desperately to return to the playful texting and chitchat they had exchanged before the accident. The tragedy had changed the parameters of their courtship. She had forgotten how it made her feel to see him; it pierced her grief, the sight of him, fired a jolt of joy through her stomach and up her spine. She gathered her dressing gown around her neck, anxious not to reveal her pyjamas and feeling incredibly shy, like a half-dressed teenager caught putting the milk bottles out by Ronald Clayton, the boy everyone in Blondin Street fancied.

'Grab your coat, Miss Plum.' He smiled.

'What? My coat? It's five o'clock in the morning!'

'Yes, I know what time it is. I thought you bakers were early risers, no pun intended.' He rocked on his heels.

'We are, but still, five o'clock!'

'Come on. Time and tide and all that.' He clapped his hands together and rubbed his palms. 'We are going out for the day.'

'Where are we going?'

'Aha, you shall have to trust me. But you'll need sturdy shoes, a windcheater and a jersey. The weather might be changeable. I'll wait in the car.' He pointed to the black Jaguar that was parked illegally on the kerb.

'But I haven't had a shower or anything.' She sounded like a nervous schoolgirl. 'And it's a bit tricky, I don't know if I feel up to it and I can't just leave Milly and Meg.'

'Who's Meg?'

'It's a long story.'

'Good, we've got a long journey. I'm not taking no for an answer. Leave a note if you must, don't want anyone to think you've been kidnapped. And we are leaving in precisely ten minutes.' He tapped his watch and climbed into the car.

Pru closed the front door and leant against it. Milly poked her head out from the corridor that led to the café.

'What are you making a racket about at this time of the morning?'

'Oh, you're talking to me then?'

'I might be talking to you, but it doesn't mean I like you.'

'The feeling is entirely mutual.' Pru smirked.

'What are you doing up? Do you know what time it is?'

'Yes I do, Mills,' she shouted, untying her dressing gown as she went. 'I'm going out for the day and I leave in ten minutes, apparently.'

'Out for the day? Where?'

Pru craned her head over the banister. 'I don't know, but it's a very long way and I'll need a windcheater as the weather might be changeable.' She disappeared from view.

'Blimey, sounds like a barrel of laughs. And don't think I'm going to be checking on your houseguest, cos I won't!' Milly shut the door with a little more force than was entirely necessary.

Eleven minutes later, Pru settled into the passenger seat of the Jaguar and eased off her navy pumps. 'I like your car.'

'Thank you. I've heard a nice car helps attract women, so that's why I got it.' He patted the steering wheel.

'I see. How's that working out for you?'

He gave her the once-over. 'I'd say pretty well.'

Pru smiled. Only weeks ago, his humour would have had her rolling with laughter, but not today, not now.

'Do you drive, Pru?'

'No. I never learned, and living in town, it's always felt easier to jump on the Tube or in a cab.' She didn't mention that in her youth learning to drive had been way beyond her means. She hadn't known anyone that owned their own transport and she couldn't have afforded lessons let alone a car. Despite her success, she had never really caught up.

'I could always teach you?'

'At my age? I don't think so.'

'Forgive me. I didn't realise there was an age limit. And I seem to remember you chastising me for using that phrase a little while ago. How old are you anyway, eighty-four?'

'No, I just look it and feel it. You know perfectly well what I mean.'

'Actually, no I don't. And I have a new philosophy. I have decided that life starts when you let it, whether you are twenty or seventy. It's a state of mind and I am choosing to let this chapter of my life begin today, right now! Because you know what, Pru? William and Bobby had their whole lives ahead of them and pow! In one second, one wrong move and it was gone, extinguished in the blink of an eye.'

'I know. I can't believe it. I still can't believe it.' Pru put her head in her hands and let the tears fall. She had planned on being tough today, but it was harder than she thought. She cried hard and was instantly embarrassed. 'I'm sorry,' she spluttered into her hands.

'That's okay. You go ahead and cry. You are allowed one sob every hour, so your next one is due at…' He looked at the clock on the dashboard. 'Six fifteen.'

She smiled at him through her tears.

He shook his head. 'I have to joke or I'll cry too. It's

terrible, just terrible. How's Milly doing? I thought she was very brave at the funeral. You both were. Remarkable actually. I don't remember much about Ginny's funeral, it was and still is a bit of a blur, but I'm fairly sure I wasn't as contained as you and Milly.'

Pru gulped down the hard ball of tears that had gathered at the back of her throat. 'Milly's not doing great, but she's making out she is, it's what she does. Things have got a bit complicated and I may not have handled it in the best way.'

'Complicated how?' Christopher looked across at her as he navigated the empty streets of Knightsbridge and headed west towards the M4.

'Oh, Chris, I don't really know where to start, so I'm just going to say it. I wanted to wait until I saw you in person, but now I'm wishing I'd told you over the phone. Because this feels awkward.'

'Told me what?' He glanced to his left again, trying to gauge her news from her expression.

'I know William was your nephew… and Bobby really loved him, she really did. He was good to her, in some ways, but—'

'But what? Spit it out, Pru, the suspense is killing me.'

Pru exhaled and told him everything, watching the waves of shock and disbelief cloud his face. By the time she had finished, they were approaching Heston Services.

Christopher furrowed his brow, trying to take it all in. He was silent for a good minute, and for a moment Pru thought he was furious with her. Then he spoke.

'And she's genuine?'

Pru nodded, emphatic. 'Yes, definitely.'

'I'm not going to tell Isabel, not yet. I don't feel it's my place and she has so much going through her mind, the poor love. She's not what you'd call a coper. It's destroyed her, it really has – well, you saw her at the funeral. William was always her golden boy, her soldier. I don't want anything to tarnish that for her; it's pretty much all she's got left, isn't it?'

'I guess so, but Meg's carrying her grandchild and that might be wonderful for her, a little silver lining.'

'You're right, it might be, but I think I'll let the ground settle first before springing that on her. Do you think that's wrong?'

'I think I don't know her, Chris. You do and you should do what you think's best.'

'Do you know, you are quite an incredible woman, Pru.'

'No, I'm not.' She felt the creep of a blush over her neck.

'Yes, yes you are. I don't know many people that would open their hearts and their homes to a stranger in need, especially at a time like this. You are amazing and I am very lucky to know you.'

Pru coughed away the shout of happiness that bubbled in her throat and stared out of the window. *I am very lucky to know you!* His words were encouraging and felt very much like a step forward, an endorsement, and this thought filled her with a burst of excitement.

Eventually Christopher pulled the car off the motorway and into the narrow, winding lanes that took them deep into the Devon countryside. The thick wide hedgerows holding dog rose and rowan bounded undulating fields that spread like a rippling patchwork. The sky was big, uncluttered and the palest blue. It was beautiful. Pru sat up straight and held her breath, wondering how they would manage if they met a car of similar width coming in the opposite direction.

Christopher saw her flinch and laughed. 'Look at you, you are such a townie! You can relax. As long as everyone goes slowly enough and we all breathe in, there is always enough room to pass!'

'I can't help it, I'm London born and bred. I've got the Thames running through my veins and I feel a bit queasy if I go near fields and cows. All this fresh air hurts my lungs.'

At last the hedgerows became shallower and Pru could make out a dip in the hills and water glinting beyond.

'Welcome to Salcombe.' Christopher hummed as he drove down towards the harbour and pulled into the car park. It was mid morning; the salty breeze that blew in from the estuary tempered the sun. The main street twisted away from them with cobbles at its centre and terraces of pretty shops and coffee houses on each side. It was quaint yet classy, busy without being crowded.

'This is lovely.'

'Yes, one of my favourite places. It's where I come to escape. My friend has a pub here, my favourite pub.'

'It's a long way to come for a pint.'

'Ah, but it's not just the best pint, they do the best fish and chips as well. And we shall get fudge from Cranch's to eat on the motorway.'

They sat and watched the boats bobbing around on the choppy water. Rigid-hulled inflatable tenders chugged back and forth to deposit sailors of all ages on to their yachts.

'It's peaceful here.' Pru liked the delicate sounds of the

rigging knocking against the masts and the gulls swooping overhead.

'Yes, I breathe properly here.' Christopher took a big lungful of air. 'It feels a world away from Westminster and the hassle of town. The moment I step out of the car, my shoulders un-knot and my worries drift away. I'd like to live here one day – a slow, simple life. I'd buy a little boat and go fishing in the afternoons and then cook my catch for supper. In the winter I'd warm my feet in front of a log fire and drink red wine until I fell asleep.'

'That sounds nice.'

'Do you *mean* it sounds nice or are you just being polite?' He nudged her with his elbow.

'I'm not being polite. I never think of a world outside of London, but then I come somewhere like this and I can see me pottering, baking and sitting in the sun. I've never had a garden and I think I'd really like that.'

'I think I'd like that too.'

He gripped her hand as they sat on the quayside. Two seagulls squabbled over a long-abandoned chip, just feet away. 'Now, this is how to spend a day off, don't you think?'

She nodded, allowing the swell of happiness to sink down to her stomach. It was replaced instantly by guilt. How could she be enjoying life, sitting in a state of bliss when Bobby...

Christopher looked first at her face and then his watch. 'It's okay, go ahead, you are due one.'

Pru didn't want to use up her tear allowance, but she couldn't seem to help it. It wasn't so bad when she was busy at Plum's, but here her grief just seemed to flow out

136

of her, like a tap on a tank full of sadness that she couldn't switch off. She resolved to try harder to follow Christopher's new philosophy. She dashed away the tears that slid down her cheeks, and spoke through her distress. 'I've decided to follow your advice. Life will begin when you let it.'

He squeezed her hand in sympathy. 'Right, a slow walk and then lunchtime, methinks.' Christopher jumped up and helped her to her feet.

He linked her arm inside his as the two of them ambled along, giving Pru time to compose herself as they strolled along Fore Street towards the Victoria Inn. It looked welcoming: a row of vast hanging baskets hung against the exposed stone of the front and the window boxes were full to bursting with vibrant blooms that spilled over, fighting for space. The brass sign was polished, and the dog bowl full of water was a clear message that all were welcome whether on two legs or four.

'Christopher!' The landlady hurried out from behind the bar and threw her arms around his neck.

'Hello, Liz. Long time no see.'

'Too long. And who's this?' Liz stepped forward to appraise Pru.

'This is Pru, my friend.'

Liz smiled and nodded, then gave Pru a watered-down version of the same hug. 'Hello, Pru, his friend.'

It was inviting and warm. Christopher nipped off to the loo, leaving the two women alone. Pru took in the cosy tables, fireplace, freshly painted wood and stunning flowers in vintage pitchers. 'I love your pub, it's beautiful, even if it's a little too far away to be my local.'

'Rubbish, it's Christopher's local and that's a ten-hour round trip!'

'He says he's brought me all this way for your fish and chips.'

'He's a darling. It's lovely to see him looking happy, especially after that terrible business with his nephew. Tragic.' Liz shook her head.

Pru nodded, unable to give Liz all the facts, not wanting to cry again.

Liz continued. 'I haven't seen him for months and he looks different, you're obviously very good for him. He had a tough few years back there, and now losing the boy... He deserves good things.'

We both do. Pru nodded. 'We do get on well, but, you know, it's early days, we're just friends really.'

Liz turned in response to a shout from the kitchen. 'I'm coming!' She put her hand on Pru's shoulder. 'It might be early days, Pru, but I've got a feeling you might be just what the doctor ordered. And judging by the colour of your cheeks, I'd say he's doing the same for you too.'

Christopher approached the table, rubbing his hands together with gusto as he took up a stool opposite her. 'We are in for a treat.'

Pru looked into her lap.

'You know, Pru, grief and punishment are two very different things. It's okay to miss her and to feel sad, but you can't feel guilty every time you have a happy thought, because life does go on.'

She nodded. He was right.

Christopher looked at his watch. 'And I'm sorry, but

you're not allowed any more tears for another forty-five minutes. Can you sniff them back up?'

She smiled and sniffed. Yes she could.

With their stomachs full of the best fish and chips Pru had ever tasted, the two of them lay on the sand at East Portlemouth, beached and sleepy. Liz had packed them off with a bottle of wine and two plastic glasses and the ferry had delivered them across the estuary. It was perfect, a chance to collect their thoughts.

'Liz is nice.'

'Yes, she is one in a million. And she approved of you, so that's good.'

'Is it?' She propped herself up on her elbow, watching him lying there on the sand with his eyes closed.

'Yes, for me. I don't have many friends, so it's nice to think that those I do have are all going to get on.'

Friends? Is that what we are?

Christopher continued. 'I'm a fairly open book, Pru. Been involved in politics since university, married young, widowed young, no kids, sadly.'

Pru thought of her own childless state and pictured Bobby. She was so lucky to have had her for the time she did. Pru could still hear her mother's disdainful little jibes, dished out at every opportunity – '*Why don't you get yourself a nice fella, get married and have a baby. It'd do you the world of good*' – as if she was suggesting a brisk walk or an early night. Pru would pooh-pooh the idea, change the subject, make a joke – anything to stop the sadness rising to the top like cream and rendering her speechless, clogging her throat with regret.

Pru had spent decades longing for a baby, considering every avenue from fostering to adoption, but knowing that once checks had been run, that door would be closed to someone like her. Despite her advanced years, she would still often wake in the grip of a nightmare, screaming out that she could hear her baby crying but couldn't find it. Milly would rush in, knowing from the years spent sharing a room that the only way to deal with it was to hold her tightly and say, 'It's okay, Pru, the baby is safe, sleeping soundly.' In her dream-like state, Pru would believe her and go back to sleep.

Christopher was pondering. 'Funnily enough, I don't think I really mind not having children, but paradoxically I can see that I will mind not having grandchildren.'

As if on cue, a fat-legged toddler waddled over from the dunes with a bucket in one hand and a tiny fist full of sand in the other. Her little pink sun hat flopped down over her eyes as she tottered. Her grandma jogged behind in hot pursuit, her linen trousers rolled up above the ankle. She raised her hand in a wave and rolled her eyes in mock anger, clearly loving every second.

Pru waved back before turning her attention to Christopher. 'I understand that completely. When you're our age and have more time, it feels a shame not to have a little one to love. It's one of the reasons I'm so sad for Bobby. She never got the chance to be a mum, to have part of her carry on, and it's the same for me.'

Both paused and thought of Bobby and William. Recalling the fact that they were dead was like lancing the bubble the two of them had been in all day. It also threw up the question of Meg. Pru sighed, once again preoccupied by the complexity of the situation. 'And William not seeing his little baby... I feel sad about him missing out and that makes me feel very disloyal to Bob.'

'Meg's child will only know the life it has, Pru. You can't worry about what it won't have, because it won't know any different. Lots of kids don't have dads, or mums, but as long as they have someone that has their back, they will do just fine.'

'I know that. I know what it's like to grow up without. My family was poor, very poor. Not like today, when you might not have the right brand of trainers or you struggle to buy a car. I mean sharing a single mattress on the floor, not enough food, and being a bit grimy – that sort of poor. But as clichéd as it sounds, we were happy.' Christopher reached over and touched Pru's arm. She stared up at the sky, followed a seagull gliding on the thermals. 'My dad died when I was little and my mum battled her whole life just to put a loaf on the table. Milly's dad, my uncle, got killed in an accident in the docks and so my aunt and her two kids moved in with us and it was chaos! I picture my mum, scraping around for the rent every week, doing anything and everything; selling whatever she could get her hands on, including her wedding ring.'

The day her mother had slipped the thin gold band from its niche on her finger had been a terrible day. She had sobbed with the ring in her hand and her head on the table, then marched up to the pawnshop and handed it over without so much as a blink; chest out, chin up. Pru instinctively twisted the diamond band on her own finger – symbol of all that she had achieved, reminder of the poverty she had risen above. 'I watched her work her way into an early grave.'

'Oh, Pru, that must have been so tough.'

'I suppose it was, but it's like what you were saying, when you don't know any different, you just get on with it, don't you?'

'I guess you do.' Christopher blushed a little. 'And you are right, you really don't know any different. I had a very expensive education, holidays on the Riviera, a pony! At school, I was being pushed towards the law, lured by the prospect of a huge salary. My parents had a pink fit when I told them I was going to study politics.'

Pru leant back into the sand, watching the clouds drift lazily overhead. It was so easy to open up to Christopher, especially on a day like today with the sun shining and the quiet hum of families enjoying the beach. Not that she could be entirely open. The thought of what she would have to divulge sent a wave of sickness spinning through her stomach. She sat up straight and exhaled.

'I could have done well at school, I think. I was very keen. But I left at fourteen and started work at the Bryant and May factory – that was horrible, but we needed the money more than I needed an education and so that was that, no debate or discussion. It was a given.'

She closed her eyes briefly, picturing Milly and her, top to toe in their sagging bed, plotting their future far away from Bow and the factory.

'There was only one thing we knew how to do really well: make fairy cakes, just like our nan had shown us. So we thought, well then, that's what we'll do! We were so naive, but strangely that helped us; we didn't see most of the barriers that should have held us back.'

Their plan was to raise money to fund their tutelage under Monsieur Gilbert. He was the most celebrated patissier in England – they collected articles about his work and his protégés, who regularly found work in the finest kitchens in Europe – and they would not settle for anyone else. To be the best they needed to be taught by the best. It was decided that once they had both mastered the requisite baking skills, Pru would run the baking business and look after the PR and marketing while Milly would concentrate on staff, the accounts and the building. This had proved an unbeatable set-up, with each able to listen to and advise the other whenever necessary. Pru remembered that they weren't talking at the moment. She couldn't wait for their disagreement to blow over.

'My God, Pru, think of what you've achieved. You are remarkable.' Christopher leant forward, eager to hear more.

Pru ignored him; she didn't feel very remarkable. 'We decided to take a risk and leave home. We figured that if we left Blondin Street, got out of Bow and got different jobs, we could become different, better, reinvent ourselves a bit – and it worked. We moved up to Earls Court and shared a flat with a wonderful woman called Trudy.' Pru's eyes shone at the memory of her friend. 'I'd never met anyone like her, Chris. All the women I knew were downtrodden, grubby and old before their years, with too many kids hanging off their skirts and nails bitten to the quick with nerves. But not Trudy; she was phenomenal. Tall and

143

confident and beautiful – like a model or an actress – and so glamorous in her glossy red lipstick and high heels. But she'd always laugh when I complimented her, saying it was all just "smoke and mirrors". Then one day she showed me how. She brushed my hair till it shone – not this thinning barnet, no, in those days it was a deep auburn, long and wavy. And she made up my face and put me in her high heels and one of her fur coats. I can still remember how I shrieked when I saw myself in the full-length mirror. I looked like a painted doll, I felt like a different person.'

'I bet you looked stunning.'

Pru shrugged, but her hand was shaking and a tear was trickling down her cheek. Her voice was quiet now. 'I don't know if I did, but I felt like a film star. It was the first time in my whole life that I felt beautiful.'

Chris didn't look at his watch. Whether allowed or not, these tears were coming thick and fast.

'What happened next, after you'd moved? Or did you just jump straight from wearing Trudy's borrowed clothes to owning one of Mayfair's finest establishments?' He was teasing, but Pru could see that he was genuinely curious.

'Oh, you know, life happened!' Pru tried to smile. She sniffed. 'It's getting late, Chris, we've got a bit of a drive, haven't we?'

He stood and dusted the sand from his trousers. 'You're right. Come on, Miss Plum, let's get you back to the big smoke.'

The car purred along the lanes, heading to the motorway and back to the complications of life in London.

'I've had such a lovely day, thank you, Chris.'

Christopher glanced to his left and studied her face. 'That's what your mouth is saying, but you look a little sad.'

Pru stared out of the window. 'I must admit, I feel a bit guilty. Selfish, even.' She thought of Bobby jumping with excitement in the wedding shop, her whole life mapped out. 'I feel guilty that I have a future and she doesn't.'

'Pru, you have just opened up your home to a complete stranger in need. You are anything but selfish.'

'I don't think Milly would agree with you.' Pru gazed into the middle distance and for the first time in as long as she could remember, she dreaded going home.

Nine

Pru wandered down to the bakery. She had to dig deep to find a smile. Saturday had been wonderful and the Salcombe air still flowed through her veins. She had lain awake wondering about the exact nature of her relationship with Christopher. At first it had felt like the beginnings of a heady love affair, but more and more he seemed to treat her as a friend. Maybe she had misread the situation, or maybe the accident had altered the course that fate had intended. This idea saddened her greatly.

She tested the bottom stair and was happy to see it repaired and creak-free. Pushing open the swing door, she found the team working frantically on a corporate order of fat cookies that had to go out boxed and ribboned by 8 a.m. On one counter, giant pretzels flavoured with fresh chilli, smoked salt flakes and mixed seeds were being turned and shaped by hand. She watched the skilful fingers that stretched and plaited the elastic dough, pulling it wide before sprinkling each portion with the right spice mix. A second batch of *boules de pain* crusted in the oven and trays and trays of muffins and scones were cooling in the racks.

Guy saw her enter and rushed forward. Reaching into a tray, he knocked on the bottom of one of the cooling loaves as he turned his ear to hear the dull thud against the thick, dark-brown crust. '*Parfait!*'

'Delish!' Pru, like him, admired nothing more than a perfectly turned-out loaf.

'Oh, Guy, you have been busy. What did they choose in the end?' She nodded towards the cookie boxes for their corporate client.

He extended his finger and addressed her as though she were a potential purchaser. 'Good morning, Madame. Today we have a divine selection of hand-made cookies. Hazelnut and milk chocolate, dark chocolate and bitter orange, cranberry and white chocolate, and honey and oat. They are guaranteed to melt in your mouth and have been blended using the finest organic ingredients and soft-baked to perfection!'

'Wow! I'll take them all. They smell wonderful.'

'And they *look* wonderful, *non*?'

Pru laughed. She had taken a risk, employing Guy. He had a reputation for being brilliant but difficult, getting through six employers in as many years. She had learned that all he needed was freedom – freedom to express his creativity and space in which to vent his wide range of emotions; which he did, daily and loudly. They both had a deep respect for the other's ability and their friendship proved to be the glue that saw them through any turbulence.

She eyed the cooling cookies. 'Yes, they really do look wonderful.'

Guy's mouth twitched. He had something on his mind. 'I hope you don't mind me asking, but how is that little girl today, the one who is *enceinte*.' He drew the outline of a bump on his stomach with his cupped palm.

'Meg? I haven't seen her yet today. But she's good, I think. Why?'

'Oh! I didn't know if I should mention it, but on Saturday, when you were out all day, she was in the street, crying. In fact, screaming! I felt very sad for her. Milly went off to The Dorchester and I didn't know what to do for the best. Eventually I coaxed her inside and gave her hot chocolate – there is nothing it won't cure. But my heart bled at her distress. It bleeds for you all.' He placed his hand on his breastbone as if to emphasise the point.

'Well, thank you for looking after her. I don't know what that was all about, but I'm sure something and nothing.' She swept her eyes over the counters. 'Everything seems fine down here, will you excuse me?'

'But of course!' He gave an elaborate bow, as he did on occasion.

What on earth had gone on? Pru climbed the stairs to the top floor and knocked on the door of Bobby's flat. It would always be Bobby's flat to her. There was no answer. She used her key to let herself in and listened. It was silent. She hesitated at Bobby's door, resting her face against the cool wood. How she wanted to knock and walk in, like she used to. Sit on the edge of her bed and stroke the blonde hair away from her niece's forehead; even without make-up and in the middle of the night, she was always so beautiful. 'How's my girl?' she'd ask. 'I'm okay,' Bobby would answer drowsily from under her duvet.

Pru felt a sudden pang for Meg, just as she had all those years ago when Bobby had first come into her life – worried and motherly and with a need to check on her. She popped her head into the kitchen, which was immaculate. Further down the hallway, she hesitated at Meg's door before rapping quietly. She heard the bounce of the mattress springs, then Meg cracked the door a fraction and peered through.

'Morning, Meg. Can I come in?' Pru tried to sound bright and cheerful.

Meg nodded and opened the door. The window was thrown wide to allow the morning sunshine and a slight breeze to stir the room. The pillows on her bed were stacked on top of each other and held the imprint of her body. She was wearing sweatpants, part of the haul of clothes that Pru had ordered for her. They would have dwarfed her tiny frame had they not been filled at the front by her ever-expanding bump. Her skin looked almost translucent, her eyes dull. The duvet was pulled back in a neat triangle and the television was on but muted. She was watching a programme about interior design.

Meg sat back down on the bed and looked out of the window. She knew what Pru had come to say. 'Don't worry; I'm not staying here, Pru. You've obviously realised that it hasn't worked out.'

'What do you mean, it hasn't worked out?'

'Well, it hasn't, has it? I shouldn't be here, I should never have come in the first place.'

'Of course you should! I want you here. Besides, where will you go?'

Meg took a deep breath. 'I don't know, but somewhere, anywhere, that isn't like a prison!'

Pru cocked her head. 'Like a prison?' She couldn't hide

her surprise. 'But I thought you liked it here?'

Meg let her chin drop as her shoulders shook. Pru had to concentrate to hear the words, muffled through her tears. 'Milly said I mustn't go in the kitchen when she's around, and I know that if I see her, then she'll just go mental at me again and I can't cope with it.'

Pru felt a rare flush of anger towards her cousin. She left the room without replying, her jaw set determinedly. Meg stared after her with red-rimmed eyes.

Pru stepped purposefully down the stairs, took a deep breath and knocked gently as she entered Milly's bedroom.

Milly was lying on her bed in floral pyjamas and white socks. She was hugging a pillow into her chest and had the irregular breathing pattern of someone who had only just stopped crying.

'Is it okay if I come in?' Pru tried to keep the edge from her voice.

'If you like.' Milly didn't look up, sounding like a miffed teen.

'Actually, I would like. I think we need to have a talk. I know this is a difficult situation, but we need to do the right thing. You know how things operate: we do what's right, Mills, we always have. There is no room for hatred in this little space, there's enough of that beyond the door. We've always said that, haven't we?'

An image from Kenway Road flew into Pru's head just then: the two of them sitting on the wide bed, Pru gingerly patting at her bruised jaw and sobbing, '*I didn't see it coming, it took me by surprise.*' And Milly's voice, soothing, with her arm across her shoulders, '*It's okay, Pru, we just need to stick together and make sure that the bad stuff stays on the other side of the door. As long as we stick together, we will always be all right.'*

Milly raised her head. 'Yes we have, but it's not me that's forgotten that one golden rule, about keeping the bad things on the other side of the door. It's not me that's let that girl come and move in among Bobby's things, trying to live her life.'

'Trying to live her life? Are you serious? Is this what that was all about on Saturday?' Pru was astounded.

'What has she said?' Milly sat up.

'She said that she feels she can't leave her bedroom. She thought you might have told her to stay in there, which I doubt, because that would be cruel and hateful and I know you are many things, Mills, but not that.'

Milly propped herself up against her pillows. 'I don't trust her, Pru! Don't you think it's just a little bit odd that she came out of the woodwork when she did? We don't even know if she is carrying William's baby, she could be some floozy who's trying her luck!'

'Did you really just call her a *floozy*?' Pru felt anger bubbling in her throat. 'Mills, I love you very much and you know that if I could have Bobby back by trading places with her, I would, I'd do it in a heartbeat! But I can't and neither can you and neither can Meg. All we can do is deal with what is left behind and that means Meg. She is what's left behind and she's our guest and she needs some kindness. I am asking you to show it to her. I want you to take a good look at her and without too much imagination you should be able to see that she could *be* Bobby! If we hadn't

151

stepped in when Bobby was little and taken her in, who knows? She might have become just like Meg and I for one would have been very grateful that someone was helping her.'

Both of them were silent for a moment, remembering how helpless Bobby had once been, how fierce as she howled, and how Alfie had peeled her skinny little arms from his legs before hugging his sister and kissing his daughter one final time.

'Do you think I don't know that? Of course I do!' Milly banged her palm against the mattress.

The two fell silent, mentally reloading.

'I blame myself actually.' Milly looked down, her voice much quieter now. 'I should have stopped her driving; she was too excitable before she left, distracted. I should have stopped her driving.'

'Oh, Mills. She wasn't even driving, William was.'

'I know that. But she might have distracted him, being fidgety, you know how she got.'

Pru gave a wistful smile at the image of Bobby in her wedding dress on the podium in Spitalfields, jumping all over the place. Yes, she knew how she got.

'But putting Bobby aside, what I don't understand is why *we* have to fix Meg's problems, why she has to live in our flat. She's nothing to do with us!'

Pru rubbed her temples. She felt too old for this fight. 'I've done many things I'm not proud of, Mills. We both have.' She let this linger. 'But in my whole life, I have never, ever turned anyone away that needed my help and I am not about to start now!'

Pru stamped back up the stairs, intending to go in and comfort Meg, but first she stopped at Bobby's door. She listened, as she always did, before slowly turning the handle. The first thing that she noticed was the smell. It smelled of her, a heady combination of her perfume, shampoo and the scented candles that she liked to light when William stayed over. The room was neat; she had cleaned and tidied in readiness for her special evening. Pru picked up a water glass that sat on her bedside table and held it up to the window; she could see the faintest smudge of lip balm against the rim. She pressed it to her cheek, like a final kiss. It brought her unimaginable happiness.

Running her fingers over the pillows, her hand touched against a piece of paper, a heart-shaped notelet that Bobby had stuck to the pillow with a blob of Sellotape. Pru pulled it from its sticky anchor and held it up to her face, reading slowly.

Welcome home, Captain! I just wanted to tell you that I have never ever ever been as happy as I am right this very moment and it's cos I've got you! B xxx

Pru held the note to her chest and cried. These tears felt different; the sadness was tinged with joy. Bobby had been happy! She left the house happier than she had ever been and that was a wonderful thing. Pru crept down to Milly's room and placed the note on her pillow, so she would find it that evening.

Late next morning Pru was sitting at her dressing table, applying her blush and spritzing her perfume. Her phone beeped and shuddered against the wooden surface. It was

Christopher, a text: *Meet me in the park!*

Chores and work deadlines flew out of her head. She knew which park and she knew where. Slipping on her pumps, she poked her head into the kitchen. 'Just popping out, Mills, back in a bit.' She didn't wait for a response.

Pru walked as quickly as she could without running, navigating round the amblers and smiling at those ensconced in deckchairs, enjoying this little slice of countryside in the middle of the city. She slowed when she got near, so she wouldn't appear breathless or too flustered. In her hand was a Plum Patisserie carryout bag, with two large almond croissants nestling in the bottom, individually wrapped in PP monogrammed waxed paper.

Her heart somersaulted when she saw him; she wondered if it always would. Being in close proximity gave her faith that everything would work out. How could it not when there was this strength of feeling? She just hoped it was mutual.

He stood on their blue bridge, dressed in a navy suit and a white shirt, leaning over, staring down into the water with a Styrofoam cup in his hand. Pru gazed beyond him, across the lake, taking in the view towards Buckingham Palace framed by trees. He looked like he was in a painting.

'There she is.'

She loved the way this sounded as though he had been waiting for her, not just today, but for ever. He handed her a similar cup. She took it and stood next to him. 'Thank you. I brought these – *croissants aux amandes.*'

Balancing her coffee on the edge of the bridge, she opened the waxed paper to reveal the plump golden pastries scattered with dark toasted almonds and topped with a syrupy blanket.

'Oh my, they look delicious. Are you trying to make me fat?' He patted his generous stomach.

'Wouldn't dream of it.'

Christopher held the sweet flaky crescent up to his mouth and bit down, savouring the crunch of the almonds and licking his lips free of the powdery confectioner's sugar that spilled over his tie.

'This is heaven! Did you make them?' He winked.

'No, I didn't, but I can.'

'Really? What's the secret of something that tastes this good?'

Are you testing me? 'I think it lies in the *crème d'amandes*, because let's face it, a good croissant is just a good croissant without the right enhancement. But for me the trick is getting the filling and almond syrup just right. I add salt to the almond mix and finely grind the nuts before adding generous amounts of butter and then the eggs; then I blend it again until it's creamy. And for the syrup...' She checked behind Christopher's back and then over her own shoulder to make sure no one was listening. 'I pop in a tot of dark rum.'

'You clever old stick!'

'Well, you don't get to be Chief Whip without a bit of knowhow.' This time she winked at him.

'How did you learn how to bake?'

'Well...' Pru swallowed her bite of almond croissant and took a deep breath, concentrating on her words. This wasn't the time or place for too much information. 'Life in Kenway Road was in many ways one of the happiest times I'd ever known. I loved the freedom of being out from under my mum's roof and my nan's disapproving eye. And Trudy's kitchen was a real cook's kitchen, full of fancy equipment. We were amazed that we had found somewhere where we could bake every day.'

Pru still remembered every inch of that kitchen. The cupboards were of the palest blue and the dappled glass fronts allowed glimpses of blue china, dainty teacups and fancy teapots. French blue and white bistro curtains hung on brass rails halfway up the sash windows and a square table covered with a matching cloth sat in the middle of the room. There was a rack full of knives, and china buckets full of spoons, measurers and pastry crimpers. Large copper pans hung from hooks on the ceiling. A small, open-fronted dresser was crammed with platters and china mixing bowls and a large Kenwood Chef took pride of place on the deep, white Formica worktop.

'Poor old Trudy was our guinea pig. She'd be trying to watch her weight and we'd present her with plates piled high with French toast, homemade baguettes cut into thin rounds and smothered with butter and jam, or tiny éclairs with piped double cream and slivers of glossy chocolate sitting on top.'

'She must have loved it! I know I would have.' Chris laughed.

'She did.' She turned to Christopher. 'We'd always dreamed of owning our very own bakery, which we knew we'd name Plum Patisserie. We studied and practised our skills during the day, paying every penny we earned to Monsieur Gilbert at his École de Patisserie in Knightsbridge.

Oh, Chris, it was another world. I was like a fish out of water, sitting there among all the debs.'

Pru wondered, briefly, if those horse-faced debs might have been the sort Christopher socialised with. During their breaks, the girls would gather in cliques and recline on the padded, water-silk-covered benches along the walls of the parlour outside Monsieur Gilbert's classroom. Ornate china pot stands holding unruly aspidistra stood between them. A hum of conversation – which tended to be about boys, frocks and parties, rather than roux and pastries – would echo off the black and white tiled floor and domed ceiling. She and Milly would always stand slightly apart from the cliques, discussing that day's lesson. Later, top to toe in bed, wiggling their toes inside their long nighties and with Milly's giant sketchbook between them, they would try out designs for the entwined Ps that would become their logo. Together they'd chant the French terms they had learned – *le façonnage, le pétrissage, nougatine, pâte à choux* – almost like a spell, until the unfamiliar words became part of their vocabulary.

'That must have taken an enormous amount of dedication.'

'Well, if you want something that badly, Chris, you work hard for it, don't you? And you don't let the obstacles block you, you find a way around them.'

'I guess you do.' He turned to look at her full in the eyes. 'You seem a bit different today – perkier, more like the Pru I met at Mountfield, standing on her own, talking to herself.'

'I am a bit perkier actually. I found a note that Bobby had written William. It said that she was the happiest she had ever been and I take great comfort from that.'

Chris squeezed her hand. 'You are right to, that's wonderful. And how is your houseguest?'

Pru's face fell. 'I don't think her and Mills are ever going to be bosom buddies. It makes for a horrible environment, all the squabbling and hiding in darkened rooms. I don't want to sound insensitive, Chris, but I wish just for a day we could lift the blanket of misery and let joy sweep over the place, like a good breeze in a musty room. The atmosphere is quite depressing.'

'I remember, after Ginny died, feeling exhausted by the grieving process. It was relentless. I wanted to sleep all the time. I understand the thing about hiding away in a darkened room; I did a lot of that too.'

'When did it stop? Did it stop? Please tell me it did!' She sipped her coffee. Black, no sugar – he had remembered.

He laughed. 'Yes, it did, eventually. I can't remember why or when exactly, but one day I woke up and she wasn't the first thing I thought about. I felt instantly guilty of course, but then quite relieved, as if I'd reached a milestone. That day my mourning went from fifth gear into fourth and then slowly it was third, second and before I knew it, I was back in neutral.'

'It's good that we can talk about her, isn't it? I'm sorry about what I said at the funeral – it just bothered me and that's ridiculous, because we are friends and she was your wife.'

'Yes, she was and will always be a huge part of my life, but that doesn't mean that I can't move on, with friendships or whatever.'

Yes, 'or whatever' sounds good. 'It's good that we can talk about anything.' She gave an involuntary shiver.

The two of them sat quietly, one imagining the pain of closing the door on a happy future, the other remembering the pain of losing a wife.

Christopher looked at his watch. 'Same time tomorrow?'

'Is this a ruse to get more *croissants aux amandes*?'

'No! Of course not.' He held his hand to his chest, offended. 'But if you had any of those éclairs you mentioned earlier going spare, the ones with the glossy chocolate on top, I would be happy to sample them.'

'Oh, so you are doing me a favour, like market research?'

He chortled as he trotted off the bridge, away from her, and shouted back over his shoulder, 'Exactly! Market research.'

That night, Pru pulled the blind on the café and locked the bakery, then trod the stairs and tiptoed along the corridor, nervous as ever of what she might find in the flat above hers. From the sitting room came the low hum of the television. She padded along the carpet, bent her head round the door and was met with a sight that warmed her heart. Meg was in her pyjamas, slumped on the sofa with her feet up on a stool, a cushion behind her head and an empty plate beside her on the floor. She was watching an episode of *Friends*. Pru didn't hear the joke, but Meg suddenly laughed out loud, and gulped as it turned immediately into a sob.

Pru crept forward and gave a little cough. Meg looked up and closed her eyes as her grief poured from her. There was no sign of neutral here; not yet. Pru sat down on the edge of the sofa and placed her arms around Meg, who collapsed forward into her lap.

Pru stroked her hair and patted her back. 'Don't cry, love. Come on, it's okay.' Her voice was soft and soothing, the voice she had used to lull Bobby back to sleep in the early hours and the voice Meg had dreamed of as she watched the floral curtains of a dozen foster homes shifting in the night breeze of a dozen temporary bedrooms.

Finally, Meg's sobs turned to words. 'I wonder when he would have told me. Would he have actually married Bobby and left me on my own? Or worse still, had the baby with me and then married her, seeing both of us behind the other's back? What would have happened at Christmas, birthdays? Can you imagine, nipping off to see her when my back was turned and then coming home to play happy families? I feel so stupid. Angry and stupid! I should of known that someone like me doesn't get to play happy families!'

'You have a right to be angry, but you're not stupid, love. He deceived you – he deceived you both, he lied to us all, and he was very convincing.'

'I need a bit of sorting out, Pru. I haven't got anyone else.'

'Don't you worry, love.' She stroked Meg's hair away from her forehead. 'I'm not going anywhere.'

Once Meg had finally fallen into a deep sleep on the sofa, Pru tucked a soft blanket under her chin and returned downstairs. She lay in bed and watched the hands of the clock slowly turn. It was impossible trying to sleep with so much whirring in her head. She got up to make a cup of tea.

As Pru headed back to her bedroom with her mug of Earl Grey between her palms, Milly called out. 'Can't sleep?' Her voice came from the sitting room, where she sat in the dark.

Pru laughed as she rubbed her eyelids, which felt as though they were full of grit. 'No.' She took a sip of tea and sat down in her chair opposite.

'Did you see the note I found?'

Milly nodded.

'I thought it was wonderful; it made me so happy to know she was happy! Because that's all I ever wanted for her, all *we* ever wanted for her.'

'I keep thinking I can hear her...' Milly held her cousin's gaze through the gloom, not commenting on the note.

Pru stared right back, suddenly tired at the prospect of another weighted conversation with Milly. All she wanted was to go back to bed.

Milly took her silence as a cue to continue. 'You know how she used to call out, "I'm just nipping out!" Or "I'm making a cup of tea", like we needed a running commentary on her life.'

Pru smiled weakly. She could hear that voice clearly inside her head. 'I was saying something similar to Alfie earlier.'

'I haven't been able to go into her room and I have this thought that the longer I don't go into it, the more likely I am to find her there, all warm and crumpled from sleep, but if I do go in and the room is empty, it means she is really gone. I guess her note is a reminder that she's not there.' Milly buried her face in her hands.

Pru leant forward in her chair. 'It's okay, Mills.'

'I just keep wondering what Bobby would think about you letting that girl come here.'

'Oh God, Milly!' Pru was weary of the topic. 'What would you have me do, throw her out? She's got nowhere else to go and she is having a baby!'

'That's not the point.'

'That *is* the point!' Pru shouted.

'No, Pru! The point is you always think you know best. You make a decision and you go for it, without ever listening to anyone else, without listening to me.'

'Yes, and that's how we've made it as far as we have, because I did just that. If we'd waited for you to act, we'd still be planning things in your bloody sketchbook!'

'Is that right? What gave you the right to plan my life? What gave you the right to take me along with you?' Milly was sitting forward in her chair now, her face contorted.

'Take you along with me?' Pru felt physically winded. 'We were a team – we are a team!'

'Are we, Pru? Really? Or am I a silent partner that knows her place? I feel like I've never had choices, I just did what you said, always, even when we were kids. Christ, one minute I'm getting a smack across the knuckles from Nan and the next I'm meeting Crying Micky in a dark alley to hand over cash. All because I went along with what you said, always!'

'Are you serious?'

'Yes!' Milly shouted. 'I'm bloody serious. I never questioned anything, I never have. I just did it, all of it, everything, because you said it would be okay.'

Pru felt as if she had been physically attacked, each word striking her as surely as a blow from a fist. 'That is not true,

Milly! We've always done everything together, but you're making it sound like I held a gun to your head!'

'There are many types of gun, Pru. There's ones made of steel, and ones made of loyalty.'

That was so unfair. Milly had been so excited when they'd left Bow; she had packed before Pru had. All of a sudden Pru felt sick. What had their nan said? *And if Pru told you to jump off Tower Bridge, would you?'* Supposing Milly was right; supposing she had forced her into this life, into making those choices, shoving those skeletons in her closet.

Milly wasn't done. 'And just the same where Bobby was concerned. I loved her!' The words set off a new flood of tears. 'But you took over, not leaving her alone for a second, going to her new school, introducing yourself to the staff, buying her clothes and making sure you were her confidante. You kept me away from her. Even chatting to her bloody dead dad, like you had an exclusive phone line. How could I match that? But the thing is, Pru, she was my chance at motherhood too, did you ever think of that? And even now, people keep saying to me, "How's Pru doing? Give her my love." As though you count more; as though you loved her more.' Milly's voice finally cracked. 'But I loved her too, so much.'

Pru stood from the chair. She knew that she had to walk away now, knew that the words that were forming inside her head had to be contained and removed from this scene; allowing them to escape would be just too horrible to contemplate, the retorts too vicious, the attack too brutal. She stormed from the room, a whirling tornado of angst and anger, blindly stumbling along the hallway. Her heart hammered inside her chest. She pondered her exit and her cousin's cutting comments in equal measure. This was not how it worked, this was not how it was meant to be, she could not be in receipt of such an accusation and fail to deliver a response.

As if gripped by an impulse stronger than reason, Pru found herself back in front of Milly, back in the situation where she would deliver the most hurt. It was her turn to shout.

'Yes, you are right about Bobby, she was mine! Like everything else in our so-called partnership. I needed to be the best mum I could to her, just like I have to be the best baker and the best business woman. Not through any conscious choice but because you are totally fucking useless. And I didn't take you along with me, I have dragged you like a weight for all these years!'

'I have worked hard all my life! How dare you!'

'What do you mean, Milly, how dare I? I'm only confirming what you know!'

Milly shrieked. It was a loud guttural shriek as she hurled the china mug past Pru's head. Pru felt it whistle through the air as it skimmed her hair by millimetres. It shattered into a thousand pieces against the creamy wallpaper; mud-coloured droplets ran down the wall and splattered the carpet. Pru hadn't ducked or moved, almost wanting to feel the force against her face.

They stood in stunned silence. They had both gone too far and they knew it.

Ten

At 5 a.m. on Saturday, Pru stood on the kerb, waiting for the Jag to swoop into view. Despite being mid June, she had a fleecy jumper over her arm; this was a British summer, after all. She had spent the last few days and evenings in her bedroom and Milly had done the same, both smarting from their exchange. The flat had taken on a different atmosphere, as though the discord had seeped into the walls, ready to waft out every time they walked into a room; it was far from pleasant.

The only thing that had kept her sane was Christopher. The day after her row with Milly they had met in the park at their usual spot.

Christopher put his hands on his hips and shook his head. 'You're late, Miss Plum!'

Pru trotted over the bridge to make up the time. 'Only by a couple of minutes. This might help, a bribe to assuage your anger.'

She placed the little box tied with gold ribbon on the blue railing and watched as his big square fingers nimbly teased the knot until it fell apart.

Chris grinned at her. 'You are entirely forgiven.'

He carefully lifted the lid to reveal three tiny, puffy

éclairs: one topped with a square of shiny dark chocolate and bursting with fresh cream, as promised; another filled with mascarpone cream and tiny morsels of fresh peach, glazed with Amaretto icing and peppered with crushed macaroons; and the third bulging with coffee-infused crème patissière and with a thick pale coffee fondant on its lid.

'Wow! Did you make these?'

'Yes, actually, I did.' Pru folded her arms, feeling rather smug.

'I could get used to this. Assuming I can find a tailor who will let out my waistband on a weekly basis. Did you see me on TV this morning?'

'No! I was making those.' She nodded at the nest of cream cakes.

'I've told you, Pru, you should be watching how your country is governed; you might learn something interesting. I'm honoured to be a regular contributor. Luckily for me, I'm one of the more presentable members of the party – I sit nicely in the middle and don't ruffle too many feathers. I'm predictable, or so I'm told. Had a rather engaging debate with Tristram Monroe. I came out of it very well; the Prime Minister is tickled pink.'

'Oh, sorry I missed that.'

'I detect a note of sarcasm.'

Pru laughed.

'Are you okay, Pru? You seem a bit distracted and whilst still looking lovely, you do look tired, like you might have lost a little bit of the sparkle you had yesterday.'

Pru rested her elbows on the railing, propped her chin on her hands, and told him about her fight with Milly. She

166

watched the ripples work their way out towards the bank, caused by a fat duck paddling around under the bridge. 'It's our first really serious fight in all our years together. We bicker all the time, always have. But this was different.' She turned her head to look at him. 'I don't know how we'll move forward from it. And the worst thing is, I think a lot of what she said was true. I wish I could run away.'

'Well, I can help with that. Let's go to Salcombe on Saturday!'

'Chris, it's not that simple.'

'Ah, but it is! This is another fine example of over-thinking things – do you remember our first dance?' Pru's cheeks dimpled. She would never forget it. 'Well this is a bit like that: we are letting life start! Let's do it, let's go, this weekend. You know the drill, I'll pick you up at five on Saturday morning.' He smiled as he popped an éclair on to his tongue.

And now here he was, pulling up in front of Plum's almost to the minute. Leaving the engine running, he jumped out and opened her door. 'Morning, ma'am. Your coffee is in the central cup holder and there is a pillow on your seat, should you wish to sleep.'

Pru felt an overwhelming desire to cry. 'Thank you,' she whispered.

'Oh cripes, are we going to have to put you on an hourly tear allowance again?'

She shook her head, she was determined. 'No. Not today.'

Pru did sleep. The movement of the car lulled her into a deep slumber and she woke feeling more rested and clear-headed than she had in a long time. Chris negotiated the winding lanes and pretty soon they were driving down the hill, with Salcombe's harbour glittering at them in the distance.

'Look at that, Pru!' said Chris, pointing at a flotilla of small boats in the estuary. 'Isn't it beautiful?' With white sails full and arching against the breeze, the dinghies looked almost stationary as they raced across the water in formation. 'That's not a sight you see in London every day. Stress, be gone! Away with you!' He opened the windows and let the mid-morning breeze whip around the car. 'This is called blowing away your cobwebs!' he shouted as paper napkins billowed off the dashboard and Pru's hair streamed over her face.

Pru laughed, loudly and without restraint, until she remembered that she was grieving and stopped, placing her hand over her mouth. Chris put the windows up and spoke slowly. 'She wouldn't want you to be sad forever, you know that, don't you?'

Pru looked out of the window and nodded. Yes, she knew that.

They paired their shoes neatly beside them on the wall, rolled their trousers against their calves and dangled their feet from the dock. Sitting close together, they licked at honeycomb-flavoured clotted-cream ice cream in fancy waffle cones and listened to the distinctive ping of rigging knocking together in the breeze. Boats rolled gently in the harbour swell.

Pru flexed her toes in the sunshine. 'I like it here.'

'I'm glad. It would be a shame if you didn't. I hate the thought of dragging you somewhere you'd rather not go.'

'I think I'd like anywhere you dragged me, as long as I was with you.' Pru didn't know where she'd got the courage to say it, but she had.

Christopher stared at her. It was hard to read his expression and she wished she could rewind.

'Come on, fish and chips are calling!' He jumped up.

'But we've only just finished our ice cream!'

'Ah, first rule of Salcombe: there is always, always room for ice cream, any time of the day or night, no matter what else you have eaten or are about to eat. And for the record, Miss Plum, I intend to drag you everywhere I go, for the foreseeable future – like baggage, but better company and with the ability to make extraordinary buns.' With that, he strolled ahead, a little embarrassed.

Pru did her best to stifle the firework that had exploded inside her, happy that she was considered better company than baggage.

They walked into the Victoria Inn, which was buzzing. Liz spied them from behind the bar and pointed at a little table by the fireplace that had just become free. 'Ah! Chris. And Pru, his friend! How are you, lovelies?'

'We're good,' Christopher answered.

'Are we? Well I'm jolly glad to hear it.' Liz smiled, noting the 'we'. 'I don't see you for months, Chris, then two visits in quick succession! I'm not complaining, but what's going on?'

He winked. 'Must use the bathroom!' And off he nipped.

'Typical politician, evasive as ever. It's lovely to see you again, Pru. So come on, spill the beans, are you two an item?' Liz leant forward across the table.

'We haven't had that conversation.' Pru felt her cheeks go red.

'You don't need to have that conversation, you just know, don't you?'

'I guess so.'

'And do you?' Liz pressed.

'Do I what?

'Just know!' Liz tutted.

Pru looked up as Christopher entered the bar and stopped to chat to a group of men sitting on bar stools, nursing pints. Her heart gave the familiar lift that it did every time she saw him and she saw an image of Alfie, smiling and giving her the thumbs up. 'Yes. Yes I do.'

'Well it's about bloody time!' Liz clapped her hands in joy.

Pru fought the desire to bombard her with questions, realising that it would be wholly inappropriate to behave like a fourteen-year-old with a crush and pump this woman for information. She wanted to ask if she had known Ginny, what had she been like? Had they really been happy? Again, wholly inappropriate. Instead, Pru ordered the famous house fish and chips, twice.

Christopher returned to his seat. 'Bit busier today; I think the holidays must have kicked off properly. I break up quite soon too – mid July, can't wait!'

'What do you do in the summer break? Go on hols, sit in your garden, watch daytime telly?'

'Ha! I wish. No, I still work, I just don't have to attend Parliament. There's still a lot going on, but I usually find time for a little break at the beginning. To be honest though, what with spending more time with Isabel and whatnot, it's rather crept up on me. I don't have anything planned yet.'

A family barged the pub door and rushed in: a nervous woman, like a frantic mummy duck with too many chicks, followed by her brood of five children.

'Five! Can you imagine?' Christopher nodded his head at the noisy group. 'What do you think? No TV? Too many power cuts?'

Pru giggled. 'When I was little I remember being taught how babies were made. I spent the next two months assessing the neighbours and everyone I knew in my own private survey – Mr and Mrs Morris, three children; that meant they'd done it three times. Mr and Mrs Guttmann, one child; they'd done it once. My own mother, oh my word, four living and the two babies she lost; six times. I thought this was terrible, *disgusting*! Then there was Mr Peterson, who always smelled of freesias, and his best friend Mr Patrick, who lived together at Number 8 Blondin Street; they kept the most beautiful window boxes and they had a white poodle called Trixie who used to wear a little bow on her head. They were both single and had no children and according to my survey had never done it. I used to wonder if they ever wished they could try it – like jellied eels, not everyone's cup of tea, but a must just once in your life, especially if you lived in the East End. As my mum was so fond of saying, "How do you know you don't like it if you've never tried it?" I wanted to ask Mr Peterson this, but I never had the courage.'

Christopher laughed. 'Between you and me, I suspect Mr Peterson and Mr Patrick had tried it – just maybe not in the fashion described to you at school.'

'Oh, I know that now! Funny though, isn't it, the ideas you have then?'

'It sure is. My mother told me if I swallowed chewing gum it would wrap around my intestines and I'd die. So when I did swallow some, by mistake, when I was coughing and laughing on a school coach, I couldn't sleep for weeks from the worry. I was so certain I was heading for a grizzly end that I even wrote a goodbye note and stuffed it under my mattress for my parents to find. Or Isabel, of course – there were two of us, my parents did it twice!' He laughed.

'Eeuuw!' Pru chuckled at the thought.

'I hope no one is listening to us, they'd think we were mad.'

Pru sipped her chilled white wine spritzer. *I feel mad as a box of frogs, giddy and happy and I love it!*

With stomachs full of fish and chips, Pru and Chris walked along Cliff Road to South Sands, the beach at the mouth of the estuary. The beach was a fat U shape, with greenery and cliffs to either side. Small boats, windsurf boards and sails were clustered together in one section and the rest of the beach was dotted with sun worshippers and children, some hiding behind striped windbreaks and inside half-moon fabric sun huts, others intent on digging huge, pointless holes and trying to fill them with buckets of seawater.

They flopped down on to a patch of damp sand the colour of old tea and stretched out side by side.

'What is it about this place, Chris? I feel like a different person, as if I leave all my worries and most of my heartache on the motorway.'

Chris propped himself up on his elbow. 'I'm glad. It's good to have a break from grief. Take it from one who knows.' He tutted. 'Gosh, listen to us! Enough maudlin reflection. Right, what can I tell you about me that you don't already know?' Pru raised her eyebrows but otherwise stayed stock still. 'Oh yes, I love to garden, I probably drink too much wine, in fact there's no probably about it. And I didn't realise what my life was missing until I met you. Now I realise that there was a Pru-shaped gap in it that you have filled quite admirably!'

Pru turned towards him now; this required her full attention. 'Were there any other Prus in the running?'

'No, just the one and so you were almost guaranteed success.'

They lay there facing each other.

'Has there been no one in your life since Ginny?' She took a large gulp of air; she felt bold asking.

He shrugged his shoulders. 'No, no one. It's never really occurred to me to look. I know that sounds bonkers, but that's just how it's been. And then you popped up and, quite frankly, it's floored me rather.'

'In a good way?' She wanted to hear his compliments, and the beach setting and their earlier flirtation gave her the confidence to ask for them.

'Yes! In an incredible way. I feel rejuvenated and happy, despite what has happened over the last few weeks. I feel happy!' He shook his head as though this was a feeling he had quite forgotten.

'Do you... Do you miss Ginny as much now as you did, or has it lessened with time? If you don't mind me asking.'

He dug at the damp sand with a discarded stick. 'No, I don't mind at all. I miss her less, yes, but the sadness, the tragedy of losing her remains the same. Although time has diluted that a little, made it more bearable.'

'It's a lovely testament to your wife that you miss her still and think about her.' Pru fought back the spike of envy that shot through her system, silently chastising herself and knowing she would feel the same way about Bobby, forever.

He looked out to sea. 'Ginny was sick for a very long time and to be truthful, when she died, it felt like something closer to relief. I hadn't counted on the loneliness though. Having to eat lonely microwaved meals and scooting around the supermarket on my own of a weekend, it was all rather miserable. We always had a very full social life, and so it was horrible. It still is horrible in that respect.'

'Surely your social life didn't stop just because you were alone?'

'No, it didn't stop, but it changed things. Even good friends seemed to treat me differently when I turned up alone; I could sense an underlying embarrassment, as though they didn't know quite what to do with me. Should they mention her, should they not? And acquaintances were very keen to invite spare extras: women from the Home Counties who wore too much lipstick, showed too much cleavage and who read the political columns for the first time en route to dinner, where they would offer a disjointed little insight. God, that sounds mean, but it's true. I think these "spares" made my host feel more comfortable, but it certainly didn't help me. It made me feel awkward and set up. So I stopped going out, pretty much, threw myself into my work!'

'I've never been married, so I can't imagine what that felt like. I understand the workaholic bit though; I've worked hard all my life.' She felt awkward.

'I can't believe someone like you has never married. Why is that? If you don't mind *me* asking?'

Someone like you, someone like you... Pru replayed his words inside her head and concentrated on containing her smile. She mulled over her answer. *I've never met anyone who wanted to marry me. Especially once they knew who I really was.* 'I suppose I never met anyone that I wanted to marry,' she said. It was as close to the truth as she wanted to get.

Christopher looked at her and held her gaze. He delivered his words slowly. 'Well, if that situation changes any time soon, you'll let me know, won't you?'

Pru felt her head spin as a swirl of excitement fluttered through her body. Her breath caught in her throat and her mouth was dry. *So this is what it feels like.*

'I don't know what's happening to me, Christopher. I feel like a teenager!' Pru considered the ache in her stomach as she dashed off to the park to snatch a few minutes with him, the agony of waiting for her phone to buzz and the euphoria when it did. She groped for the words with which to explain it. 'It... it's as if there is this whole other world that I didn't know about. A world that's been hidden behind a secret, locked door that no one told me about and even if they had, I didn't have a key or know where to find one. And suddenly here I am stepping through it, at my age!'

Christopher threw the stick up into the dunes and gave her his full attention. 'It's called love, Pru.'

'Is it?' she whispered.

'Yes. I think you might love me and I think I might love you and that's pretty much all there is to it.'

He leant forward and kissed her full on the mouth. It was without awkwardness or embarrassment; it was as if they had been kissing forever. And once they had done it, they wanted to do it again and again! It was so lovely; she couldn't begin to remember what her life was like before they had kissed.

As they reluctantly walked back to the car, Pru catalogued every small detail of the day, storing it away for dissection later – the way he had held her hand, sitting on the quayside, their incredible lunch in the pub and that kiss, oh, that kiss! She felt like she might burst. Strangely, even though they had moved their relationship forward, she also felt inexplicably shy, as if the openness had somehow exposed her, leaving her feeling more than a little vulnerable. Her joy, however, was tempered with something close to fear. How would things move forward? She wasn't an innocent about to set up home for the first time with her beau, choosing toasters and lamps with matching cushions; she had a home, she lived with Milly. She had spent decades carving a life as an independent single woman – how did you begin to reverse that? And above all, she had a past, a past that lay buried in the deepest recesses of her mind. Which was where she wanted it to stay.

Christopher steered the car up the hill and Pru watched the harbour getting smaller and smaller behind them. 'Oh Chris, I feel very muddled. I'm having the time of my life and yet it comes at a point when my heart is literally split in two over Bobby. How can that be?'

Christopher seemed to have heard only one bit of the conversation. 'Are you really having the time of your life?'

She nodded. 'I really am.'

'I am so glad because I am too and it would be terribly sad if it was all one-sided.' He looked across at her. 'I want to spoil you rotten, Pru!'

'Well, if you insist...'

They both laughed and held hands over the centre console of the car, like a couple of teens that didn't want to be parted. It was lovely.

Pru had once again fallen asleep in the leather passenger seat that cocooned her, rocking her into slumber, allowing her to catch up after such an early start. She was woken by the sound of Christopher's voice, loud and stern. He had pulled into a lay-by near Chiswick and was talking into his phone.

'How has it got to this stage without intervention?' He covered the mouthpiece and whispered to her, 'I'm sorry!'

She flapped her hand. 'It's fine!'

'I can be there in half an hour, tops. No, it's not bloody ideal, it's Saturday night and it's a bloody nuisance, actually. But the sooner we contain it, the better for the new bill. Have you called the others?'

There was a pause.

Pru had forgotten about his job, the responsibility, and this was a stark reminder.

'Good. I'll see you in a bit.' He pushed his phone into

his top pocket. 'Pru, I am so sorry, I need to go into the office. Bit of a crisis looming.'

'Anything I can help with?' She didn't know why she said that, unable to think of a single parliamentary crisis that could be fixed with a batch of brownies or a multi-seed loaf.

Christopher laughed. 'No, you sweet thing, but I love the fact that you asked. I'll drop you home.'

'No, Chris, don't be daft. Drop me in Westminster and I'll jump in a cab. It's only five minutes, but a round-trip for you will be a pain at this time of night. Anyway, it sounded like you need to get a wiggle on and I'll only delay you.'

'I don't like the idea of abandoning you.'

'You're not – I suggested it. It's fine. Really.'

Too quickly, he indicated and pulled in by the gates of the House of Commons. Pru leant over and kissed him one more time before jumping out of the passenger door. She watched as he turned down the ramp and out of view.

'That's my man,' she said aloud.

Her phone buzzed as she jumped in the back of a black cab. She looked down, hoping for a text from Christopher. Her face crumpled as the initials CM came up on her screen. *U bettr pay me this wk or else.* She deleted the message immediately, with shaking hands.

Pru tried to concentrate on the sights beyond the taxi window, attempting to decipher buildings through the dark night. She read the no smoking sign, watched the silent advert for a credit card on the screen on the back of the driver's seat, studied her nails. In fact she did everything other than consider the ache in her heart and the quiver to her lip that she knew was waiting for release. *What were you thinking, girl? Why did you think you could be enough for someone like him? How was it ever going to work? You've been kidding yourself.*

She paid the cabbie and got out. Pressing her handbag against her Curzon Street front door, she rested it on her raised knee and ferreted for her keys. Was it really only seventeen hours ago that she had set off from here, practically skipping down the stairs? She had jumped into Christopher's car with a bubble of excitement in her throat and a happiness that verged on madness. Her head had been full of possibilities.

Now she climbed the stairs slowly and sighed as she let herself into the flat. She didn't want to encounter anyone, least of all Milly, so she headed straight for the bathroom and slid the bolt. She slipped down until her bottom was against the tiles. Her body convulsed as sobs rippled through her. She sat there with two blackened smears around each eye and her head in her hands. The words from all those years ago reverberated in her head. '*A chain that you will wear around your heart and a sadness that will sit behind your eyes, filling your mouth with sourness. It will taint all you do.*'

'I know,' she whispered into the empty room. 'I know.'

Pru looked around her opulent bathroom. She stared into the vast full-length mirror behind the double sink unit; the chrome vintage-style taps gleamed under the array of lights that were angled just-so, to highlight the designer chic. All this wealth, all this luxury and yet she still felt like the little girl from Bow who shared a bed with her cousin and slept in her clothes, trying to ignore the twist in her stomach that groaned with hunger. She had achieved everything she had ever dreamed of in business and yet when she woke in the middle of the night, as she often did, she was just as frightened as she had been when she was ten; she was simply in a different postcode. Filling her mouth with candies and sugar-coated pastry would do nothing to dispel the sourness. She should know that; she had been trying her whole life.

Pru heard the soft tread of her cousin's shoes on the carpet outside.

'Please go away, Mills.'

'You're not still sulking over that thing the other night?' Milly sounded resigned, not angry.

'No,' Pru managed through her tears.

'Good, cos that was probably about fifty years overdue, but I'd had a horrible day. It isn't worth brooding over. You and me are stronger than that, aren't we?'

Pru nodded. 'Yes we are.' She cried again, harder, with instant, sweet relief that she and Milly were back on track.

'Come on, open the door, come out!' Milly knocked.

'No, Milly, I don't want to see anyone.'

'I'll put the kettle on.' This meant hurry up.

She showered, hoping that the water would wash away some of her sadness. It didn't. Wrapping her head in a fresh white towel and pulling her soft grey dressing gown tightly around herself, she cleaned her teeth and headed out to the sitting room. Milly sat in her chair in her tiger suit, with a mug of tea between her palms and the newspaper open on her lap.

Pru rolled her eyes at the sight of her cousin's attire, and nodded at her drink. 'Are you going to throw that one at me as well?'

'No, this is just the right temperature; that other one had gone a bit cold.'

'I didn't like us fighting, it didn't feel right.'

'No, it didn't, it was horrible.' Milly flicked her eyes at the space over Pru's shoulder. 'I got the carpet and the wall cleaned.'

Pru laughed. 'I can't believe you threw a bloody mug at me!'

'Lucky for you I'm a crap shot.'

The women smiled at each other.

'What's all this in aid of, love? Locking yourself in the bathroom, it's not like you. What's wrong?'

Pru took a deep breath and tucked her feet under her legs on the wide wingback chair. It was upholstered in a cream and olive stripe, chosen to complement her cousin's one in check; both fabrics had been recommended by the interior designer, who'd selected them to match the hand-printed feature wallpaper that hung either side of the fireplace. She shook her head. This was a hard conversation to start. 'I think it's all suddenly hit me today.'

'What has? Bobby, you mean?'

'No, not really. Although partly that, yes. I feel so confused. I don't honestly know how I can be chasing happiness with Chris when Bobby and William are gone and Meg is in such a mess. It feels wrong.'

'Yep, I get that. But the point is, you're not chasing it – *it's* caught *you*. And that's different. These opportunities aren't going to be around every corner.' She smirked at her cousin. 'That's my polite way of confirming that yes, you are in fact, old.'

'I know that. And I do worry about what Bobby would think.'

'She'd say go for it. She'd tell you that you only get one life and that what happened to her was proof of that.'

'And what would you say, Mills?'

Pru watched as Milly's fingers agitated the newspaper on her lap. This gesture was the closest she would get to saying, '*I can't imagine being without you, you're my family, my business partner, my best friend.*'

'I'd say the same.' She nodded.

'Thanks, Mills. Not that I'm going anywhere. We come as a pair, right? A team.'

'Yep, a team.' Milly's shoulders relaxed and she folded her hands together calmly.

'I feel like I've been kidding myself and today I've suddenly seen quite clearly what I've been trying to avoid. I can't have a relationship with someone like Christopher. I can't have a relationship with anyone.'

'Don't talk rubbish, course you can!' Milly sipped her tea.

'No! No I can't. If I were meant to be with someone, live with someone or marry someone, then I'd have done it years ago. It's not a coincidence that I've been single my whole life.'

'But you love him and he loves you, it's obvious.'

Pru cheered up, remembering. 'He told me that today actually.'

'Well there you go!' Milly tutted.

'But he doesn't know me and that's the trouble. He loves the bits he sees and he loves the person I am now, but he doesn't know me, does he, Mills? And I can't tell him and he mustn't find out.'

'I think you might be worrying a bit prematurely.'

'Am I? I heard him on the phone to his office this evening and it made me realise that he has an important position, a public position, and if I'm his girlfriend, then that might make me more public too. Not just me, but the name Plum's as well, the whole business. And if people start digging... It could ruin him and it could destroy our business. Our reputation is all we've got, Mills. I don't want him knowing about my past. I couldn't stand to look at his face and see disgust or disappointment. I love the way he looks at me now, no one has ever looked at me in that way, ever. And so it's best I call it a day, for both our sakes.'

'There is always a solution, Pru. Don't overreact—' Milly offered this by way of solace, but Pru saw the flinch in her eyes, as if the possibility of losing Plum's had occurred to her for the first time.

'I'm not overreacting!' Pru shouted as she dashed at the tears that slid down her cheeks. 'Don't you get it? I've just been kidding myself. Can you really imagine Sir Christopher Heritage being with someone like me?' Pru thumped at her chest.

Milly rolled her eyes. 'Listen to me, Pru. You are a very successful businesswoman, we both are. Look at what we've achieved.' She waved her arm in an arc. 'All this. Our lovely home, the business, magazine articles every bloody month in every glossy mag, a client list that reads like *Who's Who*. And look at what a great job you did with Bobby, she was incredible!'

'What *we* did with Bobby. She loved you, Mills,' Pru corrected.

Milly smiled. 'Chris knows how wonderful she was and that was entirely down to you. Whether I like to admit it or not, you two had a special bond. You're a success, love, and no one and nothing can take that away from you.'

'But that's just it, he can! Crying fucking Micky can! I feel sick, Mills. Like I am standing at a delta trying to hold back a flood, but it's just me and the weight of the flood is coming towards me and there is not a thing I can do to change or stop events unfolding, but I have to try, even if it feels pointless. One word in the right ear and he can take everything from me, from us. It's a bloody mess.' Pru ran her hands over her face.

'Only if you let it be a mess, and you can't. You're made of stronger stuff than this.'

'Am I? I'm not so sure. We went to Salcombe today and it was perfect. I felt so happy. I felt like one of those women who swings their bag and holds their husband's hand, smug, because they've got it all and they know it. I was happier than I've ever been. And then we get back to town and it's like a veil's been lifted. I am not one of those women and I never will be.'

'Blimey, if I were you, I'd pull your veil back down then; it seems that your life was much nicer when you were looking through it! Or failing that, sort it out, talk it through, tell him about your worries.'

Pru was silent, considering her cousin's advice. It was a little while before she answered. 'It sounds so easy when you say it like that, as if all I have to do is talk to him and it will be like it was today – perfect.'

She looked up. Milly had made a veil out of her newspaper, with two eyeholes poked out, and she was sitting there with the sheet over her face.

'Silly moo.' Pru laughed into her soggy tissue. Milly was right; she had to face this head on.

Eleven

At 9 a.m. Meg entered the café with her hair tied back in a wide black ribbon and wearing smart trousers and sensible shoes. The crisp white shirt strained rather across her bump, and her movements were measured, but she was ready for business.

The previous evening, Pru, Guy and Milly had been standing in the workroom, bent over at right angles with their faces inches from the marble-topped table, peering at a selection of sugar-paste flowers.

Pru pushed her glasses further up her nose, Milly sniffed and Guy used his pencil to prod at the pale pink flowers, which lay in various states of collapse.

'Is this really the best they could do?' Pru straightened up and sighed.

Guy shook his head and rubbed his fashionably stubbled chin. 'We need to find someone fast! Things here are falling apart. My team are stretched and we can't cope. We are the *Titanic*!'

Pru had laughed and rolled her eyes at Milly. 'We are not the *Titanic*! It's not quite that bad, Guy. Yes, we are short-staffed and yes, it's tough. But no one is lowering the lifeboats and striking up the band for a final waltz just yet. We may have to juggle some of our less urgent jobs, but it's not the end of the world. I'll speak to Lady Miriam and The Dorchester about delaying their sample tastings. It'll be fine.' She reached for the order book. 'I have some more CVs coming in and a recommendation from one of our delivery boys – his aunt's friend, or something, who is a whizz with a piping bag. She might be useless, but at least she's available!'

Milly coughed. 'That's all well and good, but we want the right person, not the available person. How hard can it be, for Gawd's sake?'

Guy held up a bedraggled rose that looked more like a cone. 'Well, if this is the level of skill the agencies are sending us, *mon Dieu!*, harder than you might think.'

There was a tentative knock on the doorframe and in crept Meg, looking nervous. In her hand was a platter of exquisite china-white sugar-paste roses, so thin they were almost translucent and yet shaped to perfection. With the light shining on them, they took on a greenish hue, reminding Pru of real roses. They were delicate, uniform and perfect.

Guy spread his hands under his chin. 'Oh my, oh my! These are beautiful, *parfait*! Who made them?'

Meg was embarrassed. She tucked her hair behind her ears and shuffled from one foot to the other. 'I did. I was wondering if... maybe I could work in the café, help you all out... maybe. Just to learn how the shop works and everything.' She chewed her fingernail and looked at the floor. 'It's just that I've always worked. I like working. I don't want wages or nothing; you've already given me too much. But if I could help out, just till the baby's born. Can I do that?'

187

Despite Milly's angry raised eyebrow, Pru and Guy had said yes immediately.

And now here she was.

'Ah, Miss Meg! You are beautiful!' Guy kissed her on both cheeks. 'Today we set you to work!' He clapped his hands.

'That's the idea.' Meg hesitated. 'I'm a bit nervous actually, Guy,' she whispered.

'No need, *chérie*. You are under my wing.' He winked at her and grabbed a menu. They sat down at a corner table and he started to talk her through everything they served.

She was a fast learner and spent the rest of the day taking orders and ferrying plates and cups back down to the kitchen for washing. If she was being honest, she was rather enjoying herself. It was exhausting, especially with the extra weight she was carrying, but made a pleasant change from counting the minutes from the confines of her bedroom.

By 4 p.m. she was on her last legs. A man entered and hovered by the counter, obstructing anyone trying to pass and making his presence felt. Then he took a seat at one of the back tables. He was thin, with pointy features and a squinty eye. Pushing seventy, Meg guessed. Despite the heat of the day, he was dressed in a dark suit and a black trilby. He stretched out his legs under the vacant chair opposite and slouched in his seat, leaning backwards.

'Can I help you, sir?' Meg recited, just as she had been taught.

'Do you know, I think that's what I like most about coming to this sort of place. It's the level of respect that is shown. And yes, my dear, you can help me. I would like a pot of tea, some sandwiches, and a really nice cake or two. Posh ones with a big fat dollop of cream inside.' His voice was loud and sarcastic. He tried to disguise his cockney accent, but only succeeded in sounding strange, as if he was playing a game. His words were pleasant, but his tone was mean.

'I can get that for you, but we have lots of different sandwiches and cakes. Would you like to choose something from the menu?' Meg reached out for a menu to place in front of him.

'No, I would not. I would like you to do it for me. Surprise me! We all like surprises, don't we?'

Meg smiled nervously at the customer. He was weird and he kept staring at her chest, which bulged over the starched white half-apron that was wrapped around her enormous, taut stomach. It made her feel sick. She shuffled down to the kitchen. Guy was at the counter.

'There's a man upstairs who is a complete weirdo, says I should choose something for him to eat! He didn't want to look at the menu. He really gives me the creeps.'

'Maybe he is nervous and you just need to put him at his ease. Plum's is a fine establishment and people sometimes feel a pressure to behave in a certain way. Try a big smile – it usually works!' Guy drew a large semicircle between his ears with his finger. He was keen to keep all their customers happy.

'Maybe, but it didn't seem like that.'

Meg made a selection of tiny crust-less sandwiches and miniature cakes and took the tray up to the café. Balancing the tray on the edge of the table, she carefully decanted the plates of goodies and the teapot on to the space in front of the man.

He twisted the little china teacup round on its delicate saucer until the handle faced him. 'Be a dear and pour for me, would you?' He grinned, revealing stubby brown teeth that were neglected and chipped.

Meg's hand shook as she lifted the pot and leant over the table. She tried not to let the tremor affect her pouring.

'Oh now look at that, you're shaking! It's quite understandable, my dear. I have been known to have that effect on women.' He reached up and placed his hand on the back of her thigh, his thumb nudging against her bottom.

He had touched her! She wanted to shout that no one had touched her since Bill and no one would, and that she was pregnant! Instead, she jumped back, shocked, and dropped the teapot. It tumbled to the floor and shattered into a hundred jagged pieces.

How was it possible there could be so much tea inside a small pot? It spilled all over, spreading like a golden lake on the wooden floor. She stared at it and concentrated on not crying as she knelt down, awkward with her huge belly, and used her linen cloth to mop at the mess.

Guy had heard the smash and fluttered into the room like a bird. 'Oh, *mon Dieu*! What has happened? Sir, I am so very sorry. It is Megan's first day and she is a little nervous. There will of course be no charge for your tea and it would be my pleasure to bring you another pot.' He gave one of his bows.

'No charge for the tea?' the man sneered. 'I think you'll

find, my good fellow, that there will be no charge for any of it.' He picked up a sandwich and folded it in half, cramming it into his mouth and using his index finger as a poker. He smacked his lips open as the little triangle of brown bread and egg mayonnaise churned against his tongue and teeth, then followed it with a mini éclair. It was quite revolting.

'No charge, sir?' Guy was confused.

'You heard me, sunshine. I am an old friend of the proprietor, Miss Plum, and I can guarantee that she would not want to see a single penny transfer from my pocket into your shiny till. In fact, quite the reverse.' He gave an irritating nasal laugh.

'Go and fetch Miss Plum, please, Meg.'

Meg was glad of the excuse to escape the café, still flustered by the man's wandering hand and foul demeanour. She found Pru in her office behind the workroom.

'Pru, there's a man in the café who is a complete creep. I dropped a teapot and he's saying he doesn't have to pay for anything because he's a friend of yours! I'll pay you back for it, I promise!'

'It's all right, Meg, calm down. It doesn't matter a jot. A friend of mine? Sounds like a nutter. I'll come and sort it out. You go upstairs, get showered and relax a bit. I think Milly is cooking our tea later. You've been absolutely brilliant today. Thank you for all your hard work.'

'I'm sorry about the teapot.'

'Don't give it a second thought.'

Meg beamed and trudged up the stairs, glad her shift had come to an end. She felt strangely fulfilled. It was a nice feeling being tired after working hard all day and there had been minutes if not hours that she hadn't thought about Bill, she'd been that busy.

Pru closed the file she'd been working on and replaced it in the top drawer of the desk. She walked through the kitchen and up the stairs to the café. As she neared the door, she heard his laugh even before she saw him. She felt her bowels shrink and her blood run cold. *Crying Micky – here, right now, in my business, in my home.*

She walked into the café, trying to keep her expression impassive, clasping her hands in front of her to hide their shake.

'Well, well. *Now* look at you – the one and only Miss Plum! Apart from the other Miss Plum!' He guffawed. 'Long time no see!'

'It's all right, Guy, I can take it from here.' Pru nodded at her loyal manager, who hovered, disconcerted by the presence of the rude man in the hat. He retreated behind the counter and busied himself with the emergency counting of doilies. She crossed over to the table.

'What do you want?' Her tone was clipped, her volume low. She didn't want to alert any other customers to his presence.

'Do you know what? I think I preferred the tasty little pregnant piece who called me sir. Can I have her back again?' He laughed and raised his handkerchief to wipe the tear that trickled from his puckered eye.

'I don't want you here, Micky. I want you to leave, now.'

'Is that right?' He drew a deep breath, slowly. 'Thing is, it's not always about what you want, is it now, Miss Plum?

Sometimes it's about what other people need, if you get my meaning?'

'We have an agreement,' she whispered, gripping the back of the empty chair at the table, unsuccessfully trying to steady her hands.

'Ah, but that's the thing about agreements, the terms can change, just like that.' He clicked his fingers loudly above his head. Several patrons at nearby tables whipped round to look at him.

'Please, Micky, just go. If you need to talk to me, you can do so over the phone.'

'Please is nice. At least I'm getting a bit of civility now – and that's all people want in life, isn't it, Miss Plum. Civility, respect, status. Some would say it can make a business.' He glanced around the room, taking in the ornate cornicing, brass fittings and grand antique chandelier. 'Some would say that if you remove that respect and status, it can destroy a business and a reputation.' He dug with his fingernail at something trapped between his front teeth.

'If this is about money, I can't give you any more.' Her tongue had stuck to the roof of her mouth and she was finding it hard to get the words out.

Micky laughed until he wheezed then coughed. 'If it's about money? Why else would I haul my arse all the way up here to see you, Prudence? What did you think? That I'd come all this way to reminisce about old times? Well, why not! And how is that nasty tranny you lived with over in Earls Court? What was his name... Trudy, wasn't it? Still up to his old tricks? If you want to blame anyone, you—'

'Please! Micky!' Pru felt like she'd been punched in the stomach. How dare Micky foul the memory of her dear friend – what did he know? She flushed with fury at the horrible, casual way in which he'd sneered at Trudy's biggest secret. Clenching her teeth and biting back her retort, she braced herself. He had the upper hand and she couldn't afford to lose control; not here.

Her voice quivered with emotion. 'I can't give you any more.'

He made a fist and thumped his chest. 'In my book, can't means won't and won't means a whole heap of trouble.'

He stood up slowly, allowing the chair to scrape along the wooden floor, attracting the attention of the other customers. Drawing closer to Pru, he leered at her, only inches from her face. 'Another thousand a month or you *will* be seeing me again. And I might bring some of my associates; they like a good time, if you get my meaning.' He winked at her and straightened his hat. Then he grabbed a pale green pistachio macaroon from the display counter, shoved it behind his teeth and sauntered out.

Pru put on a bright smile as she cleared away the table, scooping the stray crumbs into her palm and straightening the menu against the flowers. She even managed to hum a little. She'd dealt with that quite well, all things considered. It was only when she reached the safety of her office and sank down into one of the comfy chairs that she allowed herself to register her thundering heart and quivering hands.

Her phone buzzed. She let out a little scream and trembled in the chair. 'You silly moo,' she muttered to herself, 'calm down.' Pulling the mobile from her pocket, she read the one-word message – *Park?* – and pressed the screen against her forehead.

She breathed deeply. *How can I do this? How can I pretend? I have to tell him.*

Christopher approached the bridge at the same time as she did, both of them walking along the slight curve and meeting in the middle.

'A late-afternoon bridge appointment? This is a bit of a departure, Sir Christopher.'

'I know, I like to mix things up a bit!' He laughed. 'Keep you on your toes! No, it's just been one of those days. I couldn't escape before, but I've been thinking about you. It's been a real pig of an afternoon.'

'Tell me about it.' Pru pushed the image of Micky's leering, sneering face from her mind, happy that they weren't going to compare notes.

Christopher leant across and kissed her and it felt like the most natural thing in the world, as though they had been doing it for years and not just that one day in Salcombe. She blushed and felt the knots leave her shoulders.

'I'm pleased to see you.' He smiled, as if it needed confirming.

'I'm pleased to see you too.'

'I feel different, Pru. Like we've moved forward. I couldn't have imagined meeting someone at my age, didn't know what starting out again would feel like, but it's quite a relief to know it feels the same as it did when I was sixteen. But instead of worrying about spots and whether I'll be able to borrow my father's car for a date, I now worry about

195

whether I might bore you and what to do to keep you surprised and interested.'

'Luckily for you, the answer is very little. You don't have to keep surprising me, Chris. I'm interested anyway. I think I've had more than enough surprises over the last few weeks. In fact, promise me, no surprises!'

He took her hand. 'You're right. These last few weeks have been a bloody rollercoaster. But I didn't get you to schlep all the way to the park so we could be depressed! Although I'm afraid it might be a little too late for my "no surprises" promise.'

'Too late? How?'

'Before I realised that I actually didn't need to try so hard to win you over…' He winked and pulled an envelope from inside his suit jacket. 'I got these.' He waved the envelope in front of her. 'Tickets to Barcelona. We leave on Saturday – it's that long weekend we discussed. I called Liz, but sadly the Victoria Inn was fully booked, so Barcelona it is!'

Pru put her hand to her throat. 'I can't just up sticks and go to Barcelona!'

'Yes you can.'

'I can't!'

'Do you remember what we said – life starts when you let it! And we are going to let it, aren't we? Come on, come to Barcelona. It's only a weekend. I'm sure Plum Patisserie won't fall down and Meg and Milly will be squabbling just as you left them, they probably won't even notice you've gone.'

That was all probably true, but a weekend away, together… 'I'll have to have a think about it, check with Milly.'

'Well you can think about it and check with Milly as much as you like, but I am not taking no for an answer. We are going to Barcelona.'

'Are you always this bossy?'

'Yes.' He laughed and kissed her once again. 'I love you, Pru. Just in case you were in any doubt.' He looked at his watch. 'Oh, shoot! I am very late!' He started to jog away from her, backwards. 'Barcelona! In four days! Pack sensible shoes!' he shouted with his arms spread wide, narrowly missing a teenage boy carrying a skateboard. Pru heard him muttering 'So sorry!' as he broke into a run.

Pru woke in the middle of the night with a buzz of excitement. He was taking her to Barcelona! But she was darned if she would wait four days before seeing him again. She sent her text and set her alarm. Two could play at being bossy.

Christopher looked a little bleary-eyed as he stepped into the gleaming kitchen. 'I'll have you know, I haven't had breakfast and I'm missing my morning run!' He patted his stomach.

'Not to worry, you can eat what we make and there's another morning tomorrow, so you can just run twice the distance.' She smirked as she fastened the apron around her waist before securing Christopher's tightly with a bow. She spun him around until he was facing the counter and took up her place opposite him on the other side.

'You look lovely!' She chuckled; it was good to have him here in her workroom and funny to see him in one of the Plum Patisserie aprons. 'So you've never baked anything before, ever?'

'Nope.' He shook his head, looking smug, as though this was some kind of achievement.

'Not even biscuits when you were a kid or salt dough at school?'

'No, nothing. My mother used to make cakes with Isabel while Dad and I went off and did other things. More boyish things.'

'More boyish things?' Pru put her hands on her hips. 'You are unbelievably sexist and out of touch. Some of the greatest bakers in the world are men.'

'Is that right?' Christopher put his hands on his hips too, imitating her stance.

'Yes! Richard Bertinet, Tom and Henry Herbert—'

'Ooh, Mr Kipling!' Christopher interrupted.

Pru stared at him in silence, then said sternly, 'Baking is an art and you have to concentrate and learn. Monsieur Gilbert used to say that a half-hearted baker would only ever have half-eaten cakes, and he was right.'

'I don't want to incur the wrath of Monsieur Gilbert.'

'Well it would be the ghost of Monsieur Gilbert, which would be much worse! Now listen carefully.'

Pru set a large ceramic bowl in front of him and placed a fine, pointed sieve over it. She handed him a scoop of flour and showed him how to gently tap the metal rim using the side of his palm. Christopher watched as the fine powder drifted through the tiny holes. 'Why do we have to sift it? It looks pretty lump-free to me,' he said.

'It loosens up flour that might have been sitting around in storage for a long time; it also adds air, which means your baking will have a lighter texture.'

'It feels like a lot of work.' He grimaced.

'And that's part of the reward, Sir Christopher. You get out what you put in.'

Pru watched closely as he added the bicarbonate of soda, ginger, cinnamon and nutmeg, his clumsy fingers more used to gripping a fat fountain pen than the fiddly little measuring spoon. Then she poured the mixture into the food processor, added the butter and set it to a gentle whir. 'Look.' She pointed at the bowl and Christopher dutifully peered more closely. 'You see it looks like fat breadcrumbs? This tells us it's time for the sugar.'

'I'm meeting the PM this afternoon, I shan't tell him how I spent my morning.'

'Why not? I'm sure he'd be impressed!' She laughed.

Christopher picked up the little scoop and dumped the sugar unceremoniously into the mixture. He did a better job of beating together the egg and the stretchy cords of golden syrup, which Pru then poured into the food processor.

'Ooh, that smells lovely! Gingery!' He inhaled.

'Yes.' Pru smiled. 'We're making gingerbread.'

'Are we? Goodness gracious me!'

'Do you know the best thing about making gingerbread?' she asked.

'Oh God, no, but I feel like I should have some textbook baking answer up my sleeve.'

She laughed. 'The best thing is that you get two coffee opportunities – one when the dough is chilling in the fridge and the other while it's baking! So stick the kettle on and I'll get the cafetière out.'

She glanced at him while she set the dough to chill; it felt lovely to have him in such close proximity.

They sipped at their coffee before rolling out the dough. He was pretty good with a rolling pin, Pru would give him that. She handed him a man-shaped cutter. 'You need to cut out your shapes. Press it into the dough quite firmly and then we'll use a spatula to transfer it to the baking tray.'

Christopher fumbled with the thin metal shape, his tongue poking from the side of his mouth in concentration. He didn't hear the door open.

'What *are* you doing?' Milly asked, standing in the doorway with her arms folded across her chest.

Christopher straightened up and adjusted his apron. 'I am making gingerbread men.' He blushed.

'Blimey,' Milly said. 'And to think I voted for your lot.' She left, shaking her head and tutting.

Half an hour later, Pru and Chris studied the cooled gingerbread figures and looked at the piping bags and pots of sparkles, chocolate buttons, jelly drops and other goodies lined up ready to decorate them.

'I'm going to make *you*!' Pru announced, picking up the icing cone. Her nimble fingers worked deftly as she drew a tie, a suit and even his cowlick of a fringe. The delicate white lines glistened on the smooth pale surface of her honey-coloured gingerbread figure.

'Two can play at that game,' said Christopher. And he proceeded to blob and squidge until he'd produced a Pru-figure with a thick line of smudge that combined nose, mouth and eyes.

'Do I really look like that?' she asked.

'Yes, exactly like that.' He smirked.

She showed him how to use icing to glue in place the sweetie gems and jewels, and he duly covered her figure with them. It looked hideous. But Christopher was clearly delighted. 'Look at that, it's uncanny!' he said as he lifted up his creation.

Pru made a pretend swipe at him and as he defended himself, his gingerbread woman dropped to the counter and broke, losing an arm – and her head.

'Oh no, I'm broken!'

Christopher walked to her side of the counter and wrapped her in his arms. 'I'd love you even if you were broken. I'd carry all the little pieces of you around in my pocket, forever.'

Pru closed her eyes against his chest and enjoyed being held.

Twelve

The taxi pulled up in front of three ancient buildings on the harbour front. All three listed slightly to the left and their wooden doors and shutters had been bleached bone dry. They looked like working buildings. Through an open door Pru caught sight of a boat and piles of nets and floats that looked abandoned, as if a fisherman in a hurry to get home had forgotten to tidy them away. A man with a weathered face sat on a small three-legged stool outside. He raised his hand in greeting as he worked on a battered basket. He was wearing a flat cap, which made her smile. Did all old men the world over, whether from Yorkshire or Catalonia, eventually graduate to wearing this particular sort of hat?

The building in the middle appeared slightly less dilapidated. Its walls were a faded white, but its peeling woodwork still held remnants of bright blue; a large fishing net hung over the bottom-floor window and the top floor had a wrought-iron balcony. It belonged to Christopher's friend Raul, a painter, who had taken on the fisherman's cottage, renovated it and lent them the keys for the weekend. It looked lived-in and perfect.

Pru and Christopher glanced nervously at each other as

they retrieved their luggage from the boot of the taxi. The Mediterranean heat warmed their bones and gave them both a jolt of holiday joy; this was just what they both needed. Christopher pushed on the shabby wooden door and immediately tripped on the step, just managing to right himself before he went sprawling.

'Blimey, don't break your neck! We couldn't even blame a fall on cheap vino at this time of day!' Pru laughed as she clutched at her chest.

'Don't you worry, I'm fully insured.'

'That's the least of my worries – you're holding our duty-free gin!'

He opened the front door wide as he held out his hand to take hers, guiding her over the rather elaborate step configuration. Pru found herself in an artist's studio. Canvases in various stages of completion were stacked against every surface. There were brightly coloured sploshes all over the whitewashed walls and the floor was a rainbow of droplets. The ceiling was low but the large window flooded the space with light. Christopher patted one of the weathered roof beams as he ducked his head beneath a blackened hook. 'Ships' timbers,' he said. Pru loved how clever he was.

From some of the hooks Raul had hung twists of rope with shells threaded through them: one held a small net filled with coral, another was strung with corks whose ends were stained with red wine. They were quite beautiful. A pale wooden easel stood in the corner, near a battered chaise longue with wiry-looking stuffing coming out of it. The long, scratched work table was scattered with tin pots holding brushes, chisels and pencils and glass jars full of every shade of powder. Pru wanted to run her fingers over the unfamiliar objects, smell the powders and strange items. It looked like the artist's equivalent of a well-stocked larder.

Christopher made his way over to the open-tread wooden staircase in the far corner. Pru followed him, trying not to step on the tacky blobs of paint. She watched as his clumpy deck shoes filled the depth of the first stair; it creaked and groaned under his weight and unconsciously Pru gasped loudly at the sound. She placed her hand on the wall to steady herself.

Christopher reached backwards and grasped her hand. 'Hey, no need to look so frightened. If they take my weight, they are certainly going to take yours. Come on, it's okay, I won't let you fall.'

Pru put her hand against the small of his back. *I won't let you fall...* She desperately wanted to believe him. She forced a smile and ploughed on up, trusting the worn planks as Christopher did.

The upstairs apartment was a single open space that ran the length of the building. The wooden floor sloped towards the back and fans of light pierced the gaps between its broad, waxed, golden-hued boards. Pru took in the wide wrought-iron bed and starched white bed linen and tried not to pay it too much attention. Instead, she focused on the rickety bedside tables and their oversized lamps, the patchwork cushions and the small red velvet sofa that sat alongside a crowded bookcase. To the left of the window was the kitchen area, with two green-painted stools underneath a breakfast bar. On the bar sat a fancy-pants chrome coffee machine that wouldn't have looked out of place in any high street coffee shop, and the obligatory microwave.

Pru looked straight ahead and inhaled sharply at the scene that greeted her. 'Oh my word, Chris! Look at this.' She put her hands to her neck.

Christopher beamed. This was obviously the reaction he had hoped for.

The large sash window, a replica of the one on the ground floor, opened on to the wrought-iron balcony. It was high enough to give the most amazing view over the restaurants that lined the marina, and beyond the harbour wall you could see the sea, glinting with sun diamonds. Pots of trailing geraniums, heavy with scent and an abundance of scarlet blooms, hung in metal troughs along the sides of the balcony, and in the middle sat a rather battered blue metal table with two mismatched wicker chairs. The only way to access it was to manoeuvre through the open sash window, scissor-legging over the sill, which was maybe two feet high.

'You like?' He asked the question as though he already knew the answer; it was halfway between a question and a statement.

'It's perfect.'

He gave a small nod. It was. 'I've been meaning to come here for years, but never got around to organising it. I think I knew it was the type of place that would only be half as good if I came alone.'

Pru suddenly felt inexplicably shy, hit by the reality of being in such close proximity to Christopher and sharing a living space. This felt very different from meeting for short bursts in the park. She needed the loo and tried to picture getting into her pyjamas and cleaning her teeth in front of him. She was sure it would have been easier in her teens, when she had yet to assume the cloak of self-doubt and awkwardness that she had carried with her since her forties. She remembered being very young and wishing that she weren't so tall, hating the fact that she was always a head taller than any boy she wanted to dance with. Hers was always the first face detected in a classroom or on the factory floor when the person in charge was looking for the troublemaker. Yet now, at sixty-six, her height was the one thing she did like; it was everything else that let her down: the stretch marks on her abdomen, her small boobs, which were now less than pert, the tributary of lines that ran from her mouth to her jaw and teeth that looked aged and worn.

As if reading her thoughts, Christopher made his way to the corner, to what Pru had thought might be a cupboard. Instead, the wooden louvre door opened on to a cramped but clean and shiny white shower cubicle and loo.

'Okay, we are going to have to implement a system. With no lock on the door and only this one room, I propose to whistle "Dixie" very loudly when I'm in situ. That's your warning not to enter and to cover your ears. What, might I ask, will your song of choice be?'

'I don't know. I can't whistle and my singing is terrible,' she whispered.

'How about, "Hey Jude"? That's in an easy key and everyone knows the words.'

Pru shrugged. 'Okay, "Hey Jude" it is. I need the loo now, actually.' She chewed her bottom lip.

'In that case, start singing, while I unpack at the other end!' He glanced across at her. 'You look anxious.'

'I am anxious.'

'Why?' He stepped forward and folded her against his chest.

'I think I'm a bit nervous. Not just the loo thing, the whole thing.' She closed her eyes. 'I don't want to disappoint you, in any way.'

He grazed the top of her scalp with a kiss. 'Oh, Pru, you couldn't disappoint me in any way. You are an incredible woman.'

'I'm not twenty any more.' She hoped that this would convey her fears and her self-consciousness about her aged body, her many foibles and the peculiar habits of a single woman that had been a lifetime in the making.

'Neither of us are, my love, that is why this is rather special.'

She smiled against the fabric of his shirt. 'In that case, I'd better start singing.' She disengaged herself and headed for the louvre door.

After a stroll around the marina, as the day drew into dusk, Pru and Christopher made their way back to the fisherman's studio.

'I'm shattered!' Christopher patted the space next to him, to the left of where he lay on the bed.

So that was her side then. Easy. Pru kicked off her shoes and sidled over to where he rested. Placing her head on his chest, she felt his arm encircle her shoulders. She could hear his heart beat and smell his unique, intoxicating scent. They sank into the gloriously soft mattress as the sounds of the marina drifted up through the window. Pru felt a welcome calm spread over her. This wasn't awkward at all, just lovely. Christopher's chest rose and fell as he dozed. She couldn't sleep, but listened to the clatter of tables being set, cutlery and crockery clunking together as it was placed on the linen tablecloths below. Waiters called instructions to one another in Catalan. Music was starting to play; guitars strummed amid the gentle hum of laughter and conversation as lovers and families strolled along the waterfront, looking for friends or seeking the perfect table from which to watch the harbour.

Pru felt at peace as she hugged Christopher's form into her chest.

He stretched as he woke, smiling, happy to see that she was next to him. 'Well, not a bad first day, in fact half a day, as we only arrived this afternoon.' He stroked her hair.

'It's been great. I'm quite exhausted. I don't think me and afternoon bottles of wine mix very well!'

'God, you wouldn't last five minutes in Westminster.'

'I could have told you that, wine or not!' She laughed.

'Right, you stay here. I'll be back in a bit.' He sat on the edge of the bed and pulled on his deck shoes.

'Where are you off to?' She tried to sound nonchalant.

He turned and kissed her nose. 'Never you mind! I am a man of mystery!' He struck a pose that was part Flamenco, part magician, then disappeared down the stairs.

Pru lay back on the pillows. As soon as he left, she let the cold creep of concern wash over her. *I need to tell you something, Christopher, but I don't want to spoil things. I don't honestly know how to start.*

208

She reached for her phone and punched the icon that meant home. Milly answered immediately.

'It's only me. Everything okay, Mills? Plum's have a good day? Meg all right?'

Milly sighed loudly across the miles, refusing to answer the questions. 'How long have you been gone?'

Pru looked at her watch. 'I don't know – seven hours?'

'Precisely. And just what do you think might have occurred in that time?'

'I don't know. Have you seen Meg? Is she okay?'

'No. I haven't heard a peep out of her. But here's how it is. If she's quiet, it's because nothing has happened and therefore you have nothing to worry about, all is as you left it. If on the other hand she has in fact found the combination to the safe, robbed us blind and left with our worldly wealth stuffed into that fake bump, then there is absolutely nothing you can do about it.'

'You're not really helping. I was just checking in, that's all.' Pru sighed.

'Well don't. Bugger off, drink sangria and have a nice time. I don't want to hear from you again. If anything out of the ordinary should occur, then rest assured that I will call you.' Without a farewell, Milly ended the call.

'Well that's me told.' Pru stared at her handset and laughed as she wriggled down further on to the bed and waited.

It was nearly an hour later that Christopher poked his head above the stairs, his arms raised high. In each hand he held a thick terracotta platter. One was piled high with sardines and wedges of lemon, the other with slabs of fresh crusty bread and two fat peaches.

He walked past her with barely a sideways glance and made his way out to the balcony, climbing through the open window with the deftness of an expert. He placed the food on the table. Then he came back into the room, retrieved the bottle of plonk they had bought earlier and gave an elaborate bow that reminded her of Guy. 'Dinner is served, ma'am.'

Pru clambered from the bed, her clothes crumpled, her hair mussed, but she didn't care. She followed him through the open window and sat down at the table, marvelling at the sights below. Lights twinkled and the smell of garlic-infused dishes wafted up to them.

'This is amazing!' She ran her palm over the table.

'Oh! Wait a mo!' Christopher hopped back through the window and reappeared almost immediately with a glass lantern. The large cream candle inside was already lit. He set it on the floor and then produced two glasses and two linen napkins. She noted that there was no cutlery.

'Now it's perfect.' He sat down to join her.

They ate with their fingers and minimal conversation: like two people that were so familiar, nothing else was needed. Pru had never shared such intimacy with a man. They gorged on the garlicky fish, which they smothered in lemon juice and wrapped in the warm bread. It was delicious. She thought of the conversation they had to have and her throat tightened. She wiped her mouth with her napkin.

'You okay there, Miss Plum?'

'Yes, I'm great; full but great.' She patted her stomach. 'I was just thinking how lucky we are to be here, with all this. And we get along so well, don't we?'

He nodded. 'We do.'

'But we are still strangers to each other in a lot of ways, aren't we?'

'Well, yes, that's always the way when you're starting out on an adventure, whatever one's age. We are getting to know each other every day and I must say, I am more than enjoying our journey.' He squeezed her hand inside his own as it lay on the table.

'Me too. But I guess we should make time for frank chats – that would be good, wouldn't it?'

'Yes, of course, but that will all happen in time. You can ask me anything, anything at all, whenever you wish. I have nothing to hide.'

Unlike me. I have to hide my whole life. 'I don't know what to ask you.'

Christopher sipped at his foggy glass of chilled wine. 'We are not in any hurry, Pru.'

'I guess.'

Christopher reached out and took her hand again. She stroked her fingers against the back of his hand and marvelled at the warmth of this one small act.

'Right, don't know about you, but I'm shattered. Think I'll have a quick shower and we can call it a night.' Christopher raised her hand to his mouth and kissed her fingers before climbing back through the window.

Pru nodded and sipped at her wine, glad of the encroaching darkness. *Oh my God, nearly bedtime.* She felt a shiver of nerves running along her limbs. It had been a long time and never, ever like this. Her palms were damp with sweat and her hands shook. 'Get a grip, woman,' she whispered to herself as she stood up and watched the horizon. The sky had turned a very particular mauve and the sinking sun seemed to make everything it touched instantly more beautiful.

She scrambled inelegantly through the window as Christopher emerged from the shower in his dressing gown. His hair was damp and curled around his neck and she noticed for the first time the tufts of grey that sprouted at the top of his chest and poked from his dressing gown. It made him look older, yet also masculine, sexy. She felt shy of the man standing in front of her.

'It's a little cramped in there, but a good temperature. Shall I get it running for you?'

Pru nodded. No one had ever prepared her shower for her before. She let the water wash away the grime of the busy day and scrubbed her face until her skin glowed, then slipped into her vintage silk kimono with its swirling turquoise patterns and pink flowers. It had once belonged to Trudy and Pru treasured it. With a towel around her head, she left the safety of the cubicle.

Christopher was on the balcony. She watched him scrolling through the news pages on his phone, his equivalent of a quick call to Milly, no doubt. Pru patted her legs dry and tousled her wet hair with her fingertips, raking it into its bob shape. Goose bumps peppered her warm flesh as she felt his gaze on her through the open window. She was unsure why she wanted him to see her, really see her and yet she was certain that she did – the real Pru, the Pru without worry, without history, stripped.

She completed her routine as if she were alone. Rubbing lotion into her limbs and torso, she managed to reach her lower back by moving her hands inside her beautiful kimono. She was glad of the cool silk against her skin. She turned to look at Christopher; he was a handsome man and in the dying Mediterranean light his eyes looked bright and his skin olive. She imagined looking at him every night while she got ready for bed and she liked the idea very much. Knowing there was someone to chat to in those final minutes of the day would make her feel less lonely. This thought surprised her: for the first time, she realised that, despite being surrounded by people and having a full and busy life, she was indeed lonely.

She decided against underwear and ducked out of the window to where Christopher now sat in deep contemplation. Without speaking, he pulled the overstuffed cushion from the wicker chair and threw it on the floor between his splayed bare feet. He gestured for her to sit on it. As she lowered herself down, he twisted her shoulders gently so that she was facing away from him. She knelt on the cushion, arranging the kimono over her lap to preserve her modesty. When he was happy with her position, he returned to the studio, leaving her alone.

'Is this where I'm sleeping?' she called through the window.

He placed his finger on his lips, the universal sign for hush.

Pru felt her heart rate increase with a combination of nerves, anticipation and embarrassment. What was he doing?

He re-emerged quickly, holding her jar of body cream. Then he retook his seat and pulled her backwards slightly, until she sat snugly in the space between his knees. Placing his hands inside the neck of her kimono, he gently eased the fabric down over her shoulders. The slippery silk fell instantly down to her waist, anchored only by the tie belt about her midriff. Pru wished she hadn't fastened it so tightly, aware of the smallest bulge of fat that sat over it. The material billowed over her forearms and pooled in her lap. Her upper body was naked, skin exposed to the evening air. Modesty felt pointless and so she simply closed her eyes, thinking herself away, a habit she had perfected in her younger days. She couldn't quite identify what she was feeling, at first. She felt reckless, daring and expectant. And then she recognised that delicious combination – she felt young! This was how it had felt in the days before Plum Patisserie, when she had planned and pictured her future; a time when the world had been hers to discover and everything felt possible.

Christopher dotted the cream into his palms and rubbed them together to warm the lotion and grease his hands. Placing his flattened palms against her exposed shoulder blades, he waited for her to stop shivering and for their temperatures to sync before he started to massage her skin. His fingers kneaded the knots from the muscles at the nape of her neck. Working his hands down and around her back, he covered every inch of skin with circular movements of his palm. Using his fingertips, he probed and manipulated her spine with his fingers. Pru fell into an almost trance-like state of bliss, not wanting him to stop. Despite her near nakedness and the level of physical contact, the whole encounter was far from sexual. It was instead deeply moving; personal without any of the shorter-lived instant gratification she associated with sex.

The pleasure for Pru was intense. Christopher pushed her head forward and exposed her neck. He massaged up under her hairline and behind her ears, it was wonderfully unhurried. Pru felt herself slump as sleep tried to envelop her; she felt his hands gently restore the kimono over her shoulders as he helped her stand and led her through the open window. In a dream-like state she lay on the vast bed and Christopher covered her legs with a soft grey blanket.

Pru lay face down in the favoured pose of the inebriated or exhausted and welcomed the heat of his hand through the thin fabric of her gown. His touch was lighter now. Gone were the small deft strokes; instead, his hands worked in long sweeping gestures, caressing her skin through the slippery gossamer silk. She couldn't fight the deep sleep that pulled her into another world – and she didn't want to fight it. She welcomed the tunnel of escape that had appeared before her. It felt wonderful to sleep with someone watching over her, just as she had always dreamed of.

Thirteen

Pru woke the next morning to find Christopher propped up on one elbow, staring at her.

'You look lovely when you're asleep, very young.' He traced a finger across her cheek.

She stretched her arms over her head. 'Oh no! Don't say you've been watching me. I'm torn now between the embarrassment of being watched and wanting to repeat it, if it makes me look young! Was I drooling or snoring?'

'Both. I've just had complaints from the neighbours on both sides; they wondered if I had a camel in here. You were very loud and drooly.'

'That's so embarrassing! I hope you apologised on my behalf – the poor neighbours. Was it me or did you actually have a camel in here?'

'You got me! I had two camels in here actually; they've just left.'

'I can see the headlines now: *Prominent Politician Caught with Two Camels in Spanish Loft!*'

'Oh, I rather like the idea of that – gives me an air of eccentricity, rather than the dull truth.'

'I don't think you're dull.' She ran her fingers through her hair. 'Actually, I know I don't snore, you fibber. Milly would have told me – in all these years she's never held back from pointing out my many faults and failings. The list of which is long and ever changing.'

'I don't believe that.'

'It's true.' She nodded.

'You did say "Bobby", though, just as you were waking up. I think you must miss her in your sleep as well.'

'Yes, I think I do. She's on my mind all the time; maybe she always will be. I think my loss of her will be like a tiny stone that I carry in my shoe, always there and never letting me forget. And now I worry about Meg, or more specifically, Milly and Meg. I do hope she'll be okay. The poor love's been knocked for six and her baby is nearly due. I know that taking her in might have seemed irrational and, according to Milly, disloyal, but it felt like the right thing to do.'

'I can understand that. She's lucky to have you.' He stoked her arm.

'Oh, on the contrary. She's a lovely addition to my life and I'm loving every minute of having her around. Even if it doesn't exactly make me flavour of the month.'

'That was an extraordinary thing to do, bringing her into your home. I'm still amazed by it.'

'D'you think I was wrong?'

'No, not at all. I just don't think I've ever met anyone who would reach out like that to a complete stranger. It's remarkable. I'm not sure I could have done it, and William was my nephew, so it was probably more my responsibility, thinking about it. I still don't know what he was playing at. It's dreadful, isn't it? It's the level of deceit that's so shocking. I can cope with most things, but deceit for me is the worst.'

Pru pulled the sheet up over her shoulder. 'When it first came to light, I felt like I hated him, seeing the mess and hurt he'd caused. But now, even just a few weeks later, I don't feel like that any more. I actually feel a bit sorry for him. I'm not condoning his behaviour or forgiving it in any way, but I can see how if you are weak and scared, then you might only do what pleases others and not yourself. You might not be able to follow your heart and that is very sad.'

'Don't you think he was following his heart?' He let his fingers travel down over her arm.

'I think he thought he should marry Bobby, but I've listened to the things Meg says, the way she describes the little things – she really knew him. They didn't have the flash, exciting, Mayfair life that he and Bobby did, but it seemed a bit more authentic. She told me he bought her a hot water bottle and cashmere bed socks, as there was no heating in her flat. And I know it sounds ridiculous, but that's the act of someone who is taking care of you, even if he was a shit.'

'Poor William.' Christopher looked momentarily downcast. Pru wasn't sure whether that was at the memory of how William had died or because he hadn't had the courage to chase happiness.

'Poor everyone,' she said. 'No winners in this one, I'm afraid, least of all a little baby who will never know it's cheating dad.'

Christopher reached across and lifted her with surprising

ease, his arm muscles flexing as he did so, until she was lying on top of him. Her silk kimono covered them both. And just like that, her age, her less than perfect physique, even their future and the words that sat in her stomach like rocks, didn't matter. Nothing did. They entered a space where only the two of them existed.

'I don't want to talk about William or Bobby, in fact I don't want to talk about anything.' He kissed her then and the anxiety of the previous day slipped from her like a second skin. Together, they were natural, at ease and blissfully, blissfully happy.

It was a hot day. Christopher donned his crumpled Panama as they reluctantly left the studio and walked hand in hand along the streets, grinning at each other as they stepped over the cobbles and stopped for coffee and pastries only minutes into their outing. Pru sat opposite Christopher at the little table on the quay and watched as he popped cubes of almond candy on to his tongue and gobbled the lightly fried fluffy round fritters that had been dusted with powdered sugar and filled with pastry cream.

'Oh, these are delicious!' He spoke with his mouth full, delighted and relaxed.

Pru wrinkled her nose at the greasy fare and raised her hand to decline the offer of her own little cream-filled doughnut. She had standards to uphold.

Christopher pushed his hat up on to his brow. 'Pru! I don't believe it! Are you a food snob?'

She shrugged. 'I am a bit, but I promise it's the only thing in the world I am particular about.' Pru rather liked the idea of being thought of as discerning and she decided not to confess to her love of sweets and junk food, especially pink shrimps and strawberry laces, dandelion and burdock pop and, most shameful of all, her occasional craving for a Pot Noodle.

'You must be easy to live with.' Christopher's face coloured and he coughed, embarrassed at having voiced his thoughts and worried it might have frightened her.

'Well, apart from my snoring, drooling and singing "Hey Jude" off key, I suppose I am.' She watched as he stared at her, smiling. 'What?' she asked.

He shrugged his shoulders and laughed. 'Nothing. I just like looking at you and I am happy, really happy!'

'Me too.'

'I haven't even thought about the mountain of paperwork on my desk, or worried about the job once – not once! It's a bloody revelation!'

'Where are we heading?' She looked up and down the long, tree-lined street.

'Do you mean in life or in the next hour?'

'The next hour, clever clogs.' She sipped at the minuscule bitter espresso, which jolted nearly every one of her senses.

'I thought we could take in the National Art Museum of Catalonia.' Christopher pulled a pamphlet from his pocket and perched his reading glasses on his nose. 'Sitting on one of the highest points in the city,' he read, 'the building itself is spectacular, commanding the most incredible views of Barcelona, where you can take in the elegant city sprawled out before you.' He looked up at her and caught her eye. 'How does that sound?'

'It sounds lovely.' Truth was, she would have been just as happy to sit in that little café and chat to him all day. Anywhere with him by her side was precisely where she wanted to be.

Pru felt a swell of nervous anticipation as they climbed the steps and entered the rather grand building. It was a bit intimidating entering an art gallery with someone clever like Christopher. She had very particular taste and was sure of what she liked and didn't like, but her preferences weren't based on any deep artistic knowledge and she hoped that she wouldn't embarrass herself.

She needn't have worried. The two of them ambled from room to room at a measured pace; if she saw a picture that she liked the look of, he consulted his guidebook and gave her the background. His easy manner and encouragement bolstered her confidence.

'I think if Westminster doesn't work out for you, you could always get a job as a museum guide.'

'I'll bear that in mind.' He patted her bottom.

Some rooms didn't hold them for long and there were certain works of modern of art that neither of them particularly warmed to, eliciting a mutual wrinkling of noses. Others they positively disliked: still lifes and animals in oils that were a bit too chocolate-boxy for both their tastes.

But then they turned a corner into a rather unassuming little room and Pru stood transfixed. Her heartbeat quickened and she was rooted to the spot. The painting was relatively small compared with some of the huge pictures that dominated the other walls, but Pru was unable to take her eyes off it. It was quite simply the most beautiful and

221

saddest painting that she had ever seen. Others passed by, seemingly unaffected. But for Pru it was as if it called to her. She wanted to drink in every detail.

It was a painting of a woman sitting on the cobbles in the moonlight. She was wearing a torn gauzy white night-gown and was lit from behind by the glow of a candle. Her dark curly hair was haphazardly piled on top her head and she looked as if she had been recently disturbed from sleep. A man on horseback threw gold coins, a couple of which fell into her lap, the others scattering around her on the ground. One hand clutched the thin material of her gown across her chest and the other was stretched out against the wet cobbles. Her shoulders sagged and she looked exhausted and beaten. Her face had the most haunting expression: there was a remorseful twist to her mouth and her eyes were deep pools that seemed to speak of shame and regret.

Christopher handed Pru his handkerchief. She hadn't realised she was crying. She blinked as she examined it, a small square of cotton embroidered with his initials.

'Th... thank you,' she stammered.

'Do you like her?' he asked as he put his arm across her shoulders.

Pru nodded as she blotted the tiny rivers that carried the remnants of her mascara down her face. She tucked the white square into her pocket, not exactly stealing it, but knowing that she might need it later. 'She is so beautiful and so haunted; she looks like she needs help.'

Christopher gazed at Pru's profile. 'Yes. Yes she does.'

'I do love you, Christopher.' Her tears fell even harder.

He kept his eyes on her. 'And I you.'

He leant forward to look at the title of the painting. '*Puta*,' he read aloud. 'Whore.' He squeezed her arm and guided her towards the sunlight. 'Come on, let's get you some fresh air.'

Hand in hand, they made their way back to the marina, their mood reflective. Pru was nervous, knowing what was about to come and Christopher silently wondered at the change in her demeanour, anxious not to do or say the wrong thing at this early stage of their relationship.

'You okay there, Miss Plum? You are rather quiet.'

'I'm fine.' She wrapped her arm around his.

Sitting on their balcony, she watched the hustle below, storing away each sight and smell. The scent of pine resin and garlicky roasting meat mixed with the tang of the sea was intoxicating. She knew that long after they left Barcelona, those smells would transport her back to this warm Mediterranean evening, where everything had still been perfect.

'Hello, hello!' Christopher called as he appeared from the staircase with a basket full of goodies.

Pru could see a fresh loaf sticking from the top and a large slab of cheese in waxed paper. She turned in her chair and called 'Hi!' through the window. Christopher collected two glasses from the little square china sink before joining her in the dusky evening light. This was her favourite time of day.

'Now, before you go all foodie on me, we have locally produced goat's cheese that smells wonderful and a tub of spicy pickled peppers. The bread, I'm afraid, isn't quite Plum Patisserie standard, but it's hot, fresh out of the oven and looks wonderfully rustic. More to the point, I'm bloody starving! All that walking is enough to give a man an appetite.'

He handed her a glass of chilled white wine and stood with his arms resting on the balcony rail. His long legs were straight, his wide, muscular back taut under his pale pink linen shirt. Pru wished they could stay like this forever; it was peaceful and a world away from the life that awaited them back in London. Christopher took his place at the small table and stretched, making the wicker chair creak against his body. The two smiled at each other as they shared the bottle in companionable silence, happy in the knowledge that there was nowhere else they would rather be.

He turned towards her slightly. 'I bought you a present,' he said as he reached into his shirt pocket. 'A picture, a postcard of the painting you liked.'

He handed her the card.

'Oh! Thank you, Chris; she's beautiful.'

'I wanted you to have a memento of our trip and I know she moved you.'

'Yes, she really did.' Pru nodded.

'We should go to exhibitions in London; I'd really like that. I'd forgotten the pleasure of walking around a gallery, I thoroughly enjoyed it.'

'I'd like that too.' Pru sipped her wine.

'This trip has been incredible. I feel like we've been away for weeks, not just a couple of days. I want us to spend more time together, Pru. I want to spent all my time with you, if I'm being honest!' He laughed, cautious with this line of conversation. 'And now I'm feeling very nervous because your smile has faded and for the second time today I'm wondering if I've overstepped the mark or offended you in some way. I have to confess, I want to get this right, but I am so out of step. You can always tell me to shut up, or better still, give me pointers—'

'You don't need pointers, Chris, you're amazing. Perfect in every way.'

'Well that's good to hear, but forgive me, if I am as you say, could you look a little happier about it?' He grinned at her, baring all his teeth as though asking her to follow suit.

Pru sighed and placed her wine glass on the table. 'I'll try. You make me so happy, happier than I can ever remember, but I also know that I'm not perfect, and that's the problem.'

'Ah, but that's the beauty of it: you don't have to be perfect. You only have to be perfect for me, and you are.'

'Supposing I'm not?' Pru stared at the postcard on the table in front of her.

'Well, I think you should let me be the judge of that.' He paused for a couple of seconds and stroked his chin. 'Right, I've had a think and yes, I now judge you fit for purpose!' He laughed.

Ordinarily, she would have joined him, but not tonight. 'I want to tell you about me, Chris, I want to tell you all about me.'

'I'd like nothing more.' He angled his chair towards hers and took her hand inside his own.

She nodded and took a deep breath. 'It's difficult to know where to start, so I'm going to go back to the day I moved to Earls Court from Bow, me and Mills, trudging across town and on the Tube with one battered suitcase between us.'

'Oh good, will there be time for questions at the end?' he joked.

She ignored him, concentrating on getting her words out.

'Are you going to keep me waiting all night?' Chris chuckled and swilled the last of his wine around his glass, then reached for the bottle and poured himself a generous refill.

'No, I'm just figuring out how to start.'

Christopher's phone buzzed on the table. 'Damn. Sorry, Pru, I have to take it, might be work. I'll be as quick as I can.'

'Of course.' She waved her hand, crossed her legs and sipped her wine.

He stood and walked to the front of the balcony, facing out towards the harbour.

'Christopher Heritage.' He looked over his shoulder and winked at her, smiling, with one hand on his hip and the other holding the phone to his ear. 'Yes. Here.' He sounded firm.

She watched his eyes flicker as his lips parted. The colour drained from his cheeks and his face seemed to slip, drooping down, despondent, shocked. His pupils dilated and he gripped the balcony rail as if to stop himself from falling.

'Everything okay?' she mouthed. It was clearly bad news.

He turned away from her gaze and spoke into the corner of the balcony. She stared at his back, his shoulders rising and falling with every deep breath. 'When?' His voice faltered. 'Is it accurate?' He waited for the response. 'Are you sure?' Again the silence. 'I see.' Christopher straightened his spine and exhaled. 'Thank you, that can't have been easy. I will see you in the morning. Yes, right now, tonight.' He looked at his watch. 'Thank you. Goodbye.'

He ended the call and placed the phone in the breast pocket of his shirt. Holding the balcony rail with both hands now, he stared out to the dark sea beyond, looking over the heads of the revellers below.

'Are you okay, Chris?'

He snorted through his nose and shook his head. 'Am I okay? I'm not sure really.'

'What's happened, can I help?'

'Oh no, no. You've done quite enough, thank you.' His tone was cool, clipped. Pru shrank back against the wicker chair.

They were both silent for a minute. Then Christopher spoke. 'I've been floored once or twice in my life. The last time was sitting opposite a consultant in a dusty room in Harley Street on a rainy Thursday in November. It was when he told me Ginny had run out of options. It felt like this, just the same as if I'd been kicked in the gut.'

'Chris, for God's sake, what's going on?' Her breath came in shallow pants.

'Good question! What the fuck is going on? I'll tell you what's going on, shall I? My staff received a call and then a visit from a certain "associate" of yours who is threatening to go to the tabloids with a snippet of information that might be of interest.'

Pru closed her eyes. The moment he used the word

'associate' she knew it was Micky. 'Oh God!' She wrapped her arms around herself and gripped on tightly.

'Yes, "oh God" indeed. You know what's funny? All these snippets of information that you let slip over the last few weeks – a life of hardship, the little match girl angle – all very endearing, but not once did you see fit to mention that you were on the game, a whore! Not once! Don't you think that one small fact might have been good to share?'

'I was going to tell you, Chris. I wanted to,' she replied in a small, cracked voice. 'I knew I had to. I just didn't know how to start.'

His shoulders straightened and she watched as he assumed a sober, collected expression.

'When, for how long?' he said tersely, as if addressing a suspect.

Her voice was quiet. 'It was in my late teens and early twenties, for seven years. Seven years of saving and learning patisserie when we had enough money. We worked with Trudy. But at the same time we started catering for functions and we were good, really good. Our reputation grew and when we could afford it, we moved into our first little shop off Oxford Street. The rest is history.'

She looked up and tried to catch his eye, but he determinedly fixed his gaze elsewhere.

'I never talk about it and I have never told anyone. I still have nightmares about it. I was a little girl in so many ways. I wasn't worldly when I left Bow; I'd never even been kissed. And then there I was, sitting in that room, waiting for a man old enough to be my granddad. He walked up the stairs and I knew he was coming for me. And I knew that once I'd done it that one time, I would be changed forever. And I was.' She paused, dug her nails into her hand, willed herself to get it all out. 'I remember he smelled of cloves. The top stair leading up to our flat was broken and it creaked as he trod on it. It's almost like a reflex now. If I hear the creak of a stair under my foot, my heart jumps like it might fire out of my body and I feel like I'm going to fall. It petrifies me. Every time I heard that creak, I knew that it would only be a minute until I was on that bed, losing part of myself all over again. I still hear it, I still dream about it. I see all their faces as a group, bearing down on me, and sometimes, in the middle of the night, I have to sit up and put the light on, just to check I'm alone and safe.'

She looked up and saw a flicker around his eyes.

'I knew that being part of a couple was not for someone like me. Deep down, I knew that. But I wanted so badly to be the kind of person that could be. I think the world of you, Chris.' Her tears came thick and fast now. 'I really do. But from the moment you took my hand, I knew that I would have to tell you that I've slept with hundreds of blokes for money.'

Pru blew her nose and tried to compose herself. 'I've always been a bit fascinated by people in love, you know. I worked with a girl at Bryant and May, her name was Dot Simpson and she couldn't talk about the bloke she loved – Solomon, I think his name was – without grinning. She couldn't say his name without her eyes sparkling and her cheeks glowing. Even the thought of him made her happier than I had ever known. I envied her that and I've never forgotten it.' Dot would be a grandmother now, probably, she thought with a jolt. Still living in Bow with her Solomon, most likely. 'And even though I've shared a pillow with many men, I have never felt even a twinge of intimacy, of love; those things both felt very separate from sex. But with you, it's different. I want to breathe the air you breathe; I want to touch your skin. I love the way you smell, your walk, the way you laugh, everything about you. And strangely, the sex is just a small part of that, not as important as the other stuff for me. It's like it's come full circle.'

'I wish it were that simple.' Christopher finished his wine in one gulp. Holding the stem, he set the glass back down on the table with such force that both of them glanced at it to see if it would break.

'I can't help it, Chris, and I can't change it. That's me. My life wasn't university and an early marriage, but a hard life, a difficult life. I made choices that I have lived to regret. Every day of my life I regret them, but hindsight is a wonderful thing.'

'Isn't it just.' He sounded curt, distracted.

'I've never had to tell anyone I cared about before, because I've never cared about anyone in this way before. Never.'

He snorted a small laugh through his nose. 'Do you think that makes a difference? The fact that you've let things get this far might make it okay?' He ground his teeth together. 'You are so mired in how tough you've had it, but you have no concept of just how hard I've worked. I have clawed my way up, with every man around me willing to strip the shirt from my back to get a step ahead of me. I've given everything to my career, even put my marriage second...' He paused. 'And you could be the thing that takes me right back to square one; forty years of bloody hard graft and sacrifice wiped out. Do you have any idea of the position you have put me in?'

'I'm sorry,' she whispered.

'You're sorry?' He laughed.

'I love you, Chris. I love you and I don't know if that's enough, but it's the truth. I didn't want to have any secrets from you. I wanted you to love all of me and I *know* that this could hurt your career.'

'Hurt my career?' Chris laughed into his palm. 'What about hurting me?' He shook his head, as if still sifting her words to find meaning. 'My people will deal with your friend.'

'He's not my friend! He's a sleazebag – he just wants money out of all this, surely you can see that?' She watched as he gave an almost imperceptible shrug, as if it was of little consequence. 'These last few weeks have been amazing; spending time with you has made me so happy and so sad. It's made me see what I've been missing all these years. I knew we'd have to have this conversation and the thought of it has been sitting like a rock in the base of my stomach. I was afraid that you'd leave me and now I can see it in your face, I know that's it.'

'It's a lot to take in, a lot to think about.' His tone had changed. He sounded like he did when he was on the phone to work; that same dispassionate, angered tone. 'I don't honestly know what to think.' He shook his head and sighed.

Pru's voice was quieter now; he had to strain to hear her.

'It's easy to judge from here, but when you are poor and you want desperately to find a way out, you'll do anything. I did anything. It wasn't the day and age where a poor girl could waltz into a bank and ask for a loan. I didn't know anyone that had a bank account even. My mum had different jars in the kitchen cupboard, one for rent money, one for food, one for the meter; hard to imagine now, but that's how it was. So that's what I did. I sold my body and at the time I didn't think of it as prostitution, not until it was all over. I'm not proud of my early life and it taints all that I've achieved. But I can't erase it. I wish I could. I wish a lot of things. I wish I'd been born into a family that sent me to school and gave me hot dinners and a bloody pony. I wish I'd had a mum and dad that helped me achieve my dreams. But I wasn't and I didn't. And that, Chris, is just how it was.'

'Don't you dare try and make me out to be the bad guy! Being born into money was not my fault and you are labouring under the misconception that it meant everything was easy for me, which it certainly wasn't! You have kept me in the dark, you have lied to me!'

'I have never lied to you!' She almost shrieked.

He smirked. 'In my book, omission is deceit and that is the same as lying.'

Pru looked up, her face streaked with tears, her eyelids swollen. 'You said you would love me even if I was broken. You said you'd carry all the little pieces of me around in your pocket, forever.'

He shook his head. 'We both said a lot of things. And this is real life, Pru, not fucking gingerbread.'

He grabbed the phone as it buzzed once again in his

shirt pocket. Pru watched as he scrolled through the screen. 'Flights are booked, I need to get back to London.'

'Now?' She sat forward in her chair.

He reached across, grabbed the postcard from the table and tore it into pieces, letting the bits fall to the floor around his feet.

'Yes, now.' Christopher walked past her, leaving their supper untouched on the table. He climbed through the window and started to gather his belongings.

She nodded; she understood. 'I'm sorry,' she offered once more.

He shook his head as if to emphasise the impotence of those two words.

The two of them placed their bags on either side of the bed and silently folded their clothes.

'You know what?'

'What?' He focused on scooping up his loose change, watch and passport from the bedside table.

'I may have slept with men for money, but I have never felt so dirty and humiliated as I do right now.'

Chris walked briskly past her and shut himself inside the louvre-doored shower room. Pru listened to the sound of running taps; she couldn't hear him whistling 'Dixie', but she could have sworn that she heard the sound of crying.

Fourteen

Pru looked at her reflection in the window of the cab; she looked lost. There was a remorseful twist to her mouth and her eyes were deep pools that seemed to speak of shame and regret. *Puta*.

It was the early hours of the morning when she alighted from the cab in Curzon Street. The engine seemed loud and invasive, cutting through the purple-tinged hush of the summer night. She placed her key in the lock and trod the stairs. She was about to walk into her flat, picturing her bed, or more specifically, her pillow, when she heard shouting from above. She paused with her hand on the banister before climbing the next flight of stairs, digging deep to find the energy to put one foot in front of the other as she let herself in. The noise was coming from the sitting room. She could hear both Milly and Meg's voices and was able to make out the odd phrase.

'You have no idea how much Bobby loved him! They were getting married—'

'And I am having our fucking baby, what's that if it's not commitment?'

'That's not commitment; you wouldn't have seen him for dust. Bobby knew his family!'

'Well good for her. I knew his pin number!'

It was the final straw at the end of a long and horrible evening. The plane journey had been horrendous. They'd sat in near silence, Christopher's body angled away from hers, his arms tucked into his lap. She felt small and dirty and would have given anything to be free of his company sooner, wishing she could have clicked her heels like Dorothy and woken up at home. The formality with which they had said goodbye at the airport couldn't have been more different from the way they had greeted each other there only two days before. She could hardly bear to recall it.

She walked into the sitting room and stood by the door. Both women were standing in front of the fireplace. Milly staggered and wobbled – she looked as if she had been drinking. And Meg too looked a little unsteady, exhausted.

'You knew his pin number? Oh well that's practically a proposal!' Milly gave a derisory laugh.

'I didn't need a proposal, we were buying a house, a house that we would raise our child in!' Meg screamed.

'You're a liar!' Milly growled. 'And you might have taken Pru in, but not me, I'm watching you.' She pointed her fingers at her own eyes and then directed them towards Meg.

'Am I? Is this a lie?' Meg patted her swollen stomach. 'And what about the photos I've got, and all his letters, talking about our future? Am I lying about them n'all?'

'Enough!' Pru screamed from the doorway.

Both women looked round, shocked by her presence and her tone.

'What are you doing back here, Pru?' asked Milly, taken aback. 'I thought you weren't due home till tomorrow?'

Pru ignored the question. 'Sit down, both of you.' She spoke as if she were addressing kids. Her voice was stern but her hand trembled as she pointed first at them and then the sofa. They made their way across the room in silence and sat at either end of the oversized sofa. Pru stood in front of them, shaking with anger.

'I've had enough!' she yelled. 'This stops, tonight, right now!' Her voice was croaky from the effort of holding in her tears for the last few hours. 'You have both been through an ordeal, but to further torture each other is futile and cruel. And I will not live with this sort of behaviour any more. I will not! Is that clear?'

Neither woman reacted. 'I cannot and I will not put up with it. Why should I? I want peace. I deserve peace. You seem intent on destroying any harmony that we have here, but it's pointless. William is to blame for all the deceit. He's the one that let you and Bobby down, Meg; he kept you in the dark and he lied to you. But he's dead; he is dead and he's not coming back. And neither is Bobby.' This she addressed to Milly.

Both Meg and Milly started to whimper. 'That's it! More bloody tears. Perfect.' Pru ran her hand over her face. 'You, Milly, have had a wonderful life, admittedly a good few heartaches and struggles along the way, but in the end a lovely life, a charmed life. You are a grown woman. No one is responsible for your life choices, not me, not anyone, just you. And yes, this terrible thing has happened, it's happened to us both. We lost her! But it cannot be what defines you. It can't make you bitter. You must not let it.'

Milly nodded into her lap, sobered by her cousin's outburst.

'And you, Meg. I have invited you into our home and I expect a certain standard of behaviour. If this situation is going to work out, you need to find a way to live here as part of the family, not skulking around the edges of it and only coming out to fight with Milly behind my back. This is no way for any of us to live. This is not the example you should be setting for that baby. Okay?'

Meg nodded.

'Good. And finally, I would like to say to you both that some people go through their whole miserable life without ever loving or being loved. And it's a very lonely way to live.' She didn't notice that she was crying, her body finally seeking the release that she craved. 'So instead of screaming at each other and sobbing into your pillows, try being thankful for the fact that you loved someone so much that you miss them now they're gone. And you, Meg, that someone loved you enough to give you a baby. Because some people have neither of those things, ever, no matter how much they want it. Some people live alone, when even a little love would have made a huge difference to them. Do you understand?'

Both women nodded and looked from her to one another.

'Good. I'll see you both tomorrow.'

Pru turned and walked from the room, leaving them to stare at the space that she had vacated. The echo of her words spun around the room then settled over them like a fine mist, seeping slowly into their consciences.

Turning the handle of the shower, Pru allowed the water to run hot. Steam filled the glass-sided cubicle as she gingerly stepped under the deluge; she felt the hot hard jets pummel her skin. The temperature was more than a fraction too hot and ordinarily she would have lowered the gauge until it felt comfortable. This, however, was no ordinary night and she didn't want to feel comfortable. Standing with her face tilted upwards, she let the water cascade over her body. Her skin flared red and angry at the scalding. It was some minutes before she reached for the lavender-scented soap and started to work up a lather. Using her loofah brush, she scoured every inch of flesh until she tingled with pain. Then she started the whole process again. She scratched at her scalp with her fingernails, again painful but necessary. She wanted to scrub away the touch of every man that had laid his hand on her skin, every punter who had paid money to take pleasure from her body, every person who had used her.

It had taken Pru two weeks of listening to Trudy traipse up and down the stairs with a never-ending parade of men – every sort, from senior policemen to Fleet Street's finest – before she realised how Trudy earned her living. At first she naively thought that she just had a lot of friends. But once she understood, she asked Trudy immediately if she thought it would be a good way of earning money for Plum's.

Trudy had sat herself down at the kitchen table and taken a deep drag on her cigarillo. Her voice had a gorgeous husky growl, and she always sounded kind when she spoke to Pru.

'It's up to you,' she said. 'The fact is, you are either cut out for this or you're not. There ain't nothing glamorous about it. When I started out at sixteen, it was about survival, but I'm twenty-six now and let me tell you it ain't about survival no more, it's about money. A lot of money. I'm very picky about my clientele, I don't walk the streets, but I do have a fixer. He makes the arrangements, but I don't work for him, I don't work for anyone. It's a partnership. I have some that come here, regulars, or I go to where they are staying, top hotels in the West End, mainly. And there's the occasional party or private function, if you get my drift.'

Trudy's fixer turned out to be Crying Micky. He wasn't much older than Pru and Milly, but he vetted the punters, made the introductions and took a cut. Pru had never liked or trusted him, and she kept her distance as much as she could. He mostly left her alone, but he had always looked at Milly as if she were meat, making her shiver with fear. The first time they met, he had crouched close to Milly and pointed to his eye injury. 'Y'see this, Mills? A bear did it!' There was a pause while the girls stood there, waiting for the punchline that Trudy had heard many times before. Micky grinned. 'It was a bear all right, a bare fist holding a knife!'

'How much could you make if you had an extra girl or two?' Pru had asked Trudy that day in the kitchen at Kenway Road. She had been direct. If this was something she was going to do, it had to be worth it. It was the first time she could see a clear path to bringing their dream alive.

But nothing had prepared Pru for the flicker of fear she felt when, alone in her bedroom, she listened as her first punter climbed the stairs. His foot creaked on the wood, and she shivered. When he entered the room, she was shocked at how old he was. He was wearing a wet wool coat that smelled, and when he opened his mouth to kiss her, his breath smelled of cloves. It felt all wrong. It felt horrible.

As if in a dream, she took his calloused hand in hers and led him across the room. She imagined it was a game, a dare, part of her elaborate adventure. His near nakedness had brought her close to tears, more than the act itself. And the memory of it still could.

After he had gone, she was too numb to cry. She lay there and looked at the coins that he'd put in a pile on the chest of drawers, and she thought about the bricks it would buy. Maybe one brick, maybe two, but each one of those bricks would one day build her freedom.

Fifteen

Pru left the flat mid morning with a file tucked under one arm, giving the impression that her excursion might be business-related. In the other hand she clutched a brown paper bag containing two *croissants aux amandes*, which this time she had made herself. She walked quickly, keen to get to the park, forgetting that there was no plan. She had to remind her racing heart to calm down. Christopher hadn't answered her calls and so she had texted her intention to be in the park. She knew he probably wouldn't be there, but she'd smoothed her fringe and applied her scent nevertheless. She felt a bit stumped when the bridge came into view. What was she to do now she had arrived?

Conscious of being observed, of being so obviously abandoned and loitering aimlessly in this public space, she looked at her watch and sighed, as though the person she was meeting was late. She did this a few times and walked from one side of the bridge to the other, craning her neck as though trying to spot a certain someone in a crowd. This act was genuine enough. She was searching for a certain someone who might or might not have been visiting his favourite London landmark that day. He wasn't, not today.

Pru took a seat on the bench and set down her file with

the little paper bag on top. She watched as couples and families sauntered past, stopping to admire the ducks or to kiss in the shadow of a weeping willow. She studied their grins, their interlinked hands and their slow blinks. She knew how they felt; she had been one of them, just for a little while. Her mouth trembled and her shoulders sagged. *I miss you. I miss seeing you and I miss having you to think about. I am lonely again, just like that. I am lonely all over again.*

A chubby dark cloud blocked the sun and threw the park into shadow; the chill crept into her bones and caused her to look skywards as fat droplets of rain began to fall. Pru closed her eyes and let the water run over her. The paper bag disintegrated and rendered her croissants to mush. Looking around, she saw that everyone had dispersed, leaving her quite alone and feeling more displaced than ever.

She sat on the bench for two hours and thought, ignoring the showers that started, stopped and started again. It wasn't as if she could ever have had a future with him. She couldn't exactly see him taking her to a do at the House of Commons – her, sitting between Lord and Lady Lahdeedah, chatting about growing up in London. While they were at debutant balls, she was taking paying customers up to the flat for a couple of bob a time. That'd be a conversation stopper, right there! Pru allowed herself a rueful smile. What would she do if they did get married, sit him next to Crying Micky on the top table and make out he was a friend from the country club?

Pru shook herself and smacked her forehead into her palms. Unbidden, the memory of her and Milly discussing their perfect wedding sprang into her mind. Milly had always wanted a proper church, with peach-coloured confetti, the lot. But Pru had scoffed at that, preferring something extraordinary. A woodland fairy canopy with stars twinkling, that's what she had always longed for, a wedding fit for a forest princess. She twisted the diamond on her finger and gulped back a sob. She wasn't a princess. She wasn't even a businesswoman. She was nothing but an old brass. No wonder Christopher Heritage didn't want to be associated with her; she couldn't blame him, not really.

Pru stood up from the bench and dusted off the small twigs and leaves that dotted her clothes. She took one last lingering look at their bridge and with her head down returned the way she'd come. She didn't look back, didn't see the grey-suited man step from beneath the cloak of the weeping willow, didn't see the expression that swept across his face. A look that some might interpret as regret, wishing that the world were a bit more like gingerbread.

As she walked back to Curzon Street, she decided to try and put him out of her mind for good. She wouldn't go looking for him in the park any more, or attempt to call him. How pathetic was that? No, it was less distressing and far easier to accept that that was it; ties cut, fling over.

It was easy enough to say these words in her head, but so much harder to banish the images and memories that went with them. Pru lay in her bed, exhausted, but sleep would not come. Only days before, she had slept so soundly, within touching distance of Christopher and gently comforted by knowing he was close by. She imagined sleeping like that every night – she couldn't help it. So many of the men at Kenway Road had uttered promises against the rented pillow in the aftermath of sex. Before they headed home to the wife and kids they adored, they would tell her she was beautiful or that they wanted to run away with her. They made a mockery of the shiny gold band that had briefly lain against her naked shoulder or stroked her hair. But she believed none of their promises. Who did they think they were kidding? She had never allowed herself to be taken in, never smudged the line between paying for sex and romance. With Christopher it had been different; she'd believed his sentiments, had wanted to hear his terms of endearment, his promises.

Eventually she fell asleep, but after an hour she woke and sat bolt upright, momentarily confused, not sure where she was. Barcelona? She jolted at the recollection of what had happened. A fresh wave of regret was right there waiting to sweep over her, as it always was.

A few days later, just as Pru was closing up the café and about to make her way upstairs, she noticed a fan of light poking from beneath the kitchen door. She walked in, expecting to find Guy and his sketchbook.

'Oh, Meg! Hello, love. I didn't expect to see you here at this time of the evening.'

Meg froze. She was still slightly wary of Pru after the shouting match the other night. 'Guy said it was okay. I'm just playing a bit, baking stuff.' She wiped her arm first across her face, smudging her nose with flour, and then over the Plum Patisserie apron, which was tight across her stomach. She looked worried that she might be in more trouble.

'Yes, that's fine, of course. You carry on. What are you making?'

'Madeleines. My first batch isn't quite right.' She glanced at the pale sponge offerings that lay abandoned on the counter.

'Let's have a look.' Pru sat on one of the bar stools by the stainless steel central island.

Meg groaned and reached for the wire rack on which sat eight little butter sponges.

'They look pretty good to me.'

Meg shook her head. 'No, the grooves aren't right. They're supposed to be firmer and fan out more – like a scallop shell, it said. And mine don't; they look more like mussels.'

'How do you know about madeleines?' Pru was curious.

'Guy told me about them and he gave me his book.' She held up the laminated cover. He had fixed a typed label to the front: *La Cuisine pour les Débutants*. 'I don't know what it means, but the recipes are good. He's written them all out in English and his handwriting is beautiful.' She tipped the page to show Pru, who smiled at his neat italic script and ordered rows of measurements, weights and cooking times set towards the right of the page. 'I'm working my way through all of them. Guy said it's the best way to learn, to just get stuck in.'

Pru nodded. Guy was right and a good man for entrusting this girl with his own beginner's recipe book. She broke off a corner of sponge and popped it into her mouth, squashing it against her palate before biting into it. 'This is very good, delicious!'

'Oh, you're just saying that.' Meg blushed as she kicked at the tiled floor.

'Meg, there is one thing I will never lie about and that is the quality of anything baked that leaves this kitchen.

245

That's my name above the door and if something isn't good enough, you'd know.'

Meg grinned. 'Really?'

'Yes, really.'

'I like making things and I'm rubbish at everything else.' She instinctively placed her hand on her enormous bump.

'How are you feeling?' Pru was worried. Meg looked tired and ready to burst.

Meg flopped on to the stool on the opposite side of the counter. 'I'm a bit scared actually.'

'What are you scared of?'

Meg considered this. 'Having the baby – everything. And the closer it gets, the more scared I feel.'

'That's understandable. I know this isn't what you planned—'

'Nothing is what I planned, what we planned.' Meg closed her eyes and dropped her head on to her arm, propping it on the table. As she told Pru about how she and William had planned for their baby, choosing paint for the baby's room and picking out names, her eyes misted over. When she got to the part about moving in together to a new house, she stopped and gave a wry little laugh. 'There was always a voice in the back of my mind telling me that it was too good to be true, that I was too lucky. Things like that don't happen to girls like me. Turns out the voice was right.'

'Where are your parents, Meg?'

She snorted. 'They're divorced. My dad's remarried and lives on Canvey Island. I haven't seen him since I was about twelve. And my mum, well, let's just say she hasn't really got room for me in her life.' Meg told Pru how she went into care when they divorced, and about the times her mother had come to visit her. 'She only came twice, but she told me she was saving up to take me on a little holiday. I used to think about it before I fell asleep, planning what we'd do, digging in the sand and eating ice cream. One of the older girls gave me a pair of flip-flops that she'd outgrown; they had little ladybirds on them. I thought they were wonderful. A size too big, but that didn't matter. I never wore them; I was saving them. I'd line them up under my bed every night, so that I'd be able to put them on in the morning, ready to go to the seaside. I thought if I wore them in the garden or around the house, I'd jinx things and wouldn't get to wear them on the sand. Of course she never came and I never got to put them on. But I don't think it was her fault really. She always had a lot going on, things weren't easy for her.'

It saddened Pru to hear Meg forgive her mum so easily, when she didn't sound like she deserved it. But who was she to judge? Many a similar comment had been directed at Alfie. Perhaps this woman too had been waging battles too complex for those on the outside to comprehend.

'Does she know about the baby?'

'I told her, but I haven't seen her. Don't think she's that fussed, to be honest. Mind you, I'd be more shocked if she was!' She let out a long sigh. 'I have to keep busy, Pru, so I don't do too much thinking. I'm worried that if I stop and think, I might go a bit loopy.'

Pru nodded. This she understood only too well.

'Pru, I hope you don't mind me saying this...' Meg chewed her lip. 'But I'm really sorry things didn't work out for you and Christopher. You seemed to really like him.'

Oh, I did that.

'Don't give up on the idea of finding someone. Don't let him put you off. You just have to hang on for the right one. And maybe it is him, maybe he is your one; things might work out for you both, you never know. I've forgiven William. I still get mad at him, but really I've forgiven him, otherwise it'll just make me feel rotten for my whole life and I don't want that. I think you're more likely to find love now you are back in practice, if you get me. Not that I think I'll ever meet anyone, no one will want me.'

Both were silent for a moment, and Pru could see Meg's emotion rising. She changed tack, tapping the mixing bowl with her finger to draw her focus. 'You need a dot more flour. If the mixture was thicker, it would stick to the tin a bit better, and hold its shape. Another minute on your baking time and they will be Plum standard.'

Sixteen

Pru pressed her lips together, trying to blot her over-zealous application of gloss, and ran her tongue over her teeth; she wanted to look her best. She hadn't been able to decide whether to take a little square raspberry and frangipani bun as her offering, or a mini gooseberry meringue. Although she had sworn to herself and to Milly that she would never go looking for him again, she had listened to Meg and knew she had to try one more time. Her stomach churned as she put her left hand inside the pocket of her white linen jacket, partly to hide its tremor but also to wipe her sweaty palm on the fabric. She was nervous. Trying to look casual, she walked with a measured pace until she came to the park. She checked the ribbon on the patisserie box in her right hand. In the end she had opted for a delicate *tarte au citron*, the base of which was the finest, crumbliest sweet shortcrust she could muster. The filling was sharp but fresh, with twirls of lemon zest running through it, and it was covered with a lattice of icing infused with *sirop de citron*.

She approached the curve in the path and looked ahead towards the bridge. As ever, lovers walked arm in arm, strolling along the paths and across the grass, only today she didn't feel they were kindred spirits. Instead, they were to be envied, part of a secret club from which she was barred. It was as if the whole other world that she had only recently learned about was once again locked behind the secret door and even if she had known where to find it, she no longer had a key.

In her imaginings, she and Christopher had arranged to meet, but the truth was that she hovered near their bridge on this busy lunchtime in the vain hope of catching a glimpse of him in his favourite place. She had practised how she would look – surprised but delighted – and had pulled the face a couple of times in the mirror.

Approaching slowly, she scanned the crowds and every time her eyes fell upon a dark suit or a head of grey hair, her heart stuttered. Closer inspection would reveal the man to be an imposter. She took a seat at a spot a little way around the bend but with a perfect view of the bridge to her right. An hour passed before she had to accept that he was not coming, not today. Reluctantly she placed the *tarte au citron* on the bench and left, looking back over her shoulder until the bridge had almost disappeared from view.

Even though he had not been there, she still pictured them finding each other, him laughing, saying, 'There she is,' and the two of them standing close together, sipping coffee and planning their weekend away. Even this false memory, almost a dream, was enough to lift her spirits.

'Hello.' His voice came from behind. She stopped and turned and there he was, two feet away from her, his complexion a little flushed, whether through embarrassment or exertion she couldn't tell. Two dark circles of fatigue sat beneath his eyes. His hair was a little more unkempt than she had seen it.

'I... I brought you a lemon tart.' She pointed to the bench, wondering if it was too late to go and retrieve it.

He nodded; he had seen.

'Shall we sit for a while?' he asked.

She nodded. *Yes! Yes, my love! We will sit for a while and we can make everything good!* She hadn't counted on the rush of desire and warmth she felt at seeing him; it took all of her strength not to jump into his arms.

Pru noted how he walked with his hands in his pockets, awkward. The two of them sat either side of the cake box; it became a barrier and not the gift she had intended.

'I've thought about seeing you, tried to bump into you and now we are here I don't know what to say. I feel quite tongue-tied!' She giggled.

Christopher knitted his hands in his lap and sat, straight-backed, looking ahead. 'How have you been?' His voice was hoarse. She noticed he had lost weight. His cheeks were a little jowlier and his chest smaller; it didn't suit him. Nothing a few good meals wouldn't sort out.

'I've been terrible, actually. Very, very upset and lonely.' She decided not to sugar-coat the truth, no more lying via omission.

He nodded. This was his story too.

'But here we are!' Her voice lifted and her face broke into a smile. 'Open the box! I made it myself. I couldn't decide between—'

'Pru,' he interrupted, still unable to catch her eye, 'this isn't a reconciliation.'

'It's not?' she whispered, unable to keep the edge of sadness and disappointment from her voice.

'No.' On this he was firm, jutting his chin and pulling back his shoulders. 'I've done something terrible and I am sorry. I wanted to see you to say that in person. I am truly sorry.'

Tears slid down the back of her throat. She couldn't find any words. She had thought she was being given a chance and the joy she'd felt at the prospect had filled her completely. Meg's words floated into her head. *'It was too good to be true, I was too lucky. Things like that don't happen to girls like me.'* Pru simply nodded. She understood. He had chosen his career over her and there was very little she could do about it, no matter how much it saddened her.

'I have a team of advisors and… sometimes things are taken out of my hands. Do you understand that?' He looked at her now, his expression doleful.

She shrugged, caring little how his precious career worked, wanting to be alone but at the same time wanting this meeting, possibly their final one, to last as long as possible.

'Why don't you go away for a while, Pru? Take a holiday, get out of town.'

She stared at him, perplexed. Did she repulse him that much that he wanted her gone? Removing the chance for any accidental encounter. He needn't worry; she wouldn't be hanging around his park, not any more.

'I would happily buy you a ticket,' he mumbled.

Pru stood, stole one final glance at the bridge and took a deep breath. 'It's been a long time since anyone has paid for me, Christopher.' With that she turned and walked away without looking back. Her tears finally fell and she let them, whimpering as she made her way back to Curzon Street.

By the time she reached home, Pru had decided that she'd done enough moping. As she hung her linen jacket on its hook, she resolved to turn her humiliation and hurt into fuel that would drive her forward.

'Right, Alfie, enough is enough.' She glanced at the photo on the wall in the basement office. 'I've had a good old think and it's about time I got my arse in gear. So I have decided, no more pining, brooding or thinking about what-ifs. I'm a grown woman with a business to run. And I can't keep apologising, can I? So as of now, I will spend more time with my clients, more time with Guy and I am going to push myself.' Pru stretched and looked at the diamond on her right hand. She didn't need to rely on a man for her success or her happiness.

'And it all begins... with syllabub.' She clapped.

She went into the workroom, fastened her apron around her waist and pulled the cold metal bowl from the giant fridge. She held it under her nose and inhaled the mixture that had been infusing since early that morning.

'Oh, you smell wonderful!' Pru closed her eyes and breathed in the heady sweetness, a combination of brandy, sweet white wine, the juice of a whole lemon and dissolved caster sugar. She fished out a hand-wrapped muslin bundle of spices and a long curl of orange peel and tossed them into the bin. The mixture was ready for stage two. Pru pulled the lid on a fresh carton of double cream and poured

253

the required amount into the bowl, before reaching for her balloon whisk.

She started to whip, moving the mixture slowly yet steadily against the sides of the metal bowl. Then she changed the angle of her wrist and started again, making sure she incorporated the mixture at the bottom of the bowl. Over and over she did this, watching as the cream started to thicken and the mixture bloused under the slow, rhythmical movement. After a while she set the bowl on the counter and, using a fine grater, added the zest of a fresh lemon. Once the pale yellow cream was peppered with its golden flecks, she picked up the whisk and continued.

She observed the pale mixture intently, continually folding and whisking until it began to rise in the bowl. Finally it thickened and gained weight, like a plump pillow beneath her whisk. This was the point at which to stop; just one or two more turns of the hand and the mixture might curdle. She recalled this very thing happening to Monsieur Gilbert and the tirade of blasphemous French that had bounced off the walls as a result. Her mouth twitched at the memory.

Pru spooned the syllabub into fancy cocktail glasses and dotted each one with a generous dollop of *compote de framboises* and a sprinkle of crushed and toasted hazelnuts. She placed the desserts on a tray and climbed the stairs, dropping one off for Milly, who was lying under a mountain of bubbles in the bath.

'Ooh, how lovely, syllabub in the tub! Is there anything nicer!' she garbled, a large spoonful having found its way into her mouth with lightning speed. 'Shut the door on your way out.'

Pru tutted. 'What am I, the waitress? Blimey, I'm going!'

She knocked on Meg's door. 'I brought you pudding!'

'That looks lovely, what it is it?' Meg lay in the middle of the bed; she looked tired.

'It's syllabub.'

'Never heard of it.' She spooned the mixture into her mouth. 'Oh, that's delicious. Kind of winey, with cream, and very citrusy.' She licked her lips. 'Can I taste orange as well as lemon?'

Pru nodded. The girl had a palate on her.

Milly was on the early. Pru, in no hurry to go to bed, where she would be at the mercy of her dreams, wandered around the flat with her syllabub balanced on her palm, resigned to another disrupted night without Bobby – or Christopher. She wondered when this ache for him might disappear. It was one thing to recite the words of detachment in her head, but her heart hadn't quite caught up. The disappointment left a nasty aftertaste to everything she swallowed, even her delicious syllabub. *'A sadness that will sit behind your eyes and fill your mouth with sourness.'*

Seventeen

Pru was up early, sitting in her office, going through invoices when Meg rushed down from the café, clearly flustered, red in the face and flapping her hand, trying to indicate without words what was going on.

'You all right there, Meg?' Pru placed her pen on the desk in front of her and studied Meg, who nodded and rolled her eyes over her left shoulder.

Following in her wake with a determined stride and a thin-lipped expression of disgust was Lady Miriam.

Pru did a double-take; she hadn't scheduled any meetings. 'Ah, Miriam! What a lovely surprise. I wasn't expecting you! Let me get you some coffee.'

She stood up to call for Guy, who was overseeing the creative team in the workroom next door. They were rolling tiny pink sugar-paste roses and hand-shaping the petals which Guy would finish painting later. He had perfected the art of applying shadows and hues to make the flowers look as if the sun was falling against one side of the cake; it was a stunning effect.

Lady Miriam flicked her hair back over her shoulder. 'I don't want coffee, thank you.' Her tone was clipped.

'Oh, right. Well, do take a seat.' Pru indicated Lady Miriam's usual chair and sat down opposite, her hands on the desk. She tried to guess: Bunny was having second thoughts on the colour scheme, or maybe Lady Miriam required an extra tier in response to a sudden rise in her daughter's popularity.

'This is rather delicate, Pru, but I need to discuss this.' Lady Miriam unfolded the red-top newspaper from the top of her leather tote and laid it on the desk. Her eyes shone.

Pru stared, confused. Her eyes scanned the front page, which described a drunken brawl between two footballers' wives and carried several photos of someone she didn't recognise having a glittery frock malfunction on a red carpet.

'I'm sorry, Miriam, I don't quite follow.' She smiled.

With an alacrity bordering on excitement, Miriam flipped to a well-thumbed page and slid the double-page spread across the desk towards her. Pru popped her glasses on her nose and squinted at the black and white picture of a rather leggy woman climbing into the back of a taxi. It took a while for her to recognise the woman as herself.

'Oh!' she giggled, 'that's an old one!' She wondered why they had printed this particular picture of her, which must have been at least twenty years old, taken as she left a function in the West End and revealing a little more thigh than she was usually comfortable with. Pru raised her eyebrow at the headline – *SHE NEEDED THE DOUGH!* – and then started to read. As she raced through the opening paragraphs, her smile faded – *Under a veil of respectability… Catering for Hollywood A-listers… Cakes costing thousands of pounds…* The colour drained from her cheeks. There it was in black and white: the story of her life – a hooker who used her ill-gotten gains to fund the start of the prestigious Plum Patisserie. In each sentence lay a kernel of truth, enough to make challenging or denying it impossible. She felt sick and her legs shook underneath the desk.

Pru gasped for breath. *'I've done something terrible,'* he'd said in the park. She had thought he was referring to breaking her heart. But now it was clear. He had sold her out, told her story before someone else did. She wouldn't have believed it possible.

'This leaves me in a very precarious position.'

Pru looked up at Lady Miriam; she had forgotten she was there.

'I understand.' Pru nodded. Lady Miriam was the least of her worries. She was suddenly overwhelmed by the thought that everyone she had ever known would now have access to this information, stripping her bare, exposing her shame.

'You are without doubt the finest baker in London, if not Europe,' Miriam continued, 'and it's not that *I* will judge you, far from it... But it's what others think and that's what matters.'

Pru stared at her. 'Is it, Miriam? Is that what matters? What others think? What about what you think?'

Lady Miriam put her hand to her chest. 'Well... I...' She was speechless.

'Please excuse me.' Pru walked from the room. She passed Guy and Meg, who had a copy open on the table in the workroom, delivered to them from the café. Everyone at Plum's had now seen it.

Guy caught her arm, stopping her in her tracks. 'I am, as ever, devoted to you, Miss Plum.'

Pru patted his hand where it rested on her arm. Dear, sweet Guy. His words, no matter how genuine, couldn't dilute the sickness that sat in the pit of her stomach.

Milly met her on the stairs, coming in the opposite direction. She spoke with urgency. 'Go up to the flat and stay there. There are a bunch of photographers outside; go upstairs and stay away from the windows.'

Pru took a step up and threw her arms around her cousin. 'Oh shit! I'm sorry.'

'Sorry?' Milly peeled her arms away. 'Don't make me punch you! This is no time for going bloody soft. You never have to say sorry to me. We just need to stick together and make sure that the bad stuff stays on the other side of the door, right?'

Guy stepped into Pru's office, to find Lady Miriam jabbing her finger at a text on the screen of her phone.

'I am sorry, Miss Plum has been called away.'

'I bet she has. I truthfully don't know what to do. I don't want Bunny's fourteenth blighted by association with this!' She rubbed her brow.

'Quite.' Guy's jaw tightened. 'Oh, Megan,' he called through the open door, 'could you please pack the cupcakes for Kensington Palace. I am a little detained with Lady Miriam.'

Meg piped up, 'Yes of course.' Her eyebrows twitched; she hadn't the foggiest idea what he was talking about.

Lady Miriam apparently noticed the rather pale, rough girl for the first time. 'Kensington Palace? What's going on there then?' She dropped her phone to her lap and sat forward in her chair.

Guy placed his splayed fingers against his cheek. 'Nothing! Nothing is going on there. Oh, *mon Dieu*, I should really be more discreet. Please do not say anything to Madame Plum, our clients' confidentiality is of the upmost importance!'

Lady Miriam licked her lips. 'Oh, I wouldn't dream of it.'

Guy bent low, speaking loud enough for Meg to hear. 'We deliver at *least* a batch a week to Kate, although I should probably not share that. Please excuse my indiscretion.' He lowered his eyes.

Lady Miriam sat up in the chair, gripping the arms. 'Really? You do? What colours does she have?' Her mouth hung open in fascination.

'I really couldn't say, it's a closely guarded secret. Besides, Meg handles that particular order. What colour does she favour, Meg?'

Meg didn't flinch. 'She particularly likes the pale pink and white ones, with sparkly glitter on top.'

'Ah!' Lady Miriam clutched at her chest. 'The same colour scheme as *my Bunty's* cake!' She gasped.

'Yes.' Guy nodded. 'Just the same as yours. And can I ask, Lady Miriam, are you planning to cut the cake at the venue?'

She nodded. 'Absolutely. We shall cut it and give slices with a glass of fizz for the toast. Why do you ask?'

Guy paused and looked upwards, as though envisaging the day itself. 'I'm just picturing, wouldn't it be lovely if every little girl got to take home a miniature version of the birthday cake?' He laughed. 'I don't mean an exact replica.' Miriam laughed too. 'I'm thinking a mini-cupcake, like the ones favoured by you-know-who.' Guy tapped the side of his nose. 'But graced with a miniature pastel-pink bloom and a good shot of glitter, and presented in a tiny square box, with a pale pink ribbon, tied just so.'

Lady Miriam stared at the space into which Guy had been looking. 'Yes! That's perfect! Oh, I love it. How much will the cupcakes cost?'

'How many do you need?'

'Let's say two hundred.'

Guy didn't falter. 'They retail at five pounds in store, but I am certain that for that size order, we can come to some arrangement. Maybe throw in the packaging for free?'

'Wonderful! It will be exquisite, won't it?'

Guy gave a small bow. '*Mais oui!*'

Lady Miriam turned to Meg. 'I want them to be absolutely identical to the ones that a certain someone is rather partial to, which of course no one will hear from me.' She mimed zipping her mouth closed and throwing away the key. 'It's perfect!' she repeated as she clapped her hands and stood up. Turning to Guy as she left, she said, 'Thank Pru for me, won't you.'

'But of course.' Guy bowed politely as he escorted her up the stairs and out via the café.

She didn't seem to notice the clutch of hairy men with lenses trained on the shopfront. Guy listened and watched as she pulled out her phone and before she had cleared the step and her foot had touched the pavement, she was speaking in hushed tones. 'Hello? Maudy? It's Mims. I have the most fabulous bit of insider gossip for you! Not a word to anyone, but firstly, you won't believe who I saw today and secondly, guess who takes delivery of a batch of cupcakes every week and guess who knows what colours?'

It was agreed that Pru would stay out of sight, away from the shop, café and workroom, letting Milly, Guy and the team handle things until the storm had blown over. Pru didn't like the idea of being idle upstairs, confined to the flat, but she had little choice. Milly tried to cheer her up by making their favourite supper – extra-strong cheddar cheese melted on to thick granary toast with thin slices of tomato gracing the top, accompanied by huge mugs of tea, all of which was balanced on their knees and the arms of their chairs. They had spent their entire childhood eating every meal, no matter how meagre, sitting up at the table with its thick beige table protector and patched cotton tablecloth over the top. The parlour had always been cold and in shadow, even at the height of summer, and its drabness had made the food less enjoyable. To eat like this, even after all these years, felt warm and comforting. It wasn't quite enough to soothe Pru's fears of what would happen to Plum's, but Milly and Meg were also doing their best to be friendly towards each other and keep the conversation light.

'I was looking at myself in my bra and pants today.' Milly broke the silence.

'That's nice, Mills.' Pru put her cheese on toast back on the plate. Her appetite, already meagre, had suddenly vanished.

'No, it wasn't nice actually. I remember Nan telling me that if you are very thin, you get a bit wrinkly. You can't have it all, she'd say; you are either a grape or a raisin.

Well, I always liked being a raisin, until now. I'm wondering if it's too late to become a grape.'

'What are you on about? You sure it's just tea in that mug?' Pru raised an eyebrow at Meg.

'Yep, just tea.' Milly took another sip. 'I suppose I've realised I'm getting old. I'm sixty-five, so I expect a bit of wear and tear, obviously, but I've just been pootling along not thinking too much and today I caught sight of myself in the full-length mirror and I was quite shocked.'

'What did you expect at your age, to be working as Rihanna's body-double?' Pru managed a laugh.

'Of course not, you daft cow, but I thought for a split second I had laddered tights on: my skin's gone droopy, it's horrible!'

Meg shuddered. 'Ooh, don't. I don't want that to happen to me. It's bad enough having stretch marks on my tummy now!' She ran her hand over her bump.

'Oh, Meg love, that's not the worst of it.' Milly shook her head and rolled her eyes. 'I can't tell you how many hours I spend staring into a magnifying mirror with a pair of tweezers. I am waging a war against facial hair and if I pluck one, the next day my enemy has planted two more that I swear weren't there before! It's like they regroup and plan their strategy.'

Meg unconsciously touched her hand to her top lip.

Milly laughed. 'You can look horrified, Meg, but it will creep up on you too. One minute your biggest concern is whether you've enough cleavage showing and is there lipstick on your teeth? The next it's have I tucked in my thermal vest and where have I left my teeth?'

'You're scaring her, Mills!' Pru looked at Meg's appalled expression. 'Ignore her, darling. *I* don't look like I'm wearing laddered tights.'

'Well, let's just hope I'm more like you then!'

The three women giggled their way through the evening's TV, a rubbishy programme about deep-sea fishing. The blanket of misery had been lifted, and Pru went to bed feeling sunnier than she had done in weeks. The thing she had been dreading the most had happened and so, mixed in with the shock at having her past exposed and the concern at what people might think, there was also a sense of relief.

'Oh, Alfie, I can't believe he did that to me. I thought he loved me. I feel stupid; old and stupid. What will people think of me, what will our customers say? I wish I could explain to them the circumstances – not to make excuses, never that, but I'd like to ask them if they'd ever been desperate, ever made a mistake? I can't believe he did it, Alfie, I can't.' Pru buried her face in her pillow and cried until, exhausted, sleep finally washed over her.

Eighteen

With Pru ensconced upstairs, Meg, Guy and Milly opened the shop and ran the bakery. It made a pleasant change for Milly to be so involved, taking the helm. Apart from Milly flicking the V at a rather persistent photographer, they simply ignored the dwindling throng of reporters. Thankfully, the new season of a reality show had just started, which meant that the general public had far more important things to worry about than how a London baker had spent seven years of her youth. Life went on. For Pru, however, it was difficult to relax into her enforced rest. Despite having no reason to rise early, she was up at the crack of dawn, pacing and thinking before most of the city had even stirred.

Downstairs, Milly pottered behind the counter, polishing the glass of the display cabinet and arranging the various plates into neat stacks in order of size. She took pride in keeping the workspace immaculate. A couple of regulars scanned the broadsheets while enjoying their breakfasts. One was sipping his coffee in between bites of his morning pastry, which today was filled with fat apricots and finished with toasted almonds and a generous dusting of icing sugar. Another was devouring her favourite eggs Benedict, served on plump homemade toasted muffins and speckled with freshly ground black pepper that clung to the glossy, butter-coated spinach. This was what Plum Patisserie's customers cared about: good food served in a pleasant environment. On this bright morning, with the sun shining through the window and the coffee machine giving off its rich aroma, how the proprietor had raised the funds to start up seemed of little consequence.

Guy was instructing Meg in how to make a good basic white bread dough. They wore matching Plum Patisserie pinnies and Meg was bent over the workbench, rapt by his demonstration. Guy worked better when he had an audience.

The ingredients were lined up: strong white bread flour, softened butter, yeast, salt, olive oil and water. Guy held the jug of water up to Meg.

'This, chérie, is very important. Dip your fingers in and feel the temperature. The water is not cold, nor hot, it is the same temperature as your fingers, like feeling nothing, okay?'

Meg nodded. 'Like feeling nothing. Okay.'

Guy placed the large china mixing bowl on the counter top and tipped in the flour and the butter. 'Watch, Meg. On one side we put the salt.' He poured a little salt mountain on to the left-hand side of the pile. 'And then on the other side we place the yeast.' He tipped the yeast on the opposite side.

'Why can't you just tip it all in together?'

'Non, non, non!' Guy shook his head. 'The salt will kill the yeast!' This he almost shouted. 'Keep it apart until we have mixed it.'

He took a large metal spoon and gently stirred the

ingredients. 'Now, we add the water that is the right temperature – and we know this, how?'

'Because it feels like nothing, not too hot or too cold!'

'*Exactement!*'

Guy ditched the spoon and, using his fingers, turned the mixture against the bowl, incorporating half of the water. He continued to add the water in small drizzles, working it in with his fingers, gathering the flour from the side of the bowl, until eventually he'd formed a fat blob of dough and the bowl was clean.

'You've still got some water left. Shall I put the rest in?'

Guy shook his head and took the ball of dough from the bowl, placing it in Meg's palms. 'This is what you listen to: the dough. Let it speak to you, it will tell you whether it is too sticky or soggy or dry. It will tell you what it needs. It doesn't matter how many ingredients you have – you listen to your mixture! Okay?'

Meg nodded but looked petrified, far from okay. She wasn't sure what she could learn from listening to her dough.

Guy painted the work surface with olive oil and took the dough from Meg's hands, placing it in the middle.

'You work the mixture between your fingers, use the knuckles of this hand and with the other you pull the other half of the dough towards you, *comme ça*.' He worked quickly, using both his hands in a hypnotic action. 'We then lift the edges over and back to the middle, and turn the dough, before starting again. Do you see?'

Meg nodded, watching the muscles cording in his forearms, fascinated by his skill.

'Find your rhythm, Meg, and once you have, the dough starts to become elastic. And that is when the dough comes to life. As you push it away, it will push back, challenging you. You must not let it win, ever!' Again he shouted. 'Master your dough and it will become your bread!'

Guy flicked his hand over his head like a dancer and held the pose. Meg felt the beginnings of a giggle, but respected him too much to give into it. Besides, he was a master of his craft and she wanted to learn all she could.

An hour later, Meg returned to the covered dough and it had doubled in size! She couldn't believe how exciting that was. But nothing was as wonderful as the finished product that was pulled from the oven later – crisp, golden and shiny, with floury crosses cut into the top. Meg felt her mouth water as she waited for it to cool. The smell was intoxicating.

Guy held the loaf close to her ear and knocked on the bottom. 'Can you hear? It sounds hollow.'

Meg nodded.

'That means it's cooked!'

Milly was called down and presented with slices of warm bread smeared with a hint of good salted butter. She smelled the bread and pushed at it with her finger before placing a chunk on her tongue. 'Oh, Meg! This is really, really good.'

'Guy did most of the work, I only helped a bit.' Meg cracked a big smile as Milly reached for another slice.

Guy looked at his watch and grabbed his coat as he left. '*Merde!* I am late for my zumba!'

'Sounds painful!' Milly whispered.

Meg laughed.

'Fancy a cuppa?' Milly asked.

'Yes please.' Meg nibbled more of the loaf and could have quite easily folded slice after slice into her mouth until it was all gone. 'I can't believe I helped make this. I've never been good at anything and now I'm learning to bake! Thanks to Guy.'

'He's one in a million, more like family.' Milly nodded.

'Well, it's the nicest little family I've ever been a part of.' Meg felt the blush creep over her face. She didn't want to assume she was part of the family; that wasn't quite what she had meant.

'Me too!' Milly sipped her tea. 'Do you not see your mum and dad?'

Meg shook her head and twirled the apron tie between her thumb and finger. 'Nah, not really. But you don't miss what you never had, that's what they say, isn't it?'

'That's what they say, but I don't think it's always true. At least not for me. I miss being a mum and I've missed being a wife; I've never had either, but I still ache for it sometimes. I wonder what it would be like to have a different sort of life, a more conventional life.'

Milly's kindness and honesty chipped away at Meg's stiff upper lip and she found she was crying. 'Sorry, Milly.' She sniffed and wiped her nose on her arm.

'You cry, girl, if you want, that's okay.'

'I'm all right most of the time because I don't think about it, but when I do, it takes me right back. Every night that I was in care I prayed that tomorrow would be the day that she came and got me. I'd get my flip-flops ready just in case she was coming to take me out, but it never happened. I used to invent stories as to why she couldn't make it that particular day, like she'd missed the bus or she'd got the flu. I never gave up on her. I believed that one day she would come for me and she'd take me to the seaside, just like she promised.' Meg used her sleeve to wipe her tears. 'And a couple of years ago, she did turn up and it didn't matter that I was nearly nineteen. When she pitched up, I was over the moon. It meant I hadn't been lying to myself for all those years, I was proved right. It meant she did love me after all.'

'What happened?'

Meg sucked her teeth and took a deep breath. 'She told me she was going to open a B&B in Margate and asked me if I wanted to go with her. I didn't have to think about it, I was so excited. I'd saved eight hundred quid from working at The Savoy and I drew it out of my savings account, thought it would be a nice little start for us. We got to Victoria Station and were looking to see what coach went to Margate. She said we'd have to see how much the tickets were, and when I told her about the money, her face lit up. I thought it was because she could see a future for us. She told me she'd go and sort the tickets. She took my bag – my phone was in there, my purse, all my savings, everything – and left me sitting on a little plastic seat.'

Meg threw a little half-smile at Milly, who was already dreading how the story would end.

'I wondered where she had got to. I thought there might be a queue and so I waited and I waited. After an hour or so, I think I knew she wasn't coming back, but I didn't want to believe it, so I made up more excuses for her. Maybe she really had been taken ill or had got lost. But deep down I knew. I knew she'd lied to me; it was all about her on the make, seeing what she could get. I fell for it because I wanted to believe her. I haven't seen her since then.'

'I'm so sorry, Meg.' Milly reached out and gave Meg's hand a sympathetic squeeze. 'You've really not had it easy, have you?'

Meg gulped and stared up at the ceiling, trying hard not to open the floodgates again.

'Someone told me once,' Milly continued, 'that there are only two ways to be a parent: you either learn from your own mum and dad and copy them or you learn from your own mum and dad and do it differently. But I imagine it's a whole lot more complicated than that.'

'Bill used to say that we'd figure it out as we went along,' Meg said, her voice quivering. 'I never thought about how I was going to be as a mum, because I thought with him as a dad, this baby couldn't really go wrong.'

'I think you're going to do a great job.' Milly patted Meg's arm. 'You're already taking such care of the baby and it's not even born yet.'

Meg looked up at her. 'You're right. My mum never made me feel safe. Never. I don't want my little one to ever feel like that.' Her lip trembled and her tears fell again.

Milly put her arm across Meg's shoulders and held her tight.

Pru was going a little stir-crazy. Normally she enjoyed the odd day when she didn't venture outside, when she'd laze around wearing her pyjamas and watching TV or pottering in her bedroom. But being told she couldn't go outside meant she instantly wanted to. She flung open the double doors of the French windows in her bedroom and stood at the Juliet balcony looking down over Curzon Street.

'I can't see any photographers, Alfie. Do you think I'm out of the woods?'

Evening was biting on the day. The lights from the restaurants and bars were blazing, inviting passers-by to step inside. Marco the Italian chef, who worked in Shepherd Market, stood in the alley wearing his chef whites and blue dogtooth-check trousers. In his right hand he held a cigarette, gesticulating wildly with it as he shouted in Italian into his mobile phone. She couldn't tell from his tone if he was arguing or chatting. A tall Asian man was counting bank notes as he tucked them into his wallet, concentrating as if his life depended on it. A cab crawled past with its hire light giving off the distinctive orange glow, hugging the kerb, eager to pick up the customers that spilled from pubs and offices. The cinema hoarding stood out, the word 'Blockbuster' written larger than any other. A skeletal-looking girl with white-blonde hair that skimmed her waist tottered on towering heels. She wore oversized sunglasses despite the encroaching darkness and held a designer bag under her arm, out of which poked the head of a dog so small it looked like a prop.

Pru watched the lives unfolding on the street below her, wondering how many of them had dark secrets lurking in their past, tales and predilections that they would take to their grave. Not her; no such luxury. The whole world knew her business, and she felt bruised by the revelations.

The next day, Meg was working in the café when Milly popped up from the kitchen. The two of them stood behind the counter.

'Sorry for going all teary on you yesterday, Milly. I think it must be my hormones. How's Pru? I was going to pop in and see her last night, but I didn't want to disturb her and it was a bit late.'

'She's doing okay. Bored stupid, but a couple of days of resting and hiding won't hurt her. It's nice to have her out of my hair!' Milly laughed.

Meg hesitated and looked at Milly. 'I feel so sad that she went through those things I read about. Sad that she had to, but I understand why.'

'It was a very long time ago.' Milly gave a small sigh.

'I wanted to ask you, Milly, did you... were you...?'

'Was I on the game too?'

Meg nodded.

'I didn't know what was going on for a long time. I was naive; we both were. We moved in with an amazing girl called Trudy; she'd had a bit of a life, to put it mildly. Pru twigged long before I did how she made her money. She saw it as the answer to our dreams, a way to get the cash we needed. By the time I found out, Pru was already making good money and that was that, the path was set. I'm only a year younger than her, but she's always felt responsible for me.' Milly smiled at the truth of that. 'She didn't want me to follow the same path, but I didn't want her to be the

273

only one going through that; I wanted us to be equal, in everything. So I got a couple of clients and did what I did.'

'Oh, Milly, I don't know what to say. I feel sorry for you both.'

Milly stuck out her chin. 'It was hard, yes. Horrible, in fact. Scary. Disgusting sometimes. There's a reason neither of us have ended up married.' She sighed. 'But no one forced us. We made the decision – Pru made the decision – and we saw it as a price worth paying.' She stood a little straighter. 'And now we've got this amazing life. For two poorly educated girls from Bow, that was probably the only way we could have done it back then. When it comes down to it, I don't think I'd change a thing, not really. Except for losing Bobby, of course. I'd give anything to have her here.' She swallowed.

Meg nodded guiltily, all too aware that she was only there because Bobby wasn't. 'What happened to Trudy? Is she still in London?'

Milly shook her head. 'No. Trudy fell in love with an American who was over here on business. His name was Frank. He was a short, bald New Yorker, a salesman. Lovely man. They made an unlikely couple but he adored her, treated her like a queen. She packed up the flat in Kenway Road and went back to the States with him, to Florida. It was as if she knew she wasn't coming back; she gave nearly everything away. She gave Pru her beautiful kimono and me a silver hair brush and comb, which I still treasure.'

Milly and Pru went to Heathrow to say goodbye, and the memory would stay with Milly for a long time. Even now she could picture the two of them: Frank barely reaching

Trudy's shoulder as they stood together in Departures, and Trudy draped in a silver faux-fur collar, despite the clement weather. Frank went off to the loo, leaving the three old friends alone to say goodbye.

'Look at you, Mrs Big Shot in her Chanel jacket!' Trudy had said, playfully hitting Pru on the arm with her gloves. 'Quite a turnaround for those two little match girls who pitched up at Kenway Road all those years ago.'

'We've had funny old lives, haven't we?' Milly reflected.

Trudy nodded. 'Yes we have and I've a feeling mine is going to get a whole lot funnier. I mean, Florida, it's hardly Paris!'

Pru rolled her eyes affectionately. 'You'll have a ball, course you will.'

'I don't know about that, but right now I could do with a smoke!' Trudy dug into her clutch bag and pulled out an empty cigarette holder. 'I shall hold this for comfort.' She removed her passport and opened it at the back. 'What do you think, you two, is it a good likeness?'

They both squinted and read the name: *David Parkes.* 'It's not bad.' Milly smiled at the photo, remembering the certificate she had spotted in the hallway of Trudy's flat that first day, and Trudy's oblique comment about a brother who'd 'died' a couple of years earlier. In all the years since, they'd never discussed Trudy's past, and Milly and Pru were both immensely touched by this parting gift of their friend's most precious secret.

'You are an amazing woman,' Pru said, 'and I owe you so much.'

'We both do,' Milly added.

'Oh for God's sake, don't start with all that, you'll set me off and I don't want this foundation smudged. I intend to arrive in Florida looking absolutely immaculate.'

'You always do.' Pru was sincere.

'Smoke and mirrors, love. Smoke and mirrors.' Trudy laughed.

Frank reappeared and took Trudy by the arm. As they walked towards the gate, Trudy looked back over her shoulder. She gave her friends one of her legendary winks. 'I love you, Prudence and Millicent Plum! Bakers of the best bloody bread and cakes in London!' she shouted as she waved over the heads of the fascinated crowd.

Pru nodded and held Milly's hand. They were unable to reply, their throats too clogged with emotion.

'Did she not come back then?' Meg's question drew Milly back to the present.

'To London? No, no she didn't. For six months she was happy. For the first time in her whole life, I think, she was happy. But then she got sick. Those bloody little cigars that she was never without finally did their job.' She paused to remember their formidable mate. She had passed away in her adopted Florida well over a decade ago, with her beloved Frank by her side. 'Her cancer spread quickly and she died just before her sixtieth birthday.'

The jingle of the café door opening roused them. A man entered, weighed down by a black satchel, a briefcase and a holdall. He hovered. It was clearly his first time at Plum's.

Meg walked forward. 'Good morning, sir. Table for one?'

'Yes.' He nodded and followed her to a quiet table in the window.

He spread his bags around his feet, making it nearly impossible for anyone to pass between the tables. Meg said nothing; it was quiet and the man would probably be on his way before the lunchtime crowd descended.

'What can I get you today?' she delivered with her biggest smile, remembering that everyone should be made to feel comfortable.

'Coffee, I think.' He smiled back.

She used her pen to indicate the list on the blackboard behind the counter, which started with French roast breakfast blend and ended with a decaffeinated frappé.

'I'll take a normal flat white with two sugars.'

'Coming right up!' She nodded and turned to head for the kitchen.

The man spied Milly behind the counter. 'Phew, been a manic morning!' He raised his eyebrows in her direction.

'Well, a nice cup of coffee should put you right.'

He leant forward. 'Are you one of the Plum sisters?'

Milly's instinct kicked in – a journalist or a pap. Either way, she wanted him gone. 'No, I don't have a sister.'

'Millicent, isn't it?'

'Well, if you know, why are you asking?' she snapped.

'I just want to talk to you. I can make it worth your while, or if that's not of interest, it's a good opportunity for you to set the record straight, put your side of the story.'

Meg approached with the coffee to see Milly standing beside the man's table, her hands on her hips. 'I have nothing to say to you and would like you to leave now.'

'I think I'll have my coffee first.' He smirked, drumming his fingers on the table.

Meg set the coffee on the counter and walked over. She bent low behind the man and spoke into his ear. 'Did you threaten me when you came in?'

'What? No! Of course not!'

'I think you did. Me! A pregnant woman! How dare you!'

'I hardly said a word to you!' He looked at her as if she was nuts.

'There you go, threatening me again. What kind of man does that to a vulnerable girl! Did you hear him, Milly?'

Milly nodded. 'Loud and clear.'

'I think I better take your name and who you work for. I'm not letting this drop!' Meg rubbed at her stomach. 'I don't feel too good; your words have upset me. Now, if I were you, I'd fuck off before I call the police and take things further.'

The man pushed his seat away from the table and gathered his bags. He left rather quickly.

Milly stared at Meg. 'Where did that come from?'

'You don't grow up in care and not learn a thing or two.' She grinned at Milly, who was still shaking her head. 'I do feel a bit wobbly though.' Meg slumped on to the chair the man had vacated.

'Are you okay?'

'Yes, I just feel a bit sick.'

'You'd make a crap henchman, coming on heavy one minute and then feeling sick straight after! You're going to need to practice.'

They both laughed. It was only ten o'clock and they'd already had quite a morning.

*

Pru did as she had done with regularity: tuned in to watch Christopher on the screen. She brushed her hair and spritzed herself with perfume; ridiculous that she should want to look her best, but she did. Sitting in a ladylike pose, with a file on her lap awaiting her attention, she picked up the remote control and perused the channels. And there he was, Christopher. His face loomed large on the screen and his name and title were written in the bottom right-hand corner: *Sir Christopher Heritage, Chief Whip*.

Pru watched as he smoothed his hair and gave a small cough into his bunched-up fist. Even the sight of him had the power to make her heart flutter and her stomach contract; she had forgotten how he made her feel. She felt a wave of sadness wash over her, mingling with fury at his betrayal. The weeks she had spent in his company had been the happiest she had known and to see him was like reopening an old wound. No matter how much it hurt, she was unable to turn the TV off, or change channels.

She listened to his voice and wished that things could have been different; she wished she was heading to the park or popping the kettle on, waiting for him to come home.

'You all right, girl?' Milly asked.

Pru looked up. She hadn't heard her enter and didn't have time to swipe the tears from her cheeks or change her expression. She nodded at her hands folded in her lap. 'I'm fine.'

Later that evening Pru stood by the open window in her bedroom and scrolled through the contacts in her mobile phone. She stopped at the initials CM and pressed the number.

He answered almost immediately. The sound of his voice set her teeth on edge and made the little hairs on her neck stand up, but her hand remained uncharacteristically steady, something she could not have envisaged even just a few weeks ago.

Crying Micky snorted down the line. 'Well, well, well, if it isn't the elusive Miss Plum! I am honoured to be in receipt of a phone call. You're lucky to have caught me, just back from a little trip overseas, stocking up you might say. Seen sense have we?' He followed this with his irritating nasal laugh.

Pru dipped into her memory bank and pulled out the voice of her youth, the one she'd used before Trudy had so patiently coached her in how to 'talk proper', as Milly called it.

'Hello, Micky. Yes, I have "seen sense", as you put it.'

'I'm glad to hear it. I thought that little display of defiance went on longer than was necessary. You could have saved us both the bother and rolled over sooner, if you'll excuse the pun. You've got my account details, I expect to see a payment within the next twenty-four hours or there will be repercussions.'

'What kind of repercussions?'

'You need me to spell it out for you?'

'I do,' she whispered.

'Well for a start that shopfront ain't going to look too pretty with a dirty great lump of concrete sticking out of the window and a few choice words sprayed here and there. Might make your stuck-up punters ask a few questions, do you get me?'

Pru sighed loudly. 'Oh yes, Micky, I get you. Or should I say, I've got you – this whole conversation – recorded, just in case. I don't think extortion and blackmail are looked on very favourably.'

'You can't scare me, you fucking old bike.'

'No, and you can't scare me any more. I have stopped your payments and I shall pass this recording on to a close friend of mine. I shall tell him to do nothing yet, but to store it away for safekeeping. But if you contact me or any member of my family again then it will go straight to the police and I mean it.'

'Is that right? You think you're so clever! I'll go to the press – sod the money, I'll do it just so your customers know what you are! I'll bring you down.'

Pru looked around her bedroom. Her eyes lingered on the photos of the people that she loved, the people that mattered, and on the stunning bouquet from Lady Miriam with her handwritten note of thanks for having made Bunny's birthday so perfect.

'You do that, Micky! Although I think you'll find no one is really that interested. You're about four days and a few hundred thousand copies too late.' She pressed the button with her now trembling finger, ending the call. Then she wiped the sweat from her top lip, took several deep breaths and smiled at her reflection in the dressing-table mirror: she wouldn't have the first clue how to record a telephone call.

For the first time in an age, Pru fell into a deep, worry-free sleep. Her phone shattered the peace in the early hours.

'What's up, love, are you okay?' Pru spoke through the

fog of sleep; a quick glance at her alarm clock told her it was three in the morning.

Meg's voice came in short, breathless bursts. 'Oh God, Pru! I think I'm having the baby! I've just had this watery stuff come out all over the kitchen floor and I've got waves of pain. I don't know what to do!'

Pru sat bolt upright and closed her eyes. 'Well the first thing is to keep calm. It will all be okay.'

'It will all be okay!' Meg repeated for her own benefit.

'That's my girl. Now listen to me very carefully, Meg.'

'I don't want to listen to you very carefully!' Meg shouted. 'Can't you just come here?'

'Remember about keeping calm?'

'Yes,' she squeaked.

'Good. Now here's the thing. I've been sick all night. I've got a terrible bug and I can't risk giving that to you or the baby; that would be dreadful. You'll have go to the hospital with Milly. I'll call you a cab and the two of you go downstairs.'

'What? No way! I'd rather go with you. Please, Pru!'

'It'll be fine. Just make sure you keep warm and stay calm.'

'Oh God! I'm really scared. Can't you just not breathe on me or something? Please.' Meg's breath was fast and nervous. She and Milly had started to break down barriers over the last day or so, it was true, and they might even have laid the kindling for a friendship, but the way Milly had treated her originally was still fresh in her mind. She wanted Pru by her side.

'You have to keep calm, Meg. I'm sending Milly up now.' She clicked off the call and looked at the photograph of

Alfie. 'Don't look at me like that!' she protested, then hurried along to Milly's bedroom.

'Mills?' she hissed into the darkness.

'What? What time is it?' Milly clicked on her bedside lamp.

'It's three o'clock. Listen to me, I've got a terrible bug, I've been sick all night.'

'Well I don't bloody want it!' Milly sat up in bed and shooed her away. 'Get out!'

Pru held a flannel over her face. 'Here's the thing, Mills. Meg has gone into labour and you need to take her to the hospital. I would go myself, but I can't risk giving this to her and the baby.'

'Are you kidding me? You want me to go?' Milly shook her head, casting around for her slippers.

'Yes and hurry! She's upstairs and starting to panic. I'll call you a cab and it will all be fine. Just trust me on this, all right?'

'Last time you said that to me it was when you were trying to make me jump over the chicken coop with a pair of pants over my eyes as a blindfold. You said it'd be fine and I ended up with eight stitches in my leg.'

'I was nine, for God's sake!'

'You were a silly cow then.'

'And you were a daft moo. Still are,' Pru whispered back as she crept from Milly's bedroom.

Fifteen minutes later Pru stood in her dressing gown with her ear pressed to her front door. She heard the two of them descending the stairs.

'Careful now, watch your step,' Milly coaxed.

'Have you got my bag?' Meg asked.

'Yep, don't worry about a thing. I've got your bag right here. You're going to be just fine.'

Pru smiled into her cup of tea, nibbled her toast and honey and closed her eyes. Special bonds sometimes had to be nurtured.

Nineteen

Pru donned her sunglasses and then removed them, deciding they made her far more conspicuous at this time in the morning. She glanced up and down Curzon Street: no one stood out and she couldn't see any lenses pointing in her direction. She calmly hailed a cab and jumped in, her first public outing since the story had broken.

It was with a twist to her stomach that Pru walked the corridor of St Thomas's, remembering all too vividly the last time she had been inside the building on that dreadful night a couple of months ago. In truth, it felt like a lifetime ago. God only knew how it would make Meg feel being under this roof again.

She rode the lift to the sixth floor and took a deep breath before the lift doors opened. She sometimes felt almost guilty in the company of women who were mothers, as if she hadn't quite fulfilled her purpose. At the age of twenty, she'd felt the slight stir of panic at the fact she was still single. By thirty, with the constant haranguing of her mother echoing in her ears, that slight swell had become a mini tornado, the swirl of which made sleep impossible and fuelled bad dreams. In her forties, it had been quashed, coming full circle, replaced by a calm acceptance. But still it had the power to overwhelm her with a jealousy so acute it could make her weep. Christopher had been right, you did actually miss them the most in your later years, when you had time on your hands and were able to draw up a list of regrets, successes and maybes. Pru knew that for her list of regrets she would require at least one extra sheet of paper.

She wandered past couples sitting with heads close together, staring at their tightly wrapped pink-faced new arrivals as if in a bubble, looking bewildered and ecstatic in equal measure. As directed by the smiley nurse, she stopped at the foot of the bed at the far end of the ward. Her heart lifted with joy. Meg lay against the pillows and slept. She looked pale and tired, but peaceful. Milly sat in the tall green vinyl wingback chair to the side of the bed. In her arms lay a little bundle from which poked a tiny arm and fingers coiled into a fist that punched the air. Milly kissed the miniature fingers and smoothed the fine covering of hair on the baby's head. 'Sssssh,' she cooed, even though the baby hadn't made a sound.

Pru crept forward and bent down, hovering by the side of the chair. Milly didn't take her eyes off the baby. 'Hello there, Aunty Pru. Meet Lucas William.'

Pru looked at the crumpled face and squashed nose of the little boy who slept in her cousin's arms.

'Isn't he absolutely beautiful?'

Pru nodded. 'Yes, he really is. Are you okay?'

'I am. Meg was amazing.'

'Was she?' Pru choked back the tears that threatened to spill. She wished she had been there to witness it all.

'She was. She was frightened, we both were, it was really

scary. But they talked us through everything and she kept calm. Little Lucas couldn't make up his mind whether he was coming or not, so things kept slowing down and then speeding up and then they slowed and finally it was a sprint finish! It's been the most amazing night of my life. I'm exhausted and ecstatic all at the same time. I've laughed and cried and, most amazing of all, I got to see this little fella arriving in the world!'

'You are very lucky, that's a rare thing.'

'It is that, mate.' Milly continued to talk quickly, partly through excitement and partly because she was running on nervous energy. 'It got pretty terrifying at times and I wasn't even at the business end, if you get my drift.'

'I get your drift, Mills.'

'What you and Bobby had was special, Pru. I guess I was a bit jealous. You were her mum and I was always her aunty.' Milly looked Pru straight in the eye. 'I can see that now and it's okay.'

Pru was unable to speak, storing away the sweetest words she had ever heard.

'And you know, Pru, last night, seeing Lucas arrive, it's kind of put things into perspective. It's what life is, isn't it? Being born and then dying, with a chunk in between that you have to make the best of, because that's all we've got, isn't it?'

'Pretty much, love. Yes.'

'Oh, you brought muffins!' Milly licked her lips at the sight of the wicker basket full of little white-chocolate muffins, artfully stacked, with blue ribbons streaming from the handle. 'They look gorgeous, what a great idea.'

'I'm sure Meg'll love them, won't she?' Pru felt a pang of sadness for her darling Bobby, remembering how she'd practically demanded just such a basket of muffins for her own baby... Henry, that was it.

'Meg was very calm. Even when it got bad, she was incredible. A real trouper!'

'I couldn't have done it without you, Milly,' Meg piped up from the bed.

'Hey, she's awake!'

Pru bent over and gave her a hug. 'I am really proud of you, Meg. I'm really proud of you both.'

'Do you want to cuddle him?' Milly held Lucas up.

'Is that all right?' She checked with Meg.

'Don't be daft, course it is!'

Gingerly Pru took the baby into her arms. It felt wonderful. It didn't matter that her childbearing days were behind her; her pulse raced and her womb pulsed as she nuzzled him close to her skin, inhaling the gorgeous scent of him. 'Hello, Lucas, hello darling!'

He made a small mewling noise.

'He's due a feed actually.' Milly looked at her watch.

Pru handed him to his mum and watched, fascinated as he latched on and started to guzzle. 'Look at you, you're an absolute natural.'

'I'm not so sure about that. I'm shit scared actually.'

'I'm sure it's the same for everyone in this room. It's just that some are better at hiding it than others.'

'I've been lying here feeling quite sad. I mean, happy, obviously, that I've got Lucas. But I feel a bit like I've let him down already.'

'Well of course you haven't, he's only just arrived!' Milly shook her head.

'I know, but I keep looking at all the other babies, who are lying there with mums and dads and already I've short-changed him, haven't I? He's only got me.'

'No, he's got us!' Pru insisted. 'You're not on your own, Meg.'

'I want to thank you, Pru, for everything. You've been amazing to me and you didn't have to be. I don't know what we'd have done without you, I really don't.'

Milly sat down on the edge of Meg's bed. 'I was thinking we could turn the little room into a nursery. We could paint it and get him nice things. I'd love that. I can help you!'

Pru turned to her cousin. 'I don't think I have ever been more proud of you than I am at this very moment. You are wonderful.'

Milly grinned and rubbed Pru's back. 'You look good, Pru. How's your bug?'

'What bug?'

'I thought as much!' Milly shook her head.

'It's funny how things work out, isn't it, Pru?' Meg smiled at Lucas, who was starting to look a little sleepy. 'Who'd have thought we'd have ended up here, hey, mate?'

'Life is never what you plan, trust me.' Pru blinked away the image of waking up with Christopher watching over her.

'I wish…' Meg stuttered.

'You wish what, Meg?' Pru asked.

'I wish Bill was here and I wish Lucas had someone he was related to – apart from you two of course.' She beamed.

'But a proper blood relative like me. It's what I wanted all those years when I was in foster care, someone who had my blood in their veins. I know it sounds stupid, but when you haven't got it, it becomes important.'

Pru breathed in the cool evening air as she scrolled through the contacts in her phone, locating not Isabel's number but Christopher's. Her finger hovered over it. She had the perfect excuse for making contact. But then she thought better of it; why sprinkle salt on her wound? Hearing his off-hand tone and cool, staccato delivery would only make her feel worse and she was in no mood to forgive him.

She sighed, rattling the phone in her hand, half hoping it would tumble out of her palm and shatter on the pavement below. She didn't really want to have this conversation. Pru stared at the keypad, trying to find the courage, unsure how to start. She shuddered at the thought that Christopher might have shared her story with Isabel; God only knows what she would have made of that. She drew her shoulders back and took a deep breath. This wasn't about her, it was about Meg and Lucas.

Pru pushed the call button and closed her eyes. It was picked up instantly. The voice at the other end sounded old and croaky. It was the kind of voice a pantomime witch might have, or a feared old crone; nothing about her tone or manner suggested it was the same woman who had chatted to Pru over the scrubbed kitchen table some three months earlier. That woman had been excited about her future, clapping as she held court and so energised that she practically sang. Pru had been intimidated and irritated in equal measure by her vitality and energy, and had laughed at her preoccupation with wedding bows and centrepieces. This woman sounded broken, unrecognisable. She had hoped that she might have healed a little since the funeral, but that didn't appear to be the case.

'Isabel? Hello, it's Pru here, Bobby's aunt.' Pru closed her eyes. *Am I still Bobby's aunt? How I miss her.*

'Hello, Pru.' She sounded flat and unsurprised to be hearing from her, as if nothing could surprise or interest her ever again, not now that the very worst had happened.

'How are you?' Pru cringed. It was a question she asked automatically, but she knew how Isabel was and to make her search for the words felt cruel.

'I'm, you know…' Isabel offered.

Yes, Pru did know, which was precisely why she had shied away from calling before. She preferred to write a card and then a letter, penned from the safe distance of her office desk. It felt easier to write down what would otherwise have stuttered in her throat. Easier or more cowardly, she suddenly wasn't so sure.

'I am so sorry to disturb you, Isabel.' She paused, giving Isabel the chance to say, 'That's okay' or, 'You are not disturbing me'. She offered neither. 'This is a very difficult conversation to start and I would come and see you and talk to you in person. But, well, here it is—'

'What's happened? Is it Christopher?' Her voice was again level, almost as if she expected something bad to befall her last bastion of support.

'No! No, not Christopher.' Pru paused, wishing that she *were* the person closest to him, the one that would call in

291

an emergency, but quickly quashed the happy flicker at Isabel even thinking she might be. 'There's no easy way to tell you this and please forgive my being blunt, but as I said, I don't really know where to begin.'

'Go on.' Isabel sounded uninterested and slightly impatient.

'Just after William died, I met a young girl called Meg...'

Pru closed her eyes and told Isabel the full story, trying to make the situation sound positive, choosing words that painted William as hapless rather than duplicitous. She paused only when Isabel's sob broke her rhythm.

'And is she saying it is William's?'

'Yes. It is William's. She gave birth a few hours ago to a little boy who she called Lucas William, your grandson.'

'What utter rubbish! The girl is obviously after something, although what she thinks she can get out of it, God only knows!'

'I understand why you might think that, but I can assure you it's not the case. Meg is genuine and she has given birth to your grandson. I've seen photos of her and William, and letters.'

Her revelation was met by silence.

'I thought I should call you to let you know of his existence, and to tell you that he will be here with us in Curzon Street, if you would like to come and meet him. You would of course be made very welcome. I know it's an awful lot to take in, but it would be lovely to see you.'

'Why are *you* involved with this girl? I don't understand how she is connected to you.' Isabel ignored the invite.

'It's a long story. I met her once and stepped in to help

her; she was having a very hard time.'

Isabel made a noise that sounded like 'Hmph', reminding Pru that no one had had as hard a time as she had.

'I can only imagine how this must sound, Isabel, and I know it's a big shock. Believe me, it's not easy being the one giving you this news.'

'It's not news,' she interrupted, 'it's lies. William would not have done that, he wouldn't. He loved Bobby. I know he did. He was so excited about the wedding. We had that party! You were here, it was a perfect day, absolutely perfect.'

'Yes it was. And he did love her and she knew that. But I do believe he also loved Meg and—'

'No. Stop it, Pru! Just stop right there! I don't want to hear any more. It's not true, he's gone and I won't have any grandchildren. That possibility died with my son.' She sobbed. 'To suggest otherwise is very cruel and more than I can bear to consider.'

'But that's just it, Isabel, that possibility didn't die! Lucas is here and he's wonderful, he—'

Pru stopped talking as Isabel clicked the phone into the receiver and was gone.

'He could do with a link to his daddy.' Pru looked skywards. 'Oh, Billy-boy, the things I do for you!'

In the space of just a few days, Lucas, the newest resident of Curzon Street, had become the biggest time sponge Pru had ever encountered. All three women in his life spent hours watching him, bathing him, dressing him up and allowing him to sleep in their willing arms. It had sent all their normal routines into disarray.

So when Pru heard the doorbell ringing early one morning, she was still only half-dressed. She looked out of the window and saw a shiny fat silver Mercedes parked on the double yellows with its hazard lights on. Her heart soared as she recalled the last time someone had called for her at such an early hour, parked illegally and giving her ten minutes in which to get ready. She shoved her dressing gown on over her slip and ran down the stairs, brushing her hair with her fingers as she went.

She opened the door, trying to look casual and alluring at the same time. Her shoulders sank and her smile faded at the sight of Isabel clutching at her handbag and looking close to tears, but she quickly rallied and rushed forward.

'Oh, Isabel, it's so lovely to see you!' She held her arms out to the woman who would have been Bobby's mother-in-law and the two stood in a silent embrace. 'I am so very glad you came.' Pru stood back and held her hand, sincere.

There was a scuffling behind them and Meg appeared with Lucas in her arms.

Pru let go of Isabel's hand and gestured to Meg – slight, pale, pretty Meg, who hovered in her jeans and a floral shirt. 'This is Meg, who I told you about.'

Meg stood shaking, trying to contain all that she had been told and unsure of what to expect. She knew she was a million miles from everything that Bobby had been and was nervous about how she would measure up. 'Hello,' she said, extending her hand. Isabel ignored it and instead pulled her into a hug.

'I've come to see the little boy,' Isabel whispered, hardly daring to believe that it was true.

'Your grandson,' Meg said, lifting the sleepy Lucas up towards his grandma for closer scrutiny. He sighed and mimed feeding in his mother's arms. His little tummy rose and fell and he placed his scrunched fist against his cheek, angelic.

Isabel nodded as tears filled her eyes. 'Yes, my grandson.'

'I was just taking him for his morning stroll in the park. Would you like to come with us?'

Isabel nodded. 'I'd like that very much.'

The next morning, Meg was in the bath as Pru fed Lucas his bottle and watched as he lay with his eyes closed and his milk-filled tum rising and falling in rhythm with his sleep.

'There we go, little man.' She held the empty bottle up to the light. 'You've guzzled that. Won't be long till we get you on steak and chips or one of my lovely cakes, how about that, Lucas?'

His perfect pouty mouth was open and milk dribbled over his dimpled cheek as he smiled through his dream. Pru stroked his face and wondered what someone so new to this world dreamed about. Her stomach ached with love for this little helpless thing, who at that moment was lying with the posture of a drunk, sprawled with arms wide and head lolling against the cushion. A familiar voice broke the lull, and Pru looked up quickly, recognising the outline of the face on the TV screen. It was Christopher, addressing the House in his confident baritone. Pru's tears came quickly, without invitation or consideration. She clutched Lucas against her chest and cried into his sweet-scented scalp.

Pru didn't see Milly standing in the doorway and taking in the scene, a fierce anger burning in her eyes. Neither did she hear her slip out of the flat and jump in a taxi.

'The Palace of Westminster, please. And be quick about it.'

Twenty

It was unseasonably cold for July, but at least the sky was bright blue. Wisps of cloud floated by on a determined breeze and birds circled overhead. It was peaceful, far away from the city and the noise of traffic and people. The grass was well tended, with just the odd patch of gorse poking through. The grey and green landscape was broken up by clumps of wild ox-eye daisies that grew tightly packed in abundance, providing pockets of white and yellow that drew your eye. It was a good place to come and have a think, away from the hustle and bustle and a useful reminder of the fragility of life. Meg liked it there.

The small, simple gravestone stood under a sprawling oak tree. The spot had been chosen deliberately for the sense of protection it offered. Meg used one hand to gather her coat closely around her neck and hesitated before dropping to her knees, not caring about the sap and damp soil that clung to her legs and stained her tights. She didn't care about much as she sank down, staring at the arc of granite before bowing her head. She ran her hand over the simply styled young stone, touching her fingers lightly against the words that were so beautifully inscribed: *Much loved, always missed*. It was perfect.

'I miss you, you know. I miss you every day. I know we didn't get a lifetime together, but what we did have changed my life and you changed me. You were the best thing that ever happened to me. Ever. I want you to know that. I love you. I love you now and I'll love you always.' She swiped at the tears that trickled down her cheeks. The sound of footsteps snapping a branch underfoot made her look up.

Isabel approached and squatted down next to Meg. 'It's a lovely spot, isn't it?' She patted Meg's back.

Meg nodded. 'Yes it is. I'm really glad you chose this place.'

'It brings me peace, coming here.' Isabel gave a small sad sigh.

'I can see why.'

'They're all waiting, if you're ready?'

Meg stood up and brushed the dirt from her coat and palms, then ran her fingers through her hair. 'I'm a bit nervous. How do I look?'

'You look lovely, like the mother of a little boy about to get christened.'

Meg cocked her head. 'Poor little sod. I can't believe you talked me into letting him wear Bill's old christening gown – he looks like a girl!'

'He doesn't! He looks absolutely beautiful.'

'I think you might be a little biased.' Meg laughed. 'It's amazing you arranged all this so quickly!'

Isabel allowed herself a smile. She had thrown herself into organising the christening with almost the same gusto she'd lavished on the engagement party. It had dusted off her old spirit, given her a jolt. She had been relieved to find her old self emerging through the fog of sadness and confusion. She doubted she would ever be free of grieving for William, but Lucas was a wonderful little bonus that she could never have imagined. She turned and flicked her head in the direction of the church. 'See you in there.'

Meg knelt down again, kissed her fingers and touched them against William and Bobby's gravestone. 'I don't 'arf miss you. Especially today. Oh, Bill, if you could see that boy of ours, you'd be so proud. But you're always with us, aren't you, watching over our shoulders. Milly told me that. And I know your dad was always with you, wasn't he, Bobby? Anyway, I've got to go. Wish me luck.'

She turned and walked towards the little church, smiling as she made her way through the heavy door and up the aisle to where Lucas was wriggling in his Aunty Milly's arms. Milly was cooing back at him. Meg's cousin Liam and his flatmate Rocky stood beside them, looking dapper in bow ties and snug suit jackets over their jeans.

The vicar nodded at the little group and began the service. Just as he spoke the words, 'This baptism is recognition of the inherent divinity of this child, and our commitment to love him,' the door creaked and in hurried Pru. She mouthed 'Sorry!', flustered that her meeting had overrun, leaving her transport plans in disarray. She slotted in next to Milly and blew a kiss at Lucas, who was dressed in a rather ornate white lace nightie. He looked beautiful.

After the church ceremony, the little crowd gathered in Isabel's kitchen at Mountfield, sipping champagne and devouring the cakes that Plum Patisserie had created to celebrate the day. There were mini doughnuts filled with crème anglaise and dusted with powdered sugar, individual ginger and rhubarb cheesecakes topped with elaborate baskets of gold sugarwork, and, of course, the christening cake. The large square fruitcake was covered in white royal icing and decorated with piped ropes of icing along the edges. Across the top, in a fine rolling script of the palest blue, was written *Lucas William Fellsley* and in the top right corner there was a single gold star, to represent his daddy.

Milly rocked Lucas on her hip and looked out of the window.

'Hello there, godmother!' Meg approached with a glass of fizz in her hand.

'Ah, hello, we were just having a chat.'

'Oh yeah? What are you chatting about?'

'About my godmotherly duties. The first one being to make sure his mummy doesn't get so pissed that she throws up in the car on the way home – that kind of thing!'

'Ha ha! I've only had one!' Meg raised her glass.

'Sure you have and I'm Madonna.'

'Well, Madonna, when you've quite finished, his bum needs changing.' Meg placed the clean nappy on Milly's head, which she wore like a hat. It made Lucas gurgle.

Rocky and Liam sauntered over. Liam touched his finger to Lucas's cheek. 'All right, little mate?'

'Do you want to hold him?' Milly offered.

'Nah!' Liam took a step backwards. 'I might drop him.'

Milly shrugged. 'Doubtful.'

Rocky stepped forward in his place. 'Is it true that christenings are like weddings, where the best man gets off with the main bridesmaid? So like the godmother and godfather have to get together?'

Milly looked him and Liam up and down: they had a combined age that was still decades younger than hers. 'It most certainly is not!' She smirked, however, despite herself. 'Cheeky sods.'

The boys left the kitchen a bit sharpish, laughing and looking for somewhere they could have a sneaky fag.

Milly tickled Lucas under the chin and thrust the nappy back at Meg. 'I've been meaning to tell you something, Meg.' She hesitated, looked out over the grass. 'I think that you end up with the people in your life that you are supposed to have and I think I'm meant to have you and Lucas in mine. And I'm so sorry for how we started, Meg, truly sorry. I was so messed up over Bobby, but I should never, ever have taken it out on you. I shall regret it, always.'

'Oh shut up, Milly, you're stuck with us now!' Meg pecked her on the cheek.

Pru and Isabel sat side by side at the kitchen table.

'He's a poppet, isn't he?' Pru looked at Isabel, who nodded.

'He really is.'

'Does he look like William?' Pru wondered.

William's mother sighed. 'Not identical, but bits of him, yes. His little smile is similar and he's the same type of baby – placid, sweet. William was always like that – until he got to school, and then it was a whole different story!'

'I'm glad,' Pru said. 'I like to think William was a bit naughty, lived a life!'

Isabel gestured to Meg, who was fooling around with the nappy and making a fuss of Lucas. 'I'd say she's evidence enough of that!' She inhaled sharply and sipped her champagne. Then she leant in. 'I want to tell you something, Pru.'

'Fire away!'

'On the day of the engagement party, when people were leaving, I couldn't find William anywhere. Bobby was dancing away, having the time of her life!' Isabel paused at the memory. 'I came into the house and I don't know why, call it instinct, but I went up to William's old room and he was sitting there on the bed. He looked like he had been crying. Apart from when his father died, I hadn't seen him like that since he was a child and it was awkward for us both. I sat next to him on the bed and asked him what was wrong. He was very vague, but he said something that stayed with me.' She drew breath. 'He said he wanted some peace. I put my arm around him and I said to him, "What on earth could be making you so sad on a day like this? Are you missing Dad?" Because to be truthful that's all I could think of, I guess that's because I was missing him too, always do at any function.' Pru saw the flicker across her eyes. You would never have guessed, Isabel, the life and soul.

'But he shook his head and turned towards me. I could smell that he had been drinking, but it was that sort of party, wasn't it? I didn't think much of it. He tried to smile at me, but it was difficult for him, as though he had too much going on in his head. I tried to guess then what the problem might be. I asked him if he had last-minute nerves or felt things were going too fast. I was trying to work out how I could make it better for him.' She paused. 'Again, he shook his head and then he said, "No, Mum, nothing like

302

that, but I've messed up." That's what he said, "I've messed up," and then he said it again, "I just want peace."'

Pru listened, not knowing how to relieve the guilt that dripped from her every word. Isabel continued. 'I didn't know what he meant of course and put it down to the drink talking. I thought maybe he was referring to the overly long two-day party; maybe he was tired, wanted to sleep. Maybe he had something going on at work. I thought all sorts, but never, ever that he had got himself into real trouble. Then when you called, it was as if every word that he had spoken on that night came sharply to my mind. I think this was what he was talking about.'

'Probably, Isabel, but it wouldn't have made any difference. They had an accident and everything else is incidental.'

Isabel shot her a sideways look. 'I know.' She twisted her fingers together. 'But maybe his cluttered head led to that accident, maybe they were fighting? And I keep thinking that if only I'd been there for him, talked to him about what was really bothering him, intervened, he might not have crashed.'

'It doesn't work that way.'

'I know it doesn't, but that won't change how I feel.' Isabel emptied her glass and reached for the bottle. 'For the last couple of months, it's felt like I've been trapped in a black hole and I couldn't see how to climb out. Then Lucas popped up and it's as if he has brought me back to life.' Isabel smiled, warmly this time. 'It's almost as if William left me an amazing gift.'

'That's exactly what he did, he left you an amazing gift.' Pru patted her hand.

'I do wonder if he would have come clean eventually. He'd have had to, wouldn't he? One way or another.'

'Maybe. Who knows.' Pru sipped at her glass.

'Not us, I guess.' Isabel looked at Pru. 'It's a shame Christopher couldn't make it.'

'Yes,' Pru muttered, thinking the exact opposite. She didn't know how she would have faced him in front of all these people.

'I had high hopes for you two, you know.'

'You weren't the only one!' Milly slapped the table with a plate laden with goodies and sat down to join them. 'I thought I'd finally got her off my hands!'

'Well, it just didn't work out.' Pru gave an insincere grin. 'These things often don't.' *Oh, but I wanted it to, I wanted it so badly. I loved him. I love him.*

'I have intentionally avoided the papers, Pru. I think your business should remain just that, and let's face it, who among us hasn't got a few tales rattling around in the back of the wardrobe. I know William certainly would have.' Isabel looked over at Meg and Lucas. Pru gratefully acknowledged her acceptance. 'It's a shame though. You seemed very natural together. He seemed so happy.'

Pru fixed her smile again, trying to remain calm as her pulse raced and her heart ached at the wasted opportunity. Isabel wasn't done. 'He phoned me when you got back from Salcombe and he sounded full of the joys. I hadn't heard him like that before. He said you had "raked the embers of his heart", which was most poetic for an old pragmatist like Christopher. I thought it was quite beautiful.'

'Will you excuse me?' Pru almost ran to the loo, where

she splashed her face with cold water and stared at her reflection. 'You silly moo, Pru, get a grip. You're sixty-six, not sixteen. Hiding in a loo with a broken heart! Come on, girl.' She straightened up, reapplied her lip-gloss and brushed her hair. She wished for the first time that she had never met Christopher. It would have been easier. It was somehow worse to have been shown the prize and then had it snatched out of sight.

As she made her way back along the corridor, she stopped at the sound of a voice she recognised. *Oh dear God, please no, no!* But her God wasn't listening. She looked through the kitchen door and there he was, being introduced to baby Lucas.

'And this is your Great Uncle Christopher!' Isabel scooped up the baby and plonked him in her brother's arms.

'Hello, little fella. How are you doing?' He handled the baby awkwardly, embarrassed to be responsible for him, unsure if he was doing it right.

'I thought you couldn't make it?' Isabel trilled.

'I didn't think I could, but I finished a little earlier than I expected and got my driver to take a detour, so here I am! Just a flying visit, but enough to say hello to Lucas.'

'He's happy to meet his Uncle Chris,' Milly interjected, 'aren't you, darling boy?' She leant in and kissed the baby in Christopher's arms.

'And you must be Meg?' Christopher said.

Meg nodded; quiet, aware that she was being scrutinised.

'He's a lovely boy.' Christopher smoothed Lucas's tufty hair.

'He is usually,' Meg said, 'but today he's been dressed up like a girl!'

Christopher gave his ready laugh. 'Yes, he has rather.'

'I didn't want him to wear that horrible frock, but Isabel insisted. I mean, who in their right mind would put a boy in that?'

'Ah, I'm afraid that would be my mother's fault. This was my christening gown originally.'

'Oh shit, sorry.' Meg grimaced. The champagne had more than loosened her tongue. 'Hey, here's Pru!' she announced over his shoulder.

Christopher turned and the two stared at each other. It was an almost instinctive reflex: his face broke into a smile at the sight of her, which she returned. *'There you are,'* he seemed to be saying. And just for a second it was as if there were just the two of them and they were happy to be in close proximity. Like it had been in Salcombe, lying on the beach, or holding hands across the console of the car.

Lucas squirmed and Christopher turned away to deal with the task in hand, concentrating on not dropping him. 'I think you better have him back, I'm not used to babies!' He laughed.

'Not used to babies, but would have loved to have been a granddad,' Pru murmured. She didn't realise she'd said the words out loud.

Christopher turned to her as Lucas was lifted from his arms. 'That's right.' He smiled. 'Something else for me to lament in my old age.'

'Oh yes, I'm sure. What else will you "lament", as you

306

put it? Telling my story to the world? Betraying my trust?' These last words she whispered.

Christopher stepped forward and gripped her by the top of her arm. 'Come on.' He practically marched her out to the garden. Isabel, Milly and all present watched, the conversation lowered to a hush.

They walked at pace until they reached the edge of the lake, where they had spent that first glorious afternoon. Finally he released her arm and put his hands on his waist inside his suit jacket. 'I tried to explain to you, that day in the park. I told you that it wasn't my doing. There are a team of people that work on damage limitation and it was taken out of my hands.'

'Damage limitation? Listen to yourself, Chris. I'm not one of your political hiccups, a piece of legislation or a debate, I'm a person! A person who has worked very hard her whole life, and your "team" could have taken all that away from me.' She shook her head. 'It might just be a salacious story for people to ogle over breakfast, but it's so much more than that to me, Chris, it's my life! My whole life laid bare!'

'I'm sorry. I'm truly sorry.' He looked out towards the water.

'What exactly are you sorry for? Sorry you hurt me? Sorry we ever met?'

He rounded on her quickly. 'Sorry we ever met? I loved you! I thought we had a future. I was making plans, I—'

'Making plans? Me too. But now I'm making different plans. I'm planning never to let anyone close to me like that again. Not that anyone would ever be interested, because I'm broken, aren't I, Chris? And this is real life, not fucking gingerbread.'

Pru left him by the side of the lake and stalked back to the house. There was nothing more she wanted to say and nothing she wanted to hear. It was done.

Milly nipped out to the driveway and waited by Christopher's chauffeur-driven car. She thought about the last time she had seen him, when she'd managed to get as far as the wide corridor in the Palace of Westminster, all decked out with oil paintings featuring pointy-nosed men sitting next to miserable-looking dogs. Christopher had come out to meet her.

'I just got a call from the front desk. What on earth are you doing here?' He was in full-on pompous work mode, and Milly wasn't having any of it.

'You look like shit, Christopher.'

He rubbed his hand over his face and carried on walking down the ornate corridor, which was tiled in pale greens, blues and gold. Milly had to trot to keep up.

'Milly, lovely as it is to see you, I have a very busy day ahead, which doesn't allow time for listening to how bad you think I look. And the state of my appearance is, incidentally, quite unconnected with how I am actually feeling, which – as anyone will tell you – is fine.'

'Yes, so you say. Pru says the same thing; she says she's fine, but she looks like shit as well, even though I tell her the opposite. She thinks I don't know, but she routinely goes over to the park and leaves you cake parcels on the off chance you might saunter by and pick them up. Now that is nuts. Fine indeed!' She shook her head.

'I really can't discuss this with you, Milly. Did Pru send you?'

'Good God no! She'd kill me if she knew I was here. I'm just worried about you, Chris.'

They had stopped under a carved wooden arch that curved up to the church-like roof. Christopher seemed to be hiding from his colleagues.

'That's kind, but there really is no need.' He had given Milly a brief, false smile and walked back to his office.

She wasn't about to let him get away with that a second time. As he strode across the gravel, she stood squarely in front of the car door.

'Oh no, Milly! Whatever you have to say, I haven't got time to hear it.' He raised his palm.

Milly folded her arms and leant back on the car. As if a raised palm would stop her. 'Well you better make time, mister. I said I was worried about you – and I am. I'm worried that you are making the biggest mistake of your life. You are knocking seventy, you're not twenty and neither is Pru. How much longer do you think you've got on the planet? Ten years? Twenty? That's all, that's it! This ain't no rehearsal and you have to choose very carefully what you do with the time you have left. You were both lonely, then you found each other. And the way she was that night after she came back from meeting you here, down there by the dyed bloody swans...' She pointed towards the lake. 'I have never seen her look that way. Never. I think it's rotten luck for you both that she needs to be punished for something she did over four decades ago, especially as she has been punishing herself ever since. I should know because I

309

punish myself too. But here's how it is: you can't rewrite your past, no matter how much you want to. You can only make sure that the mistakes you made don't define your future; you let yourself live. Otherwise, what's the bloody point? What's the point of any of it?' She threw her arms in the air for added theatricality.

Christopher was speechless. He watched as Milly walked back towards the house. She turned her head and shouted over her shoulder, 'You ain't stupid, Chris. I am trusting you to think things through and come to your bloody senses.' She turned quickly and continued back to Mountfield, praying that Pru hadn't seen her.

Pru hadn't seen anything. All she could think about was the way Christopher had feebly apologised. It wasn't enough; it wasn't nearly enough. Who did he think she was? How could her life and her feelings count for so little? As if she were invisible, or, worse, not worthy of consideration. *Puta*.

Pru sank into the chair at the kitchen table and closed her eyes, wishing she could disappear, wishing she had never come. Mountfield held so many deeply emotional memories. It had the power to strip her to the bone, exposing her for all to see.

Milly walked over and stood behind her cousin. 'Reckon we ought to get going ourselves, eh, girl?'

Pru nodded, grateful that her cousin knew when she needed rescuing, without her having to say a word.

Twenty-One

When Milly strolled into the kitchen mid morning the next day, Pru was dressed ready for action and eating her muesli.

'Blimey, look at you all done up to the nines, where you off to?'

'I'm hardly done up to the nines! I'm off on a little holiday, Mills. I'm getting out of London. I am leaving my phone so I can truly escape. I'm going somewhere I can breathe and eat ice cream and just think about me for a change.'

'Do you want me to come with you?'

'No I don't, thanks. I want to be on my own.'

'Charming.'

'Sit down, Mills.'

She sat. 'Oh God, what have I done now?'

'Nothing!' Pru pulled out a cream envelope and tossed it at her cousin.

'What's this, your last will and testament? Please tell me you've left me your Gucci loafers?'

'Similar. It's the deeds and legal documents that hand everything over to you – the flats, the business, the building, the whole lot. It's yours, just yours.'

Milly stared at her. 'Have you gone loop the loop? What have you gone and done that for?'

311

Pru stood. 'Because, Millicent Plum, I have steered this ship for long enough. I'm going to be a passenger for a while. You can do what you like – grow it, sell it, run it into the ground. It's yours!'

'You are coming back, Pru? You're not going to do anything daft?'

'Course I'm coming back! Of the two of us, I'd like to remind you that it's you who has the reputation for being daft.'

'Point taken.' Milly nodded. 'It's just that you've got that look about you.'

Pru tutted. 'What look? And where else would I end up, you silly moo?'

'I don't know, you daft cow!'

The two women hugged. 'We did it all, Mills, didn't we? We achieved it all.'

Milly squeezed her tight and spoke into her ear. 'We bloody did, girl. We did it all.'

A car beeped from outside and Pru popped her head out of the window. 'That'll be my cab. See you in a bit, Mills. I'll call you.'

'What do you mean, "a bit"? How long is "a bit"?' Milly shouted after her.

'Who knows! A while!' Pru practically skipped down the stairs.

Milly shrugged, walked into the sitting room and switched on the TV. She turned the envelope over in her hand. 'I don't want to steer the bloody ship,' she muttered. 'I'm more of a navigator, not the bloody steerer!'

The voice on the TV announced that it was the last day

of parliamentary business before the summer recess. And there he was – Christopher, large as life on the screen. 'Morning, Chris, you silly old tosser.' Milly lifted her mug towards him.

Meg came into the lounge and plonked Lucas into the nook of Milly's arm. His head rested against her and he started to doze.

'Hello, beautiful little man,' Milly cooed. 'Mummy is making your bot-bot so we can fill up that tum, make you big and strong. You are magic, do you know that? You have made us all so happy, who'd have thought it? Even that Uncle Liam of yours can't keep away, can he?' She kissed his face and Lucas wrinkled his nose in dislike.

'I don't know, Billy-boy,' Milly continued, addressing the ceiling now. In recent days she had taken to conversing with William, telling him about his son and any other bits of news she thought he might find interesting. It was a bit like having an exclusive phone line, she thought, though she never once acknowledged the paradox, after all the times she'd scoffed at Pru's chats with Alfie. 'Things have a funny old way of working out, don't they?'

Lucas fell into a snooze and Milly turned her attention to the television, with the volume turned low.

Chris looked ready to speak. Milly turned the sound up a fraction.

'My lords, ladies and gentlemen of the House, I thank you for this opportunity to address you all today.' He paused. 'It has been suggested to me that if my career at Westminster doesn't work out, I might like to seek employment as a museum guide.' Milly laughed, as did the hundreds of MPs present. 'And today, I welcome the chance to deliver some momentous news. I am not about to seek a role as a museum guide…' The camera panned round to show the faces of the backbenchers, many of whom were muttering behind cupped palms. This was clearly not the speech they had been expecting. Then it zoomed in on Tristram Monroe, Chris's old adversary, who looked bemused. 'But there will be a vacancy for the position of Chief Whip with immediate effect. The Prime Minister has today accepted my resignation. It has been my honour and my joy to serve you all, but after much consideration and with a happy heart, I must tell you that I am indeed resigning.'

Milly sat forward. *Resigning?* There were collective gasps from both sides of the House.

'Pru? Pru?' she yelled. 'Oh tits!' She shouted even louder, remembering that Pru had left.

'And the reason I am resigning is that I am in love!' Everyone present erupted into fits of laughter, followed by thunderous applause, foot stamping and the odd whistle. This had to be a joke.

'Order, order!' The Speaker of the House banged his gavel and tried to make himself heard over the guffaws and titters.

Christopher continued, undeterred. 'Yes, indeed. I am in love with Miss Plum. Who I am hoping is watching, and if she is, she will know where to meet me. She is the purveyor of the finest éclairs this side of Paris. You may have read the intrusive stories about her past in the tabloid press…' A chorus of lewd comments and wolf-whistles echoed from the backbenches at this point. 'But circumstances sometimes force people into making unpalatable choices and no one should have to keep paying for mistakes they have made. This, I am ashamed to admit, is something I have only recently come to realise.'

Finally! thought Milly. *The old sod gets it! At last.*

'I have decided,' Christopher went on, 'that life starts when you let it, whether you are twenty or seventy. I believe it's a state of mind and I am choosing to let this chapter of my life begin, today, right now! I thank you all for your friendship, support and service over the years; it's been a blast. Adieu!'

'Aaaaagh!' Milly screamed. Lucas woke with a start and started crying. 'Oh my God! Meg! Take the baby! I've got to find Pru!'

'What's the matter?' Meg rushed in from the kitchen.

'He's come to his bloody senses, that's what!' Milly whooped with joy and swept from the room.

As he sidled along the crowded bench, Christopher Heritage held his tie flat against his stomach with one hand and returned a series of hearty handshakes with the other. MPs pressed forward to embrace him, kiss him and slap him on the back, pumping his hand as he made his way towards the exit. When the heavy wooden doors eventually slammed behind him, he could hear the cheers and laughter of his colleagues and the faint cry of 'Order!' as the Speaker tried to regain control.

Milly shoved on her slippers and ran down the stairs. She flew out of the front door and looked up and down Curzon Street. Of course, Pru was long gone.

'Shit!' she screeched. Pulling out her phone, she began

scrolling down to 'P' when she remembered with a jolt that Pru had left her phone at home – to 'truly escape'. 'Oh, you daft cow!' she shouted. 'Truly escape? I'll shove it where the sun don't shine when I catch up with you!' She ground her teeth in irritation. 'Oh Christ,' she muttered, 'if she doesn't meet him, she'll blow it! I have to go and find him. Think, Mills, where is their special place?' She closed her eyes and tried to remember. A bike courier whistled at her as he sped by. She tutted in his direction, but the neatly wrapped packages on the back of his bike were the clue she needed.

'The park!' she yelled. 'Please God, let it be the park!'

Milly ran, clutching at her bra-less chest. She ran until she thought her lungs might burst. She ran faster than she'd known she could, dodging pushchairs, tourists and slow-paced lovers en route. She dashed across Piccadilly and sprinted through Green Park, ignoring the whistles and shouts that she seemed to be attracting this morning. Finally she hurried over The Mall and into St James's Park. She made it in a record-breaking fifteen minutes and as she rounded the bend, there it was, the blue bridge. And there Christopher was, nervously waiting.

Milly ran towards him with her arms spread wide. 'Christopher! How lovely! I came as soon as I could! I had no idea you felt this way and when you said you loved Miss Plum, I had to come!'

Milly watched the colour drain from his face. She bent over and laughed until tears gathered and she wheezed for breath. 'Don't look so worried, you silly sod, I came to tell you that Pru has gone!'

His shoulders relaxed. 'Gone where?'

'I don't know, mate, but she said she was going on a little holiday and she wanted to be on her own.'

Christopher shook his head. This was not how he had envisaged his grand plan working out. 'I don't believe it! When is she coming back?'

'I don't know. "A while", whatever that means. She said she'd call, but she hasn't taken her phone and she said she wanted to go somewhere she could breathe and eat ice cream.'

Christopher threw his head back and laughed. 'Milly, you beauty! I know exactly where she is.'

'You're not the first person to call me a beauty this morning – I've had wolf-whistles, the lot. It's quite made my day!'

Christopher took a step closer to her and almost whispered. 'You do know you are wearing a rather short nightdress and nothing else?'

Milly looked down and gulped. 'This is like being in one of those bad dreams when you think you're out in public with no clothes on – only this time it's for real! Help me!'

'Tell you what, Mills, I'll help you, but I need a little help in return.' He smiled and removed his jacket, placing it around her shoulders as they walked through the park to find a cab. 'Nothing to see here!' he shouted. 'Certainly not a lady who forgot to put her clothes on, nothing like that at all!'

Milly turned around and punched him in the stomach. 'You get double if you flinch, that's the rules!'

Pru pulled the little floral curtains and bent down to look out of the deep-set window. The sun was already high over the harbour and boats were busily chugging out of the estuary. The gulls were squawking their timeless greeting and dining on leftovers discarded by the milling tourists. She opened the window and took a deep lungful.

'Beautiful this, isn't it, Alfie? This'll do me good. I was thinking yesterday, on the train down, I'm better off single. I don't think coupledom is for me. Anyway, I've got you to talk to, haven't I? Do you know what, I deserve more than to be judged by someone who doesn't have the first clue what it would have been like to live my life; someone who had a bloody pony! What did I have? A dolly made out of a sock stuffed with straw and two buttons sewn on for eyes. Anyway, my day beckons. Give Bobby my love.'

Pru pulled on her white linen trousers and floaty white top and trod the wooden stairs that twisted down to the bar. There was a creak to nearly half of them; she smiled and placed one hand on her chest, trying to calm her leaping heart.

'Morning, Pru – or should I say, good afternoon! How did you sleep?'

'Like a log, Liz. I just zonked out. I can't believe it's midday already, what a layabout! The journey must've taken it out of me. Thank you for putting me up.'

'Any time. A friend of Chris's is a friend of mine.'

'We're not exactly friends, Liz. Not any more.'

'Oh no!' Liz pulled up a chair and sat down at Pru's table. 'I'm sorry to hear that. You seemed so good together. What happened?'

'It's a long and complicated story. Let's just say I wasn't perfect for him.' She toyed with her napkin.

'I truly am sorry to hear that, love. What's your plan for today?'

'I'm going to go wandering – stroll the streets. And I shall stop for ice cream and whatever else takes my fancy. I might even jump on the ferry and let it take me there and back, just to be on the water.' She didn't know if she could handle retracing their steps of that first perfect afternoon.

'That sounds like a plan, would you like a packed tea?'

'Ooh yes, thank you.' A packed tea made it a proper outing.

A vast brunch was deposited in front of her: thick rashers of smoky bacon, glossy fried eggs, mushrooms, crispy hash browns and the obligatory dollop of baked beans.

'Wow!' Pru was impressed. Next, a side plate with two slabs of fresh crusty white bread was delivered.

'In case you want to make a sandwich.' Liz winked, a woman after her own heart.

The phone behind the bar rang.

'I better get that.' Liz jumped up and grabbed the receiver. 'Hello, the Victoria Inn... Hey! Well, what a coincidence, I

was just... Oh, right... No... Oh... Okay... No... Yes...
Yes... What...? Seriously...? Really...? Oh my God! Yes...
Yes, do... Okay.' She put the phone back in its cradle and
looked at Pru, who was about to tuck into her full English.
'Wrong number.'

With that she disappeared into the kitchen. Only to
emerge a few minutes later, looking a little flustered.

'Bad news, I'm afraid, Pru.'

Pru was mid mouthful. 'Oh no! Anything I can do?'

'No, nothing like that. It's just that there's a bad weather
front coming in over Salcombe, whole place will be covered
in dark clouds and rain. And it'll be very cold. Rainy and
cold.' She nodded.

Pru looked out of the window, swallowing her bacon
and egg. 'Really? But it looks beautiful out there.'

The bright blue sky was dotted with wisps of cloud and
a heat haze shimmered above the water. Kids in shorts
carrying multi-coloured buckets and crab lines were running
along Fore Street to commandeer a good spot.

Liz nodded. 'Yes, yes it does, but I'm afraid that's what
it's like here! I tell you what, I have a few urgent chores
to run in Kingsbridge this afternoon – why don't you come
with me and then I'll take you for tea in Hope Cove?'

'How far is it?' Having only arrived the night before,
Pru didn't want to spend hours in a car.

'Not far at all, couple of miles.'

'Won't the weather be rubbish there as well then?' Pru
was thinking a day on her bed with a box of chocolates
and a good book might be preferable to wandering around
in soggy linen.

Liz looked through the window and after the slightest hesitation said, 'No. It's on a different system.'

'A different system of weather?' Pru wrinkled her nose.

Liz nodded. 'Yes, that's right. A different system of weather. God, you townies, you don't know anything, do you?'

Pru shook her head. Apparently not.

By late afternoon, the two women had investigated practically every retail outlet in Kingsbridge, filling Liz's basket with all sorts of essentials, including hand-made birthday cards from the craft shop and a new sink plunger from the hardware shop. They hardly seemed to qualify as urgent chores and Pru wondered if Liz was simply being kind and getting her out of the bad weather.

'Thanks for this, Liz. It's lovely just to have a mooch – and to be out of London, if I'm being honest.'

'Any time. Spot of tea?' Liz looked at her watch. 'Or perhaps that should be G and T, given the time.'

Pru was in holiday mood. 'Why not?'

They jumped into Liz's little car and headed for Hope Cove. Stopping at The Harbour Light, they found a table on the terrace, making the most of the early evening sunshine.

'I can't believe that the weather here can be so different when we're only around the corner from Salcombe!'

'I know.' Liz nodded as she scrutinised the drinks menu. 'It is unbelievable.'

The two sat and nattered like old friends, enjoying the last of the rays and the most refreshing glass of Pimm's Pru had sampled in a long time. The sky was beginning to lose its blue.

'Think I might go for another Pimm's.' Pru scanned the terrace for a waiter.

Liz looked at her watch. 'No!' she shouted.

'Sorry?' Pru was a little taken aback.

'No more Pimm's. There's no time, they're closing.'

Pru looked up as another two couples arrived and sat down at a nearby table. The waitress handed them menus and pointed at the specials board. 'Really? It doesn't look like they're closing.'

'They are, plus the weather system has done its thing and the rain has now moved on from Salcombe; in fact it's probably heading over here. So we should go back and enjoy the sunset.' She nodded again.

'How can you tell that?'

Liz pointed at the clouds on the horizon. 'I can tell by the cloud formation over there.'

Pru looked at the clouds and then at Liz; she wasn't sure what to make of it all. But they paid their bill and left anyway.

As they drew into Salcombe, Liz parked the car near the harbour and killed the engine.

'You look lovely, Pru.'

'Thanks! I can't see any puddles, in fact it looks very dry.'

'Pru, forget about the weather. Have you got your lipstick on you?'

Pru nodded.

'Might want to pop a bit on and give your hair a bit of a brush.'

'But you just said I looked lovely?'

'You do, but...' Liz sighed, as if exhausted. 'Just do it.'

Pru applied her gloss, ran her brush through her locks and touched her temples, as was her habit.

'Thinning?' Liz asked

Pru nodded. 'Yep, every part of me is either thinning or sagging and if it ain't thinning or sagging, it's stopped working properly.'

'Tell me about it!' Liz chuckled.

Pru spritzed herself with her perfume.

'Now you look lovely and ready to face the world.'

The two women trotted along Fore Street and approached the pub.

'Thanks for today, Liz. It's been really lovely, just what I needed. A day of girlie gossip. I won't ever forget it.' Pru couldn't help sounding a little wistful, mindful of the wonderful hours she had spent with Christopher in the very same place.

Liz laughed. 'I'm sure you won't.' Just outside the front door, she paused. 'Have you got any plans this evening?'

Pru shook her head. 'No. I think an early night after a hot bath and a chapter of my book.'

'That sounds perfect. Before you go up, though, have you seen our terrace?'

'I didn't know you had a terrace. No, I haven't seen it. I promise I'll check it out tomorrow. I'm done in, Liz!'

'Oh you must see it, it's beautiful.'

She took Pru's hand and led her to a side gate. Lifting the latch, Liz stepped back to allow her entry. Pru took two steps forward and placed her cupped palm over her mouth. It was beautiful. One of the most beautiful things she had ever seen.

Sparkling white fairy lights had been strung in a canopy of stars around a tiny secluded arbour. Dark leaves of ivy and camellia had been wound into a bower and illuminated with tea lights suspended in glass pots. There was a single wooden bench beneath the arbour and beyond it a wooden door. It felt like a secret world.

She heard a cough from behind her. She turned her head slowly – and there was Christopher, waiting in the shadows.

'Hello, Miss Plum.' He stepped forward and took both of her hands into his. 'You look beautiful. I've missed looking at you.'

'I've missed looking at you too.' She grimaced. 'Although I did see you on the telly.'

'Not yesterday you didn't.'

'Oh?' Pru's heart was racing so hard she thought she might collapse. What was he doing here? And where had Liz disappeared to?

'Yesterday, Pru, I announced to the nation – on live TV, no less! – what a fool I'd been.' He heaved a sigh. 'But naturally you weren't watching.'

'I'm sorry, Christopher, I have no idea what you're on about.' She peered into the darkness, catching sight of a figure – a crowd of figures – skulking in the flickering candlelight, beyond the door. 'What's going on, is this another one of your set-ups? A bit more damage limitation? What are you planning? You've really got some nerve.'

Christopher winced and seemed to choke on his words. He clutched at her arm. 'Pru, listen to me. I know I can never fully apologise for what I did. I was such an idiot and I panicked. I was so caught up in that ferocious, self-absorbed Westminster world. It made me blind to what's really important. Blind to what you'd had to put yourself through, for all those years. God! What an ignorant tosser. I am so very, very sorry.'

Pru stared at him. He was practically on his knees at her feet. 'Okay, Christopher,' she said slowly, gulping down the lump in her throat. 'I accept your apology. I know you're not a bad man.' She reached down to kiss his forehead. 'You finally understand – thank you.'

Christopher cleared his throat and stood up straight. 'I want you to reach into my top pocket.'

Pru did as she was asked. Stepping forward, she placed her two fingers inside the silk-lined square and pulled out three pieces of honey-coloured biscuit, with a smudge of icing.

'It's me!' she whispered.

'It's you,' he confirmed. 'I will carry you in my pocket forever, no matter how broken.' He took her hand. 'Will you marry me, Pru Plum?'

'I... I...' She was in a state of confusion. 'What?' In her head she replayed snatches from her furious speech to Meg and Milly that horrible night. *Some people go through their whole life without loving or being loved.* She bit her lip, nervous. She didn't want to be one of them. A little love, that's all she wanted. As her tears pooled, she looked up at Christopher. 'It's changed.'

His face dropped. 'What has?'

'My situation. You said that I should let you know if I ever found someone that I wanted to marry. And I have.'

His face lit up, radiating relief and happiness, and he pulled her close – before pushing her away almost immediately. 'It is me, right?' He placed his index finger on his chest.

'Yes.' She nodded. 'It's you. It always was.'

'In that case, Miss Plum, please walk this way.' He took Pru by the hand and unlatched the door at the back of the arbour. For the second time that evening, Pru was struck speechless by the sight before her.

The door opened on to a bigger, more elaborate version of their little arbour. A tapestry of twinkling lights and glittering tea lights was woven through a vast awning of glossy dark green leaves. Flaming torches in aged sconces were set around the exposed brickwork walls. Beneath the woodland canopy stood a dozen round tables, each one dressed in stiff white linen and with a candelabra at its centre. Fat white candles dripped wax over the ivy and camellia leaves that decorated them.

Pru let her eyes sweep over the white china that sparkled and the pristine glasses that gleamed under the fairy lights. Glancing to her left she noticed a beautiful white cake, which looked very much like the one Guy had been working on for the gallery space. It was stunning. The whole thing was magnificent, breathtaking. What, she wondered, was the occasion?

Pru let her eyes wander from the decor to the people sitting in groups around the tables. Her breath snagged in her throat as she caught sight of Meg, holding baby Lucas. She pointed at her, but couldn't quite voice the words. 'Meg?' she mouthed. 'What... what are you doing here?'

Her eyes darted from table to table. Guy, Isabel, Milly, Liam, Rocky... Everyone was there, but how? Why?

'What's going on?' she asked the faces as they all turned to smile at her.

Then she spied the wide willow arch at the side, beneath which hovered a rather nervous-looking lady vicar. And finally she twigged.

Christopher gathered her into his arms and held her close to him, kissing her gently on the mouth. Meg stood up and pressed a small bouquet of wild flowers into her palm, and the lady vicar walked over. Christopher held out his hand and they stood side by side, their heads bowed. As Pru took the hand of the man she loved, the chain fell away from her heart. The sadness disappeared from behind her eyes and her mouth filled with sweetness. She was no longer alone; she had her husband by her side.

As night fell, the terrace became even more magical. Milly cradled Lucas in her arms as Meg chatted to Guy. Pru surveyed her family and friends, watched them drinking and laughing under their canopy of stars. She couldn't have felt more loved.

Milly had been in charge of the decor. She had been determined to give Pru her wedding fit for a woodland princess, the one she'd dreamed about since they were teens. Even if it was all very last minute and meant having to call every damn florist in the whole of Devon.

Guy had worked all through the previous night in the basement kitchen at Plum's and then all afternoon with Liz's team. He had pulled together the most amazing spread, not least of which was the magnificent cake, which he had made sure took pride of place on the terrace, so that everyone had to walk past it. Meg had been allowed to ice the middle tier and on the third attempt he had deemed it acceptable – progress indeed. Its flat surfaces were immaculate, blemish free and decorated with clusters of lily of the valley made from sugar paste in the palest ivory, clinging to pale green stems. The miniature bell-shaped flowers, with stamens a shade darker than the petals, lay in tiny sprigs in the top right-hand corner, as if thrown there; others hung down to the tier below, a waterfall of minute blooms. Each of the three square tiers was supported by four squat white pillars, which gave the cake form and depth without being overly grand. It was simple and perfect.

Guy tried to enjoy the party, but for him it was a busman's holiday of sorts. He fluttered around, asking for feedback on the patisserie, giving out linen napkins and rearranging the buffet to show it off to its best advantage.

'Guy, you have done the most amazing job! The food is wonderful and the cake looks absolutely magnificent!' Christopher patted him on the back before walking away, leaving him flustered and blushing.

'I like him,' Guy said from the side of his mouth to Pru.

'So do I!' she countered.

'Pru?'

'Yes, love?'

'I wanted to say that I think you are marvellous.' He crossed his hands across his chest.

'Well, I think you are pretty marvellous too.'

Guy shook his head. 'No, I don't just mean how we

work. I mean because of your past and what you endured. You are a *source d'inspiration* for me. Even more so now I know all about you.'

Pru accepted his compliment, offered with sincerity. 'Thank you, Guy.' She was keen to get back to the party, but he wasn't done.

'Keeping secrets is not easy. It is a burden and I should know, because I too have something that I do not share, something that I would like to share with you today.'

Pru breathed in, bracing herself. 'Oh?'

Guy gave a little cough and knitted his hands together. 'I will never marry a woman.'

Pru stared at him a little confused. 'I'm sorry?'

He wiped away the sweat that peppered his top lip, looking over his shoulder to check no one was within earshot. Then he reached for her hand, as if this physical reassurance might help with the shock. 'Pru...' He paused. 'I am, in fact, a gay man.'

Pru blinked quickly. She felt her mouth moving silently as she tried to compose an appropriate response. It wasn't often that she was speechless. What else was he going to reveal, that the Pope was Catholic, that bears prefer the forest floor to porcelain?

'Well,' she managed, 'I am honoured that you feel you can share your secret with me. My lips are sealed.' She leant forward and planted a kiss on his cheek, fuzzed with designer stubble.

Guy smiled at her, then jumped forward, flapping his arms. 'No! No! No!' He waved at a young girl who was replenishing the depleted macaroons on a three-tiered silver platter. 'Never, ever place the cerise next to that lavender colour. That, *ma chérie*, is the food equivalent of wearing glitter or sparkles before eight p.m. – a complete no-no, as well as social suicide. You must break them up with pistachio green or pale lemon! Can you see the difference?' His fingers worked quickly, creating an artful stack of colour-coordinated perfection. 'We want to make a subtle rainbow that grabs the eye and tempts the tastebuds.' His hand rolled in the air as if giving a royal wave. '*Mon Dieu*, if I allowed that kind of colour clash, I would be the laughing stock of London... and wherever this place is!'

Dear, dear Guy, your secret's safe with me.

'I wonder what Trudy would have made of all this?' Milly said as she approached her cousin.

Pru giggled and imagined Trudy standing on the terrace with her cigarette holder between her fingers, sizing up the other guests and offering a cutting commentary on all of them. 'She'd have hated it.'

Milly laughed too. 'Yes she would. She'd have left as soon as possible, sloping off and hoping you hadn't noticed. And she would have known just where to slope.' She winked.

'That she would.'

'Ooh good, he's alone!' Pru watched as Milly sped across the terrace and plonked herself down next to Christopher. 'I want a word with you.'

'Oh God, not another word!' His eyes twinkled at her. 'The last time you felt the need to reveal your innermost thoughts to me, it caused a whole lot of bother.'

'I can see that,' said Milly as she looked around the

terrace, at friends, family and colleagues dancing under the stars with glasses of champagne in their hands. 'I wanted to say, Chris, that because Pru loves you, we all love you – that's how we work.'

'Thank you, Mills.' He patted her arm.

'But if you ever hurt her, you'll need more than a few stitches in your shin.' She winked and then spied someone else she wanted a word with.

Meg sat down next to Pru and sipped her champagne. 'You look amazing, Pru. It's been the loveliest wedding.'

'It really has.'

'I've been thinking. I loved Bill, I really did.' She blinked away the slight sparkle of tears in her eyes. 'But he can't of been "the one", can he? Because if he was, he'd have been perfect for me and he certainly wouldn't have been seeing anyone else, lying to me or hiding me away. I'd have been enough for him, wouldn't I?'

'I think you are very smart to take that on board. And talking of you being very smart, Mills and I want to give you a bit of a promotion – and a rise, of course. I might be around a bit less, but Mills will be on hand to help you in any way she can. Besides, I think I've given that place enough of my life. I won't abandon Plum's and I'll always love it, but it's time for a new broom.'

Meg clapped her hands together. 'I don't believe it! Really? I've spent hours drawing up plans. I was going to present them to you – my ideas for world domination. I want there to be a Plum Patisserie in every capital city!'

'You'll do it, girl. You can do anything if you put your mind to it. I'm proof of that.'

'I know you're not my relative and I haven't been around that long in the scheme of things, but I really love you, Pru.'

'The feeling, Meg, is entirely mutual.'

Chris sought out his wife. 'I think your cousin just threatened to kneecap me if I put a foot wrong.'

'Well, you are well advised not to mess with us tough East End birds. Consider yourself warned, Sir Christopher.'

The delicate sound of a spoon hitting the side of a crystal glass reverberated around the terrace of the Victoria Inn and the chatter hushed to a whisper.

'Ladies and gentlemen, please welcome on to the dance floor, your bride and groom!' Liam announced.

Thunderous clapping rang out. Lucas yelled in response; he didn't like the big noise one bit. Meg rocked him from side to side before handing him over to Isabel, who had the knack of quieting him. Meg had noticed how, however much he might be bawling in the car, as soon as Isabel hurried down the driveway at Mountfield to meet them, as was her habit, he would pipe right down. She would scoop him up and smother his face in kisses, and he would become quite calm.

'Come to your grandma. That's it, my darling boy.' She kissed him and patted his back against her chest and sure enough he stopped crying.

'I don't know how you do that, Isabel, but I wish you'd teach me!'

Milly laughed. 'I could do with you around at three in the morning, when Meg can't hear him crying over her own snoring.'

'Funny, Milly. I may snore, but at least I don't sleepwalk in the middle of the night and eat cheese!'

'I did that once, you daft bint!'

'Yes, but that's once more than normal people, you nutter.'

Isabel laughed. 'Look, stop it, you two – Pru and Chris are going to dance.'

'Oh, God help us!' Milly whispered to Meg and the two of them collapsed into fits of giggles behind their hands.

Christopher put his hand on the small of Pru's back and held her right hand in his, at an angle.

'I can't believe you are making me do this, Chris.' She burrowed her face against his chest.

'Well, if I want a first dance with my wife then I shall jolly well have one. Remember, don't over-think it, just let me lead you.' He twirled her round, catching her before she slipped. She giggled loudly. They tripped across the floor, laughing, pressed close together, oblivious of all who stood watching.

Meg felt a tap on her shoulder.

'I can't bear to see a pretty girl all alone – would you like to dance?'

She beamed into the face of the handsome chap in a suit. As they made their way to the area where people smooched and swayed, she introduced him to Pru. 'Have you met Piers Parkinson-Boater?'

Pru nodded. 'Yes, I think I might have, once or twice.' She smiled at him, remembering how sweet he had been to her once before, and watched as Meg slipped into his arms quite naturally, almost as if that was where she belonged.

Christopher nodded at Meg and Piers, who were laughing as they waltzed across the floor. 'Looks like things are moving forward, Pru.'

She reached up and kissed him. 'Actually, Chris, I think it's better than that, I'd say they had reached neutral.'

Twenty-Three

The white-painted shutters of the rented apartment were thrown open to reveal the bright blue Salcombe morning. The gauzy curtain panels arched in the early breeze as the gulls screeched their morning greeting. Beyond their window and the ornately scrolled iron balcony they could see nothing but the white tips of the waves, breaking in the estuary, the masts and rigging of boats bobbing around like impatient pets, waiting attention and the patchwork shades of green on the cliff top hills beyond. Even at this early hour, the sun was giving off warmth and there was the distant ring of bells from the Holy Trinity church. He reached out and traced his finger over her shoulder.

'It's like looking at a painting isn't it?'

'It is. It's beautiful and so peaceful. I think I rather like this life.'

'Me too, but do you know the very best thing?'

Pru shook her head and sank further into the downy pillow.

'It's knowing that I get to wake up with you every morning for the rest of my days. And no matter what the day or night brings, that prospect fills me with unimaginable joy.'

She grinned up at him. 'You're an old softie.'

'Less of the "old" please; my joints don't need any reminding.' He rubbed at his elbow, which had a nasty habit of locking in the morning.

'This is really real, isn't it?' Her voice was a whisper.

'Yes, this is really real.'

'I shan't ever forget a single detail of yesterday, not ever. It was the most magical thing I've experienced. I keep replaying snippets in my head.'

'I'm so glad, I wanted it to be perfect for you.'

'It was, and to see everyone together, dancing, laughing, coming together for us,' Pru shook her head, 'it feels like a dream. I didn't know I could feel like this.'

'Me neither.' He laughed. 'To find you now is like being given an incredible parting gift for my twilight years. I would of course have liked to have met you when I was twenty, virile and handsome.'

'Okay, so you're not twenty, but two out of three ain't bad!' She kissed his arm and ran her fingers over his chin, which was peppered with grey whiskers.

'Ha! In all seriousness, you were worth waiting for. I think I've definitely saved my best years till last.'

'Thank you for loving me.' She beamed.

He gathered her against his chest. 'It is my absolute pleasure.'

'We should look at fishing rods while we are here, there's a shop on Fore Street.'

'Fishing rods?' he asked.

'Well that's the plan, isn't it? Aren't we going to potter about in Salcombe, buy a little boat and go fishing in the afternoons and then cook your catch for our supper? Then in the winter, warm our feet in front of a log fire and drink red wine until we fall asleep?'

'That sounds perfect, Mrs Heritage.'

Pru squealed and wriggled down the bed. She looked at the thin gold band that sat on the third finger of her left hand, a simple piece of jewellery that was so much more than the sum of its parts; a symbol of love and commitment, given to her by a man that wanted her by his side. 'Mrs Christopher Heritage! It doesn't have quite the same ring as Pru Plum!'

'You'll always be Pru Plum.'

'Yes.' Pru smiled. 'I will, won't I?'

Christopher raised her hand and kissed her palm.

Their bedroom door opened without warning and in bustled Milly, wearing her tiger onesie and apparently unconcerned that it was the early hours of their honeymoon morning.

'Jesus Christ! I've been all over this bloody place and there's not a bakery open anywhere. There are several people watering hanging baskets, fetching newspapers and walking little dogs, but not a loaf to be had. Luckily, I brought a packet of digestives with me, so who's for a cuppa?'

'Mills, we are having a lie-in. We are on our honeymoon, you silly moo!'

Milly backed from the room. 'All right, all right! I was only offering, daft cow.'

A Little Love

Notes for your bookclub

- Pru is a successful businesswoman, but she also talks of her sadness at being childless and unmarried. Do you think she is happy with how her life has turned out?

- Were you shocked by Bobby's and William's deaths? What effect does this have on the overall novel?

- How does the author use the characters' childhood experiences to inform the events of the present day?

- What role does age play in the novel? Would Pru and Christopher's romance have had the same impact if they were much younger characters?

- Sometimes the author uses cakes and baking to express her characters' emotions. Did you find that successful? Do you find that food and mood are closely related in your everyday life

For more information, and to sample a tasty gingerbread recipe, please visit www.amandaprowse.org

Amanda Prowse

Will You Remember Me?

Prologue

I often think about the day we got married, replaying the best bits in my head. I picture us laughing as we walked to the pub afterwards and the way he held my hand, tightly, possessively, stepping slightly ahead as if leading me. I was happy to follow. It felt safe and comforting. The bloke that owned the local café drove past in his van and shouted out of the window, 'Oi oi! It's Mr and Mrs!' It was the first time we'd been called that and we exploded with giggles. I thought I looked very average – dreadful, really. It wasn't like I had the posh frock and all the trimmings. But when I look at the pictures now, of the younger me, I can see that I looked far from dreadful. I was glowing, as if my joy shone out of me; no fancy dress could match that.

Later that night I climbed into the rickety bed alongside my husband. The gas heater hissed, doing its best to take the chill off the damp room. My face ached from all the laughing and the permanent grin I'd worn. We were both tired. I was about to drop off. My eyelids were drooping and I was really, really comfy, when suddenly he flicked on the lamp and sat up. I opened my eyes, wondering what was wrong, thinking that maybe those seven pints of Guinness and the kebab on the way home had finally caught up with him.

He lay back down and turned over, positioning himself on his side, with this head propped up on his elbow. And then he said, 'I love you so much. I want to give you the moon with a bloody big bow tied around it. My wife! I've got a wife and not just any wife but the best bloody wife in the whole wide world!'

I laughed as flames of happiness flickered inside me.

'Tell me,' he said. 'Tell me what you want and, one way or another, I'll get it for you.' He reached out and knotted his free hand with mine.

I remember looking at the bumps of our knuckles side by side, with our little wedding bands sitting next to each other, shiny and new. 'I don't want anything, only you,' I whispered, which was the truth.

He shook his head. 'Nah, that's not the answer, girl. If you could have anything, and everything was possible, what would you want?' His expression was bright, hopeful and child-like.

I lay back and closed my eyes, trying to picture a world for us where I could have anything, and everything was possible. 'Well...' I swallowed. 'I'd like two kids, a boy and a girl, who are happy and secure. I want them to be like us, but smarter and cuter.'

'Well that wouldn't be too difficult!' He laughed.

I didn't open my eyes; I stayed in that world that he'd created for me. 'And I'd like a swimming pool shaped like a kidney—'

'Why like a kidney?' he interrupted again.

'Because, apparently, rectangular pools are the cheapest design, but a kidney takes some doing, with all them curves.

Costs more. So everyone would know how much dosh we've got, just by its shape.'

'Gotcha. What else?' He moved closer. I could feel his minty breath against my face.

'I'd like a diamond ring. Not just any old diamond, mind, but one the size of an ice cube. And I'd show it to everyone from school and on the estate who has ever laughed at me or made me feel like I was nothing.' I felt his lips graze my neck and a shiver of joy travelled down my spine. 'And I want to lie on a tropical beach and feel the soft powdery sand slip through my fingers and the hot sun on my face.' This was the wish of a girl who had rarely left the postcode of her childhood.

'So, not Southend?' He kissed me again.

I opened my eyes and turned to face him. 'No, not Southend.'

'Are you done?' he asked as his hand travelled up under my nightdress and rested on the flat of my stomach.

'Nearly.' I placed my hand on top of his. 'I want to dance with you in the rain, wearing a lovely dress, and I want it to be a proper dance, like a waltz, old fashioned and romantic.'

He rolled over then until he was lying on top of me, resting on his forearms. He smoothed the hair from my forehead and kissed me gently on the mouth. 'Then a dance in the rain you shall have.' He covered my chest and neck with tiny kisses, making my heart beat faster.

'And what about you?' I managed. 'What would you want if you could have anything, and everything was possible?'

His expression was suddenly solemn. He looked into my eyes and spoke in a soft voice. 'I want us to live in the countryside, just like we've always wanted, and I reckon if we lived somewhere nice, everything else would fall into place.'

I nodded agreement against his shoulder. The countryside was our dream.

He wasn't finished. 'And I want to give you everything that you've asked for. That'd be enough for me: to make you happy. That's a world I'd like to live in.'

'Well, congratulations!' I beamed. 'You do make me happy, so maybe we've arrived there already!' I laughed and wiggled down the bed with my arms wrapped around him.

'There is one more thing...' I added softly into his ear.

He paused his kissing and gave a small sigh. 'You're sure it's the last?'

I nodded. 'I'd like to know who my dad is.' I had felt the absence of this special man on this, my wedding day. Unexpectedly, a tear found its way to the surface and trickled down my cheek, which he kissed away.

'Don't be sad,' he whispered. 'Not tonight.'

I sniffed and smiled. He pulled the duvet over our heads and it felt like we were in our own little bubble, sheltered from the world; like no one could get to us and we were safe. And I remember thinking, if I get to feel like this every night of my life, lying in bed with the man I love, knowing that nothing can touch us, then we *have* arrived at that place, we really have. And I was right.